THE
SECRET
OF
BOG LANE

Dear Rosa,
Happy Reading!
[signature]

THE
SECRET
OF
BOG LANE

AN ANCIENT EVIL REACHES FROM A SEASIDE
AMERICAN TOWN INTO THE HEART OF THE
AMAZON JUNGLE

Americo Tulipano

PARAGON HOUSE

Paragon House
1925 Oakcrest Avenue, Suite 7
St. Paul, MN 55113
www.ParagonHouse.com

Library of Congress Cataloging-in-Publication Data

    Tulipano, Americo, 1954-
      The secret of Bog Lane : an ancient evil reaches from a seaside American
    town into the heart of the Amazon jungle / by Americo Tulipano. -- 1st ed.
       p. cm.
      Summary: "A family moves into a house with a horrible secret near Cape Cod
    Bay and an explorer in Brazil courts Amerindians with scientific miracles.
    This suspense novel alternates between a family in present-day Massachusetts
    and the natives in Amazon rain forest as an evil connecting the two
    unfolds"--Provided by publisher.
     ISBN 978-1-55778-900-6 (pbk. : alk. paper) -- ISBN 978-1-61083-043-0
    (e-book) 1. Haunted houses--Fiction. 2. Indians of South
    America--Fiction. 3. Cape Cod Bay (Mass.)--Fiction. I. Title.
     PS3620.U55S43 2012
     813'.6--dc23
                       2011045712

Manufactured in the United States of America
  10 9 8 7 6 5 4 3 2 1

To Lucia
Who taught me the meaning of
"faith that works through love"

THE SECRET OF BOG LANE

PART ONE

PART TWO

PART THREE

45: The Good Neighbor 261
46: Lex. 268
47: Emergency 274
48: Council 279
49: The Number 287
50: Flailing in the Deep 291
50: Muriel's Secret 300
52: Executive Decisions 309
53: The Searchers. 315
54: Sole Survivor 321
55: Sanctuary 326
56: Tequila Sunrise. 330

57: Plymouth Monday 334
58: Building Blocks. 340
59: The Lesson 346
60: S-53 350
61: The Bog 355
62: What If?. 359
63: Remains. 364
64: The Incarnation 367
65: Death Struggle 375
66: The Promise 385
Epilogue: The Medallion . . . 394

PART ONE

Nothing begins at the time you think it did.
—Lillian Hellman, *An Unfinished Woman*

PROLOGUE

SIX ACRES OF EDEN

LIKE A VIPER SLITHERING SLOWLY DOWN a VINE, the danger wormed quietly into our lives. There were no omens or cries of alarm. In fact, my family's troubles started with nothing more ominous than a light-hearted Latin melody. It was an annoyingly perky version of *La Macarena,* and it was coming from my wife's unseen cell phone. While I finished drying the supper dishes, she hurriedly searched the usual places: her coat pockets, her purse, the large bowl by the front door. Laine followed the recurring melody and found the phone just as it played its final, sparkly chord. Of all the unlikely places, it was sitting on the re-charging unit.

From the kitchen I heard her say "Hun-nee," so I knew that she was talking to Jean. My wife had customized a slightly different style of speech for each of her oldest friends, and I'd learned to identify each friend by the inflections and tone of Laine's voice. I was surprised when the call ended within a matter of minutes. Her conversations with Jean seldom ran less than an hour.

When Laine returned to the kitchen there was a determined but happy gleam in her almond eyes, and her cupid face flushed with excitement. She tossed me the car keys with one hand while pulling Gabriel along with the other. "Darlin', rev up the engine," she said, mimicking Jean's Tennessee drawl. "You won't believe what a beautiful birdie just whispered in my ear…"

Over an hour later, as the sun set on that early August day, we turned down a dead-end road in the grand old shire of Plymouth, Massachusetts. "Look, Mom!" Gabriel cried from the back seat. "They named a street after you!"

"Well it's about time they got around to that," I said. "Do you see any statues of her, Gabe?"

He pointed to a street sign that heralded our destination: *Bog Lane.*

"Sweetie, my name is spelled with an 'i'—remember? L-A-I-N-E. What does that spell?"

"Bog." Gabriel was still looking at the street sign. "What's a bog?"

Hearing Gabriel say something that sounded like dog, Biscuit, our three year old Siberian husky, barked. I glanced in the rearview mirror just as the dog licked the side of my son's face. Gabriel nuzzled Biscuit's furry neck. A square medallion, dangling from the husky's collar, glinted in the day's final shafts of sunlight that streamed through the car's windows.

Laine didn't answer Gabriel's question. Her eyes were fixed on the stately, three-story structure that blocked the end of the road. Although Bog Lane ran for nearly two hundred feet, it contained only three houses: a white neo-Colonial on the left; a red Cape on the right; and this final abode, a gray Queen Anne Victorian with black trimmings. On its porch stood a smartly dressed woman with long, chestnut brown hair. As we approached, her comely face— brightened by a radiant smile—came into view. She jangled a set of keys in the air and bounced on the balls of her feet like an excited game-show contestant. "We're going to be neighbors!" she cried. "We're going to be neighbors!" Beautiful birdie indeed.

Happiness reigned on that summer evening, for we gazed upon Eden—six acres of Eden, to be precise. But unlike the realm described in the Bible, this garden was fronted by a furnished house with a wrap-around porch, all nestled amidst the woodlands and cranberry bogs of southeastern Massachusetts, less than an hour's drive from Boston.

Jean escorted us through thirty-five hundred square feet of sumptuous living space. From the baronial central stairway with its polished banisters, to the built-in crystal cabinets, to the decorative woodwork that framed every doorway: a genteel, 19th century American mind had stamped its sense of style on every room and passageway. There was even a wrap-around veranda on the third floor, flanked by a circular turret that overlooked the six-acre yard. Yet the house's add-ons were strikingly functional. There were three spacious bathrooms; a work-out room with large pieces of aerobic equipment and a Universal weight machine; an airy kitchen with remodeled fixtures and an island counter-top. There was even a six-burner Garland gas range. No, this wasn't the place we always wanted; it was a great deal more than we always wanted. And now this portion of paradise was inexplicably within our price range.

We felt like the luckiest people on earth.

But I'm a pessimist at heart. So, after a day or two of elation, my thoughts spiraled downward. As they descended they touched on some of the problems that might lurk in our new home: termites, radon, a porous basement, rotting support beams, a leak in the gas line, or perhaps some form of toxic mold. If I'd thought hard enough, I might even have conjured up some otherworldly dangers: territorial ghosts, ancient curses, and the like... Nothing was too fanciful for my imagination.

Or so I thought.

All too soon I would come to realize that my imagination was hopelessly outmatched. Because even if I'd scrounged around in the murkiest crevices of my mind, I could not have imagined what was waiting for us on Bog Lane.

ONE

BAD

THE MAN PRESSED THE KNIFE-BLADE TO her neck and repeatedly rammed his pelvis against her soft, inner thighs. The pounding intensified until it seemed he couldn't thrust any faster or harder. The woman's lips contorted and a pained squeak pulsed from her throat with each abrasive shove. Just when she feared she might scream in anguish, the coiled tension in his body went slack. He moaned deeply. His semen flowed inside her as beads of sweat rolled off his head and dropped on her face.

For a moment all was still.

Then he opened his eyes, reared back, and spat at her. He could only see the dim, pinkish outline of her face in the darkness. A tree loomed overhead, blocking out the moonlight, and the nearest streetlamp was hidden behind a thicket of hedges. But he was sure his glob of spit had found its mark.

The woman didn't see, feel, or hear the insult. Her eyes were shut tight, her body was numbed by adrenalin, and the sound of her own rushing bloodstream filled her ears. Terrified and humiliated, all she could do was whimper. The man glowered at her as he stood up: "Shut up bitch, or I'll cut you to the bone." He pulled up his jeans and yanked the zipper shut. He then dropped to one knee and used the knife to probe through her purse. The tinkle of loose coins rippled through the night.

Overcome with shame, she tried to cover her face but her arms were entwined by the blouse that he had ripped open and forced over her shoulders. A skirt lay crumpled at her side, and a thin trickle of blood oozed from her left nostril into her ear. She feared worse was yet to come.

The woman wanted to keep him from doing more harm, but she was afraid that he might carry out his threat. The frantic need to *do something* finally overcame her paralysis and a quivering squall of words spilled out: "Please let me go; I have children at home; they're little; I have pictures in my purse; they need me; they're just—"

His fist glanced off the side of her forehead. The same darkness that made his initial attack possible now kept him from delivering a direct hit. "Shut-up!" It was a hushed command, but his basso voice—timed with the jolt of his punch—thundered in her head like a gunshot. She resigned herself to her fate and sobbed quietly.

He examined the few bills that he found in her purse until his vision adjusted well enough to make out cameo portraits of George Washington and Abraham Lincoln. "What you working for bitch? You got nuthin! Nuthin!" He threw down the purse. "This is shit, woman! You workin' for shit!"

Anticipating another blow, she turned her face from him. At that moment a car traveled down the street. He dropped on her and clamped his hand over her mouth. The car cruised by, passing within twenty feet of their frozen bodies. He waited until its rear lights were red dots in the distance, then he slid off her.

"You open your mouth and you gonna go home in a box. Got it?"

She nodded vigorously. He removed his hand and scowled at her. "Don't even try to look at me with that ugly face!" She quickly turned her head until the side of her face pressed against the grass. Realizing he was going to let her live, the sweet fragrance of Russian

Sage filled her lungs as the tip of her nose brushed against its stalks. The flowers had been within a few inches of her head throughout the ordeal, but only now did she become aware of them. Suddenly he was off her and moving quickly away.

The man pocketed the bills and placed the knife into the hand-warmer of his sweatshirt. It was too hot for a sweatshirt, but the hand-warmer gave him a perfect hiding place for his knife. The sound of weeping faded as he jogged along the side of the road. He sliced off into a backyard and cut down a driveway that emptied out to another street. Feeling a bit safer, he moved down the sidewalk with an easy, loping stride.

"*Bad!*" he said. "I am one bad mutha fucka!" He wondered if he would make tomorrow's TV news. He imagined the Channel Seven News chicks mouthing his nick-name: "The so-called 'Rockland Rapist' has struck again…" He wished they would use words like *daring* or *bold* when talking about him. He could see the secret hunger in their eyes when they reported his feats. Someday they would know his real name, and they would mouth it with their sexy lips.

He stopped.

At the far end of the street a white car slowly turned toward him. From that distance he couldn't read the letters on the side of the car, but he knew they spelled *Plymouth Police*. Though an inner voice told him to stay cool, a bolt of fear fired through his legs and sent him sprinting down a side road. He had run about a hundred feet when he saw that the street was sealed off by a large house and a six-foot steel fence.

It was a dead end.

"Shit!" he panted. Realizing the cruiser would pass at any moment, he flew straight toward the fence. There was a sign on it, but he didn't stop to read what it said.

He jumped, clamped both hands on the top bar of the fence and swung his legs over. He rolled as he hit the ground on the other side, then flattened himself against the grass. Keeping his head down, he angled his eyes up just in time to see the police car slowly pass the mouth of the road. He let himself breathe; but before getting up, he made sure no one was watching from any of the houses on the dead end street. Shades were drawn and there were no faces in sight. The windows of the large house on his right were all dark. Either everyone was asleep or no one was home.

He took a deep breath and hissed, "Gold medal, man; gold medal for that one." He stood up and pounded his chest with his left hand. "I am *bad*! I am one bad mutha fucka!" He looked around, daring anyone to disagree with him. But the only sounds he heard were bullfrogs croaking in the night. There were no lights in the yard to guide him, but he knew that if he moved straight ahead he would eventually come to another street. His goal was to get far away from the pink-faced woman before she told her story to the police. "I am the baddest of the bad!" his fists were clenched, his arms thrust down, and his head jabbed out each word.

A lone, thin cloud smudged the moon's face and the ground was a maze of shadows. But the young man wasn't scared: he knew he was the baddest of any bad thing that might lurk in the shadows. He mixed a dance step into his loping stride. He had gone about thirty feet and was beginning to realize that the area was far too big to be an ordinary backyard. *What is this place?*

Suddenly he was falling. His arms shot out to break the fall but they went right through a layer of leaves and lily pads. His face splashed into a pool of water. Fumbling frantically, his hands sunk into murky goo as he tried to push himself up. Coughing and cursing his bad luck, he dragged himself out of the water and stared at the darkness until the formless contours of a pond came into focus.

Small glassy marbles slipped down the inside of his sweatshirt. He pulled off the shirt and pressed two of the pellets between his fingertips before realizing what they were. "Cranberries!" he whined. "Goddamn cranberries!" The berries were small and hard. One had lodged between his abdomen and his jeans; he plucked it out and flung it into the night. Then he slowly got to his feet and trudged around the edge of the bog, wringing out his sweatshirt as he went.

Though he stepped more carefully, he kept moving until he came to another fence, beyond which were clusters of trees and a poorly lit road. There was just enough moon glow for him to see a large mound next to the fence. *A pile of dirt or gravel*, he thought. Too tired to perform another gold medal vault, he walked toward the small hill. From the top of it he would be able to climb over the fence with little effort. As he approached the rising, a gust of wind swelled from behind and blew toward the fence. The August night was so hot that the breeze didn't chill his bare, wet back.

The wind eased up just as he stepped on the mound and a foul odor filled his head.

The pile of dirt felt hard and lumpy under his feet, like a heap of inflated tires. As he reached out to grab the top of the fence, the ground shifted just a little. *Can't be no earthquakes in Massachusetts.* The wind kicked up again, rustling the leaves which broke the moonlight into flickering beams. The effect reminded him of the flashing strobes in a nightclub he used to haunt. Then the mound beneath him moved again.

This ain't no pile of dirt he thought as he looked down.

A large, white bicycle seat caught his eye. It skidded on a patch of grass off to the side, then rose up and hovered about two feet off the ground. *A floatin' bicycle seat!*

It was like watching a magic show without a magician. But in the dim, pulsing light he now saw that the jumbo seat was attached to a long, thick hunk of rubber hose. It was like a big, white sewer pipe—except that this pipe could move and bend. As he watched, something deep in his brain told him to jump over the fence. But his eyes couldn't pull away from the freakish sight. The massive bicycle seat slowly turned and he noticed a large, yellow circle on one side. Then he saw another yellow circle on the other side. Each circle was centered by a black diamond that grew bigger and bigger. In the strobe-light created by the moon, wind, and dancing leaves, the seat seemed to move in herky-jerky spurts as it came closer and closer. A wire shot out of the front tip of the seat; it shot out again and again as the big, white triangle came nearer to the man's face.

Then he realized what the huge bicycle seat really was.

He spun around to leap over the fence but his legs gave out when the mound beneath his feet pushed outward. The man slammed hard to the ground, flat on his back. As he gasped for air, the thing twisted all around him. He tried to scramble to his feet but the creature seemed to slide everywhere at once: rather than just one monster, it seemed as if a gang of monsters were surrounding him. He reached for his knife, but his sweatshirt with its knife-holder disappeared between two long slabs of meat sliding in opposite directions. He tried to scream for the police to return and rescue him, but a cold limb wrapped around his face and snapped his head back, nearly breaking his neck.

The man wrenched his head from side to side, finally freeing it from the thing's grip. But as he did this, another part of the creature wrapped around his body and pinned his arms to his rib-cage. He struggled wildly to free himself, but the beast's hold was more powerful than any living thing he had ever felt. His chest was being crushed as if by a giant hand; even his heart barely had room to beat. The pressure caused his eyeballs to bulge until everything around him became blurry and twisted.

Something hard and sharp—like a crown with hundreds of nails sticking out of the bottom—clamped down on the top of his head. The nails gouged trenches into his flesh. He tried to pull his head into his neck, but the spikes only bit deeper. He felt trickles of blood flowing through his hair and down to the back of his neck. He suddenly realized that the nail-lined crown was actually a mouth—elastic jaws that slowly scraped down over his forehead. Rows of slanted fangs ripped the skin off the upper part of his face. As the pointy teeth carved onward, they sliced into his bulging eyeballs. The man again tried to scream, but with no air in his lungs his face became a silent, gaping mask. Suddenly everything went black. The thing's fangs, inching onward, had plucked his eyeballs from their sockets.

Somehow he remained alive. The thing's mouth now covered most of the man's head. Acid seeped into his ears, nose, and the holes where his eyes had been. He tried to scream one last time, but the acid scorched his vocal chords and burned away his voice. Though his brain cells were rapidly dying, the young man knew that he was being eaten alive. His last frenzied flicker of thought was a hopeless question:

How could anything be so bad?

TWO

THE LOCKED ROOM

WOODROW GOODELL WAS A NEW ENGLANDER by birth and breeding. We selected him to inspect the house on Bog Lane for one reason: prior to becoming a home inspector he had been a locksmith, and we needed his lock-disabling skills. Though shy of sixty, Woody had an ample supply of curly locks that tumbled out from under his Red Sox cap. But his hair was tinged by flecks of gray and white that stood out against the carbon hue of his skin. His mane never left my sight because I stayed on his heels throughout his top-to-bottom examination of the house. He probably thought I was an anxious first-time home buyer. But I was an anxious second-time home buyer. Laine and I already owned a split-level in Maynard, an old mill town about fifty miles northwest of Plymouth. Unlike the Maynard property, however, the house on Bog Lane would not only be an investment but our home—the place where we would grow old and someday entertain our grandchildren.

Normally it is the prospective buyer who selects the home inspection company and pays for the inspection. But in this case it was the seller who put up the money. We were still allowed to pick the company, provided that we selected one within a week. It seemed to us that the seller—a man named Richard Heinrich Hitchens—was extremely confident that we would love the place and that the inspector would find everything in order.

Jean was concerned about Hitchens's haste. But she also worried that someone else might get wind of the deal and offer Hitchens more money. Laine and I shared that particular concern, so we were happy to abide by Hitchens's hurry-up schedule.

"This place is ancient by American standards," Woody remarked as he probed the woodwork for termites. "But someone did a nice job restoring it." Something akin to pride stirred within me, as if I'd done the work myself. We hadn't yet signed papers, but I already had a proprietary feel for the place.

Woody was right: the house could've been the cover story for a lay-out in *Country Living* magazine. Someone took great care to retain its original architectural character while adding modern conveniences and stylish niceties. When I told Woody how much the house would cost us, he thought it was a joke. But my exultant smile put his assumption to rest. "That's the advantage of having a wife whose best friend is a workaholic realtor," I said.

"Foreclosure sale?"

"No, nothing like that. Jean said the owner just had to go somewhere in a hurry."

Woody gave me a sideways glance but didn't say anything. When we finally turned our attention to the cellar, I hurried to get in front of him because I wanted to personally introduce him to our special mystery. But before I got one step down the stairway he pointed to the loosely hung oak door and its mauled slip lock.

"Damn." I slid my fingers over the cylindrical bolt, which was bent.

"Someone just couldn't wait to get up here," Woody said as he stepped past me and flicked on the cellar light switch.

"You're telling me that someone was trying to get OUT of the cellar?"

"Check out the bottom of the door."

There, about twenty inches from the floor, the inside of the door was cracked and dented in several places, as if a powerful midget had punched it repeatedly.

I was flummoxed. "Why would someone need to get out of the cellar?"

Woody frowned and stopped midway down the stairs. "Maybe the owner locked himself out of the house, found a cellar window that was open, and then had to force his way in through the locked cellar door. It happens."

"Wait a sec," I caught him as he reached the bottom step. "Why would he force himself in by hitting the bottom of the door?"

He shrugged. "I guess you'll have to ask him."

Woody's response struck me as a bit too nonchalant, so I didn't say anything about the sight that awaited him in the basement. I wanted to see his spontaneous side.

The area was relatively small, befitting a 19th century cellar. A bare, gleaming bulb dangled from an exposed ceiling wire, but the room's fieldstone walls seemed to absorb the light and shroud the area in perpetual dusk. I noticed a steep, narrow stairway that hugged the wall on the opposite side of the room. Its steps looked far newer than the ones Woody and I had just descended. A much wider set of cement steps led to a bulkhead on another wall. Woody went directly to the gas heater in the center of the room. A tag hung from the heater's drain pipe, proclaiming the unit's installation date in bold print. "Not bad, eh?" I beamed. "Less than two years young."

But Woody seemed mildly perplexed.

"What is it?" I pushed my glasses up on my forehead. "Is something wrong?"

"No," he replied, tinkering with the heater. "It looks fine. I'm just wondering why the owner would've put in all these gizmos only to turn around and sell the place."

"Maybe he just needed a new heater."

"I'm not just talking about the heater," he said as he loosened a valve to adjust the water level in a tube on the side of the unit. "All the appliances—the refrigerator, stove, dishwasher—are five or six years old, tops. The electrical system was recently converted from fuses to circuits. You won't have to worry about the roof for at least ten years, and that wrap-around porch—which wasn't in the original structure—is a very personal touch." He returned his screwdriver to his toolbelt, still mulling the heater. "If you ask me, someone was planning to make a final stand here."

"Well, maybe the owner just wanted to increase the value of the place: you know, to get a better price."

"The owner," Woody quipped without turning, "could've snagged a better price without changing a blessed thing." This was an exaggeration—but not much of an exaggeration. I was faced with two conflicting adages: *"Never look a gift horse in the mouth"* versus *"If it seems too good to be true...."*

I was instinctively drawn to the latter. Yet, by a conscious exertion of will, I forced myself to dwell on the former. For the first time in a long time, I refused to search my imagination for trouble.

Woody stood up to continue his examination, and that's when he saw the steel door that was built into the eastern wall of the basement. The large silvery portal, which was sealed shut with a bolt lock, seemed out of place in this dank cellar.

"What's this? A walk-in freezer?"

"Welcome to our not-so-little mystery," I said as I unlocked and opened the door. We peered down a hallway lined with cinderblocks, which emptied out to pure blackness.

"What the hell is in there?"

"You're the inspector," I reminded him.

From the earthen stubble floor of the old cellar we stepped onto the smooth cement surface of the passageway. Woody stopped. I'd done the exact same thing during my initial walk-through with Jean several days earlier. The opaque space at the end of hallway had given me the feeling that I was walking into a black hole. Sensing Woody's uneasiness, I stepped ahead of him, raised my clenched hand, and knocked three times on the darkness.

"What the—" He slowly moved down the corridor with his hand extended until he touched a thick sheet of Plexiglas. The plastic door was rimmed by steel bars that ran along the top, bottom, and sides. The fit was so tight that a newborn garter snake couldn't have slipped through. His fingers probed the barrier, then slid to the brass plate lock that was fused into the left side of the door. Not even bolt cutters could defeat that guardian.

"What's on the other side?" he asked.

"You wouldn't believe me if I told you," I replied.

On the wall next to the lock was a light switch. Woody flicked it on. A brilliant flash from the other side of the Plexiglas momentarily blinded us, like the split-second glare from a photographer's bulb. Then it flashed again and again. On their fourth try an array of florescent lights remained aglow, and we saw what was on the other side of the Plexiglas door.

Woody gasped.

THREE

THE NURSE

THE YOUNG WOMAN SAT UP ON THE EDGE of the examining table and gazed at the nurse. He placed his instruments on a side table and sighed. "Mara, you have no infection; there is no infection. In fact, you look fine." He spoke an Amerindian language, punctuated by Spanish and Portuguese words. She responded in kind.

"I'm glad you think I look fine," she smiled warmly.

He looked away, intent on maintaining his professional poise. "No, what I mean is I cannot find anything wrong with you."

"You don't think I look fine any more?" Her smile wilted.

"No, Mara—I mean yes, Mara. Yes, I think you look fine. But what I'm trying to—"

"Oh Felipe!" She smiled and reached out for him, but he stepped back, still trying to preserve a modicum of medical propriety.

"Mara, I'm working!"

As much as she was drawn to Felipe's deep-set auburn eyes, sharply chiseled jaw-line, and boyishly tousled brown hair, Mara loved his sense of dedication even more. And she liked putting his professional integrity to the test whenever they were alone.

"I still think I have an infection. I still have that itchy feeling." Her lips pouted, but her eyes—seraphic and beguiling—continued to smile. "Maybe you should examine me again."

19

She started to lie down but he stopped her. "No, Mara, that won't be necessary."

Felipe removed his stethoscope from around his neck and turned toward his desk. His workplace was a medium-sized room that was stocked with all the equipment one would normally find in a big city's doctor's office. But Felipe's clinic was located in the Amazon rain forest, thousands of kilometers from the nearest metropolis.

With an impish grin still on her face, Mara started to remove her medical gown and Felipe heard the rustle of its papery fabric. "No, Mara, please don't do that," he said, turning back to her. She had already pulled the salmon-colored garment part way down, revealing her smooth, olive-complexioned shoulders.

"You want me to stay?" Her tiny kernel of a smile flowered into full bloom.

He was reduced to helpless honesty. "Mara, you know that I love you. And I want to teach you how to be a nurse. But you mustn't interfere with my work. So you must keep your clothes on."

"How can I put on my clothes if I can't take this thing off?"

"Okay, okay; that's a good point," he nodded. "You go ahead and change. I'll be right back." He removed his gloves and went into the only other room in the cabin. It contained a cot with a thin mattress, a small bureau, and a three tiered bookcase that fit under the room's only window.

It occurred to Felipe that his living quarters were as Spartan as those of Henry David Thoreau—the 19th century American naturalist who famously withdrew from town life and moved into a small cabin near a place called Walden Pond. As a boy, Felipe had read about Thoreau and he quickly became one of his heroes. But a few comparisons now came to mind. Thoreau had lived in the woods and contemplated nature's lessons for about *two* years; Felipe resided in the Amazon rain forest for over *three* years. During Thoreau's stay at Walden Pond he frequently visited family and friends, who lived just a few kilometers away. But

Felipe only returned to Santa Cruz—which was nearly two *thousand* kilometers away—during Christmas week to see his parents and siblings. Thoreau eventually had enough of his "life in the woods" and returned to his home town. Felipe had no plans to abandon his cabin in the Amazon.

As a boy growing up in a bedraggled *municipio* in Bolivia, hunger and want were Felipe's frequent companions. But they weren't the worst of his lot. The worst was the belief that change—*change for the better*— was virtually impossible. Nothing sapped his spirit and energy more than the premonition that he was powerless to make a real difference for himself or anyone else.

But Felipe's parents, Luis and Juana Vasquez, a manual laborer and a nurse's aide, set an example he would never forget. They made tough sacrifices, and argued with just about every local official, so that their son could attend Santa Cruz's best school. Determined to honor their trust, Felipe made the most of this opportunity and achieved consistently excellent grades all the way through to his senior year. Although his board scores were high enough to win substantial scholarships, all of the medical school slots went to well-connected families. As far as he could tell, none of the admission tickets were marked: "Reserved for the child of Bolivian peasants."

Undeterred, Felipe pressed on and earned a bachelor's of science degree from *Universidad De Lima* in Peru, as well as a license to practice health-care as a registered nurse. Within twenty-four hours of graduation, he was back in Bolivia applying for a job at *Centro Medico* in La Paz.

That's where a newspaper blurb caught his eye: "Nurse needed: Rugged conditions but excellent pay and rewarding work." At first he thought it must be a government position, though the part about "excellent pay" made him a bit suspicious. He called the number appended to the listing, but instead of talking to a government bureaucrat he was put directly through to a banker in Rio de Janeiro named Juan Ponticari. The banker asked about Felipe's age, health, and his willingness to work in a place that was "devoid of conveniences."

When Felipe finally got to ask a question, it was straight to the point: "If not the government, who is financing this job?" Ponticari said that he served as an intermediary for a wealthy American who had taken a special interest in a particular Amazonian tribe. Beyond that, he couldn't say anything else about the identity of his employer. But the banker told Felipe that if he accepted the position, he would immediately receive double the starting salary of registered nurses in one of Rio de Janeiro's finest hospitals: *Santa Casa De Misericordia Hospital Geral.* He would also receive a substantial cost-of-living increase every six months, and his checks would be wired to any bank of his choice. Felipe asked if these funds could be accessible to his parents in Santa Cruz, and Ponticari assured him that he would make the necessary arrangements with his banking contacts in Bolivia. Felipe took the job.

Ponticari told him to gather only his most essential possessions into one backpack and report to the airport in La Paz at 6AM the following morning. The pilot of a small plane would be waiting to fly him to an airstrip outside the Brazilian town of Codajas, on the banks of the Amazon River. Once there, another man would take him on a long jeep drive to the north bank of the Purus River. From there he would have to cross a footbridge and walk—alone—the last several miles of his journey. The jeep driver would give Felipe an extra backpack with fresh medical supplies, two canteens of water, and a detailed map of the area, marked with a red line showing exactly which paths to take.

This entire trip was planned so that he could reach his destination before nightfall.

"Don't dawdle along the way," Ponticari warned him. "Don't take any *siestas.* You must reach the village before the sun goes down. You don't want to be wandering around in the jungle at night. When you get to the village, the Inucans will welcome you with open arms. Good luck."

Felipe had always kept a trim, nicely-muscled physique. During weekend afternoons in Lima he played soccer virtually non-stop. But the journey into the depths of the Amazon pushed him to his limit. Through sweltering heat, clouds of voracious insects, and layers of tenacious mud, he shouldered one backpack and carried another down the map's red line. Twice he veered off the designated route and had to backtrack until he happened upon natural landmarks. Felipe had heard stories about hardy explorers who strode boldly into the jungle, never to return. Those stories came back to him as he struggled toward his destination. With each arduous step, he gained a deeper appreciation of the jungle's ability to make people vanish without a trace.

At long last Felipe made it to the outskirts of the village, but its people didn't exactly have their arms open. Several Indian warriors—their faces painted blood red—stood on the edge of a hill and glowered down at him. Machetes dangled by their sides; some held taut seven-foot bows bundled with arrows that looked almost as long. Felipe said the word *medico* four times; he also kept his hands open in front of him to show that he had no weapons. A gray-haired man finally stepped through the phalanx of sentinels and walked down to the base of the hill where Felipe stood.

"Are you the new nurse?" he asked in surprisingly clear Spanish.

"Yes. My name is Felipe Vasquez."

"Welcome to our village. My name is Yoro; I am the *Sartum*." This was the first Inucan word to fall on Felipe's ears, and he rightly inferred that it meant chief or leader.

Yoro noticed the small wooden cross that Felipe wore around his neck. It consisted of two twigs—each one less than an inch long—tied together by a piece of string. "Did you make that yourself?" he asked in a raspy voice.

"Yes," Felipe replied, but he still glanced nervously at the grim warriors on the hill.

"Don't mind them," Yoro said. "They thought you might be a tax collector." He invited Felipe into the village.

The Inucans numbered about two hundred people, and except for a few steel tools and a well for fresh water, they seemed to be living in the Stone Age. There was no electricity or plumbing, and the only fully enclosed structure was a cabin which Yoro said would be Felipe's new home. The nurse learned that it doubled as a medical clinic. His job was to deliver babies, inoculate infants against disease, clean wounds, treat sicknesses, and do everything in his power to save tribespeople from venomous snake bites. In the process he would have to learn the Inucan language, eat Inucan food, and submit to Inucan customs.

Felipe quickly settled into his new life amidst the Amerindians. Ponticari's jeep driver pulled up to the footbridge only once a week. Always waiting faithfully was a small group of Inucans. They gave the driver any mail or written requests for supplies from the nurse. The driver, in turn, gave them any mail for the nurse or supplies that had been requested the previous week. Aside from this weekly ritual, there was no contact with the outside world: no movies, television, telephones, computers, restaurants, convenience stores, in-door toilets, air-conditioning, or refrigerators.

And there was no one to call in the event of an unmanageable emergency.

None of Felipe's predecessors had lasted longer than a few months, and there were several who barely lasted a day. One young nurse immediately tried to retrace her steps back to civilization. The Sartum warned her that night was falling, but she screeched at him—nearly hysterical—and plunged back into the jungle. The Sartum ordered some of his warriors to follow her. They tracked her movements for about a mile until she crumpled into a fetal position and began sobbing between a stream and a cluster of jambu trees. Knowing that she would be easy prey for the jaguar that was also tracking her movements, one of the warriors hoisted the petite woman onto his shoulders and carried her all the way back to the village. At sunrise the following day, the Sartum ordered two warriors to safely escort her all the way back to the footbridge. When the trio arrived at their destination, they waited nearly an hour before they spotted a vehicle cruising along the lonely road. She managed to frantically hail down the car, but when she turned to thank the warriors for their patience, they were nowhere to be seen.

For Felipe Vasquez there would be no hasty retreats back to civilization. With each passing day among the Inucans he believed that he was precisely where he ought to be. A vast chasm separated this Amerindian tribe from technologically-advanced societies. But, much to Felipe's own surprise, he had little difficulty straddling that abyss. The world he left behind was a place where neighbors often remained strangers to each other; where relationships ended on the merest whim; and where an individual's entire existence—all of his or her dreams, efforts, and love—could be swallowed up in an instant by the headlines and deadlines of modern life. The well-heeled people of Rio, Tokyo, New York, and London were equipped with palm-sized cameras, miniaturized audio recording devices, and video equipment for every conceivable purpose. Yet, despite all of these gadgets that provided perfect recall, the modern mind was remarkably quick to forget the things that mattered most.

The Inucans had no recording devices of any kind. They didn't even have a written language. But they had retentive memories and a keen sense of appreciation. No kindness was forgotten, and the bonds that united people didn't continually disappear into a swirling sea of new trends and new pleasures. This rich sense of connection and personal affirmation made Felipe's labors immensely satisfying. In this primitive and secluded place he could clearly see the enduring consequences of his actions. He watched the infants that he had delivered and inoculated grow into healthy childhood. He marked their birthdays, heard their laughter, and held them in his arms. Even the Inucan warriors gradually accepted Felipe as one of their own. He may not have been a brother in arms, but he was a brother in the battle to create a better life for their families. Here, among this isolated group of human beings, he finally made a clear difference.

Thus inspired, Felipe devoted himself to a task that wasn't in his job description: he painstakingly developed a written form of the Inucan tongue. Then he offered to teach any interested villagers how to read and write their language. To his surprise, so many Inucans showed up for his daily reading sessions that he had to move the class out of his cabin and into the middle of the village.

The most attentive student in his first class was Yoro's granddaughter, Mara. At that time she was in the final stage of adolescence, replete with shy glances and bony body parts. But in the space of two years she had blossomed into a lovely young woman.

And she was no longer quite so shy around Felipe.

He sorted through his modest collection of books until he found a biology text that he had read as a boy. It was written in clear, simple Spanish and packed with illustrations. He returned to the main room of the cabin, flipping through the pages of the book. "Mara, all of these words are Spanish, but there are some anatomical diagrams that you might—" he looked up and saw her standing in front of him, completely naked.

"Are you sure you don't want to examine me again?" she flashed a bewitching smile.

"Mara—"

Before he could say another word she delivered a voluptuous kiss on his lips. The book slipped from his fingers and flopped to the floor along with his professional poise. He slowly wrapped his arms around her and they savored passionate kisses in silence.

But their intimate moment was interrupted by the sounds of movement and loud talk outside the cabin. Several people seemed to be running in all directions, and the chatter became more excited. Sarpay, one of the wisest and most respected tribal elders, burst in and breathlessly announced, "Pensador crossed the footbridge! Pensador is returning!"

She didn't seem to notice that Mara was naked. Sarpay closed the door and continued spreading the news throughout the village.

Felipe and Mara—still locked in their embrace—blinked at each other, barely able to believe what they had heard.

FOUR

THE UNDERGROUND
JUNGLE

THE PLEXIGLAS BLURRED OUR VIEW A BIT, but Woody and I could see the enormous room on the other side. Though this was my second viewing, its sheer size stunned me once again. Woody pushed against the lock with one hand and eagerly extended the other toward me. "The key; let's have the key."

"Jean didn't have one. The owner left her a key for every lock in the house, except the key for this...well, whatever this is," I cocked my head toward the brightly lit room.

"Can't you just call him?"

"Jean says he's in Venezuela or Brazil—somewhere in South America. Apparently he won't be back any time soon."

Woody turned; it almost seemed as if his brambly eye brows, aquiline nose, and thick lips formed into one loosely connected question mark.

"He works for Amilaco." I explained. "He's some sort of oil exploration guy. He goes around the world searching for oil deposits. He wants Jean to handle the sale, and she recommended you for this very reason." I pointed to the Plexiglas door.

Woody still seemed confused.

"You used to be a locksmith, right? Jean said that you had a knack for picking locks. So do you think you can undo this one?" I again pointed to the door.

This was enough to prompt Woody into action. "The oil guy was the sole occupant?" he asked as he pulled a needle-nosed device from his tool-belt.

"I think so."

He inserted the odd looking skewer into the mechanism and began his miniature fencing match. "No wife or kids?"

"Jean said something about a wife and son. The wife died and the son took off."

"Took off?"

"Ran away, I guess. Jean didn't go into detail."

Woody wiggled and twisted the instrument for several seconds, and then stopped.

He placed his hand on the translucent barrier and pushed ever so gently. The Plexiglas door slowly swung open. "Wow," I said, genuinely impressed. "If you ever get tired of inspecting houses, you could have an exciting career burgling them." I stepped into the room and the odor of rotting vegetation—or rotting something—filled my nostrils.

I caught my breath and turned towards the stairway: "Honey, we're in!"

"Fantastic!" Laine cried from the kitchen. She raced down the steps and joined us in the doorway. "I knew Woodrow could do it—" she abruptly gagged. "Jeez Louise, what's that stink?"

Her question was swallowed up by the gigantic room that loomed before us. I estimated that it was a perfect square, extending about a hundred and fifty feet from one corner to the next. But the ceiling was no higher than the ceiling of the old cellar. The immense space was crammed with plants and shrubs. The only exceptions were a narrow walkway that ran along the cinderblock walls, and another walkway that ran directly through the center of the room. This middle aisle bisected two vast fields of foliage.

The dense vegetation seemed terribly exotic—as in *tropical*—and it appeared to be dead or dying. But out of this clotted mass of desiccated flora, which was nearly five feet high in some places, a massive tree trunk arose in each quadrant of the room and merged into the ceiling, branches and all.

"Organic support beams?" Woody marveled at the functionally truncated trees. "I've never heard of such a thing."

He slowly walked down the center aisle, while Laine and I moved along the walkway adjacent to the left, or western, wall. A steam radiator was positioned about every twenty-five feet or so. My fingertips gingerly glanced off each one as we walked past; they were all cool to the touch. With each step I sensed Laine's mounting consternation. When we turned the corner we saw that no radiators lined the northern side, but the wall itself featured beveled protrusions and indentations. A section of the wall smoothly pushed out for several feet, and then smoothly turned inward for several feet. This pattern alternated all the way down to the eastern wall. At the innermost point of each indentation, a thick black line ran from the ceiling down to the floor.

"Have you ever seen a wall like this?"

"I was about to ask you the same question," Laine replied.

When we were about halfway to the eastern wall she stopped and shook her head. "I cannot believe this." Her comment was more of a lament than an angry outburst.

But then she took several steps directly into the foliage, and with each step she became angrier. She finally stopped and threw up her hands. "Look at this!" she exclaimed, "There's a damn rain forest under my kitchen!"

I wanted to put a good face on things, so I said, "Honey, look at the bright side: we finally have enough storage space for all of your shoes."

Instead of smiling, Laine screamed. She leapt toward the walkway and I caught her before she slammed into the wall. "Something crawled against my foot!" She stared back into the dense mass of vegetation.

"Your foot probably rubbed against a vine," I said.

"I wasn't moving—*it* was moving."

I was about to speak when a faint rustling sound came from the area where she had been standing. Though dry and drooping, the foliage in that portion of the room was at least three feet high and it was impossible to see through its tangled fronds. But, for just a moment, the surface of this green sea swayed as if something was moving through its depths.

"It's probably just a big insect," I said, trying to hide the hopeful lilt in my voice.

"How big?" she asked, still watchful.

Before I could answer, Woody's voice resounded from the eastern wall. "Hey, check this out!" We ran around the walkway until we found him kneeling by a steel, circular hatchway in the floor. It looked like something you would see on the conning tower of a submarine. It even had a swivel latch that could securely bolt the hatch to the floor. This locking mechanism was in its closed position, so the hatch could not be opened from underneath.

"What the heck is that?" Laine asked.

"Well," Woody pressed on the hatch, "if this were an ordinary house, I'd say this must be the sewage cleanout. But this is no ordinary house, and this is no ordinary cleanout cover." He contemplated the strange portal for a moment and then looked up at us. "Mind if I satisfy my curiosity?"

"Be our guest," I answered as Laine peered over her shoulder at the foliage. Woody undid the latch, grasped the metal handle, and slowly pulled up the circular hatch. It was larger than a man-hole cover but not as heavy. He tilted it back until the hinge held it upright. About three feet below the floor was a stream of slow moving liquid. My knee-jerk pessimism kicked into play, so I assumed it was sewage. But, when the inspector shined his flash-light into the hole, we saw that it was water—surprisingly clean water.

"Well I'll be..." Woody pulled a tape measure from his tool belt, stretched out its narrow aluminum tongue and plunged it into the stream. "About nineteen inches deep." He then leaned forward until his head and shoulders disappeared from view. If someone had taken a snapshot of him at that moment, the photo could've been titled *"Man Being Devoured by Floor."*

"It's about sixty inches in diameter," his voice echoed up from the porthole. "It runs west to east, but I can't see either end." His head reemerged from the orifice and he took a deep breath. "It must go on for quite a distance in either direction."

"Damn it!" I folded my arms across my chest. "Can you believe this? A freakin' river runs under my house!"

"Oh, sweetie," Laine sighed. She sympathetically rubbed my arm while looking down at the hole. "Look at the bright side: you finally have your very own Jacuzzi."

FIVE

THE THINKER

THE INUCANS KNEW HE WAS COMING. Two of their hunters had seen him
when he was still miles away. He looked just as he had looked several
years earlier: tall and lean, his face shaded by a wide-brimmed hat, with
thick, blond hair streaming down the back of his neck, touching his
collar. A distinctive red and white cloth was tied around his neck and
a holstered gun seemed glued to his right hip. But the rest of his attire
was less peculiar: almost all outsiders who ventured into the jungle
wore the same type of mud-colored clothes—what they called *khaki*—
with multiple pockets. Pensador was no different in that respect.

Behind him trailed a trio of hulking men. One was Anglo, one was
African, and the other was a curious hue of reddish-gold. To the Inucan
sentinels this last man seemed to be a blend of Indian, African, and Anglo
blood. The three men guided several mules that were tethered together
and laden with bags and boxes. A cage with two furry guinea pigs—
called *cuys* in the Inucan tongue—was tied to one of the mules. The
rodents jostled left and right with each step taken by their four-legged
carrier. The two largest mules were harnessed together. These beasts of
burden were attached to a big, wooden crate on wheels. Its lid was held
shut by a chunk of iron. With some effort, spurred on by an occasional
whiplash from one of Pensador's helpers, the mules pulled the massive
box along the footpath.

A woman trudged behind the men and mules. She was only a few inches shorter than Pensador and her eyes were hidden by dark-colored glasses. She kept pressing a white cloth to her mouth and swatting at a gray mist that hovered alongside the caravan. The Inucan watchers knew that this relentless fog consisted of tiny flying bugs.

Word was quickly sent to the village. Inucan women prepared garlands of flowers and baskets of fresh fruit. The children painted each others' faces orange and turquoise, the colors of happiness. The men slaughtered a fat goat, an equally plump capybara, and two peccaries. By the time Pensador and his group climbed the broad hill on which the village was located, the smell of the animals' succulent flesh—roasting on four separate spits—seasoned the air.

Upon entering the village Pensador asked to see Neko, the Sartum of the tribe. One of the Inucan women told him that Neko had died five dry seasons ago. The visitor was then introduced to the new Sartum, a graying man named Yoro. Pensador remembered him as Neko's most trusted advisor. The outsider removed his hat and gracefully tilted his head toward the Sartum in a gesture of respect. Yoro then embraced Pensador and the Inucan people broke into a chorus of yelps and whoops.

The tall woman who made the journey with Pensador stood silently and watched from behind a pair of large sunglasses. The three men who accompanied him were silent as well, but they continually glanced at the young, bare-breasted Inucan women. All of the Amerindians wore pieces of cloth from their belly-buttons down to their thighs. Some of the men gripped large bows by their sides; a few carried machetes, their blades stained and slightly warped by years of hard slashing. Several children gathered near the mules, and though Pensador's men let them touch the pack animals and the cage that held the guinea pigs, they wouldn't let them get close to the wooden container that was attached to the two biggest mules.

Pensador, accompanied by Yoro and a throng of villagers, went to the nurse's cabin. In the jungle's almost constant humidity and rain, the structure had aged considerably over the past seven years. But it still served its original purpose: medical clinic and living quarters for the village nurse. Felipe came out to greet his employer, whom he had never met. As they shook hands and exchanged the obligatory courtesies, Felipe was impressed by the quality of Pensador's Spanish. He was also struck by the man's well-formed face: it exuded strength and intelligence, balanced by piercing blue eyes.

The outsider introduced himself by the nickname the Inucans had bestowed on him: *Pensador.* His actual name was unknown to them. The tribespeople had once known him as *the outsider,* which is what they called anyone who wasn't born in the jungle. But at some point Neko referred to him as Pensador, which meant "thinker" in Spanish. Such an appellation seemed well suited to a man who mulled over every problem with exceptional thoroughness, so the name stuck. The outsider did nothing to discourage the Inucans from using the nickname. He considered it a title of sorts—*the Thinker*—and he savored the implied compliment. Over the past seven years, he even signed e-mails and memos to his U.S. colleagues with the lone letter P.

After conversing with Felipe in front of the cabin, Pensador made his way toward the far end of the hill-top. One of his muscular helpers stopped him and pointed to a large wooden structure in the middle of the village. It was an immense awning, at least twenty feet high, and wide enough to shelter every member of the tribe under its roof of hand-made wooden shingles. In the center of the open-sided shelter was a ring of hefty stones that encircled a pile of ashes. Scores of wooden stools were scattered around the slumbering fire pit. This was the closest thing the Inucans had to a community center. They called it *la recognus*—a hybrid Spanish-Inucan phrase which meant *the gathering place.* Pensador looked at it but shook his head. "There's nothing to stand on," he said to his worker in Portuguese. "I want everyone to be able to clearly see me."

With the entire tribe following behind him, Pensador walked to the village well. Its imported granite stones looked just as secure now as they had when he left the Inucans seven years ago. He ordered his workers to place a thick plank across the top of the stone structure. He stood on the board and turned toward the crowd. All eyes were on him. He stretched out his arms, and announced—in fluent Inucan—"It has been far too long, my friends, but I have returned, as I promised I would."

Pensador was the first outsider who had truly mastered their language, and that fact alone commanded deep respect among the Inucans. Many of the villagers were awed by the very sight of him. He was the subject of stories that had faded into legend. Some younger Inucans had begun to wonder how much truth the stories really contained. But now he was standing right there—as real as a rock, or a tree, or any tangible thing in their jungle cosmos.

Pensador had first made contact with the Inucans fifteen years ago. The villagers were wary of all outsiders, and initially he was no exception. But Pensador gradually won them over with his extraordinary knowledge and resources. He knew precisely when the moon would block part of the sun; he taught the Amerindians how to grow a greater variety of crops; he had medicines that could cure various sicknesses; and he seemed to understand the incarnations of their mysterious river god, *Surutas*.

Yet Pensador told them that he was not a god; he was, like them, only human. But he said that he possessed reason. His knowledge and resources were not magical. He explained that they were the products of arduous exercise in the discipline of reason. Despite his remarkable abilities, he assured the Inucans that he did not seek power over them. He only wanted to help them find a better way of life. With such assurances, he gradually quieted the rumors that were floating around the village about him.

Several years later he returned with gifts, tools, and more medicine. He also supervised the construction of the well and the cabin. He told the Inucans that a nurse would live in the cabin and help them in their ongoing battle against malady and misfortune. Before leaving them, Pensador made a solemn vow: he promised that he would someday return and share his special powers with the Inucan people. "You will be a great people," he told them. "All outsiders will envy the Inucans."

Now the villagers rejoiced, for Pensador had indeed returned, and they believed he would make good on his promise. Some of the Inucans tried to imagine how he intended to accomplish that feat: *How could he make outsiders envy them?* It was usually the other way around: the Inucans envied the capabilities and possessions of people who came from beyond the jungle. Outsiders always seemed to have so much, yet they almost always wanted *more*—more land, more trees, more gold, more information, more labor; outsiders inevitably sought to gain *something* for virtually nothing. But Pensador had never expressed an interest in anything beyond the good will of the people. So, despite their ingrained misgivings, almost all of the villagers were excited and hopeful. They wanted to see what *the Thinker* had in store for them.

SIX

THE REALTOR

JEAN HAD FLOWN TO TENNESSEE THAT morning for her family's annual reunion, which always took place on the first full weekend of August. But on Friday night—several hours after Woody completed his inspection of the house on Bog Lane—she phoned us at our place in Maynard to see how the assessment went.

Jean and Laine had first met at a restaurant in California two decades earlier. Shortly after graduating from their respective high schools they each struck out in a westerly direction: Laine from her home in Lincoln, Massachusetts, and Jean from her home in Memphis. Although raised in very different environments, they shared many of the same qualities—not least of which was a knee-jerk sympathy for lost causes and honorable outcasts. Indeed, the lower an underdog ranked on society's elusive index of social worth, the more Jean and Laine cared about the besieged soul. But neither woman played the role of dupe very well. They were adept at picking out parasitical personalities, and each woman could be as combative as a cobra when the need arose. So when their circuitous paths led them to jobs in the same San Luis Obispo restaurant, they quickly gained each other's respect. Before long, this mutual deference blossomed into friendship.

Their relationship—like other enduring friendships—was fused solid in the heat of a crisis. In this case, the crisis was instigated by the chef and co-owner of the restaurant where they worked. He was known as *Ash-Paz,* which wasn't his name but Persian for "maker of the soup." In his home country, those words served as the colloquial designation for any capable cook. But in the U.S. those words became his nickname. Ash-Paz was a pudgy middle-aged man with a bushy mustache and well-honed culinary talents. Praise for his creative cuisine had lured gourmands from as far away as San Francisco to the north, Los Angeles to the south, and Las Vegas to the east. Very few of his patrons left his restaurant unsatisfied.

But the chef seemed to think that he was entitled to a bit more than good table service from his waitresses. This became clear to Laine one night when she stayed late to cash out and balance each worker's account. Ash-Paz made a clumsy gambit for her sexual attention. She managed to fend off his advances, and the following day she warned Jean about being alone with the grab-happy Lothario. But Jean was a hostess, not a waitress, so she wasn't required to stay late and was never the last woman in the restaurant with Ash-Paz.

That all changed when Laine's father was diagnosed with amyotrophic lateral sclerosis, known to Americans as Lou Gehrig's disease. She took a leave-of-absence and flew back East to take care of her dad while Jean took over Laine's responsibilities.

Late one Sunday evening, after every one else had gone, Ash Paz celebrated the end of another lucrative week by imbibing several snifters of Grappa. Jean was leaning over the cash register, making a few final calculations, when the chef suddenly latched onto her, more-or-less the way one herd animal might abruptly mount another herd animal. Far from being frightened or angry, Jean began to laugh. The scene struck her as funny, if not pathetic. There she was, drooping after a long day's labor; and there he was, huffing and sweaty, trying to hump her through her skirt. Even if she had been naked, Ash-Paz's efforts would have been wasted. He didn't seem to realize that he was grinding his penis into her right hip. He was so plastered he couldn't have found her vagina with a compass and a spotlight. But, like a dog in heat, he pounded away with mindless zeal. All the while, his chef's hat sagged off the side of his head—its puffy, white top flopping back and forth with each pelvic thrust.

Jean couldn't help but laugh. She laughed so hard that her voice resounded over the restaurant's empty chairs. The chef was drunk enough to be uncoordinated, but not quite drunk enough to be oblivious to her reaction. He unsteadily stepped back and listened to her laughter. With each passing second his rage swelled. Ash-Paz didn't realize that Jean was giving him a get-out-of-jail-free card. She was treating a criminal act as if it were a harmless prank. But he didn't see it that way. More precisely, he didn't hear it that way. All the chef heard was her laughter—gales of hilarity that struck his ears with the force of a vicious insult.

When Jean reported for work the following afternoon, two police officers were waiting for her in front of the restaurant. They informed her that she had been accused of theft. Dismayed, Jean asked what she had been accused of stealing. They didn't answer her question, but one of the officers explained that they had to follow through on the complaint, and he asked for permission to search her car and belongings. She assented without a second thought.

Jean always carried around a large ivory-yellow bag which contained her purse, cosmetics, cell-phone, and sundry other essentials that an American woman accumulates in the course of daily life. Laine called it "the saffron saddlebag." Jean seldom had the time to inventory its contents, so there were items in the bag that she had been toting around for months, forgetting that they even existed. When one of the officers got to the bottom of the bag, he found a thick packet of twenty dollar bills, neatly wrapped in a restaurant serviette.

It was the exact amount of money she had been accused of stealing.

At first Jean was too mortified to think clearly. But as she was led off to the San Luis Obispo police station to be booked, she realized that Ash-Paz must have planted the twenties in her bag before she left the restaurant the previous night. She then explained what had happened to the officer who booked her.

"Why didn't you report this last night?" she was asked.

"I didn't know he was going to be such a schmuck about it last night," Jean said.

The other waitresses were questioned about the chef's past behavior, but each of them said he had always been a respectful employer. A few members of San Luis Obispo's Chamber of Commerce even came forward as character witnesses for Ash-Paz, and he played the role of gentle victim to perfection. Things looked grim for Jean. The theft probably wouldn't land her in prison, but she would be toting around a criminal record, along with her saffron saddlebag, for the rest of her life.

That's when Laine got wind of what was happening. She immediately flew to the west coast, drove straight to the San Luis Obispo police station, and reported her own after-hours scrape with the libidinous chef. Laine explained that he had attempted to fondle her, and when she rebuffed his advances he became more aggressive. She put an end to the episode by grabbing a butcher knife: "You put another hand on me," she told him, "and the meat I'll cut off won't be choice, but it might make a good appetizer for the rats in the wine-cellar..." Or words to that effect.

After Laine's testimony was revealed, other waitresses came forward, one by one, and told their own stories. One mousey woman, who had two children to support, revealed that in her case the chef's behavior went beyond grabbing, grinding, and sloppy kisses. Ashamed and regretful, she confessed that Ash-Paz had paid her five thousand dollars cash to keep her mouth shut—the very mouth that he had once wrenched open.

As the tables slowly turned in Jean's favor, the renowned cook quietly sold his half of the restaurant to its co-owner and boarded a plane for his homeland. Before the police could issue a warrant for his arrest, he was on his way to Iran, where extradition was all but impossible.

In the aftermath of this drama, Jean and Laine were as good as blood sisters. Jean never forgot Laine's dam-breaking testimony. And even after each woman left San Luis Obispo and took separate, meandering paths back East, they never failed to talk at least once a week.

Jean eventually established herself as a realtor in Connecticut. While attending a series of real-estate seminars in Boston, she met an up-and-coming lawyer who clarified some of the finer points of property law. He sported a smile that somehow managed to be cute, manly, and intelligent all at the same time. Like Jean, he was a transplanted Southerner, and his classroom demeanor combined professional poise with easy-going grace. None of these facts hurt Jean's opinion of him one bit. An after-class conversation led to a cup of coffee, which led to a date, which led to more dates.

All of which ushered Jean Smith and Harrison Powell to that mysterious leap of faith called marriage. They eventually had two daughters and settled down in Plymouth, thirty minutes from his office in Quincy and less than three blocks from Bog Lane.

As the years passed Harrison developed a name for himself in criminal law, and he acquired one of the prime offices in Plymouth County's District Attorney's suite. Jean's career flourished as well.

Her reputation as an exceptionally competent agent passed from mouth to ear, and she began working as an independent realtor out of her Plymouth home. Her shingle was on display in her front yard, so when the owner of the elegant Queen Anne Victorian on Bog Lane decided to sell his house, he presumably saw her sign and decided to give her a call.

Location, location, location...

When I told Jean about the underground rivulet that Woody had uncovered, she issued a series of penitential declarations. You don't know what an apology is until you've heard one delivered by a daughter of Dixie.

But no apology was necessary. Richard Hitchens hadn't told her anything about the hatchway leading to the subterranean stream. We couldn't very well expect Jean to give us information she didn't have. Nevertheless, real estate agents don't like surprises when they're introducing buyers to a property. Hitchens's omissions made it seem as if Jean hadn't done her homework, which must have stung her professional pride. Wanting to spare her a heated and potentially costly exchange with a client, I offered to call Hitchens myself.

"That's nice of you, Rick, but he told me not to give his cell phone number to anyone. He was very explicit on that point."

"What exactly do you know about this guy?"

"Not a whole lot. I told you and Laine just about everything I know last Tuesday."

"What about his son? You said he ran away from home. Did Hitchens tell you that?"

"No. I heard about it last winter, when it happened. And I don't think he ran away from home. All I know is that he disappeared. The police conducted a search; there were a lot of land-sweeps, door-to-door inquiries—they did everything possible. But the boy was never found."

"Oh, God."

"I asked Harry about the case and he says the police now seem to believe the boy was abducted."

"Abducted? How old was he?"

"Just a little kid—six or seven."

"I thought he was a teenager."

"No, no. He was just a little boy." There was a pause, and when she spoke again her voice seemed to lose its pace. "It was an awful time down here. People felt horrible for that poor kid. He had some sort of mental problem, so even the next-door neighbors didn't see very much of him. I guess his father didn't want him playing with the other kids on the Lane."

"What sort of mental problem?"

"I think he was autistic, but I'm not really sure," Jean said. "Pamela Sampson—who is gonna be one of the nicest neighbors you're ever gonna have in this life—saw him a few times, and she said he was a cute kid. She couldn't tell there was anything wrong with him."

"Was he abducted from Bog Lane? That would be pretty brazen of the kidnapper to take the chance of getting bottled up on a dead-end street."

"No one knows. No one saw him being abducted. But I remember it was an awful time down here. Parents were so afraid for their kids. I made sure that Samantha never left the yard, the gate was always locked, and the dog was always out there with her. I even gave Delaney lectures about playing it safe. It was a dreadful winter; just dreadful."

"You think maybe that's why Hitchens wants to get rid of the place? Too many painful memories?"

"Could be. But he didn't say so. He never mentioned his son. He said that he was"—her intonation became mockingly officious—"in

Brazil working on a 'top-priority' project." Despite the deep Southern lilt in her voice, Jean could deftly imitate other dialects and styles of speech. "He said that his work would keep him there for quite some time, so he decided to sell the place. He told me his lawyer would give me all the paperwork and the keys to the house."

I shook my head. "This whole thing sounds kind of bizarre."

"Kind of? In all my years I've never handled a deal like this one. Besides, I flat out didn't like the way Hitchens talked to me. I got the feeling he wanted me to say 'Yes sir' every time he finished a sentence. I was good and ready to turn the whole thing down."

"But you didn't."

"No, I didn't. When Hitchens told me the price I almost choked. I had to ask him to repeat the figure twice. Hell, if Harry and I weren't buying the winter house in Savannah we'd have taken #3 Bog Lane ourselves."

"We're very grateful, Jean."

"Ordinarily I'd have talked the seller into upping the price. But, in this case—well, I naturally thought of my soul-sister and her two darlin's in Maynard."

"I can't tell you how much it means to us, and we're still crazy about the place. I'd just like to talk to Hitchens. You know, man-to-man."

"Hmmm. You think if I talk to him woman-to-man he might break down and start crying?"

"Oh, cripes, Jean, you know what I mean."

"No offense taken, darlin.' But Richard Heinrich Hitchens, well, he's another story," she made a sound that was part groan and part growl. "That guy has been treating me like an indentured servant, and that is offensive. So I'm gonna give him a taste of his own dis-respect. You go right ahead and ring that bastard. His number is..."

Hell hath no fury like a realtor scorned.

SEVEN

THE SPEECH

MOST OF THE MEAT AND FRUIT had been devoured by the time the sun set over the Amazon. Except during the dry season, which lasted roughly from January into April, thunderheads and other dark specters were common sights in the jungle sky. But now there were only a few vaporous strands on the western horizon, and the last rays of sunlight imbued these serpentine wisps with a creamy glow. Some of the Inucans took this as a sign: heaven seemed to be smiling on Pensador's return celebration.

As the afternoon passed into evening, the female outsider removed her sunglasses, revealing a pair of thin, sloping eyes. These, along with her height and mustard complexion, made her an object of fascination. Pensador said that her name was Lynn Lee, and that she came from a faraway place called *China*. His listeners responded with a pregnant "ohhh," as if he had revealed a profound secret. But even after he introduced her to the villagers, the only person who talked with her was Felipe, who conversed in his broken English. The Inucan women were especially curious about the tortoise shell clips that held Lynn's long hair in a tightly wrapped chignon. They had never seen such devices or such a hair style, but none dared ask her about them.

As the feasting came to an end, Pensador ordered his three male helpers to build a bonfire on the outskirts of the village, near the well. When this was done, he beckoned the Inucans to gather around the crackling flames. He dispensed toys to the children. These little ones stared unabashedly at Pensador. Not only had they never seen an oriental woman, they had never seen a man with beige skin, blue eyes, and blond hair. The toys that he gave them were relatively simple gadgets—building blocks and plastic connectors—but the adults were as intrigued as the children.

Yoro, the leader of the tribe, made an elaborate display of offering his hut to Pensador. It was the most spacious abode in the village. But the outsider politely declined and said that he would sleep in a tent until "other arrangements" were made.

At that moment his three workers were already assembling three large tents on the other side of the village. One tent was for Pensador, one was for Lynn Lee, and the other was for the three male helpers.

Like Lynn Lee, the three men seldom spoke, but Pensador talked to them in Portuguese, one of the two outsider languages with which the Inucans were familiar. The other was Spanish. Over the past century a number of Portuguese and Spanish words had crept into their indigenous language, which was an off-shoot of Quechua—the language of the ancient Incas. But Pensador referred to his three male helpers by the curious names of "Larry," "Curly," and "Moe," none of which sounded either Portuguese or Spanish to the Inucans.

After gifts had been given to the children, Pensador stood on the well and addressed the entire tribe. "My dear friends, tomorrow I will give you more than toys. Tomorrow every man in the village will have his own new machete and his own new axe; every woman will have her own box of salt and new pots for boiling water; every boy will have steel hooks and nets for fishing; every girl will have new needles and tools for sewing; and you will all have many other new things as well. This I promise you." The crowd yelped and struck sticks against sticks—the Inucan version of applause. They marveled at his ability to express himself in their patchwork language. Pensador paused solemnly until the clamor subsided.

"My dear friends, when I was last here, workmen built this well so that you could always have fresh water. We also learned new ways to grow food; we enriched your beautiful language with some new words; and we learned how to defeat some sicknesses—even malaria. Now we will do even more. The foundation of a great people has been laid, just as the foundation for this well was laid—piece by piece. Now, just as we draw fresh water from this well, we will draw greatness from the Inucan people."

Excited and hopeful, the crowd erupted again. Lynn Lee stood amidst the people, her arms folded across her long, spare torso. Although she didn't understand Inucan, she had helped write the English draft of the speech and had listened to Pensador rehearse it several times. Now she nodded as he spoke, as if hearing the beat of a familiar song. She knew just when to anticipate each joyful outburst from the tribespeople.

Pensador continued: "Trust me when I tell you that the Inucans will someday become a great nation. Trust me when I tell you that your descendants will be honored by the peoples of the world—not only those who speak Spanish and Portuguese, but by all other nations. And when your grandchildren's grandchildren look back upon this generation, they will say that YOU"—he thrust out his arm, tipped by an extended index finger, and slowly turned until he came full circle— "YOU are the ones who laid the foundation for the great Inucan nation!"

The clatter of sticks on sticks again filled the night. He had used the Spanish word *nacion*. Most of the Inucans weren't even sure what a "nation" was, but they assumed it must be something wonderful. Pensador waved his arms to quiet the crowd.

"Why? Why will your descendants say these amazing things about you? I will tell you why. It is because YOU are ones who will take the first step toward something that mankind has dreamed about for thousands of generations. YOU are the ones who will lead the battle against disease, and defect, and decay. YOU are the ones who will help me to create heaven on earth: A place where there is no more sickness;

where everyone is strong of limb and sane of mind; where everyone lives for over a hundred dry seasons!"

The crowd was stunned. Most were ready to go with Pensador wherever he went, but now he had gone to a place that was beyond their reach. *How could anyone live over a hundred dry seasons?* Still, every pair of ears and eyes remained focused on the outsider. Felipe watched from the outskirts of the crowd. During the past three years he had developed a thorough command of the Inucan language. But now he questioned his lexical knowledge. Pensador's claims were so incredible that Felipe thought he must have misunderstood.

As if he had read the nurse's mind, Pensador nodded with slow, exaggerated movements. "Yes, my dear friends, I am telling you the truth: If you are willing to trust me, all of these things will come to pass." He stopped nodding and looked directly at Yoro. "These things will take time, and they will require some changes. A large flying machine will visit us tomorrow, and the day after, and the day after. Don't be alarmed by these visits. The flying machine is big and noisy, but it will do NO harm. In fact, it will bring great good to the Inucan people." He paused to let these words take hold, then he zeroed in on Yoro's face again. "A new building—much bigger than the nurse's cabin—will have to be built on the next hill." He pointed west, but kept his eyes on Yoro. "Some builders will come here again to live with us for a while. But I will stay here with you, and I will make sure that these changes do not upset your way of life. These changes will make your lives *better,* not worse. So I ask you to accept me again, just as you accepted me seven years ago. I ask you to trust me." Pensador somberly surveyed the faces around him. "You know me. You know that I do not make promises lightly. So believe me when I tell you that a great adventure lies before you: an adventure that will enrich the Inucan people. If you are willing to place yourselves—*your very bodies*—in my hands, we will defeat sickness and push back the face of death. This is my promise to all of you!"

Many Inucans still doubted their ears and weren't sure what to do. But some villagers immediately responded with ecstatic cries. This display of joyful certainty induced others to join the happy chorus. The contagion turned even more Inucans into believers, and a chain reaction gradually swept through the crowd. Soon almost all of the villagers were on their feet, creating a sustained, jubilant roar. Many hugged; some had tears in their eyes.

A deep thrill ran through Pensador's chest as he surveyed the scene. *Surely*, he thought, *the jungle has never witnessed such a spectacle. Even the animals of the forest must be stirring in their lairs.* He regretted that his father wasn't here to see this. Pensador had spoken to all kinds of groups, many of which were far larger than this primitive throng. But the Inucans' reaction was different from anything he had ever experienced. These people honored him not just because he could make them rich, and not just because he held hierarchical rank or institutional power. The Inucans perceived his inherent, self-enhanced power; they sensed his individual greatness apart from any organizational structure. They trusted *him*. They believed in *him*. They appreciated his utterly unique worth. This was the intensely personal adulation that he had craved ever since he was a boy. How he wished—dearly wished—his father were here to see this.

Charged with an overwhelming sense of power and purpose, Pensador threw caution to the wind. His voice became louder and more vibrant: "But, my dear friends, to make more progress, we must understand four truths. From these truths come great power and great responsibility. When I was last here I didn't share these truths with you." A look of regret darkened his features. "I believed that the time was not right, for these four truths are not easy for all people to hear. But now," a magnanimous smile brightened his face, "I believe that the Inucan mind is big enough and strong enough to embrace these four great truths."

Although she didn't understand the words, Lynn Lee knew that Pensador was departing from the rehearsed script. The crowd had expressed its appreciation four times, so she knew the speech should be drawing to a close. But her boss still seemed to be going strong. She looked up at him and for a moment they made eye contact. She flashed a confused expression and held her palms upward, as if carrying an invisible tray in front of her. He ignored the silent query and continued speaking. "My dear friends, I refuse to treat you like children; I refuse to keep you in the dark…"

As he spoke, she quickly walked over to Felipe and asked him to translate.

"So, my dear friends, open your minds as wide as possible," Pensador cried out, "for you are about to hear the truth!"

EIGHT

STATIC

"HELLO. MAY I SPEAK WITH MR. Hitchens please?"

"Who is this?" the deep, resonant voice was instantly defensive.

"My name is Rick Delvecchio; I'm calling from Maynard, Massachusetts. My wife and I are interested in your house in Plymouth. In fact, we'd like to buy it. We just wanted to ask you one or two questions about the place."

There was a pause. "How did you get this number?"

"Jean is ill; she can barely speak. She asked me to call for her." I had no qualms about telling Richard Hitchens a little white lie.

"Jean...Jean Powell? The real-estate agent?" His voice got louder with each word. "She gave you my cell number?"

"Well, as I said, she's very sick and wasn't able to call. Look, Mr. Hitchens, I want to make this deal. I didn't call to quibble about the price. I want to buy your house."

I didn't bother to mention that Laine had already hired Woody to change all the locks at #3 Bog Lane. "But first I need to ask a few questions about the house."

Another pause. "Is there a problem?" There were sporadic bursts of static on the line, but at that point I could clearly hear him.

"Frankly, yes. It's not a major problem, but you must admit that this is an unusual way to sell a house."

"Mr. Del—"

"Call me Rick."

"Whatever. If Mrs. Powell is sick I'm sure there are other realtors in Plymouth; just as I'm sure there are other buyers who ~ ~~ ~ interested in my house." Static obliterated part of his sentence, but I got the message.

"Mr. Hitchens, I told you that we are interested. We are very interested. I just want to ask you a couple of questions—"

"I thought a buyer would be signing papers by now."

"Signing papers? Mr. Hitchens, these things take time—"

"I don't have time. I'm involved in an extremely important and time-consuming project." His voice was clipped and curt. Jean's imitation was dead on.

"Then I'll make this brief. Was flooding ever a problem at your house?"

"This is infuriating." The electromagnetic frazzle got louder.

"Mr. Hitchens, what is the purpose of the hatch in—" the disturbance cut me off.

For a moment we heard only the sizzle of the spheres. Then his voice broke through the static: "If you want the house, you know the price!" He was shouting now. "Send the check to Maxwell Burke in Boston. He has full power of attorney and he knows where to wire ~ ~~ ~." A spate of interference blotted the end of his statement.

"Hold on, Mr. Hitchens," now I was shouting.

"Do it today," his voice was thick with suppressed rage, "or the deal is off the table."

"Mr. Hitchens," I said, struggling to remain calm and yet speak over the static at the same time, "you just have to answer a couple of questions…"

Suddenly the line was perfectly clear. I thought he had hung up, eliminating the static.

I shrugged at Laine, who was listening on the cordless extension.

She opened her mouth to speak—and I was about to hang up my phone—when Hitchens's voice oozed through our receivers with menacing intensity: "Listen, whatever the fuck your name is: I don't answer to anyone. NOT TO ANYONE. Do you understand? Comprender? Yo sou mi propio dios." I'd heard enough Spanish in my life to know that his last several words were in that language, but neither Laine nor I understood their meaning. Then, in English, he said: "I am my own ~ ~~ ~," static chopped up his last word, but it sounded as if he said decoy or debris, neither of which made any sense. Before I could think of something to say, there was a decisive click on his end, followed by silence.

I stared at the phone until I heard Laine's voice float down the hallway, "Sweetie, I was just wondering: how do you say asshole in Spanish?"

NINE

ENLIGHTENMENT

PENSADOR PAUSED TO ALLOW THE INUCANS to prepare themselves for what he was about to say. Felipe had translated enough of her boss's words for Lynn Lee to realize what was coming. She looked at Pensador and repeatedly ran her index finger across her throat. The villagers standing nearby thought this must be a form of sign language used in her homeland. She silently mouthed the words, 'No, No, No,' as if Pensador was about to step off a cliff. But he turned away from Lynn Lee. He was sure that he had the entire tribe in the palm of his hand. The Inucans watched him expectantly, and he had no intention of disappointing them.

"My dear friends, these are the four vital truths of life…

…One: there is NO truth higher than us or greater than us. There is NO spirit beyond us. There is NO spirit meaning. There is only nature and the struggle for survival. Therefore, we must make up our own meanings to suit OUR purposes.

…Two: Since there is no Spirit, there are no spirit consequences for any of our actions. There is no spirit right or spirit wrong; no good and no evil; no heaven and no hell; no karma and no nirvana; no blessing and no retribution. Therefore, we must create OUR OWN idea of goodness and create heaven on earth for ourselves.

…Three: the greatest good of all is REASON." He used the Spanish form of the word—razon—which the Inucans understood.

"Therefore all of our thoughts," he pointed to his right temple;

"and all of our feelings," he pointed to his heart;

"and all of our passions," he pointed to his genitals;

"must be guided and controlled by REASON.

"...Four: the greatest and purest form of reason is science." He had used the Spanish form of this word—*ciencia*—during his first stay with the Inucans. But the tribespeople struggled with its meaning and application. Now he sought to simplify things for them. "What does science mean? It means PROVE IT. Whenever we say something or believe something, science tells us that we must PROVE IT. We mustn't believe anything unless we can PROVE IT to be true." He sensed that he had finally found just the right words to capture the minds of the tribespeople.

"My dear friends," he continued, "I know the Inucans have been visited by missionaries in the past. They offered you faith. But faith is a big lie—it's a big, beautiful tree covered with poisonous leaves. So I won't tell you about faith. Instead of faith, I will tell you about science. If you give me your help and your trust, I will PROVE that what I have said here tonight is the truth!"

Lynn was no longer gesturing for him to stop. Felipe had translated enough of Pensador's words for her to get the gist of his ad-libbed finale. Now she held her head with both hands, as if it might roll off her shoulders if she let go. Undaunted, Pensador continued: "If we live by these four great truths that I have shared with you tonight, we will become free people. We will liberate ourselves from ignorance and all childish imaginings. And in our freedom—" his voice peaked as he raised both hands in the air—"we will become a new race of noble beings!"

But this time there was no reaction from the crowd.

"Understand?" he asked, still beaming.

Silence.

"Do you understand?" he cried out, his smile fading into the night.

The only response came from Lynn Lee. She muttered an English word which many of the Inucans heard, but only one of them understood.

"Fool."

TEN

TAKING THE PLUNGE

I'D CALLED RICHARD HITCHENS TO CLARIFY matters so that Laine and I could calmly make a fully informed decision. But my call didn't quite have the intended result. Instead, Hitchens was more of a mystery than ever, and his Plymouth property featured contrivances that continued to baffle us. So we had to make a major decision with some cards still unturned.

Realizing that Hitchens might contact another realtor at any moment, we reappraised our situation. Commuting from Plymouth to Watertown, where I worked as an architect, would be a bit more difficult than my current trek from Maynard. Laine's teaching job in Lexington would be even less accessible. But Gabriel's education took priority over such considerations, and Plymouth had a better school system than Maynard. He was due to start 2nd grade shortly after Labor Day, so he would have the remainder of August to adjust to a new environment and a new set of faces. As far as the house was concerned, it was structurally sound. Of course, it would take a considerable amount of time to clean out the basement and get rid of the other unwanted furnishings. But Woody had confirmed our strong suspicion: in purely material terms, this was the deal of a lifetime.

As for the previous owner, Richard Heinrich Hitchens had revealed himself to be a less-than-endearing acquaintance. But it's not as if we were planning to have him over for pajamas parties. Once the necessary papers were signed, his house would become our home, and we would never have to deal with him again. We had a maturing Certificate of Deposit account—fat with years' worth of interest and ripe for plunder. This, combined with various other savings, would cover the 20 percent down payment. We could have the money on the table before noon on Monday.

All too often, a swipe of brutish bad luck puts people on a detour to nowhere. But in this instance, luck seemed to be taking us in a very different direction. By a chancy series of unscripted turns, we had an opportunity to jump on the fast track to happy times. Cape Cod Bay would become our pond and its sandy shores would serve as our extended back yard. On winter afternoons we'd skate on the cranberry bog outside our door. In the summer there would be barbeques on the beach with old friends. At night we would fall asleep not to the screams of sirens, but to the chirps of crickets. And mornings would have us waking up to birdsongs and the Atlantic's salty fragrance. With such thoughts looming large in our shared imagination, Laine and I agreed to take the leap. Within an hour of my aborted exchange with Hitchens, she was talking to our accountant and I was on the phone to Maxwell Burke.

Later that evening, after all the necessary assurances had been given to each concerned party, I tucked Gabriel in and read him two bedtime stories. One was about his third favorite non-human: Thomas the Tank Engine. The other was about his second favorite non-human: Winnie the Pooh. His favorite non-human, of course, was Biscuit, who had already curled up at the foot of the bed. Half way through the second tale Gabriel too was sound asleep. He had pulled the blanket up around his head so that only his curly, brown locks were visible. Too tired to walk down the hall to the master bedroom, I laid down next to him.

The erratic but purposeful tapping of a computer keyboard sounded down the hall from the study. As I slowly nodded off, I surmised what Laine was doing. Earlier, during the flurry of deal-making discussions, it became clear that Hitchens's lawyer was eager to broker an agreement for his client. But Maxwell Burke confessed that he had met Hitchens only once and knew very little about him.

The veil of secrecy that seemed to encircle Hitchens didn't put Laine off one bit. On the contrary, it sharpened her curiosity to the point where she was determined to poke a hole in the curtain.

If anyone could accomplish that feat, it was my internet savvy wife.

ELEVEN

REASON SUSPENDED

THE CROWD WAS SILENT.

"Reason!" Pensador shouted again. "Do you understand?" He carefully scanned the surrounding faces. Some had blank expressions. A few were clearly stunned. Others seemed lost in thought. Lynn Lee was walking towards the other side of village, where the skeletons of three large tents had been erected. He knew she was angry.

Felipe stood with his hands in the pockets of his khaki shorts. Pensador had been a stranger to him for the past three years. But within the past three minutes he learned a great deal about him—more than he ever expected to know. Still, the outsider's motives eluded him. *Why come to such a remote place to indoctrinate a group of people? What did Pensador hope to achieve? If he was indeed committed to the spread of atheism, why wasn't he preaching on college campuses and writing books for the Western world's vast middle-class?*

Yoro, the old chief and resident wiseman of the tribe, contemplated a different question: *Will this man help or hurt my people?* Pensador saw the expression on the Sartum's face and thought that he looked dismayed but not angry. This gave the outsider reason for hope. Perhaps Yoro was beginning to realize that his entire world-view was about to be overhauled. During Pensador's first two stays with the Inucans he had learned to respect Yoro's incisive mind. He was easily the brightest of the Amerindians, and his people trusted his judgment. If the outsider could win over the Sartum, that would make his mission considerably less difficult.

Pensador continued to assess the faces that encircled him. As he looked, a pair of sapphire eyes caught his attention and effortlessly drew him in. They were the eyes of a young woman. For a moment he imagined a Venus flower silently beckoning a fly into its eternal embrace. Pensador instinctively shook himself to break the spell. But those seductive eyes issued an unspoken thought: *Come, come; it won't do any harm to look just a moment longer...*

So he looked.

The bonfire, which began as a raging inferno, was now a glowing heap of scorched logs. But the crackle of wood could still be heard, and the fire's radiant core kept the Amazonian night at bay. The woman stood just within the fire's dome of illumination. The ethereal light lacquered her already tan complexion and accentuated the contours of her face. As he looked her over, he could easily believe that the Inucans were the descendants of a seafaring Pacific people, for her high cheekbones and feline eyes were those of a Polynesian goddess. Her arms were folded across her waist, framing a pair of bare, harmoniously proportioned breasts. Mahogany nipples—circular stems on nature's most exotic fruit—lured him into a long stare. He finally broke away, only to be ensnared by the sight of her smooth, slender abdomen. She wore a short, threadbare skirt, which might have been a loin cloth masquerading as a skirt. A thin sheen of moisture, the jungle's froth, glazed her thighs and calves. He slowly re-examined her body, from her legs, to her waist, to her breasts, to her shoulders, to her neck... Inucan females wore a simple necklace of white beads to show that they were betrothed, and a necklace of red beads to show that they were married. He was very pleased to see that this Inucan female didn't wear a necklace of any kind.

When Pensador's re-examination reached the woman's face, he realized that her eyes had been watching his eyes the whole time. She wasn't smiling, she wasn't awestruck, and she wasn't confused. Her cool demeanor unnerved him. She couldn't have been more than eighteen years old, yet she seemed to know exactly what was going on in his mind.

He didn't remember her at all from his last visit. At that time she would have been a mere child, and would naturally have slipped under his radar. But now, having blossomed into a nubile beauty, she pulsated on all of his masculine sensors.

And she was staring *at him*.

He forgot that all of the Inucans were staring at him. At that moment he was only aware of her. With each second that her eyes met his, waves of primal hunger pounded from the animal depths of his skull and coursed through every gland of his body.

Pensador—the self-avowed champion of unsullied reason—yearned to pluck and possess that Venus flower for the crudest of reasons. Sensing this, he tried to elevate his hunger with a more refined line of thought. *Aclla* was the Quechua word for "chosen woman." The ancient Incas bestowed that title on only the most beautiful and talented girls throughout the empire. These vestal virgins were taken to one of the imperial centers where they were trained to serve Inca royalty.

Yes, Pensador thought, *this is my aclla. She will make a worthy vessel.*

TWELVE

MONSTER

The red Chevrolet pickup was heading east on the Carver back-road at exactly thirty-five miles per hour. It couldn't go any faster because it was behind a Toyota Corolla whose driver refused to break the posted speed limit: thirty-five miles per hour. The pickup edged to the line that divided the narrow road. The bearded driver at the wheel of the Chevy tried to pass the Toyota. But the street continually curved one way or the other, and every time he began to swerve around the sedan, another vehicle suddenly loomed up ahead in the left lane. The man swore every time he was forced to retreat behind the Corolla, and every time he swore his pit-bull on the passenger seat barked. The dog's muzzle, neck, and shoulders were etched with scars and its dingy, off-white fur was taut against its ribcage. Hunger sharpened a dog's aggressive instincts, so the man kept his hound on a meager diet.

Impatience turned into anger, and the man gunned the engine until his front bumper was within a few inches of the Corolla's fender. A wrinkled face peered back at him from the sedan's side mirror. But it wasn't a reproachful look—it was a frightened look. The eyes in the side-view rectangle were old, weak, and scared. When the bearded man sensed fear in the other driver, his mood gradually went from annoyance to amusement.

"Wanna have a little fun, Monster?" he asked. Sensing that its master's blood was up, the dog barked again. The man could see into the car through its back window. An arm—as wrinkled as the face that glimpsed back through the side-view mirror—reached from the passenger seat to the driver's seat. Something was being said in the Corolla; advice was being given. The Toyota's right directional blinked and the car slowly pulled over to the side of the road, next to a sign which read: *Welcome to Plymouth.*

But rather than pass the Corolla, the bearded man pulled up behind the car and leaned on his horn. He lowered the passenger-side window just enough so that his pit-bull could thrust its head through the opening and bark furiously. The Toyota quickly pulled away. The man waited a moment then floored the gas peddle. Gravel crunched under the pickup's tires and scattered across the rural road. Within seconds, the Chevy was bearing down on the Corolla again. The car sped up and actually exceeded the speed limit. The young man in the pickup grinned. He had achieved his objective: he had frightened the old man so much that he broke the law.

But now a new question formed in the younger man's mind: *How much faster can I get the geezer to go?* He accelerated and came dangerously close to the Toyota's rear fender. The Corolla's speedometer hit the forty-five mark, and the elderly driver almost lost control of the car as it swerved through a sharp turn.

The impromptu game of cat and mouse continued for another quarter-mile or so, until the sedan again pulled over to the side of the road to let the truck pass. But, once again, instead of passing, the Chevy pulled up behind the Toyota. Unable to take anymore, a stooped figure with thinning white hair slowly stepped out of the Corolla. The old man trembled in the August sunlight, but he was determined to stand his ground. His wife called out to him from the passenger seat. "Herb, get back in here! Just keep driving! Herb!"

The bearded man got out of the pickup. A tattoo of a Harley-Davidson chopper stained one of his beefy, white biceps; the outline of two massive mammary glands stained the other. "You lookin' for trouble, grandpa?' The pit-bull again seemed to sense its master's combative mood and it unleashed a string of ferocious barks from the cab of the pickup.

The old man was confused. "Trouble? I don't want any trouble," he said earnestly. "I'm just trying to get home in one piece."

The bearded man was about to speak when he saw something move off to the side of the road, behind the Toyota. A raccoon was digging at the bottom of a tall, chain-link fence. The pit-bull had smelled the creature through the opening in the passenger-side window. It thrust its angular head through the gap and snarled; saliva dripped from its bared fangs. The bearded man scanned the street but didn't see any houses or any other people. He quickly walked over to the Chevy's passenger door and swung it open.

"Go get 'im, Monster! Get 'im!"

A terrified voice cried out from the Corolla as the dog flew off the passenger seat of the pickup: "Herb! Get in the car! Get in the car!" The husband didn't need any more prompts. He quickly got back into the Corolla and slammed the door.

In an instant the pit-bull turned into a sixty-five pound canine missile that shot past the Toyota and aimed straight for the rac-coon. The tattooed man laughed as the elderly couple drove off. "There's your lunch, Monster!" he cried as he watched his hound zero in on the rodent. "Get it! Go get it boy!"

The raccoon clawed frantically at the dirt below the bottom rail of the chain-link fence. Just as the pit-bull was about to pounce, the rodent flattened its body and crawled under the steel bar. The dog couldn't fit through the trench the racoon had created, but it tore at the ground until the opening was just large enough for the hound to squeeze through.

"Get 'im, Monster! Go get lunch!"

The area beyond the fence looked like a nature preserve. A rooftop turret was visible in the distance, jutting up between some pine trees. The rest of the area was a loosely forested expanse pocked by a couple of very small ponds. The raccoon had scampered into this open stretch of land, but it couldn't outrun the pit-bull which was in hot pursuit.

"Rip him up, Monster! Rip him up!"

Moving as fast as it could, the raccoon ambled around a small pond or marsh, about thirty feet in diameter. Some bushes partially obscured this body of water from the man's view. When it was three-quarters way around the pond, the raccoon unexpectedly turned, arched its back, and hissed loudly.

"Save a leg for me, Monster!"

But as the man howled in delight, he realized that the raccoon wasn't facing his pit-bull. The rodent was facing the marsh. The animal was taking a defensive posture *against the pond* and leaving its flank exposed to the pit-bull.

"Stupid coon. He's so scared he doesn't know which way to turn."

The pit-bull closed in fast. Rather than run around the marsh, as the raccoon had done, the dog went straight at the rodent, plunging through a shallow corner of the pond.

Suddenly the marsh came to life. Water erupted in every direction—far more water than should've been thrown up by the dog's paws. Something white and sinewy rose up from the pond, and for several seconds there was a violent thrashing behind the bush. The man couldn't make out what was happening.

"Monster! What are you doin'? Monster!"

He heard a bark, followed by a yelp. The raccoon scampered away from the pond. The man pushed his face against the chain-link fence and stared. Something out of his earliest nightmares came to life before his eyes. The nightmare was so old that it didn't originate with him—he had inherited it from his human ancestors. A massive bundle of interlocked flesh slowly wheeled behind a bush. The man shuddered as he saw a coil of scaly meat wrap around the pit-bull's midsection. Except for some leafy flecks that were stuck to it, the slithery appendage was whiter than the pit-bull's fur, and it was so thick that it covered the area from the dog's neck down to its haunches. The man could hear small branches snapping as the thing squeezed the pit-bull. Then he realized that the snapping sounds weren't being made by cracking branches—the sounds were coming from his dog's ribcage.

The man opened his mouth to cry out, but no sound emerged. He felt as if his chest was being crushed right along with his pit-bull's. All he could do was watch in paralyzed horror as the dog's hind legs kicked wildly. But the horrid thing kept squeezing until the squat limbs finally went limp. Then a mouth lined with fangs slowly opened wide. The man screamed, "No!"

Jaws clamped down on the dog's scalp, quickly inched over its ears and down to its neck. The thing's mouth was big, but not big enough to fit around the canine's brawny shoulders. The thing's jaws were stretched to their limit.

But then the creature did the impossible: it somehow opened its jaws even wider.

The thing's face became a hellish contortion as it swelled to devour the dog's carcass. The flesh around each of the creature's lidless eyes stretched until its eyes became tight, horizontal slits. Yet, the tattoed man sensed that the thing could still see him; it was daring him to scale the fence. The man didn't move.

The dog's hind legs slowly disappeared into the creature's mouth.

Several cars passed by. Their occupants saw the bearded man on the side of the road, but they couldn't see what the man was seeing. A vital sensor deep in the man's mind—an inner gyrocompass that helped him differentiate up from down and left from right—slowly disintegrated. The man was unable to accept or even comprehend what had happened. The ancient horror, and the savage death of his most trusted friend, wouldn't fit into any of the stiff compartments of his mind. So the walls within his mind slowly gave way, one by one, like falling dominoes.

He staggered senselessly backward, and would have stumbled into the road if he hadn't bumped into his pickup truck. There he slumped to the ground.

One of the passing motorists called the Plymouth Police on a cell phone to report a drunken man sitting next to red Chevy, talking to himself. The passer-by was concerned that the man might attempt to drive away in his inebriated condition.

A short while later a Plymouth Police car pulled up behind the Chevy pickup. An officer stepped out of the cruiser and walked toward the bearded man. When she was within a few feet of him, she removed her hat and crouched down.

"Sir?"

The man didn't speak or move. He continued to gaze through the fence to the forested area beyond. The officer followed his line of vision, but the thing the man had seen—the thing he was still seeing in his mind's eye—was gone. She noticed a sign on the fence which read: *Danger: Area Patrolled by Attack Dog.* The face of a ferocious looking hound was sketched below the warning. But there were no dogs in sight. She leaned forward to smell the man's breath but didn't detect the odor of alcohol.

"Sir, can you hear me?"

He didn't answer.

She placed two fingers against the side of his neck and could feel a pulsing jugular vein. The officer stood up and was about to call for an ambulance when she heard the man whisper something. She crouched down again. "What?"

The man mumbled, but she couldn't quite make it out.

"Sir, what did you say?" she leaned toward him and put her ear up to his lips.

With some difficulty, his lips and tongue maneuvered just enough for him to pronounce a barely audible word into the officer's ear: "Monster."

THIRTEEN

THE EXPERT ASSISTANT

That night in the rain forest—like every night in the rain forest—a multitude of superbly adapted sensors continually swept the jungle. No movement went unnoticed. Though they remained unseen by humans, the presence of these sensory-rich organisms was revealed by their hoots, clicks, snorts, growls, grunts, rasps, shrieks, and voltaic hums, all of which blended into a sprawling symphony that resounded from the shadows. The instrumentalists in this unruly orchestra were not driven by applause or a yearning for social recognition. They were impelled by throbbing instincts: hunger, the need for a mate, or the desire to survive another night.

The Amazonian darkness ended the way it had always ended—with the sun radiating the eastern horizon. As the luminous disc peaked over the world's edge, the night's denizens retreated to their hidden lairs, and the forest's daytime cohort gradually emerged. The earliest and nosiest greeters were the birds. An astonishing assortment of winged virtuosos made their presence known in a cacophony of chirps, caws, coos, clucks, screeches, whistles, and even the rat-a-tat-tat of an industrious woodpecker. Perhaps, if for no other reason, they sang because they could soar high above the slit-eyed killers that stalked the jungle.

On that particular morning, the cry of a new arrival was heard in the Inucan village. Although exotic and difficult for the Inucans to decipher, this call was not celebratory, and it was muffled by tent fabric: "How could you be so stupid? What the hell were you thinking?" Pensador sat on his cot, staring down at the artificial floor of his tent. Lynn Lee didn't pause long enough for him to answer her questions. "I cannot believe that you would jeopardize this entire project so senselessly. We haven't got one genetic sample yet and you're already trying to impose your mindset on the locals!"

"Pipe down Lynn, they'll hear you."

"I thought you said that none of them understand English."

"They all understand anger—it's kind of a universal language, you know. It wouldn't do to have you scolding the great Pensador in his own tent." He flopped back on his cot and stretched his legs. The half bottle of tequila that he had downed after his speech the previous evening left a murky clump of brain cells clinging to the inside of his forehead. "Oh, shit," he muttered, "you don't think that nurse is around, do you?"

"Felipe? Last night he told me he was going fishing this morning with some of the kids."

"Does he speak English?"

"Well enough," she replied as she paced back and forth beside Pensador's cot, "but I'm sure he's not around. He didn't strike me as the eavesdropping type."

"Keep your voice down just the same."

Lynn Lee's firmly set chignon hairdo of the previous evening was now a loosened mass that quivered every time she moved. Errant strands of hair had escaped the grip of the tortoise shell clips and flailed off in all directions. She had slept in her khakis, and when she awoke she made her way straight to her boss's tent without a thought for her appearance.

"You know, Hitch, it always comes down to your ego. Your stature always seems to be the biggest concern."

Pensador would never allow anyone else to talk to him the way Lynn Lee talked to him. He made an exception in her case because she was indispensable to Lexel Corporation's long-term plans. So instead of unleashing a barrage of words, he parried her comments with self-evident truths. "Well, Lynn, this whole mission rides on my ego. If these people don't trust me, this thing is over. If these people don't think I'm the greatest thing since the wheel, we're not going to get one genetic sample, not a single one."

"If you're so concerned about that, why did you put your trust on the line so needlessly last night?" She stopped in front of his cot and folded her arms across her chest. "You gambled everything on a friggin' philosophical discourse for people who can't even write their own names. What the hell does it matter what they believe about anything?"

Pensador remained flat on his cot and wished that Lynn would lower her voice. He trusted her intuitions about people as much as he trusted anyone's—not very much. So he wasn't fazed by her outburst. But on matters pertaining to genetics and biology, she was his oracle. Though she was still in her forties, he believed that there were only a handful of people in the world who knew more about DNA than Lynn Lee.

As a child growing up on the island now known as Taiwan, a wealthy uncle presented Lynn with a mechanical toy tiger on her seventh birthday. She was immediately fascinated by the small creature's abilities. Why did it open and close its jaws at the flick of a switch? What made the tinny growl that came out of its mouth? How did its legs move back and forth? She sensed that the answer to all her questions lay within the tiger. So while most children would've been content to simply play with the toy, she proceeded to dismantle it until she found its battery pack. She noticed that when the battery was disconnected, the animal became silent and stationary. This gave rise to fresh questions. How did the battery get the creature to do the things that it did? Were there miniscule words written on the inside of the battery, telling the animal how to act?

She was about to take a kitchen knife to the battery when her father came upon the disemboweled toy. Little Lynn Lee was perplexed by his shocked reaction. Didn't the tiger belong to her? What difference did it make if she played with the animal or took it apart? Either way, it would eventually cease to work. Better that she learn something about it before it wore out. Her exasperated father shook his head: "Child," he groused, "you are too curious for your own good." Her parents worried that their rich relative would be angry if he found out how Lynn had abused his gift. But a few months later she received a card in the mail. On the front was a picture of a snarling Siberian tiger. Just six words were written inside:

> Dear Niece,
> Never stop being curious.

That simple piece of advice became the North Star of her existence. As a high school student in the city of Taipei, her sense of wonder moved beyond mechanical animals and focused on the real thing. But her mind was still consumed by the same basic question that had vexed her as a seven year old: Exactly what determined the nature of organisms? In the process of reading biology books and dissecting small animals, she learned about cells: the basic unit of all living things. She then went deeper to learn about the nuclei of cells—the core "headquarters" from which each cell's chemical wizardry was supervised. She went deeper still to learn about the chromosomes that were enfolded within each nucleus. The first time she saw a chromosome through an electron microscope, it reminded her of another toy from her childhood: a flexible, fuzzy caterpillar as long as her arm. And when she learned about the genes that lined each chromosome, she imagined tiny, coiled strings running along the caterpillar's body. Working through chromosomes and the nuclei which housed them, genes directed cells to perform their various life-giving functions.

But what did genes consist of?

The answer, she learned, was acid. Deoxyribonucleic acid, to be precise.

The microscopic constituents of this peculiar type of acid, or DNA, took the form of parallel spiral ladders—the famous double-helix—whose "rungs" were connected by information-rich nucleotides. Here, finally, were the "miniscule words" written deep within each organism. DNA comprised life's microscopic command structure: it was packed with chemical codes that controlled the production of proteins and told each body's trillions of cells what to do and when to do it.

Still, Lynn Lee realized that science had only scratched the surface of this mystery. It was a magnificent scratch, to be sure, but a scratch nonetheless. Many more questions about the nature, workings, and possibilities of DNA remained unanswered. She would devote her life to finding the answers.

That quest led her to the University of Michigan, where she earned a post-graduate degree from the first and finest human genetics department in the United States. From there she ventured to yet another continent where she gained her doctorate in genetic science from Cambridge University. She then spent several years working in laboratories in Europe and the U.S. At each step she further developed methods and techniques that might someday enable her to carry out ambitious projects. But wherever she went she found climates and colleagues that were far too timid for her taste.

While working in Boston, at a lab funded by the Massachusetts Institute of Technology, she became embroiled in an argument with the director of the facility.

She espoused views that—to the director's mind—smacked of elitism, if not racism.

But Lynn Lee didn't believe in the categorical superiority of any sub-racial group.

She did, however, believe in the superiority of adaptive and constructive genes over non-adaptive and destructive genes. And she firmly believed that bad genes should be suppressed, socially or otherwise. "The eugenicists of the early 20th century had the right idea," she proclaimed in an unguarded moment, "they just went about it the wrong way. In a democracy you cannot keep undesirables from breeding."

"Undesirables?" asked the increasingly-bewildered director.

"People who couldn't survive in a state of nature." Lynn thought for a moment then gave a more exact response: "Individuals who wouldn't be able to pass on their genes if it weren't for society's pity. As someone who understands evolution, you know as well as I do that it is unnatural for defective specimens to breed."

The director was speechless. Lynn assumed he was inviting further comment.

"The technology to *thoroughly* screen fetuses for maladaptive genes is within our grasp. That's what we should be working on. Once we've perfected that technology, any fetus found to have maladaptive inheritable traits should be aborted. That process should become as automatic as the test for pregnancy itself."

The director finally found his voice. "And what, may I ask, constitutes a maladaptive trait?"

"Any inheritable feature that is detrimental to the quality of society's gene pool."

"Such as?"

"Such as any genetic marker that has been identified as a probable trigger for disease, psychological disorder, physical deformity, or a below average I.Q."

The following morning she was politely asked for her resignation.

Lynn despaired of ever finding a research environment that would allow her to break new ground. But one winter morning, not long after her resignation from the M.I.T. lab, she received a phone call from a complete stranger. He had learned of her viewpoints from a mutual acquaintance, and he claimed to sympathize with her plight. He then made a series of extraordinary offers: the third highest position at a private research laboratory named *Lexel*; the finest equipment money could buy; her own assistant who would also function as her private secretary; and a salary that was nearly triple what she had been earning at the M.I.T. lab. The caller imposed two conditions: Lynn couldn't tell anyone where she was working or what she was doing.

She accepted the stranger's terms.

That was nearly twelve years ago, but Lynn never regretted her decision. Her ongoing quest had now led her to a fourth continent and the most challenging environment she had ever faced: the Amazon jungle.

Pensador reflected on Lynn's face as she stood impatiently over his cot. It wasn't beautiful or cute. Even when she wasn't angry, there was a hardness to her face that kept it from being pretty. But her eyes glimmered with intelligence, and he had always found intelligence to be singularly sexy.

When he finally answered her question, his words came slowly. His hangover didn't allow the luxury of a hasty or passionate response. "Lynn, I thought I could win them over to our way of thinking. Don't you see? It would make our job so much easier."

She shook her head. "Did you honestly think you could undo a lifetime of cultural conditioning with one night of counter-conditioning?"

"Well, it's a start."

"No starts, Hitch. No indoctrination. We haven't got time for that bullshit."

"Shhh."

"I'm dead serious. If you try to put their minds ahead of their genes one more time, you can wave goodbye to me."

"We'll have to deal with their minds sooner or later."

"They're living in the dark ages!" she cried as she resumed pacing the tent. "They haven't got one hour's worth of education between them. They don't know their ABCs, much less anything about their DNAs. The only explanation they need to hear is that, in the end, our project might benefit some of them. They've just got to trust us. They've just got to have faith in us."

"They won't believe in us if they don't believe in what we're doing."

Lynn stopped pacing and looked down at him, but he had placed his forearm over his eyes. "Hitch, these people practically venerate you. They love you so much that they will trust you; and because of that trust they will believe in your project—even if they don't understand anything about genetics."

"I'm not talking about genetics." He forced himself to sit up on the edge of the cot. "It's not about genetics. It's about believing in a set of principles that guide one's thoughts. That's what I gave them last night. A simple set of principles to believe in."

"Huh!" For the first time that morning Lynn seemed mildly amused. "I don't know what crowd you were watching, but the people I was looking at didn't seem too enthusiastic when you unloaded your 'four great truths.' It's a good thing Lex wasn't here to catch that act."

"They are *his* truths," Pensador said. "I think he would have approved."

Lynn took a deep gulp of jungle air and said the Chinese word for feces. Then she wished out loud: "I'd give five hundred bucks for a cigarette." Her non-sequitur momentarily freed his mind to recall the *accla*: the beautiful young woman he had chosen the previous night. What would he give for her? A necklace, for starters. But would it arrive quickly enough to suit his schedule? *I must find out her name*, he thought.

Lynn paced the tent again, distracting him from his reverie. He tried to sooth her frayed sensibilities. "The crowd went quiet because the people were thinking about what I said. That's to be expected. Serious thought takes time. It may take awhile, but we can win them over. Besides, we've still got our ace-in-the-hole." He glanced at the large wooden box on the side of the tent.

Lynn's sensibilities weren't soothed at all. "I thought we were going to save that thing for the first lab failure. If we show them that monstrosity before we even start experimenting, we'll have nothing left to fall back on if things start to go wrong."

"Once they see that thing," he replied confidently, "we won't need to fall back on anything else. Why do you think we lugged it along with us? It could've come in with the choppers, but I wanted it with us just in case things went bad *really fast*."

She swore again in Chinese and then reverted to English: "Hitch, don't screw this up. We had a plan, now let's stick to it. Lex can worry about the big picture."

"He won't be here for a couple of days," Pensador replied. "Until then, I'm in charge, and I don't have the luxury of *not* making decisions."

"But the decision you made last night was one you didn't have to make at all! These people didn't ask to hear anyone's philosophy of life!"

"We still need to be honest with them on some level."

"Honest? Honest?" She echoed the word as if she was hearing it for the first time.

"Just how honest are you going to be? What are you going to tell them? That we're going to play with the magic stuff inside their bodies?"

"Okay Lynn, I can hear you," he said quietly, hoping she would follow suit.

"Are you going to tell them about all the things that might go wrong?"

"Be quiet, Lynn."

"Are you going to tell them about the grotesqueries we're going to create before we produce one healthy, immuno-advanced human?"

He bolted upward and came face to face with her. "Shut-up!" Though his teeth were clenched, he spat out each consonant.

Lynn didn't flinch. "I'm putting you on notice, Hitch. I'm here for only one reason: to experiment. I'm not here to teach; I'm not here to win any friends, and I'm not going to spend one more second in this shit-hole jungle than absolutely necessary. Those are MY four vital truths, and if you overlook them again, I'm out of here. Understand?" She punctuated her final word by prodding his chest with her knuckles. Then she spun around, tore open the flap of the tent, and stormed out.

She left in such a fury that she didn't see the wizened, bare-chested man who stood next to the tent, waiting for permission to enter.

FOURTEEN

A MUTATING MIND

I AWOKE TO A QUIET HOUSE and a one-page computer printout on my chest. Across the top, written in Laine's barely legible hand, were the words: "Gone to bank with G & B, then off to Plymouth to clean! Bring the wet-vac and try to find the other scraper." Normally a buyer wouldn't have access to a new house until papers were passed. But we had the keys and Richard Hitchens was thousands of miles away.

Possession, as they say, is nine-tenths of the law.

Still, I worried that Laine was moving too fast. She had a tendency to consider the width and depth of a chasm while in midleap. I thought about calling her on her cell phone. But my wife had something in common with a cruise missile: once she was fixed on a target, there was no changing course or calling her back. So, as I'd done many times before, I resigned myself to her trajectory and hoped for the best.

Over a breakfast of tea and toast I turned my attention to the rest of the printout, which was essentially a thumbnail sketch of Hitchens's career and accomplishments. A lifelong resident of Plymouth, he displayed a remarkable talent for chess and language at a very young age. He pursued his fascination with chess until he lost the final round of a national championship match for juniors. It was the first time he had ever been defeated in formal competition, and he apparently hadn't taken it very well. At the tender age of eleven he renounced chess and hurled himself into the study of language.

Chess and language seem to involve very different kinds of intelligence, and it's hard to believe that anyone could be gifted in two such divergent realms. But by the age of fifteen Hitchens was fluent in English, German, French, Spanish, and Latin and he was also beginning to turn his attention to oriental languages. One year later he flew to Europe and won first prize at what was called "the Lexical Joust"—a bygone tournament for high school students that was sponsored by a number of academies to promote the study of language.

At twenty he graduated *magna cum laude* from Yale University. But his major had nothing to do with language. Instead Hitchens pointed his formidable intellect straight down, in the direction of geology. He went on to get a post-graduate degree in engineering from Stanford. While there—apparently in his spare time—he mastered the abstruse and nearly dead language of Aramaic. He then completed his doctoral dissertation at the Massachusetts Institute of Technology. Among other things, his thesis proposed innovative ways to find and extract oil in difficult or hazardous terrain.

Hitchens put his theories to the test in Venezuela's rugged hinterlands, with extraordinarily profitable results. Almost overnight, he became *le enfant terrible* of the oil industry. He plied his talents as a consultant for Amilaco Corporation. He was evidently a born risk-taker, because whenever he gambled his reputation in search of oil, he made sure to put his money exactly where his mouth was. Time after time he scored big for the company, and with each success he won monumental payoffs.

By the age of thirty Hitchens owned a sizable share of Amilaco stock. At company conferences and stockholder events he increasingly became the center of attention. With his dazzling intellect and bold victories, he outshined his peers in both the executive and tactical ends of the business.

Hitchens then wrote a book about philosophy. Geology and philosophy were at opposite ends of the academic spectrum. In a way, they were also at opposite ends of the ecosphere. Perhaps Hitchens had spent so much time scrounging around in the muck that he longed to soar through the aurora of rarified ideas. But his book, entitled *The Four Truths,* got poor reviews from professional philosophers. One called it "muddled"; another found it to be "turgid"; and yet another said it was "cynical." Such comments struck me as odd. Having taken a couple of philosophy courses in college, it seemed to me that all philosophers were muddled, turgid, and cynical. I didn't think you could even qualify as a professor of philosophy if you were clear, humble, and hopeful.

Laine's research also turned up a few interesting items on Hitchens's family, but not as much as I'd hoped. He married twice. His first wife, who was also a geologist, had gone into labor prematurely while in Iraq with her husband in 1973. She died in a Baghdad hospital, shortly after giving birth to a son named Steven. The boy apparently grew up without a mother and lived in some of the finest boarding schools on America's eastern seaboard. The absence of maternal warmth must have left a void in Steven's life, but he eventually revealed himself to be a chip-off-the-old-block by attending several Ivy League schools and collecting degrees in anthropology and language studies along the way.

In 2001 the elder Hitchens married a Norwegian immigrant named Sonya Kristiansund who, coincidentally, was born in the same month and year as Steven. She gave birth to a son named James in 2002, but Sonya died two years later. There was no information about the cause of her death or James's subsequent disappearance. The death of two wives and the mysterious loss of a young son would have broken most men. But Richard Hitchens wasn't most men. He continued applying his theories and expanding his profit margins as if nothing had happened. The printout ended with a blurb from the M.I.T. alumnus guide, which briefly alluded to Hitchens's latest passion: genetics. Apparently he was so disgusted by the negative response to his book on philosophy that he devoted himself to the study of biological reproduction. Once again, he had boomeranged from one intellectual environment to a completely different realm. He even founded a genetics research company which he named Lexel—perhaps as a reminder of the great "joust" he'd won as a teenager.

Hitchens always seemed ready to rush off in pursuit of another body of knowledge. But the astonishing thing was that, time after time, he was able to pull it off. He seemed to become an expert on any field to which he turned his attention. Such was the power and radiance of his intellect.

I pondered the printout in the quiet of my kitchen. Hitchens was nearly sixty years old but apparently still eager to scale greater heights. What might such an audacious mind accomplish? He might invent a form of fuel that doesn't pollute the atmosphere, or develop a cure for some insidious disease, or create a painless way to remove nose hairs. So maybe it was a good thing that he lost that championship chess match as a boy. That defeat seemed to be the spark that unleashed Hitchens's mind in all directions.

Who could say what his bristling brain would come up with next?

FIFTEEN

THE BOX

Y<small>ORO STOOD AT THE FOLD OF</small> P<small>ENSADOR'S</small> tent and watched Lynn Lee storm toward her own tent. She didn't notice the old warrior. He was often surprised at the things outsiders didn't notice. The Sartum wondered if outsiders became less aware when they ventured into the jungle.

The Amazon basin was a cauldron of sizzling moisture that leached the life-force from a person's skin. Felipe had explained to Yoro how humidity affects people, and even now, at this early hour of the day, he could feel the truth of his words. The dank air clogged his pores and ripened the jungle's fetid odors. Amazonia must have seemed hellish to outsiders who weren't accustomed to such an oppressive climate. Perhaps, Yoro reasoned, the intense humidity numbed their senses.

The Sartum heard a distinct *click* from inside the tent, followed by the rustle of movement. Then there was a quick double click and more movement, pierced by an abrupt *yelp*. The murmur of Pensador's voice seeped through the tent's thick skin; his tender, soothing tone made it seem as if he was talking to a small child. This puzzled Yoro for a moment, but then he remembered the two guinea pigs that Pensador had brought with him into the village. He assumed that the outsider was playing with these pets, which the Inucans called *cuys*. The Sartum considered leaving, but decided to be patient a bit longer.

As he waited, he looked at the sky. It had been unusually clear for the past two days, and some of the Inucans believed this had something to do with Pensador's arrival. It seemed that even the forces of nature bowed to his triumphant return. But Yoro was beginning to have doubts about the outsider's mission—doubts that weighed heavily on the old man's sense of responsibility. His sacred duty as Sartum was to protect his people from all harm, including the dangers that might lurk behind friendly visitors bearing gifts.

The Inucans were well prepared to confront hostile Amazonian tribes. They had skirmished many times against other people of the jungle for control of hunting grounds, crops, and women. Sometimes they even battled over matters of pride. But men who came from beyond the jungle brought hidden plans and invisible influences— threats that couldn't be readily checked or subdued. Thus the Inucans were distrustful of all outsiders, and over the centuries they stealthily avoided people from the wider world.

But their existence ceased to be a secret when a group of explorers accidentally stumbled straight into the village about a hundred dry seasons ago. Since then, many other visitors had made the journey into the Amazon to see the reclusive tribe. Some came to peer at the Inucans as if they were strange objects that had to be studied; some came to teach; some came to heal; and some came to find out if the tribe had anything worth taking. The Inucans did their best to shunt these people in other directions, and they almost always succeeded.

Pensador was one of the few who had managed to slip past the tribe's defenses, mainly because he first appeared in the role of rescuer. On that day, fifteen years earlier, an Inucan boy and girl—brother and sister—had been collecting fruit some distance from the village when they were attacked by a swarm of peccaries. The boy helped his younger sister climb a tree, but he was set upon by the wild pigs before he could pull himself to safety. His sister's screams brought several warriors rushing to their defense. But before they arrived, loud cracks echoed through the jungle. Moments later the warriors found the boy lying on the ground—bloody and trembling, but alive. His sister was kneeling by his side, kissing his cheek, while his wounds were cleaned and bandaged by a tall outsider. Scattered around them were the bodies of five dead peccaries; the rest of the pack could be heard scurrying away, deeper into the jungle. Those two children were the first Inucans to lay eyes on the man who would become known to the tribe as Pensador.

The outsider's heroics gained him an immediate audience with Neko, who had been Sartum at the time. Yoro was one of the warriors who had rushed in the direction of the screams, and he knew the boy would have been killed by the wild boars if Pensador hadn't happened on the scene. In the days that followed, the handsome outsider ingratiated himself to the villagers by sharing the contents of his backpack with them, and by making an astonishingly successful effort to learn their language. Yet, despite the man's apparent goodwill, Yoro remained wary of him throughout his lengthy stay with the tribe.

When Pensador returned for an even longer visit seven years ago, Yoro was a tribal elder. Like the other villagers, he couldn't help but wonder at Pensador's remarkable range of knowledge and his seemingly bottomless bag of resources. The blue-eyed explorer was more capable than anyone Yoro had ever known, and he apparently cared about the Inucans. With each passing day, the outsider slowly won the elder's grudging respect. But he never earned Yoro's complete trust. The only outsider who ever accomplished that feat was Felipe, the nurse.

The Sartum heard a triple click, followed by more movement. It sounded as if Pensador was dragging something across the ground. Then there was a dull *snap*, which was less distinct than the earlier clicks. A moment later Pensador emerged from the tent, strapping something to his wrist. The tall outsider almost bumped into Yoro, but the old warrior stepped aside.

Startled, Pensador dropped his watch. "What the... Yoro! How long have you been standing here?"

"Not long," replied the Sartum in his raspy voice. He noticed that Pensador's first two words were spoken in the Anglo tongue before he effortlessly reverted to the Inucans' mongrel language. But the Sartum pretended to be unimpressed. Instead, he looked steadily at the outsider until Pensador remembered to display the appropriate sign of deference: he tilted his head forward. This was the proper Inucan greeting, known among them as *sumidad*. It signified something between an oriental bow, an occidental handshake, and a military salute: respect, goodwill, loyalty. As Sartum, Yoro wasn't obliged to sumidad any member of the tribe. But all were expected to give him this honor. Though he was an outsider, Pensador—like Felipe—had been embraced by the Inucans, so he was expected to follow their customs when he was among them.

Pensador picked up his watch and invited Yoro into the tent. From the inside it seemed even bigger to the Sartum. It was high enough for a man to stretch without touching its ceiling, and spacious enough for several people to sit and talk without smelling each other's breath. The tent had screened flaps that admitted air but kept bugs out, and its spongy, orange floor insulated one's feet from the ground. Several fascinating devices were positioned at various places in the tent. Though their purposes were unknown to Yoro, they seemed carefully designed to accomplish some important task. A large wooden box, sealed by a metal lock, occupied one side of the tent; next to it was the metal cage that held a chubby *cuy*. But now there was only one guinea pig in the cage; Yoro had seen two yesterday.

As the Sartum glanced around, Pensador looked at him and did something unexpected. He asked Yoro—*in English*—"How are you today?"

The Sartum met the outsider's inquisitive eyes but didn't answer.

"Right," Pensador said after an awkward moment, "you don't understand English, do you?"

Yoro still did not answer. Instead, in his native tongue he said, "I came to talk with you about the words that you spoke last night."

"Aaah." Chagrin spread across Pensador's face as he sat in a canvas chair in a corner of the tent. "Yoro, I wish the party had ended twenty minutes earlier than it did." The Sartum was still standing in the middle of the tent. Too hung over to be a model host, Pensador simply motioned for him to sit on the large wooden container.

"*Obrigado*," Yoro replied. But just as his body rested on the box, a weighty presence inside of it suddenly and loudly shifted. The old man quickly stood up and stared at the container. A series of small holes dotted the upper part of the large box, and he noticed that something was moving inside. Mystified, he looked at Pensador.

The outsider didn't say anything, but his sheepish grin was replaced by a very different expression. Though he had a handsome face and gleaming white teeth, this new grin was not reassuring. He seemed gratified. Perhaps Yoro's anxious leap confirmed a suspicion—a weakness within the Sartum?—which may have pleased Pensador. This possibility angered the old warrior.

"I'll stand," he said.

Pensador's expression abruptly changed. He realized that he had miscalculated for the second time within a span of ten hours. "No, please," he got up and ushered Yoro toward the canvas chair, "take my seat."

The Sartum allowed himself to be seated in the chair.

"I apologize," Pensador said. "I wasn't thinking."

"What is in the box?" Yoro asked.

"Oh, it's...ah...it's just a pet of mine."

"A pet? Why do you keep it locked in a box?"

Pensador rubbed a hand across the back of his neck. "It, ah, it sometimes...it doesn't... the light bothers it sometimes."

"It must not like being in that box, no?"

"That's a unique container. It's lined with a special material that retains moisture. And the, ah, my pet doesn't mind the heat. It actually likes the heat."

"What is it?"

Pensador opened his mouth to answer, then smiled. "I will show you someday. Someday soon. But today won't do. There's a lot going on today." He quickly changed the topic: "How's the chair, by the way? Do you find it comfortable?" His expression of concern struck the Sartum as extravagant and false. The old man looked at the metal cage with the chubby cuy. He wanted to ask where the other one had gone, but the outsider prattled on: "I find it very comfortable. It's just a fold-out thing, but it relieves the aches in my lower back. That's one of the disadvantages of being tall. After you've been on your feet all day, you get a lot of pains in the lower back."

Yoro eyed the outsider. "I am too old," he said, "too fond of anything that relieves my aches—and too easily put off."

Pensador poured a cup of water from an insulated container and pretended that he didn't hear the comment. But the irony of his silence wasn't lost on him. With his back to the Sartum, his lips curled into a simper.

"This is odd weather," he said in his most affable tone. "What do you make of it Yoro? Two clear days in a row during the rainy season: quite strange." He didn't bother to mention that he had carefully checked local meteorological conditions before setting off from Codajas, so that his arrival would coincide with a rare break in the weather.

Yoro continued to look directly at the outsider. There was no trace of amiability in his eyes. "It happens from time to time," he said.

"Well, you would be the expert, having lived here your entire life. Have you ever had three straight days of dry weather during the rainy season?"

"Pensador," Yoro said, "I did not come here to talk about the weather."

"Of course not," the outsider replied. "You must have so many things to do today, and here I am, going on about the weather." He flashed a self-effacing smile at his guest—the same smile that had pacified colleagues, girlfriends, and acquaintances over the years.

But Yoro was unmoved. He trusted Pensador's smile a bit less than he did a moment ago; a moment ago he trusted that smile a bit less than yesterday.

SIXTEEN

BAN SIDHE

SHE ROSE UP FROM THE BOG LIKE AN APPARITION, her naked form glistening in the moonlight. Her face was so lengthened and stricken by sorrow that the water which dripped off her body might have been tears. She turned and stared at the elegant home which loomed nearby. Its windows were dark and silent. The two lives that should have warmed its rooms were absent. Two gentle souls, lost in time.

The silhouette of a turret graced the top of the house. She spread out her arms as if to embrace the entire structure. But her arms remained outstretched. She turned her face upward, above the stately dome, until her eyes gazed at the clear night sky. Then she cried out. It was an anguished, elongated sob that would have been understood by any heart that had ever been cruelly wronged.

It was a cry for justice.

An elderly woman was awakened by the forlorn wail in the distance. She reached over and turned on her bedside lamp. *It must have been a nightmare*, she thought. The howl was so other-worldly that it recalled stories from her youth: legends about the *banshee*. Her Irish grandmother had told her about spectral beings who warned of danger by issuing a baleful shriek. The ancient Celts called them *ban sidhe*. According to her immigrant ancestor, the banshee was the spirit of a woman who had died in childbirth, or lost her life while defending her child's life. The mother's spirit was allowed to wander the earth for the duration of what would have been her natural life span. During that period of time, she could warn mortals of impending harm. But the banshee's startling admonitions were heard not so much by a person's ears as by an inner sense—a hidden faculty with a frayed and fragile awareness of an unseen place.

Muriel Gray shuddered at the memory of those stories. *Did Mother O'Connell really believe in banshees? Or did she simply want to entertain her grandchildren?* Whatever her grandmother's intentions may have been, Muriel firmly reminded herself that she didn't believe in banshees or ghosts of any kind. This sober clarification brought a certain degree of comfort. She reached over and turned out the bedside lamp.

A few seconds later she turned the light back on. The old women slowly got out of bed and put on her bathrobe. She had decided to take a walk down the hall to the adjoining bedroom. Muriel Gray just wanted to make sure everything was okay in that room.

By the shore of the bog, the gaunt figure of the naked woman remained frozen for a moment longer. Then she slowly lowered her outstretched arms and looked down into the marsh. She moved forward in a trance-like state and silently descended into the water. A moment later she was gone, as if she had never been.

SEVENTEEN

THE LADY WITH
YELLOW HAIR

On my way to join Laine and Gabriel in Plymouth, I pulled off Route Three and stopped at a coffee shop to pick up some treats for them and a caffeine boost for me. While waiting in line I thumbed through a map-book of eastern Massachusetts and realized it would be some time before I learned my way around all of Plymouth. In square miles, the seaside town dwarfed other municipalities across the state. In fact, the town of Lexington where Laine worked, Watertown where I worked, and Maynard where Gabriel went to school, could all fit inside Plymouth's boundaries, with enough room left over to easily fit the entire cities of Cambridge, Lowell, and Boston.

But all of Plymouth's acreage could barely contain its history and charm. It was the second-oldest English-speaking town in the western hemisphere, and it had the commemorative chops to prove it: a replica of the Mayflower floated in the harbor; people dressed in Pilgrim garb reenacted 17th century life and language on a daily basis in a village called "Plimouth Plantation"; and one of the eastern seaboard's most venerable lighthouses—which, of course, was reputedly haunted—graced a chunk of coastline known as Gurnet Point. America's very first canal, dating back to the 1630s, connected Plymouth Bay to Green harbor. And the oldest court-house in the country occupied a central spot in the town's square, though it had long since been turned into a museum.

A bit later, as I wound my way to Bog Lane, I did what I always do when driving through a new town: I appraised its houses through the eyes of a draftsman. In Plymouth's case, this amounted to a full retrospective on New England architecture. Some of the oldest dwellings in America—small, hardy structures called "salt-boxes"—stood next to weather-beaten Colonials and Cape-Cod houses, known simply as "Capes." A number of these places dated back to more than three centuries. There were Georgian houses that revealed the town's British roots, along with airy abodes built in the Federalist style that reflected America's gathering spirit of independence. There were also elegant homes fronted by wooden columns which were all the rage in the mid-1800s, as well as a variety of Victorian houses that dominated that latter part of the 19th century. The 20th century's architectural attitudes were also represented. I even came across an example of the exceedingly functional—and, to my eyes, exceedingly ugly—Bauhaus mindset.

When I pulled up to the Queen Anne Victorian at the end of Bog Lane, my wife, son, and dog were sitting on the top step of the front porch. Laine had her arm around Gabriel, as if consoling him.

"Hey, gang, look what I have." I extended the box of sugary treats. But Gabriel ran down the steps, ignored the box, and wrapped his arms around my thighs. "What's this?" I stroked his brown locks and looked at Laine.

"He's had a bit of a jolt," she said.

"What happened?"

"A lady yelled at me." Gabriel's face was pressed against my hip, but his words were clear enough.

"What lady?"

"One of the neighbors, I guess," Laine answered. "I was just getting the details from him when you drove up." I turned and scanned the length of the street. The other two houses on the lane were at least twenty yards away and the only person I could see was a young, brown-haired girl who peered back at me. "It happened in our backyard," Laine explained.

"What was a neighbor doing in our backyard?" Ownership papers hadn't been passed yet, but it felt as if the house was already ours.

"I don't know," Laine said. "I was peeling wallpaper when I heard him shout, 'You're not my Mom.' Then I heard him run across the porch. I came out and found him hugging Biscuit." She quietly added, "He said she didn't touch him or try to touch him."

I disentangled Gabriel's arms and crouched down to look at him. He looked down at his sneakers. "What happened, Gabriel?"

He didn't answer.

"Why did the lady yell at you?"

"I don't know." His voice was almost a whisper. I'd always seen the wisdom of presuming a person's innocence until proven otherwise. But where my own son was concerned I fell into the habit of assuming some sort of guilt. It wasn't that he was more mischievous than other six year old boys. It was simply that he was my son, so his troubles quickly became my troubles. And, when faced with roughly equal possibilities, I always assumed the least desirable one was true. It all went with being a dyed-in-the-muck pessimist.

"What were you doing when the lady yelled at you?" I asked.

"Nothin'."

"You weren't doing anything at all? You weren't even moving or talking?"

"I was going to the backyard. I wanted to see what was there."

"Where was she?"

"In the backyard."

"In *our* backyard?"

"Yeah," he answered without looking up. I glanced at Laine, whose brunette bangs barely concealed her troubled brow.

"Gabriel," she placed a hand on his shoulder, "can you show us where the lady was standing?" He nodded and led the two of us, with Biscuit on our heels, around the semi-circular porch until we looked out over the backyard. Our patch of paradise was in summery bloom. Still-life explosions of verdant green covered almost everything, dotted here and there by wild roses and the softly tinged flowers of hydrangea bushes. This pastoral scene was centered by a cranberry bog, about half-an-acre in size. Lily pads and other forms of aquatic vegetation partially concealed this marsh and blended with the surrounding woodlands, but we could make out the bog's formless shape.

To our far right and left, a chain-link fence emerged from the greenery and pincered each side of the house. During our initial tour with Jean, she touted the six foot barrier as a great security feature. "Not quite secure enough," I now thought. According to Jean, the fence encircled the entire six-acre estate, with no breaks anywhere. Privacy must have been a paramount concern for Hitchens, because that steel sentinel must have cost some serious money. Standing on the porch, we were just high enough to see a few rooftops in the distance, on the outskirts of Hitchens's estate. A short distance beyond those houses, though we couldn't see it from our vantage point, was Plymouth Bay.

"Gabe, where was she?" Laine inquired.

"Right there," he pointed to a spot about halfway between the back steps and the bog.

"Where were you?"

Several steps led from the top of the porch to the clearing in front of the bog. Gabriel walked down to the next to last step. For the first time since the start of this makeshift interrogation, he turned and looked straight into my eyes. "Right here."

"What did she say to you?" Laine asked.

"She said 'no!'" Gabriel thrust out his arm like a traffic cop ordering someone to stop.

"That was it? She didn't say anything else?"

Gabriel shook his head emphatically, then pushed his open palm straight out again. "She said 'no!' Like that. Then I ran away." Laine and I exchanged puzzled glances.

"What did she look like?"

Gabriel thought for a moment. "She had yellow hair, like Ms. Lindurm."

Ms. Lindurm was the vice-principal at Gabriel's school in Maynard. When at work she always wore her blond hair in a tightly wrapped bun.

"She looked like Ms. Lindurm?"

"Sort of, except her hair was short and—," he paused.

"And?"

"And she wasn't ugly like Ms. Lindurm."

Laine quickly lowered her head and put a hand up to her face, as if deep in thought.

She did this whenever she was trying not to laugh.

"She was really pretty," Gabriel added. "But she looked really mad."

As Laine and I tried to sort out these details, all that could be heard was the chirping of birds and the buzzing of insects. We swatted away at a few mosquitoes that were trying to land on our exposed arms and faces. "Damn," Laine muttered. "We've got to screen this porch."

I nodded, thinking that the screened porch should also have a lockable door. I walked down the steps, to the area where Gabriel had pointed, to scan the ground for footprints. Seeing nothing of interest, I strolled closer and closer to the bog. When I got to within several feet of the marsh something caught my eye. There were holes in the ground, evenly spaced about three feet apart. Each one was about three-quarters of an inch in diameter and they extended in either direction around the edge of the pond as far as I could see. Loose, fresh soil formed at the rim of each hole, as if some large ants had recently created new homes for themselves. But what sort of ants burrow holes at three foot intervals? And what sort of ants could make holes of this size?

I called Laine over and pointed out these odd apertures. She faced the mystery with her customary aplomb: "You think maybe Gabriel's blond can pop in and out of those holes?"

"Well," I smiled weakly, "that would at least explain why Hitchens's fence didn't keep her out."

"Rick, I know this sounds a little crazy, but do you think that—" Laine turned and glanced at Gabriel to make sure he was out of earshot—"that this woman has anything to do with the disappearance of the Hitchens boy?"

"You think she might be a kidnapper?"

"I don't know—I'm just thinking out loud."

"If she wanted to kidnap Gabriel, why would she have motioned to him to stop? If anything, she would have told him to come closer."

"Yeah, I guess you're right." She brushed a mosquito off her shoulder. "It doesn't make much sense."

I shook my head. "Nothing about Gabriel's story makes much sense, but I'm sure he's telling us the truth."

"Me too," Laine said.

She and I stood at the edge of the bog, looking down at the pattern of holes that dotted its perimeter. But before long the mosquitoes drove us back to the porch. As we walked, a small, yellow-spotted salamander scurried into a thick patch of grass a few feet in front of us.

"What is it?" Laine cried as she jumped behind me.

"Just a baby salamander," I laughed. "It can't even bite your little toe."

"I don't care," she said, still cowering by my side as we walked. "You know how I hate creepy-crawly things. Now I'm going to have nightmares. Except the one in my nightmare is going to be twenty feet long!"

I laughed as we went indoors.

EIGHTEEN

QUESTIONS

IN A CURIOUS CASE OF REVERSE HOSPITALITY, Yoro beckoned Pensador to sit on the large box on the side of the tent—the very same container that Pensador had directed Yoro to sit on moments earlier. Unfazed, the outsider calmly walked over to the crate and sat down. But this time there was no disturbance inside the box.

He smiled at the Sartum.

Yoro met his gaze but didn't return the smile. The Sartum's stolid demeanor began to worry the outsider.

"My dear friend," he said, trying to smooth over the graceless preliminaries, "what can I do for you this morning?"

"The things that you said to the people last night—"

"Perhaps I was a bit hasty," Pensador said quickly. "Perhaps, in my eagerness, I said things that were misunderstood."

"Did I misunderstand?" Yoro's question sounded hopeful.

"Well," Pensador's shifted his posture on the box as he searched for just the right words, "I think the final goal may have been misunderstood. I may have given the impression that I want to take away the peoples' inner peace. But that's not what I want to do at all. What I want to do is give your people a better kind of inner peace—a truer form of inner peace."

The Sartum looked down at the tent's artificial floor, then back up at the outsider.

"Why?" he asked quietly.

"Why what?"

"Why do you want to give us a better kind of inner peace?"

Pensador silently berated himself for not anticipating this question, but still managed to meet Yoro's eyes. "Well…I want to help. I want to help your people."

"Why?"

"Because I've grown very fond of the Inucans."

"Do you do these things for all of the people that you are fond of?"

"No, I don't," he said with a trace of irritation. He quickly composed himself and reverted to his diplomatic persona. "Yoro, I feel as if a special bond has developed between us. You know, from the moment I found the Inucans I knew that we would—"

"From the moment you *found* us? Were you searching for us?" Though he had interrupted the outsider, there was no tension or hostility in the Sartum's voice.

"Well, yes," Pensador replied. "In a way."

"Why were you searching for us?"

Pensador didn't like the direction of the conversation, but he couldn't afford to be rude to the Sartum. He needed Yoro's good-will as much as he needed Lynn's expertise.

"It's getting late," he said in English. Then he looked up at his guest and spoke Inucan. "Yoro, do you ask these questions of every outsider who comes here?"

"Only those who offer us things."

"Why didn't you ask me these questions during my first two visits?"

"I was not the Sartum. I advised Neko to ask you those questions, but he refused. Your gifts were enough for him."

Pensador suddenly missed Neko. "Has any outsider visited the village during your time as Sartum?"

"Yes." Yoro thought for a moment. "A government doctor, a missionary, two anthropologists."

"The missionary—did you ask him the same questions that you're asking me?"

"Yes."

"And?"

"He told us that he was searching for people with whom he could share his sacred words...his message."

"His message? What was his message?"

Yoro found it difficult to accurately sum up the missionary's teachings in a few words, so he settled for one comprehensive word: "Hope."

"*Hope?*" On Pensador's tongue the word sounded more like a slur than anything else, but Yoro answered as if it were a legitimate question. "Hope in the Spirit."

"Ahh, hope in the Spirit." Pensador's sense of diplomatic restraint was fraying at the edges, and a gust of icy contempt chilled his words. "Hope is always so much more meaningful when it is vague."

Yoro ignored Pensador's tone. "The missionary was clear enough. He said that the Spirit had come to the world with a human face. It is a message we have heard before, from other missionaries. But many of our people have taken that message to heart, so we don't mind hearing it again—especially the part about redemption. The Spirit offered redemption to all people, including the peoples of the jungle." Yoro used the Portuguese word for redemption: *redencao.*

"Redemption from *what?*"

"From injustice and evil...from the despair that life too often inflicts upon us."

"Okay, okay." Annoyance was creeping back into the outsider's voice. "Did you ask the missionary the same question you asked me? Did you ask him *why* he did this?"

Yoro looked at Pensador, but his eyes peered into the past. "He said the Spirit moved him to faith. He said no one could experience the Spirit's love without wanting to share it with others."

Pensador stroked the stubble on his jaw and decided to pursue a different course. "Well, in a way, that's true for me, too." One end of his lip curled up slightly.

"Your faith inspires you?"

"That's right. My faith moves me."

"Last night you said faith was a lie, no?"

"Well, it is—the missionary's kind of faith is a lie."

"But your kind of faith is not a lie?"

"No, it's not, because I put my faith in science. I can prove my beliefs."

Yoro's eyes narrowed. "If you can prove your beliefs, why do you call it faith?"

Pensador blinked at the Sartum and realized he had a perfectly valid point. "Well, I may not be able to prove absolutely all of my beliefs. But I can *almost* prove them."

"You can prove that life has no meaning?"

"No, I cannot," Pensador said. "But no one can prove that life has meaning, so we have to assume that it doesn't."

"That's your faith?" Yoro asked.

"It's more than that." The Spanish word for crutch popped into his thoughts. "I believe in facing the meaninglessness of life with strength and intelligence. I refuse to warm myself with fantasies. I face *the hard truth* on my own two feet—without any *crutch*. I walk on my own strong legs."

Yoro considered this for a moment and then looked up. "What is wrong with using a crutch if it helps you get to a better place?"

Pensador could feel his blood pressure rising. "There is no 'better place' to go. There is nothing else."

"If there is nowhere else to go," Yoro wondered, "where are you going on those strong legs of yours?"

For all its simplicity and quietness, Yoro's question pulled at the logic of Pensador's stance. It was like a noiseless but powerful undertow that threatened to upend him. The outsider could think of no other response except to ignore the question. "I stand on my own two feet," he repeated. "No matter how ugly or bitter *the truth* may be, I face it and fight it without leaning on the Spirit." Pensador's eyes flashed as he spoke; his face was that of a warrior in the midst of an intense struggle.

"How brave you are," Yoro said softly as he studied Pensador's defiant glare. "Is this what you mean by 'inner peace'? Is this what you want to give us?"

Pensador looked at the Sartum as if he was seeing him for the first time.

"Is it possible," Yoro continued, "that what you call 'inner peace' is really a certain kind of pride?"

The outsider rubbed his jaw and stood up. "The two go together," he said firmly.

"Is that what your science tells you?" Yoro asked. As Pensador tried to think of a suitable response, the Sartum followed his own thoughts. "My friend, it is easy to boast when you are feeling strong. It is easy to live for today, when today is happy. It is easy to say 'I am content!' when you have the things that so many others don't have." Yoro gestured toward the devices and conveniences in Pensador's tent. "But it is not easy to be so proud when you are sick, or poor, or lonely, or broken. Many good people struggle for hope. And in their struggle, they find strength and meaning in the presence of the Spirit. In your speech last night, you called such people *childish*. Are they childish because of their buckled legs? Or are they childish because they reach up for hope?"

Pensador stared down at the Sartum and realized that his mission was going to be far more complicated than he had imagined. He believed that there was some sort of appropriate response to Yoro's questions and statements, but the Sartum's gently penetrating eyes seemed to freeze his tongue. Yoro's grizzled visage was that of a warrior, but behind it lurked the mind of a capable, rough-hewn thinker.

As Sartum, Yoro's face represented all of the Inucan people. Yet their facial traits varied widely. The members of other Amazonian tribes had a set of distinctive features, and after spending so many years in South America's rain forest, Pensador was often able to tell what tribe an Indian belonged to just by glancing at his or her face. But this was not possible with the Inucans. They seemed to be a mixture of mixtures.

In bygone centuries the Inucans had absorbed numerous exiles from other tribes. In more recent times they allowed outcasts from Brazil, Peru, and Bolivia—whites and blacks alike—to join their clan of extended families. All of this intermixing had created a genetically diverse tribe with widely-divergent physical features. Thus, the Inucans weren't united by race or bodily characteristics. The glue that held them together was their distinctive culture, which was mainly shaped by their language, religion, history, and tradition-based customs.

When Pensador had first encountered the small tribe, he fervently hoped it was a truly isolated and pristine group. He longed to find the holy grail of anthropology: a tribe that was utterly untouched by modern civilization. He also hoped to find something that would greatly aid genetic research: a pool of virgin DNA. Such an exotic double discovery—a culturally undiluted tribe and genetically undiluted DNA—would have made him an overnight sensation in universities across the planet.

But the moment Pensador saw an old machete in the hands of an Inucan warrior he realized that modern civilization had already paid a visit. And the tribespeoples' heterogeneous facial features confirmed that they had shared more than trinkets and tools with outsiders.

However, the Inucans' willingness to selectively absorb people, ideas, and goods from the outside world made them the perfect subjects for a much larger game. If Pensador could win their trust, a Lexel laboratory would be established deep in the jungle, far from the prying eyes of government officials. Lexel would offer the Inucans medical care, technological advancement, and a rudimentary education. In return, the villagers would allow Lexel to engage in genetic research and experimentation.

On them.

The leader of the tribe stared back at the outsider, but there was no anger in his eyes, only a desire to understand. This made Pensador reconsider his strategy. His original plan was to offer the Inucans only palatable explanations. He would spoon-feed them bits and pieces of truth as Lexel's grand design slowly unfolded. He would tell them only as much as they could understand *and accept* at any given time.

But now he wondered if he could tell their leader the whole truth. Yoro's lack of hostility, and his incisive questions, made Pensador think that the old warrior might really understand. Perhaps the Sartum's judgment could be trusted after all.

The sound of chainsaws erupted in the distance, and Yoro quickly stood up from the canvas chair. The noise was dimly familiar to him, but the memory was not comforting.

Pensador stretched out his hands in a gesture of reassurance. "Don't worry. My men are just cutting down some trees on a nearby hill."

"That's not the sound of axes."

"No, it isn't," Pensador said. "It's the sound of progress."

NINETEEN

THE GIRL NEXT DOOR

LAINE AND I WERE CONCERNED ABOUT Gabriel's yellow-haired lady, so we told him to stay on the wrap-around porch for the remainder of the afternoon. Biscuit served as his fiercely protective bodyguard. I spent the rest of the day ripping wallpaper from the rooms on the second floor. It was lime green and imprinted with tropical ferns. "Hitchens may be smart and he may be rich," I thought as I toiled, "but he has the aesthetic taste of a reptile." Ever the woman-on-a-mission, Laine had already scraped two rooms on the first floor and was applying a coat of paint to one of them.

Late in the afternoon, as I was cleaning up, Gabriel appeared at the door of the bedroom wearing an ebullient smile. "Hey Dad, this is Sophie."

I didn't see anyone but him.

"I met her out front," he continued. "She's my new friend."

I looked at the floor, thinking that maybe he had taken in a stray cat.

"She's really smart, too."

I peered at Gabriel as if waiting for him to pull a rabbit out of a hat. He grinned a moment longer, then realized something was missing.

"Sophie," he turned and called out to the hallway.

Just as the troubling notion of an imaginary friend entered

my mind, I heard the sound of movement from one of the other rooms. I walked down the hallway until I came upon a young girl standing in the upstairs study, perusing the remnants of Hitchens's library. She had light brown hair that fell below her shoulders and wore a summer play dress that ended just above a zig-zag array of scratches around her knees and shins. Before I could say anything she turned with a winsome smile and extended her hand. "Hi, my name is Sophia but you can call me Sophie. I'm eight and three-quarters years old."

"Oh," I said, caught off guard by the ragamuffin's poise. "Well, I'm Gabriel's dad, but you can call me Rick. I'm forty-four and a half years old."

"I live in the house next door: Number Two Bog Lane," she announced.

"She's really smart, huh Dad?" Gabriel said, delighted with his find.

"Yes, she is. Do you like living on this street, Sophie?"

"It's actually a lane, not a street." Before I could acknowledge my error, she continued. "It's okay, I suppose, but there aren't any kids to play with. I play with my sisters sometimes, but they're older than me and sometimes they don't want to play. My mom drives me to Alison's house for play dates. Alison is my best friend. I always wanted to play with Jimmy, but he was indoors most of the time."

"Jimmy?"

"The boy that used to live here."

"Hitchens's son?"

"Yep. Mister Hitchens's son." The young girl emphasized the consonants in "Mister."

"He was almost as old as me, but he didn't say very much. He always looked kinda' sad." Sophie picked up one of Hitchens's note-books and thumbed through it, but she didn't attempt to read any of the handwriting. She seemed more concerned with the sheer number of pages that Hitchens had filled with his thoughts. "Whew, Mister Hitchens sure liked to write!"

"Did you see a lot of him?"

"Mister Hitchens?"

"No, Jimmy."

"He was usually in the house. But sometimes he would sit on the porch, so I'd come over and say hi. But Mister Hitchens didn't like it so much when I came over."

"He would say that to you?"

"No, he wouldn't say anything to me. He would just tell Jimmy it was time to go inside."

"Did Mr. Hitchens ever talk to you?"

"No. But he talked to my mom once. He told her she was nosey," Sophie added with a seditious chuckle.

"You don't say?" I'd been trying not to sound nosey, but our little neighbor clearly liked to talk, and I couldn't contain my curiosity about Hitchens, so I pressed on. "Why did he tell her that?"

"I don't remember Missus Hitchens. I was pretty young when she died. But my sisters told me that one day she wanted to go shopping with my mom. But Mister Hitchens didn't want her to go shopping with my mom. So they had an argument. Missus Hitchens started crying—she started crying right there on the porch. Imagine that? A grown-up crying right on her own front porch: right in front of my sisters and my mother." For a moment Sophie seemed to be recreating the scene in her mind.

"What happened then?"

"Mister Hitchens yelled at her. But my sisters don't know what he said. They said he used weird words. Then Missus Hitchens went inside. Then Mister Hitchens told my mom to go home and mind her own business. My mom said he was a ric trooper."

"A what?"

"A trooper of the rics. My mom told my sisters that it was a boy-scout troop that Mister Hitchens was in charge of."

I mulled over this bit of information until another question pressed on my mind. "Sophie, does your mom have blond hair?"

"No. My Mom has red hair, and she has the beautifulest face in the whole world."

"My mom has the beautifulest face in the whole world," said Gabriel.

"You haven't even seen my mom," Sophie pointed out.

"You haven't seen my mom either," Gabriel countered.

Sensing that this friendship was about to collapse before it got off the ground, I changed the subject. "Have you always lived on Bog Lane, Sophie?"

"My whole, entire life." Then, without skipping a beat, she asked: "Is Gabriel going to live here?"

"Yes. We hope to live here for a long time."

"That's great," she exclaimed. "Now I'll finally have someone to play with on my very own street."

"I've heard that it's actually a lane," I smiled.

Unflustered, Sophie carried on her part of the conversation: "I've always wondered what this place looked like on the inside. Mister Hitchens never let anyone in except for bad worker people."

"Bad worker people? How do you know they were bad?"

"Because Mister Hitchens was always yelling at them. People only get yelled at when they're bad."

"Mr. Hitchens liked to yell, did he?"

"Yeah. You could hear him from inside our house sometimes. He knew lots of swear words. Wanna hear some?"

"Well—"

"And who might this be?" Laine was standing in the doorway,

smiling at the very first guest to our new home. With practiced assurance, the young girl stepped forward and extended her arm. "Hi. My name is Sophia but you can call me Sophie. I'm eight and three-quarters years old."

"I see," Laine replied, clasping the girl's hand. "My name is Laine and I'm...well, I'm just a little bit older than you."

"Hmm," Sophie murmured, gazing intently at Laine. "You look like you're eons older than me." The girl wasn't exactly sure what an eon was, but she knew it meant a long time.

"She's really smart, huh Mom?" Gabriel observed enthusiastically.

The smile on my wife's face slowly dissolved into something less benign. She started to speak but I blurted out the first thing that came to mind: "Say, why don't we all go downstairs and see what Biscuit is doing?"

TWENTY

SURUTAS

THE TWO WARRIORS PULLED IN THEIR OARS and let the current carry the canoe down river. They saw Felipe and a group of older children fishing from an open area on the riverbank. One of the young girls waved to the men. Destro, the warrior in the front of the canoe, nodded solemnly to his daughter. He and his fellow hunter had painted their faces a garish shade of red—the color of violent death—so it was not appropriate for them to smile or wave back. They were hunting for something larger than piranha or any other type of fish that the nurse and his students might dredge up from the Purus river.

At a bend in the twisty tributary, the warriors dipped their oars back into the water to guide the canoe away from the shoreline. The wooden paddles lapped gently against the current, which produced sounds that were as pleasing as the patter of rain-drops or the crackle of a fire.

An enormous black caiman spied the warriors as they glided past. Its body was submerged except for a few bumpy protrusions on its skull—two of which framed watchful, crocodilian eyes. From a swirling eddy on the other side of the reptile, Destro could hear the squeaks of hatchlings. The warriors suspected that the vigilant caiman was their mother, so they gave her a wide berth. Female caiman are savagely protective of their little ones.

A bit farther on Destro noticed an aruana fish near the surface

of the river. Its distinctive eyes were pointed upward rather than forward—better to see the tasty morsels that fell from overhanging tree
branches, such as insects, flecks of vegetation, and the excrement of
tree-dwelling animals. But this particular aruana had lingered at the
surface a bit too long. A black-collared hawk suddenly careened out of
the sky. The predator's trajectory was flawless: it swooped down to
pierce the fish with its talons, then swung upward in a smooth arc that
just cleared the forest canopy. Destro watched the hapless aurana take
a journey it could never have imagined, high into the darkening sky.

In a forest glade on the eastern shore, the hunters saw what they
had been searching for: a cluster of capybaras. The Inucans prized the
huge rodents for their flavorful meat. But as the two men steered
their canoe in the direction of the clearing, they noticed that a female
capybara had just given birth to several pups. Some of the newborns
were still struggling to escape from their gooey placental sacks. Their
mother was on her side, still exhausted from the ordeal. Without a
word being exchanged, the two warriors guided their canoe away from
the capybaras.

The elders of the tribe counseled against killing any mother animal
on the day that it brought new life into the world. This teaching was
first given by one particular elder when the two warriors were just
boys. But by the time they grew to manhood many of the villagers had
come to believe that *Viro*—the Spirit that had brought all of nature into
being—would eventually punish any man who preyed upon a mother-
creature in her day of life-giving weakness. Such an act was *atola,* which
meant cruelly unjust.

The hunters began heading down river when a large male capybara bounded out of the undergrowth and into the clearing. The beast
was as heavy as either man. It came upon a pup that was crawling
along the shore-line, not yet strong enough to stand. The big rodent
sniffed suspiciously at the newborn, and apparently decided the pup
was not his. The hefty rodent promptly trampled the young creature

to death. The male then proceeded to the next pup and repeated the lethal ritual. The female capybara squealed piteously, but was unable to defend her little ones. They were all dead within a matter of seconds. With a satisfied grunt, and without eating any of his victims, the bulky male tramped into the river and began swimming to the other side, where some females were munching on tender shoots.

A gangly vulture descended into the clearing, squawked loudly, then jabbed its beak into the still-warm flesh of one of the pups. Soon a noisy gaggle of scavengers convened to feast upon the lifeless bodies that dotted the shoreline.

"*Atola*," grimaced Destro. He lifted his bow, positioned an arrow, and took aim at the head of the big capybara, which was about halfway across the river. But before he could let his arrow fly, the rodent was pulled violently downward. For a moment the only thing the warriors could see was roiling water. Then two coils of matter, each as thick as the trunk of a medium-sized tree, broke through the surface. They were wrapped tightly around the capybara. The animal's entire body, with the exception of its head, was almost completely covered by these smooth, muscular coils. The capybara opened its mouth—perhaps to bite, or to squeal, or simply to breathe—but before it could reveal its intent, it was pulled under a second time.

A series of bubbles floated to the surface and popped. These air sacs became smaller and fewer until one final, tiny bubble appeared on the river; then it, too, disappeared into oblivion.

Destro turned and looked at his companion. "*Surutas*," he said grimly. His friend nodded. They knew that no part of the capybara would ever be seen again. When a caiman killed something big, bits and pieces of its victim could always be found nearby. When a jaguar killed something big, most of its victim's bones were left to dry in the sun. Even when a pack of piranha killed something big, they allowed their victim's teeth or bits of fur to float to the surface. But when *Surutas* killed, no sliver or shred of its victim was left behind. Thus, if a person disappeared in the Amazon, and if Inucan trackers couldn't find any trace of the individual, the tribespeople knew that he or she had fallen prey to the mysterious river god. That was one of the reasons why Surutas embodied the dark and unknowable side of nature to the Inucan people.

The warriors turned their canoe around and began rowing back to the village. They would have a story to tell around the fire tonight. As Destro exerted himself against the current, he heard a thudding sound in the distance. The peculiar thwacking noise grew louder with each passing second. He had heard the sound before, but never this close. Both men stopped rowing and looked up. They couldn't see anything in the strip of overcast sky, bordered by the trees that lined the river. But the steady thuds increased in volume until they became a heavy, ominous pounding. Whatever it was, it seemed to be approaching the village.

The warriors rowed furiously to get back to their home.

TWENTY-ONE

BLOODSUCKERS

ON THE FRONT PORCH, A CASUALLY-DRESSED, middle-aged man was patting Biscuit, who usually wasn't so tolerant of strangers. The visitor had tousled brown hair, square jaw lines, and a handsome face. "Hi, Dad," Sophie said, instantly ending the mystery of the man's identity. "These are my new friends! This is Gabriel, who is six years old; this is Gabriel's dad, who is forty-four and a half years old; and this is Gabriel's mom, who—"

"Laine is the name," my wife extended her hand and smiled. "More information will be given on a need-to-know basis."

The man returned the smile and shook her hand. "Fran Sampson. I hope Sophie hasn't been bending your ears too much."

"Not at all," I replied shaking his hand. "Rick Delvecchio, but you only have to remember the Rick part. We're in the process of buying this place so it looks like we're going to be neighbors."

"I'm going to have a playmate right next door," Sophie beamed and put her arm around Gabriel, whose smile mirrored hers.

"It'll be nice to have some friendly faces on the lane," Fran said.

One of my eyebrows perked up. "I take it Mr. Hitchens wasn't the warm, fuzzy type."

"You take it correctly," Fran replied. "He..." our new neighbor sighed, "well, let's just say he wasn't a people person." A squirrel appeared on the rail at the turn of the porch. Biscuit immediately gave chase, followed quickly by Gabriel and Sophie. "Don't leave the porch!" Laine called out as they disappeared around the bend.

"What kind of person was he?" As I asked the question, it occurred to me that I was referring to Hitchens in the past tense, as if he was dead.

"He wasn't an easy guy to know," Fran said. "He bought this house a long time ago, but in all those years we had no more than a half-a-dozen short conversations. My wife says that I'm not very talkative, but compared to Hitchens I'm a social butterfly." He turned and pointed to the other house on Bog Lane, "That's Muriel Gray's place. She's lived there over half a century. Raised six children."

I got the impression that Fran wanted to get off the subject of Richard Hitchens. I reasoned that last winter's tragedy was still difficult for people to talk about—especially with virtual strangers. "A few of Muriel's kids still live in state," Fran continued, "but none of them live in or around Plymouth." As we spoke, a yellow Volvo station-wagon turned down Bog Lane, traveled the length of the road and pulled up by our front steps.

"I don't suppose Mrs. Gray has blond hair?" Laine asked.

"Muriel? No, no," Fran replied. "She's well into her seventies; has trouble getting around on her own. Why do you ask?"

"Well, Gabriel just had a strange experience in our backyard. He says that he—"

"Hey there, townfolk," Jean Powell's melodic voice sounded up the steps. She closed the car door but left the engine running.

"Hi, beautiful," I called from the porch. Laine met her on the sidewalk and gave her a hug.

Jean's daughter, Delaney, sat in the Volvo's passenger seat. Laine smiled and waved, but Delaney just stared straight ahead. Jean knocked hard against the window, "Don't be rude, young lady— don't you dare!"

Delaney reluctantly lowered the window and returned Laine's greeting with a half-hearted smile; then she promptly raised the window.

As they walked up the steps, Laine cocked her head towards the Volvo, "What's up with that?"

"Oh, don't pay her any mind," Jean replied. "She's pouting because Harry won't let her date boys until she's sixteen years old."

"That's about a year away, isn't it?" Laine swatted another mosquito on her neck.

"Delaney would tell you that it's 7,536 hours and—" she glanced at her watch—"forty seven minutes away." She gave me a hug then turned to our new neighbor. "So we meet again, Mr. Sampson."

"You know each other?" Laine asked.

"Fran is the best carpenter in town," Jean said. "Maybe the best on the South Shore. And if he wasn't such a perfectionist I'd refer more of my clients to him."

Fran was clearly embarrassed. "Maybe I'm the best carpenter on Bog Lane, but that's about as far as I'd go. Even that might not be true." He looked at me. "Maybe Rick knows a few things about carpentry."

Laine laughed.

"My beloved wife speaks volumes," I said. "Fran, I can't nail two pieces of wood together without shishkebabing my thumbs."

"I thought perfectionism was a good thing," Laine said to Jean.

"Perfection takes time, darlin'," she replied, "and time is money."

"I'll promise to curb my perfectionism," Fran turned a pleasantly wry expression in Jean's direction, "if you send a few customers my way."

"Business slow?" she asked.

"Well," Fran sighed, "let me put it this way: I spent the whole day putting the final touches on a treehouse for Sophie in our backyard."

"That sounds sweet," Laine said. "No childhood is complete without a treehouse." Then she swatted another mosquito on her calf. "Damn! Why do these things love me so much?"

Jean turned to Fran. "If you built it, I bet it is one hell of a tree house. How many bathrooms does it have?"

Fran laughed and looked at Laine. "Spending a workday doing something nice for the kids is sweet. It's sweet right up until the mortgage payment comes due, and the gas bill, and the property tax, and the—"

"Wait a sec," Laine's eyes brightened. "You might just be the person we've been looking for."

"Need some work done?"

"Have you ever screened in a wrap-around porch?" I asked.

"You name the job; I've done it."

"Could you attach a deck to the back porch and screen that in as well?"

"Not a problem."

"In that case," Laine batted a mosquito that was hovering in front of her face, "we'd be happy to pay your going rate."

Jean shot a cautionary glance at her old friend and slipped into the role of concerned realtor: "You do realize that this wrap-around porch will lose some of its aesthetic appeal if you screen it up. A seasonal annoyance is a small price to pay for beauty."

"You've got it all turned around," Laine retorted. "Beauty is a small price to pay to be rid of these winged bloodsuckers."

"That's okay with me," Fran said. "When would you like me to start?"

Laine slapped at a mosquito that had landed just above her cheek, splattering its swollen viscera on her temple. "Would right now be too soon?"

TWENTY-TWO

THE VISIONARY

PENSADOR TRIED TO READ YORO'S EYES, but it was like trying to discern the hand held by a masterful card player. The craggy-faced chieftain wasn't giving anything away. The outsider poured a cup of water and handed it to Yoro, who thanked him but didn't smile. Somehow Pensador had to make the old warrior understand that it was within their power to accomplish truly amazing things—perhaps even change the course of human history.

Lexel Corporation had already done a considerable amount of work at its Plymouth, Crestview, and Prescott labs. But researchers in those U.S. facilities were hamstrung by the constant need for secrecy and by the absence of human subjects. Operating within those limitations, they had taken their work in America as far as it could go. With a new lab in the Amazon, Lexel would be able to freely press forward on three objectives.

The first priority was to continue to systematically investigate the purpose of each human gene. The exact purposes of most of the human body's genes were still a mystery to scientists. The Lexel team sought to reverse those percentages by exposing the specific functions of as many genes as possible.

The second goal was to test new techniques for gene therapy on human subjects. In some cases this would involve masking defective genes, which meant preventing such genes from harming their biological host. But in other cases gene therapy would entail the whole-sale replacement of faulty genes with functional specimens. The Lexel teams had become so adept at these transference processes that they were able to create a number of transgenic organisms: *they had success-fully and repeatedly spliced genes from one animal into another animal's cells.*

But Lexel was far from the first to accomplish that feat. Researchers had originally created transgenic organisms in the early 1970s. By 1975 genetic engineering had become such a burgeoning field that scores of biologists gathered in Asilomar, California for what became known as the "Pandora's Box Conference." The main concern was that a pioneer-ing lab might inadvertently unleash some mutant bacterium or killer virus on an unsuspecting world. But, aside from raising awareness and generating a list of guidelines, the Asilomar Conference didn't stifle genetic research or experimentation.

By building on the foundation laid by others, the Lexel researchers had developed more effective methods for gene transference, and they repeatedly used these procedures on a variety of different organisms. In fact, they had successfully transferred *more* genetic material into a greater variety of organisms than any other team to date.

As the Lexel group became increasingly adept with this technology, the possibilities became increasingly open-ended. One area of research held particular promise for the public good: By effectively inserting cru-cial strands of genetic material into foreign bodies, the team would be able to test various theories on viral infection, cancer, and other dis-eases. This was what Pensador meant the previous evening when he asked the Inucans to "put their bodies in his hands."

The third objective flowed logically from the first two, but it was also the most problematic and would probably have to be kept secret from the tribespeople. This work would focus on a few of the tribes' young women. Under the guise of a necessary medical procedure, their egg cells would be removed and fertilized with sperm cells provided by Richard Hitchens himself. Some of the resulting embryos would be kept alive in artificial environments in the Amazonian lab, where they would function as small organic factories producing fresh biological material such as blood cells, glandular cells, and even fresh nerve tissue.

Other embryos would be used to test and improve some innovative genetic screening techniques that Lynn had developed. Using her methods, an embryo would be carefully checked for various genetic defects or potential disorders. As the embryo developed, any problematic genes would either be replaced or muted in the laboratory. The embryo would then be reinserted into the woman from whom the egg cell was taken. Lexel researchers would continually check the development of the fetus. If something appeared to be going horribly wrong, they would terminate the pregnancy. If necessary, they would infect the would-be mother with an illness to necessitate the abortion. But if the pregnancy seemed to be proceeding normally, they would let it run its course. In this way they would test the effectiveness of Lynn's screening systems as well as their *in vitro* gene treatment techniques.

By exploring all of these avenues of research and experimentation, Lexel Corporation would pursue nothing less than the perfection of the human species. This goal, though far off, was not the stuff of fantasy. The human genome—the complete genetic blueprint of the human body—had finally been mapped in 2003. It had taken international teams of scientists many years to complete this project, and for good reason. The human genome consisted of three billion chemical bases or "letters" encoded in the form of DNA. If each of these biochemical runes formed just one letter of human language, the resulting book would be a thousand times longer than Tolstoy's *War and Peace*. Such an evolutionary masterpiece was inscribed within every single cell of every human body. By revealing the sequences of these genetic bases, scientists had handed humankind a gift of inestimable value. The next logical steps were to investigate the specific purposes of all these genes, and to reengineer them to the well-considered advantage of the human species. Lexel's ultimate goal was a new race of human beings free of birth defects and virtually immune to disease. Members of the reengineered race would also be endowed with a uniformly high I.Q., and their personalities would be characterized by a predilection for reason and logic. In addition, they would possess strong, agile bodies, and their cellular aging processes would be slowed dramatically, enabling each individual to enjoy a long and active life.

Pensador knew that this monumental goal was within their reach. The Lexel team only needed three things: time, freedom from government interference, and some human subjects.

As Pensador pondered the final item on that list, he looked at Yoro and again wondered if he could confide in him. He yearned to turn him into an ally. In his capacity as Sartum, Yoro had the power to provide Lexel with all of the human subjects it would need. But he also had the power to put an end to Lexel's costly and carefully considered Amazonian strategy. The aging warrior could insure success or guarantee failure.

As Pensador studied the Sartum's eyes, he longed to see keen glints of ambition, logic, and historic vision.

But all he saw was a worried old man, burdened by superstition and a deeply-entrenched fear of misfortune. At that moment, Pensador decided he could not confide in Yoro. He would be risking far too much on a flailing hope. Instead, he opted to continue his more cautious approach.

"Yoro, please understand. My work here will greatly benefit your tribe in many ways. I'm asking you to trust me. For the sake of your people, please trust me."

"Are you asking me to have *faith* in you?"

Pensador shook his head impatiently. "I'm asking you to look around at the useful things I've given to the Inucans. I'm asking you to base your trust on these worthwhile things, and the goodwill behind them. Did the missionary give you such things?"

"He gave us some medicine and a message of hope."

"That was it?" Pensador checked his watch. "Some medicine and some hope? That was all he gave you?"

"That was all he had." Yoro thought for a moment and then looked straight into Pensador's eyes. "He also told us *why* he offered us those things. He did not try to deceive us."

The outsider immediately broke off eye contact with Yoro.

In the distance there was a faint, rapid thudding sound. Pensador peered through one of the screened flaps of his tent. "Listen, I don't have much time," he said. "All I can I tell you for now is that you would be making a terrible mistake if you pass up all of the good things that science has to offer your people. Don't throw it all away for mere hope in the Spirit."

The Sartum appeared confused. "Must we choose one or the other? Are science and the Spirit at war? Why can't we have both?"

The thudding sound grew louder.

"Science and the Spirit cannot be friends," Pensador said with absolute certainty. "They can never be on good terms. *Never.* If you truly respect one you cannot truly respect the other."

"Why not?"

Pensador scratched the scalp under his matted blond hair. The staccato thwacking sounds grew louder with each passing second. When he finally spoke, he had to raise his voice. "Yoro, I want to continue this conversation, but some important things are about to be delivered here, and I must make sure that all goes well."

The steady, powerful thudding grew louder.

"What is coming?" Yoro shouted over the din.

"Come out and see," Pensador yelled as he moved toward the door flap of the tent.

"*I will do that*," said the Sartum.

Pensador quickly turned and looked at Yoro, but the old warrior simply walked past him. The roar outside the tent had increased so much that Pensador couldn't be certain of the last words Yoro had spoken. But he could've sworn his final comment was in English.

TWENTY-THREE

CARESSES IN THE NIGHT

THUNDERHEADS WERE FORMING IN THE WESTERN sky when Laine and Gabriel set off for Maynard. I worried that they might get caught in a torrential downpour, but Laine insisted they would be fine. They had to be up bright and early for their weekly Sunday swimming session at my sister's pool in Sudbury, a town that bordered Maynard.

For a few different reasons, Laine was determined to turn Gabriel into a good swimmer as soon as possible. The most compelling but usually unspoken reason was the death of her brother. As a teenager, shortly after graduating from Lincoln High School, he drowned during an impromptu midnight party on the banks of the Sudbury River. Many summers had come and gone since that awful night. But intense grief has a way of hammering imperatives deep into the mind, and the tragedy was never far from Laine's thoughts.

I, too, was planning to be up early. I wanted to get a head start on the wall-paper removal and painting tasks. Before turning in, however, I planned to sift through some of the items Hitchens left behind during his apparently hasty departure. His personal library was of particular interest. One shelf of a bookcase held a number of loose-leaf binders filled with an elegant, hand-written script. I assumed these entries were penned by Hitchens himself, and I was curious to see what they might reveal about him.

But before I could delve into them, Jean's husband called and asked if I wanted to get a bite at his favorite Plymouth watering hole. I always enjoyed Harry's company and I was eager to get better acquainted with the town, so I went along. Since we would be spending some time outdoors, I lathered mosquito repellent on my neck and arms. Laine hated the stuff, but I quickly got used to the smell, and the chemicals didn't irritate my skin as they did hers. Most importantly, the noxious potion kept nature's pests at bay.

Harry gave me a tour of the area around Plymouth Harbor, including the town's historic Rock. I'd seen it as a boy during a school field trip, and it seemed just as unimpressive then as it did now. I'd always thought the stories about the stone and its welcome-mat role in U.S. history were less fact than fiction. But after sizing up Plymouth Rock, I became convinced the account was true. If the Pilgrims had concocted the story, they surely would have found a more memorable stone to anchor the legend.

Harry introduced me to a seaside tavern named The Brigand. We ducked inside just as a thunderstorm erupted over the town. The interior was decked out like a haven for 18th century felons and outcasts. Aside from a few safety beacons required at strategic points by state law, the tavern was illuminated by a massive fire-place on one side of the room and a securely set candle on each table. Above the fireplace was a black flag emblazoned with a skull and a pair of crossed bones. Positioned just below this Jolly Roger was a long, thick wooden plank—presumably the kind of plank that had once provided entertainment for seafaring psychopaths. The other walls were festooned with the paraphernalia of piracy: grappling hooks, rigging ropes, pikes, flintlock pistols, and even a few cutlasses. One generation's instruments of deadly criminality had become another generation's quaint adornments.

We settled in at a table near the fireplace. Harry ordered a shot of Jack Daniels and something from the menu called "Buccaneer's Bacchanalia," which he strongly recommended. I followed suit on both counts.

The rumble of thunder could be heard inside the restaurant. Occasionally, the all-too-near crack of a lightening bolt caused the ornamental grappling hooks to sway and tap lightly against the walls. Sitting in the time-warped tavern, I could easily imagine that the commotion was caused by a Spanish galleon and a British frigate trading broadsides in Plymouth harbor.

I asked Harry a couple of questions about Richard Hitchens, but he told me that he knew very little about the man. He didn't even know what Hitchens looked like. At his wife's request he had made some inquiries about Mrs. Hitchens's death and the disappearance of her son, James Hitchens. As assistant district attorney for Plymouth County, Harry was privy to investigative documents. But the police hadn't turned up very much, so Harry didn't have much information to share.

Our conversation inevitably drifted toward the trials and tribulations of modern fatherhood. For Harry, the main challenge was posed by his extremely intelligent but clique-conscious and boy-curious teenage daughter, Delaney. In my case, it was a hyperactive and thin-skinned six-year-old son. Neither of us could figure out how our parents had raised much larger families.

As we commiserated, Harry had the good sense to nurse just two drinks. I, on the other hand, gulped down four.

By the time he dropped me at the end of Bog Lane it was about eleven o'clock and I had to exert all my powers of concentration to place one foot in front of the other. Harry realized that I wasn't at my graceful best, for I vaguely remember that he offered to give me a hand. But my retort was one part proud and two parts stupid. As I recall, I said something like, "Are you kidding? I could probably win an archery contest right now..." Or at least I tried to say something clever. I'll never know what actually came out of my mouth.

I somehow managed to climb the front steps, and after taking several jabs I finally inserted the key into the front lock.

When I stumbled through the front hallway I was just sober enough to realize that Biscuit wasn't there to greet me. But a pungent odor swarmed into my nostrils. I assumed this was the after-effect of all the elbow grease Laine had applied earlier as she cleaned the house. The filth she had ejected from its crevices must have left its residue in the air.

I called Biscuit several times, but there was no movement or response. Even if he had been sound asleep when I walked in, he should have immediately reacted to the sound of the door being opened and closed. I tried to remember if he had returned to Maynard with Laine and Gabriel, but I couldn't recall much of anything at that moment. I didn't even bother trying to scale the stairs to the second floor bedrooms. Instead I staggered to the first floor living room and collapsed on the ample sofa. Sprawled out on my stomach, with my face turned away from the living room, I fell asleep.

Then something strange happened.

At some point during the night, I became dimly aware of a musky odor. The miasma gradually became thicker and heavier. Suddenly Biscuit's tongue was licking the back of my neck. But even with my whiskey-drenched senses, I realized that it wasn't one of Biscuit's usual messy licks. It felt more like the lissome touch of a wet finger. His tongue flicked at various parts of my neck again and again. Then he stopped.

In my alcohol-enhanced state of exhaustion I was a virtual quadriplegic, so I wasn't able to turn around and return Biscuit's greeting. My left arm was folded awkwardly under my torso; my right arm was dangling off the sofa, and my closed eyelids faced the backrest of the couch. I was just too sodden with booze and fatigue to reposition myself. No matter how I tried, I couldn't turn around and pat Biscuit.

But that didn't keep him from licking me again. This time his tongue probed my right arm, which hung off of the sofa. His uncharacteristically nimble, staccato licks started at my wrist and probed up to my elbow. Then his appeals for attention abruptly stopped. Although my thinking faculties were almost as impaired as my limbs, it occurred to me that Biscuit had licked the parts of my body that were saturated with insect repellant. The toxic chemicals that coated my skin must have tasted vile.

This may have lessened Biscuit's interest in me, but it didn't drive him away. Although I was virtually unconscious, I sensed his animal presence near the back of my head. It was as if he was just hovering there, observing me, or smelling me, or somehow trying to take the measure of me. Maybe he was wondering if it was really me. Maybe the scent of all that mosquito repellant made him doubt that I was Gabriel's dad. Whatever the case may have been, I could feel him very near.

The odor that he emitted may have been thoroughly natural, but it was far worse than the bug juice on my skin. Had he been sprayed by a skunk? Strangely, he didn't sniff or paw at me. He just seemed to be hanging in mid-air, looming over me. Was he standing on the coffee table? It was almost as if he was waiting for me to move—waiting for me to reveal myself as...as what? A living thing?

In the few brain cells that were still functioning properly, I realized that all of this was silly. I tried to rouse myself so that I could turn around and give our family pet a frisky hug. But Jack Daniels had gotten the better of me. I just couldn't move.

Inexorably, I drifted off into a deep sleep without twitching a muscle. I might as well have been in a coma.

Biscuit would just have to wait until morning to get his dose of affection.

PART TWO

If you want to know a man's true nature,
give him power.
—Yugoslavian proverb

TWENTY-FOUR

GIFTS

PENSADOR AND YORO EMERGED from the tent as a helicopter approached out of the eastern sky. It glided overhead, then hovered above one end of the broad hill on which the village was situated. The Inucans had seen helicopters before, but always at a great distance—mechanical insects among the clouds. Now the people were awed by their close-up view of this massive machine. It had two equally enormous rotor blades: one at the front and one at the back, and their thunder was so loud that the Inucans covered their ears. Destro, who had just returned from his aborted capybara hunt, raised his bow and positioned the notched end of an arrow against the weapon's taut fiber. But Yoro put a hand on the bow and shook his head. Destro lowered the weapon.

Pensador's three male helpers—Moe, Larry, and Curly, as he called them—had cleared the western-most section of the hill and set up a landing perimeter. As the great flying beast slowly descended, the Inucans had to protect their eyes from the swirling debris that was thrown up by its twin blades. The helicopter's whirlwind blew Buriti palms off the closest thatched huts, exposing the tangled skein of branch-work beneath.

When the machine landed its large side door slid open, revealing a man in a jump suit. Behind him were dozens of neatly aligned boxes, all strapped to the wall of the aircraft. The rotor blades continued to beat furiously as Pensador, holding his hat firmly on his head with his left hand, walked up and signaled to the man with his right hand. He then pointed in the direction of a slightly larger hill about a quarter of a mile away. The Inucans knew the place as *Kalsanuk,* or "wind-block hill."

Pensador gestured to Larry, his African worker, who immediately clambered aboard the machine. He and the co-pilot unstrapped the boxes and began passing them to Moe, the Indian worker, who in turn passed them to Curly, the Anglo worker, who stacked the boxes in neat piles about fifteen feet from the helicopter.

More villagers came out of their huts and gathered around Yoro to watch what was happening. Although they stood at a safe distance, they had a clear view of the aircraft's enormous windshield, behind which sat a motionless man. The upper part of his face was covered by dark goggles, and headphones were clamped over his ears. The Inucans had never seen such devices, and some of the Amerindians wondered if the man was an extension of the larger machine. Behind the pilot sat another man who was fully and unmistakably human. His pudgy face was topped by a receding hairline, and since he wasn't wearing sunglasses, the Inucans could see that he was staring at them. They stared right back at him, and a chasm of cultural divergence was momentarily bridged in the shared glimpse.

Felipe and several older children emerged from the forest and jogged toward the hill. Some carried tattered fishing nets; others held boxes of string with fish-hooks dangling off of the sides. They soon joined the rest of the tribe, and Felipe found Yoro. He looked at him as if to ask, 'What's all this?' Yoro shook his head. The nurse thought the Sartum appeared very grim. Mara pushed through the group and stood between her grandfather and Felipe.

Working swiftly, the men finished unloading the boxes. Then Moe and Curly joined Larry in the helicopter, and the large door slid shut behind them. A second later the co-pilot reappeared in the front of the helicopter. He opened his swing-out door and handed Pensador a freshly-charged satellite phone. Then he gave him a red box that was just small enough to be carried with one hand. Pensador smiled broadly and mouthed the words *thank you*, then he handed the co-pilot his phone, which would be taken back to Codajas to be recharged. He stepped away and spun his finger skyward. The huge machine slowly lifted off the ground, hovered for a moment, then drifted toward the nearby hill. The noise of its thudding blades slowly faded and the Inucans removed their hands from their ears.

For several seconds Pensador and the villagers faced each other, separated by piles of boxes that formed a chest-high cardboard wall. The Inucans seemed to be in a mild state of shock. He noticed three teenage boys at one end of the group. They held primitive forms of fishing gear in their hands. Pensador gently placed the red box on the ground and removed a Swiss Army knife from the thigh pocket of his khakis. He cut off the end of longest box in the pile and tipped it forward until several fishing rods clattered to the ground. "This will make it a lot easier to catch bigger fish, and a lot more fun. Come and look at them," he beckoned to the boys. "Later on I'll show you how to use them."

Knife in hand, Pensador tore through several more boxes. As he opened each container he placed its contents on the ground in front of the villagers. "These are some of the things I promised you last night." He kept opening boxes until an array of goods was laid out for all to see: machetes, stainless steel pots, garden tools, canvas hammocks, axes, knives, and fishing nets made of steel mesh. The Inucans were speechless and wide-eyed; they had never seen so many useful things in one place.

Pensador took hold of a five-pound bag and slashed it with his knife. A torrent of salt poured out. "There are many more bags—more than enough for every family," he said proudly. "Come and take, my dear friends. All of this is for you."

Destro was the first to step forward. He picked up one of the gleaming machetes and touched its blade with his finger. It was razor-sharp.

He looked at Pensador and nodded. The outsider tipped his hat toward Destro. "It's yours, my friend." Other Inucans slowly walked up to survey the offerings. Clusters of people gradually followed. Soon most of the tribe was gathered around the assortment of free goods. Some picked up unopened boxes and looked tentatively at Pensador.

"Yes! Yes!" he cried. "Open them up! These are my gifts to you—to all of you!" The Inucans began to tear away at the containers with their hands. People talked excitedly to each other as they examined and handled various items. The nervous silence that held sway moments earlier was replaced by the din of happy chatter. "Share it all," Pensador shouted over the crowd. "There's no need to fight over anything. There's enough here for everyone."

Pensador presided over the scene like a doting parent on Christmas morning. For several perfect minutes the Inucans were his grateful children, and the success of his long-term plans seemed assured. He looked around for Yoro. He wanted to see the old warrior's expression; he wanted to see a deep smile crease that distrustful face. But his heart sank when he finally spotted the Sartum. Yoro was watching his people tear through the cache of gifts, and he seemed more worried than ever.

Then Pensador saw her: the young woman whose beauty was illuminated by last night's bonfire. She was standing between Felipe and Yoro. Her face was no less lovely for its pensive expression, and she wore a plain white cotton robe that went from her shoulders down to her knees. In the space of twelve hours she went from being a Polynesian fertility goddess to Athena, the Greek mistress of wisdom.

He found the combination irresistible.

Pensador considered timidity to be a self-destructive vice that should be crushed whenever it reared its delicate persona. Yet he didn't hold bullishness in high esteem either. But his father had taught him that when a man wanted something that was fair game, he should pursue it intelligently and boldly. That's what he had done his entire life, and that's what he did now. Pensador picked up the red box and approached the young woman.

Before opening the bottle of tequila the previous night, he had called Juan Ponticari in Rio de Janeiro on his cell phone. He told the banker that he wanted one more item to be delivered the following day. When he told Pontacari what the item was, the banker balked.

"How can I get that on such short notice?"

But Pensador was adamant. "Juan, you know every jeweler in Brazil. Just get it. Money is no object. There will be a bonus for you as well. Just get it done. Understand?"

"Just like your father," Ponticari muttered.

"What did you say?"

"Nothing. Just talking to my son."

As he had managed to do many times before, Ponticari had executed an impossible wish. This time he did it by raiding his own wife's safe two hours before midnight. He would make it up to her later. After making a few calls and promises, Pontacari handed a red leather box to his chauffeur, who delivered it to the bank's private pilot before midnight. At sunrise a Lear jet touched down on the airstrip outside the town of Codajas. The weary pilot left the sleek container in the care of the helicopter's navigator less than twenty minutes before the chopper set off for the Inucan village.

And now the leather box was about to exchange hands yet again.

"This gift is for you," Pensador said as he offered it to the *accla* who stood between Yoro and Felipe. "I hope you won't think me—" he wanted to say 'presumptuous,' but realized the Inucans didn't have a word that captured its meaning well enough. He resorted to the Spanish *presumido,* which he doubted she understood.

Pensador decided to let the gift speak for him. He opened the box to reveal a string of flawless white pearls, looped around a black velvet base. The pupils of Mara's eyes swelled and a gasp escaped her lips. Felipe immediately stepped back without even realizing that he had done so. When he saw the necklace, a mass of conflicting imperatives left him uncertain as to how he should react, so he looked down at his sandals and said nothing.

Mara was spellbound by the necklace. Her gut reaction confirmed one of Pensador's long-held suspicions: the mind of the human female was innately attuned to shiny baubles. This young woman, who had surely never seen any sort of advertisement for any form of jewelry, reacted to the necklace just as a Manhattan socialite might. What they shared wasn't culture or breeding. He believed it was something deep in their mutually female brains; something in their universally womanish DNA.

"Go ahead," Pensador smiled, "it's yours. It will look even more beautiful on you."

Yoro glanced uneasily at Pensador and his granddaughter. He was about to speak when Mara reached up for the necklace. But just as her fingertips touched the pearls, she stopped and turned toward Felipe. She saw that he had taken a step backward and seemed to be looking at the ground. She recognized his posture as one of instinctive submission. Perhaps without even realizing it, he was bowing out to Pensador. Without so much as a glance or a growl, he was stepping aside for an apparently superior dog. This sudden realization mortified the young woman, partly because she didn't want to believe that Felipe's love could be so easily intimidated, and partly because it made her feel like an ignoble animal. She imagined a bitch-hound in heat, its scent glands emitting a mix of chemicals that would draw sniffing males to her hind quarters. The unwelcome image disgusted her.

"No," Mara whispered, more to herself than anyone else. She stepped to Felipe's side and slipped her arm through his arm. "No," she said again, more clearly this time.

Pensador looked from one to the other.

Mara met his eyes, but Felipe continued examining the ground.

"I—I didn't realize..." Pensador said. "Are you two...?"

"Not yet," she replied. "Soon."

Felipe looked at her, but she gazed defiantly at Pensador.

"Well, then," he forced a smile, "my best wishes to both of you." He snapped shut the leather box and walked back toward the crowd. He didn't realize that he had spoken these parting words in English.

When he was gone, Felipe took a deep breath and looked at Mara. She glared back at him. "Why didn't you stand for me?"

"Stand for you? I thought you wanted his gift. It sure looked like you wanted it. What was I supposed to do? Tell you that you had no right to accept it? Order you to get away from him?"

Though she didn't speak, her wounded expression slowly melted away.

But dull pain continued to shadow Felipe's face. "Mara, if I work night and day for the rest of my life, I'll never be able to give you anything like that necklace. I will never be that rich. I hope you understand."

Yoro looked down. He knew such an admission didn't come easily to any man.

Mara thought for a moment, then looked at Felipe. "I understand," she said quietly. "Now I want you to understand something. What I love is in here," she placed her index finger on the left side of his chest. "What I want most is not in any box. What I want most is in here." Her finger pressed against his chest. Raindrops began to pepper the ground as Mara searched Felipe's eyes. Then she stood on her tip-toes, closed her eyes, and softly touched her lips to his. Though Yoro was standing only two paces away, Felipe was too surprised to feel embarrassed. He surrendered to the moment. When he opened his eyes again he saw that Mara was walking back toward her hut at the other end of the hill. Bewildered and light-headed, all he could do was watch her walk away.

Pensador's opulent gift had raised the ghosts of past humiliations in Felipe's mind. As a poverty-stricken high school student in Santa Cruz, and later as a financially-strapped undergraduate in Lima, he seemed doomed to compete with guys who could lavish money on girls. Time and again, he longed for affections that he literally could not afford. Felipe had learned that romantic love wasn't the idealistic eagle it pretended to be; its wings were feathered not by higher emotions and noble loyalties, but by colored paper. Without money, he might as well have been an ugly, earthbound ostrich. Pensador's pearls seemed to confirm Felipe's pessimism. The talons of wealth could even reach into this primeval jungle to carry away the woman of his dreams.

But Mara's reaction had stunned him even more than Pensador's boldness. He was beginning to realize that her feelings for him were thoroughly genuine: she seemed to truly love the light inside the lantern. This dawning awareness left him stunned and breathless. For a moment he thought that if he flapped his arms he might ascend into the sky like Pensador's helicopter. Felipe heard his own voice and realized that he was saying words to no one in particular: "I am the luckiest guy in this galaxy."

"Yes," Yoro nodded, "I think you might be." Mara's grandfather didn't know what a galaxy was; but even if it included everything in creation, he surmised that Felipe was—at that moment—the most fortunate of all males everywhere.

Then the Sartum turned his attention to the giant helicopter in the distance. It had landed on Kalsanuk, less than two thousand feet away, and its rotors still thudded out waves of air. The Sartum wanted to ask Pensador why the machine had landed on the unoccupied hill, but the legendary man was showing some of the boys how to use a fishing rod.

The sprinkle of raindrops turned into a downpour. The crowd scavenged the remaining gifts and dispersed toward the huts that dotted the hill. It was almost time for their midday meal. The teenage boys thanked Pensador and jogged off into the thickening precipitation, holding tight to their new fishing rods.

When everyone had gone, Pensador stood alone at the edge of the hill. Yoro watched him and noted that, unlike most outsiders, he didn't seem to mind the rain.

Instead of taking cover, he peered at the silhouette of the helicopter on Kasulnak.

"Felipe," Yoro said, still looking at Pensador, "I would like to ask you a question in your cabin."

"Sure," the nurse replied absently, "what do you want to know?" He, too, seemed oblivious to the rain. He watched Mara duck into her small hut and silently wished he could be with her at that moment.

"What is..." the Sartum paused, then pronounced the letters as if they were discrete nick-names: "Dee—Enh—Aay?"

It took a moment for Yoro's pronunciation to penetrate Felipe's mental fog. When the letters finally speared his consciousness, he turned and looked at Yoro.

"What did you say?"

TWENTY-FIVE

SEALING THE DEAL

At quarter to ten on the second Thursday of August, I strolled to Jean's office along with Laine and Gabriel to "pass papers." Ownership of number three Bog Lane was about to be formally transferred from Richard Heinrich Hitchens to us. The entire process had been speeded up by Hitchens's lawyer, Maxwell Burke, at his client's behest. Jean was a bit worried by all this haste, but Laine and I were pleased to close the deal. Burke, a thin, fastidious man who rarely smiled, was at Jean's office to represent Hitchens.

As we went through the routine of signing numerous forms and listening to Burke summarize the content of each document, Gabriel sat in the corner of the office and watched. He had brought with him a cloth bag full of small toy trains, but he seemed more interested in the ritual that was being transacted around Jean's conference table.

Laine and I had been concerned about Gabriel for the past five days. Biscuit was still AWOL, and Gabriel was sinking into a deeper state of mourning with each passing day. We assured him that our husky was probably frolicking somewhere on the heavily-wooded six acre estate, and that he would come back after he had thoroughly explored his new stomping grounds. I firmly believed this on the first day of his absence. But, when two days had passed, I began to have doubts. Now five days had come and gone with no trace of Biscuit. I was sure something bad had happened. His collar didn't provide an address or a phone number. A square medallion hung from his collar, but the chunk of metal only gave his name along with an inscription which, as I recalled, mentioned something about the bonds of friendship. Thus, with the exception of Jean, Harry, and Fran, no one in Plymouth knew that we owned a husky. Laine and Gabriel tried to solve this problem by tacking up posters on telephone poles around the neighborhood, but we hadn't received a single call.

I considered the sad possibilities, starting with the most likely: Biscuit had been roaming the neighborhood and was hit by a car. I phoned the Plymouth Police to see if they had responded to any calls involving a dead or injured husky. They hadn't. From there the possibilities became less likely but no less dreadful: Maybe he was mauled by a bigger dog or a coyote, and had wandered into some wooded area to die. Or maybe he had found his way to Myles Standish State Forest and reverted to his feral roots. Whatever may have happened, I was increasingly sure that Biscuit would not be returning to us. At some point I would have to admit this to Gabriel, but I wanted to put that moment off for as long as possible.

On that August morning my main concern was the house on Bog Lane and its owner's mercurial personality. Specifically, I worried that Richard Hitchens might have a last-minute change of heart. The more I thought about what we were getting—and the price we were paying—the more I expected Hitchens to pick up his phone and scream: "Hold everything! I've come to my senses! No deal!"

But Maxwell Burke's cell phone never uttered a peep and the entire process was finished before 11AM. As I signed the final form and passed it to Burke, Laine asked him if he had heard anything from his client during the past week. His answer was typically concise: "No, I have not."

After Burke left, Jean and Laine hugged and giggled like school-girls. They would no longer have to rely on their phones to stay in touch. From now on they would be a five-minute stroll from a face-to-face chat. To celebrate this new era in their friendship, Jean invited us to a dinner party at her home on Saturday night.

"We'll have to get a sitter for Gabriel," Laine said. "Do you know any trustworthy folks in the area?"

"Sure do," Jean smiled. "Delaney will be happy to do it."

"How do you know?" Laine asked. "Isn't Saturday the big mall night for fifteen-year-old girls?"

"No, she's not planning to go anywhere," Jean said as she led us out the door to her front yard.

"How can you be so sure?"

"Oh, I just know these things," Jean flashed an inscrutable smile. "It's sort of like a sixth sense."

"I'm impressed," Laine said.

"Besides," Jean added, "last night Delaney gave Harry some serious sassiness about the whole dating thing, and he grounded her for two weeks. So I know exactly where she'll be on Saturday night."

TWENTY-SIX

THE PEOPLE OF THE
JUNGLE

THE RAIN BROUGHT OUT VARIOUS SCENTS in Felipe's cabin. Though it had been built seven years earlier, the faint smell of freshly-cut plywood still lingered, blending with the odor of medicinal alcohol. Other fragrances mingled in the room, but Yoro's nose wasn't quite keen enough to distinguish the emollients from the ammonia-based cleansers that Felipe regularly scrubbed into the cabin's exposed surfaces.

The nurse kept a battery-operated hot plate in his cabin. Each week, along with his mail and requests for supplies, he sent two drained battery packs to Pensador's delivery man. And each week the delivery man gave two recharged battery packs to the Inucan carriers who met him at the footbridge. Now Felipe used his hot-plate to boil water for two cups of tea. The pleasing aroma of simmering black pekoe leaves blended with the other smells that permeated the room.

"Who told you about DNA?" Felipe asked before taking a sip from a steaming mug. He sat at his desk, cradling the cup with both hands. The sound of pattering raindrops filtered in through two screened windows.

"No one," Yoro answered. "That's why I want you to tell me."

"But where did you hear about DNA?"

The Sartum looked at a glistening glass ball that pressed down on a stack of papers on the desk. Then, as he sat on a fold-out chair next to the nurse's desk, he explained the conversation he had overheard that morning outside of Pensador's tent.

As Yoro spoke, Felipe noted that the Sartum was not a big man. The height of the average Inucan warrior was about five feet, six inches—short by Western standards but taller than the warriors of other Amazonian tribes. None of the Inucans were obese. Some, like the Sartum, developed a small paunch with age, but most of the villagers had to work hard even after their hair turned gray, and this physical regimen kept their weight in check. The Inucans had no horses, donkeys, or mechanical contrivances of any kind. There were only two modes of travel: walking or canoeing, both of which burned calories. They had no televisions to sag in front of while their bodies turned food into fat. Their entertainment consisted mainly of tribal dances, games, and storytelling, which usually ended when the sky grew dark. But perhaps most important of all, no Inucan had ever eaten a potato chip or a candy bar, nor had any of them ever imbibed a soda. Such delights were unknown to their palates. Whatever the Inucans ate was wrenched directly from nature's clutches.

Yet, for all of that, life as an Inucan wasn't a stroll down the avenue of good health. On that fateful day in 1902 when the tribe was finally and irrevocably "discovered" by the outside world, it numbered over eight hundred men, women, and children. But the moment the Inucans came into contact with outsiders, their numbers began to dwindle. Like other Amazonian people, they had little or no resistance to outsider-borne diseases such as measles and smallpox. Even the common cold virus could overwhelm an Amerindian's biological defenses. Thus, in the span of about one century, their population was decimated until less than two hundred Inucans remained.

Another lethal reality that faced the tribe was the sheer ferocity of the jungle's competing macroscopic life forms. For generations the Inucans had to contend with other tribes that sought to destroy them, enslave them, or steal their women. And when the Amerindians weren't fighting off other humans, they were fighting off non-human predators. Jaguars, caimans, piranha, insects, snakes, peccary packs, and parasites of every imaginable kind had all claimed Inucan lives over the decades.

But the greatest single threat to Inucan health was their health care system. Up until Pensador arranged for a nurse to take up residence in the village, the Inucans relied largely on charms, incantations, and magical potions, which were impotent against microbes, anatomical dysfunction, and constantly evolving viruses.

During Felipe's stay in the village, only one woman had died during childbirth. But, as far as he could determine from his talks with the elderly members of the tribe, it wasn't terribly uncommon "in the old days" for a woman to die while bringing new life into the world. Even if mother and child survived the birthing process, parents didn't count a newborn as "theirs" until the child had survived at least two dry seasons. Too many little bodies expired before they reached that milestone. According to the Inucan elders, the souls of deceased children returned to the infinite-eternal *Viro*, from whence they had come.

Felipe had calculated that life expectancy for the Inucans was somewhere between forty-five and fifty years old, though some lived well into their seventies. His twin goals were to improve the Inucan quality of life while extending their quantity of life. This mission absorbed all of his intelligence, skills, and determination. He frequently requested the latest medical journals from Pensador's weekly delivery man. From these periodicals he learned of new medical findings, innovative treatments for various maladies, and recently-approved medications. It was a rare month when Felipe didn't request a new gadget or medicine from Codajas. Sometimes it took many weeks for the desired items to arrive, but he always made good use of them when they were delivered. Although Felipe didn't fully realize it, during the past three years of being on duty virtually every minute of every day—and single-handedly dealing with an extraordinary spectrum of emergencies—his skill had far surpassed that of any registered nurse. At this point, his medical talents eclipsed even those of a very competent general practitioner.

As the nurse listened to Yoro's story, he estimated that Yoro was at least sixty-five years old. Felipe didn't need an insurance company's actuarial charts to know that the Sartum had already beaten the odds. The evidence of Yoro's age and hard life were plain to see. Deep lines etched outward from his eyes to his temples, and scars pocked various parts of his body. His maroon torso—once the muscular edifice of a proud warrior—now sagged under time's invisible burdens. And the thick mane that once flowed down the back of his neck had thinned to a grayish drizzle.

But Felipe knew that one thing about Yoro that had not been diminished by time: his love for his people. *Sartum* literally meant "honored one." Yoro had earned that title not just because of his cleverness or martial prowess. He cared deeply for these *people of the jungle*, and they trusted his love. Through years of self-sacrifice and devotion, Yoro had won the allegiance of every member of the tribe. Whatever the situation, his first question was always the same: "What is best for my people?" This was the question that had guided him to the nurse's cabin, and compelled him to reveal the comments he had overheard that morning.

The Sartum finished his account by repeating the longest word he had ever heard.

"*Groe-tesk-orr-ees.*" Though he had learned some English from missionaries, it was difficult for him to pronounce the words spoken by Pensador and Lynn Lee that morning. "That's what the woman said," Yoro explained. "That's what they are going to create. And when she said it, Pensador became angry." The Sartum looked at Felipe. "What is *groe-tesk-orr-ees?*"

The nurse shook his head, "I don't know. I don't think I've ever heard that word."

He got up and went into his small bedroom. He returned with a paperback Spanish-English dictionary and sat down at the desk.

As Felipe thumbed through the book, Yoro continued. "Pensador was worried that someone might hear her. He was especially worried that *you*—" pointing his finger at the nurse as if he was pressing a button—"might hear her. They are hiding something from us, no? There is something they don't want us to find out. Whatever it is, it has something to do with *Dee—Enh—Aay.* That's why I need you to explain this to me. I must understand what they are talking about."

Felipe scanned the pages of his dictionary. "It's not in here. It must be an obscure word." He began to repeat the Sartum's pronunciation; when he reached the second syllable his eyes widened: *"Groe-tesk—"* He poked his finger into the book and read aloud: *"Grotesque."* He looked at Yoro. "Does that sound like the word?"

The Sartum nodded. "That sounds like much of it."

Felipe read the Spanish version: *"Grotesco."*

Yoro frowned. He was as unfamiliar with the Spanish word as he was with its English equivalent. "What does it mean?"

The nurse was all too familiar with the Spanish word, but he silently wished that he was wrong about its meaning. His paperback dictionary only provided a one word definition, which he read aloud: *"Hideous."*

"What does *that* mean?" Yoro asked.

Felipe thumbed through the dictionary until he found the Spanish counterpart of *hideous.* The book provided two synonyms and he read both to Yoro: *"horroso; espantoso."*

The expression on the Sartum's face went from furrowed curiosity to quiet shock.

He slowly repeated the words back to the nurse: *"horrifying; dreadful."*

Yoro didn't have to ask anyone about the meaning of those words.

TWENTY-SEVEN

GETTING ACQUAINTED

DELANEY POWELL, LIKE A GOOD REALTOR'S DAUGHTER, arrived on our front door step promptly at 6:30. Though shy of sixteen she was taller than her mom, but she hadn't yet acquired Jean's physical grace. Her frame and movements were still mired in ungainly adolescence. However, she had inherited her mother's genial smile and her father's pensive green eyes. The origin of her scarlet hair was a mystery. Jean's hair was chestnut brown and Harrison's was sable brown. But their daughter sported a mane of lustrous red curls. It would take a geneticist, a genealogist, and a detailed family tree to explain how that came about.

Delaney had babysat Gabriel twice before in Maynard and they got on very well together. He was still downcast about Biscuit, but he perked up a bit when we told him that Delaney would be coming over. Biscuit had been missing now for seven days. Laine and I were equally certain that something terrible had happened to him, but neither of us had the gumption to admit this to Gabriel. We tried to cheer him up any way we could. At one point Laine even mentioned the possibility of getting a Dalmatian—a breed of dog that had enchanted our son ever since he saw the Disney film. But Gabriel looked at his mom as if she had spoken treason. "I don't want a new dog," he cried. "I want Biscuit to come home."

As Laine showed Delaney around the first floor, she explained that Gabriel seemed to be grieving the loss of Biscuit, and she warned her to tread lightly on the subject if it should come up. As they went from room to room, they had to skirt the boxes and bins that cluttered much of the area. We were still in the process of getting unpacked and finding a place for everything. Laine also showed Delaney a back stairway that led almost directly to Gabriel's bedroom. "There are some passageways in this place that we're just finding out about," Laine explained. As she showed Delaney around, she carefully went over her list of instructions: "Remember to have Gabriel in bed no later than eight-thirty. He can keep his night light on. There's a pitcher of fresh lemonade in the fridge. The popcorn's already in the microwave; it just needs to be popped. One minute and forty seconds should do it—more than that and the kernels tend to burn. He's already had his bath so you don't have to worry about that..."

Delaney smiled and nodded politely even after Laine began repeating herself. I took my wife's hand gently into mine: "Honey, we're going to be late." But she kept talking as I led her out of the house. "Gabriel, you be good for Delaney. I love you. Remember to brush your teeth. Delaney, call us if there's a problem. He should be in bed no later than eight-thirty. There's a pitcher of fresh lemonade in the fridge..."

Still smiling politely, Delaney quietly closed the front door.

Laine and I strolled to the Powell's home, which was less than a ten-minute walk.

It was a steamy evening and we were glad that Jean and Harry decided to hold the dinner party indoors, where we wouldn't have to put up with the humidity or the mosquitoes.

When we arrived, Fran Sampson and Muriel Gray were sitting in the living room, sampling hors d'oeuvres and chatting about the last time each had tasted champagne.

Jean had invited Muriel so that we could meet the most senior resident of Bog Lane, and the Sampson's had been nice enough to drive her to the Powell's door. She was a slender, elegantly-dressed woman with primped white hair. Her cane lay against the sofa on which she sat. Fran made the introductions. "Welcome to Bog Lane," Muriel said, extending a frail hand. "I hope you'll be very happy." Her smile was warm and sincere.

"I understand you raised a family here," Laine said, sitting on the sofa next to her.

"Yes; six children." Pride and longing mingled in her voice.

"We can barely manage one," I said.

"How old?"

"He's six," Laine replied. We hadn't been away from Gabriel for fifteen minutes, but I knew that she already missed him.

"Enjoy these days," Muriel said with a faraway smile. "No one gives hugs like a six-year-old."

Laine was genuinely touched by the old woman's comment, and for a moment I thought she might well up. I quickly changed the subject.

"Sophie mentioned two sisters, Fran. That sounds like a full house."

"And two others besides," he said. "A son in college and a daughter who lives in Norwell."

"Wow," Laine said. "You've got five children?"

"I can't take too much credit," Fran replied with a wry grin. "My wife did all the heavy lifting."

"Heavy pushing, you mean." A pretty woman with rolling ring-lets of tawny red hair entered the room. She carried two glasses of white wine. "You must be our new lane-mates," she surmised, pass-ing a glass to me. "I'm Pam," she said, shaking my hand. "Welcome to the neighborhood."

"Sophie speaks very highly of you," Laine said, as Pam handed her a glass of wine.

"Sophie's only eight years old," Pam replied. "But let me know if she's still saying nice things about me when she's sixteen. Just make sure there's a sofa behind me so I don't hit my head on anything sharp."

Jean appeared in the doorway that led to the dining room. "Have y'all met our new servant girl? Our maid and butler eloped, so we had to press her into service."

Pam curtsied. "Always glad to help out in a worthy cause."

"Where's your other servant?" Laine asked.

Jean tilted her head. "My other servant?"

"I think his name was Harry. He was kinda' standing around in the church that day when you got married."

"Oh, that guy," Jean grinned. "I chained him to the stove."

TWENTY-EIGHT

IN SEARCH OF A SMOKE

LYNN LEE DREAMED OF A CIGARETTE. She held it between two fingers and admired its user-friendly size and shape. In her dream she mouthed the words: "How utilitarian!" but she didn't actually hear her voice. It was as if she was watching herself in a silent film. She put the cigarette up to her lips and took a long, slow drag, inhaling deeply. She saw the swirling vapors inflate the millions of alveolar sacs in her lungs, filter through the silk-thin walls of her capillaries, and race through her body's arterial canals.

The nerve cells in her brain rejoiced as they absorbed countless molecules of nicotine. A celebration took shape on the increasingly surreal inner landscape: globules of grayish tissue were singing and dancing on a cloud of smoke. Some played ukuleles that were imbedded in their axons. Others twirled around, clacking castanets with their sinewy dendrites. How delightful it was.

But Lynn's father suddenly appeared in the background. He wore a stern expression and wagged his finger at the festive nerve cells. They immediately scampered off the screen. Then she saw herself say something to her father. Though she didn't hear the words, she knew what they were: *Live for today, Papa.* She saw the tip of the cigarette glow brightly as she took another hit. Suddenly John Lennon was on the other side of the screen from her dad. He was silently strumming his guitar and mouthing the words: *Imagine all the people, living for today...*

She smiled approvingly, took another drag, and let the ingredients of the processed tobacco plant assuage her brain cells. Then a mechanical monster encroached on the upper part of the screen. It had a glass head and long, rectangular arms of steel that swung wildly. Its flailing limbs knocked her father and John Lennon off the screen; their surprised faces gaped at Lynn as they flew out of her dream. One of the monster's spinning arms then clunked Lynn on the head. She woke up, and the image of swirling, rectangular arms was instantly converted into the audible roar of whirling rotor blades.

The racket was deafening. Pensador had told Lynn that a helicopter would arrive that day, but he didn't tell her that it was going to land on her tent. She looked up to see the shadow of the chopper against the orange fabric, and was relieved to see the dim silhouette glide over the top of the tent toward the other end of the hill.

Lynn considered rising from her cot, but she was still exhausted from the previous day's trek. Pensador had warned her that the hike would be arduous, and he advised her to take the chopper into the village. But she harbored a fear of helicopters. The long, clattering rotor blades were like delicate fingers being wagged in the eye of fate.

Lynn lingered on her cot, unable to wipe sleep's dreary tendrils from her mind. She had always imagined the Amazon jungle to be an exotic place. But now that she was actually here, it wasn't exotic at all. It was simply deadening. She could feel the thick, sweaty atmosphere suffocating her thoughts, her senses, even her will. She had always considered herself to be a tough person. But after less than forty-eight hours in the world's largest rain forest, she was revising her opinion of herself. She craved a cigarette or any stimulant that might enliven her slumping sensibilities in this wasteland.

Rain was falling when Lynn finally got dressed and emerged from her tent. She carried an umbrella, the top of which was decorated with a multicolored rainbow. In their open-sided huts, the Inucans were as visible to her as she was to them. They were intrigued by the device she held over her head, and they were bewildered to see that she seemed afraid of getting wet. Why else would someone use such a device? The Inucans sought shelter from the rain when they were eating, sleeping, or working with their hands. Otherwise they let the falling water cleanse their bodies. Some of the villagers wondered if the rain in her land was different from the rain here. Perhaps, they reasoned, the droplets in that faraway place were somehow dangerous.

As she passed, Lynn could see Inucan women preparing meals. The floor of each hut was centered by a circular piece of stonework about thirty inches in diameter. Small fires burned on these carefully fitted rocks, over which the women boiled water, flame-seared meat and fish, or created other forms of nourishment. Some of the women were boiling manioc, the starchy root of cassava plants. During their hike to the Inucan village the day before, Pensador explained to Lynn that manioc is the nutritional mainstay of almost all Amazonian tribes. It could be baked in the hot ashes of a fire and eaten like a potato, or it could be ground into flour to produce a form of bread. The stingy soil of the Amazon was not a hospitable habitat for grain, so the staple food of Western Civilization—wheat flour—was unknown to the Inucans.

As Lynn walked to the western edge of the hill, she passed the nurse's cabin. The front door was closed, but as she strolled along she got two successive glimpses of Felipe and Yoro through the screened windows on either side of the door. They seemed to be immersed in conversation. She passed several more huts and then saw an elderly man who labored under a large awning of braided branches. He had long silvery hair and wore what looked like an off-white kilt. The man sifted through a pile of tree bark and dried leaves, carefully examining each specimen. With a medium-sized knife he cut away portions of the bark, then placed what he deemed desirable in a large, ceramic cauldron. All the while, he mumbled softly and lyrically to himself.

Lynn arrived at Pensador's side just as the chopper lifted off the nearby hill. "Oh, crap," she exclaimed. "Are they leaving?"

"It would seem so," he replied without taking his eyes off the aircraft.

"Don't they have to land back here to drop off the stooges?"

"They're cutting down more trees on the hill. They'll walk back when they're done."

Lynn sighed heavily.

"What's your problem anyway?" Pensador looked at her and saw the colorful umbrella. He smiled. "Is that some sort of fashion statement?"

"Pardon me, but I have this thing about getting drenched."

"After a few more days in this place, you'll learn to enjoy that particular sensation."

"At the moment I'm in search of a different kind of sensation. I was hoping to bum a pack of cigarettes off one of those guys."

"Tom doesn't smoke. I don't know about the pilot or co-pilot."

"Well, that just sucks," she muttered.

"You know, Lynn, you picked one hell of a time to quit cigarettes."

"Yeah," she said dismally. "I figured this would be the perfect place to go cold turkey. Even if my willpower failed, I wouldn't be able to give in."

"Well then," Pensador said with an air of mock congratulations, "you can take some consolation in the soundness of your logic."

"Damn you too."

"My, my. I guess you really are addicted."

She brushed the quip aside. "You talk to Lex today?"

Pensador nodded as the helicopter banked slightly and made a wide eastward turn.

"Everything still on schedule?"

"All systems are go," he said with a noticeable lack of enthusiasm.

She paused before voicing her next question. "Any word on Jimmy?"

"No."

"Did you ask about him?"

Pensador's hat was so saturated that its brim bent all around his head. He pulled it off and squinted at her through the rain, his eyes and voice suddenly seething with emotion. "Of course I asked. I ask every damn day!"

"Okay, okay," Lynn said, "no need to explode. I was just wondering out loud."

"You wondered out loud in Miami, in Caracas, in Codajas, and now here. If there was some change don't you think I'd tell you? If I heard that he was found somewhere, don't you think those would be the first words out of my mouth?"

She held her free hand up and spoke in her softest tone. "Okay, Hitch, I'm sorry." She paused and took a breath. "It's just that you never mention him unless I ask about him."

"What is there to say? Will my talking about him—"

"No," she cut in, "but it certainly wouldn't hurt. You two were really close; and it sometimes it helps to talk..."

He stared hard at her, and she couldn't tell if the streams that coated his face were formed by rain or tears.

She shook her head and shrugged helplessly. "I'm sorry. Forget I ever mentioned it."

"It's forgotten," he said, turning back toward Kalsulnak.

"But just remember that if you want to talk about—"

"I'll keep it in mind," he said, squishing his hat in his hand.

For several seconds nothing could be heard but the dwindling thwacks of the helicopter and the steady patter of rain drops. Then, from Kalsulnak, the abrasive growl of a chain saw splintered the air. Realizing that it would be a long time before Pensador talked about Jimmy, Lynn resigned herself to his silence on the subject. But when she turned to leave, she noticed the silver-haired man she had passed earlier. "Hitch, who is that guy over there, talking to himself?"

Pensador turned. "That's Cotulko, the tribe's shaman. Ex-shaman, I should say."

"Why ex?"

"Well, I suppose he's still the shaman, but he doesn't have a whole lot to do these days."

"Why is that?"

Pensador watched the helicopter shrink into the murky gray sky as he answered her question. "Medical science has pretty much consigned him to the ranks of the unemployed. Cotulko's main job was to heal sickness and ward off evil spirits. But for the past seven years the Inucans have had the services of a trained nurse, and they've seen that medical science succeeds where shamanism fails."

"So you're responsible for putting him out of business?"

"Not entirely. He's pretty good with herbs that relieve minor problems, and he makes a salve that keeps a lot of insects away. He also creates magical-mystery-tour potions."

"What?"

"He makes his own brand of a hallucinogenic drink called *ayahuasca*,"

Lynn's eyebrows peaked. "Did you say hallucinogenic?"

"I did indeed. It's an ancient concoction that goes all the way back to the Incas. The shaman knows what plants to use, and what parts of the plant and bark are most psychoactive. Cotulko adds some of his own ingredients to give it a little extra *pizzazz*." Pensador turned and regarded the shaman. His disdainful tone was momentarily replaced by one of grudging respect. "In his own way, I suppose he's a bit of a scientist himself."

"Does the stuff work?"

"You bet. Packs quite a wallop."

"You've tried it?"

"Seven years ago."

"And?"

"It's taken me about seven years to recover," Pensador laughed. "Actually," he said on second thought, "Cotulko's brew took me for a nice ride."

"Is that what he's doing now?" Lynn asked, suddenly bright-eyed.

"I think so. The last time I was here he used to brew up a batch every couple of weeks. Most of the villagers only take it on special occasions. A few take it more often just to break the monotony. But Cotulko drank it often. He told me it puts him in touch with *the spirit realm*." Pensador laughed again. "I told him that was bullshit."

"What did he say?"

"He asked me if the shit of bulls smelled worse than the shit of other animals."

"Bullshit or not," Lynn said, "his stuff takes you for a ride, right?"

"Sure does."

"That's all I need to know." She walked over and introduced herself to the shaman. Pensador watched her make an elaborate series of gestures, accompanied by simple English words. Each gesture ended with her index finger pointing into her mouth. Cotulko stood silently, his face as furrowed and uncomprehending as the chunk of tree bark in his hand. Lynn finally called out to Pensador: "For crying out loud Hitch, will you get over here and translate."

Pensador reluctantly sauntered over. The shaman frowned as he approached. They had never been on very good terms, and after last night's speech Cotulko wanted nothing more to do with the outsider. He made a point of withholding *sumidad*, the customary Inucan sign of respect. Rather than tilt his head forward, the shaman tilted his head back a bit—an explicit sign of disrespect.

Pensador extended the middle finger of his left hand at Cotulko.

"What does that mean?" asked the shaman.

"It's a message from the spirit realm," Pensador smirked.

The shaman spat on the ground next to the outsider's feet.

"I'm glad we got that out of the way," Pensador grinned. "Now, how can I help you two close this deal?"

"Tell him I want to try some of that stuff," Lynn said pointing at the cauldron.

Pensador spoke one sentence to the man. He said two sentences in return. Pensador turned toward Lynn. "He says it's going to take hours to boil out the impurities. It won't be ready until tonight."

"I can wait," Lynn replied.

"Are you sure you want to do this? You don't smoke this stuff—you drink it. And it doesn't taste like champagne."

"What does it taste like?"

Pensador pointed to the large kettle. It was half-filled with bits of tree bark and flakes of leaves. "What does it look like?" he asked.

Lynn peered into the pot. "It looks like mulch."

"Right," he nodded, "and that's what it tastes like."

Lynn frowned. "Can't he put sugar in it or something?"

"Where are you going to get sugar around here?"

"Maybe I can mix it with some of your tequila. You didn't drink all of it last night, did you?"

"I've still got a bottle or two squirreled away. But I think you might be sucking up more than you can swallow. Cutolko's recipe for *ayahuasca* is extremely potent. You'd better check with the nurse first. I'm sure he can fill you in on the possible dangers."

"Yoro's got his ear right now. I'll talk to him later."

Pensador's smile faded. "Where? Where did you see them?"

"They were in Felipe's place a few minutes ago," she said. "Looked like they were having a real heart-to-heart."

"What were they talking about?"

"I have no idea. I couldn't hear them. Even if I had heard them, it's not as if I could've understood what they were saying."

"I wouldn't be so sure," Pensador replied.

"What?" a puzzled expression spread across Lynn's face. "Hitch, what the hell are you talking about?"

"We might have a problem," he said, staring at the cabin in the distance.

TWENTY-NINE

LINDORM

GABRIEL WAS AT THE KITCHEN TABLE, drawing on a piece of poster board with dry erase markers, when Delaney entered the room. She noticed that he was sketching the same creature in different sizes and colors, over and over. But with each rendering he added more detail to the animal's face. She sat down next to him and was about to ask "What is that?" when she remembered what Laine had told her about Biscuit. Not wanting to venture into such uncertain and painful territory, she used her most buoyant voice to suggest that they play a game.

Jean made a point of seating Laine and me at the end of the dinner table, across from each other. We assumed she and Harrison would occupy the head seats at opposite ends of the table. There was no particular seating arrangement for the other guests. Harry had yet to make an appearance, but the aroma of honey-lemon sauce—which we knew to be a crucial part of his culinary specialty—wafted from the kitchen.

Jean handed me a chilled bottle of champagne and asked me to liberate its cork.

I looked around the dining room and noted the delicate objects that adorned its walls: portraits, china, and polished mementos of one kind or another. "Jean, this has all the makings of a scene from a Jerry Lewis movie. Mind if I do this on the front porch?"

"With my blessin's, sir," she said in her most mellifluous drawl.

I walked through the living room and opened the front door. Standing on the other side were two women whose expressions were no less surprised than mine. One woman held her clenched fist in front of her shoulder, frozen in the act of knocking.

"No need for violence," I said. "I'll let you in."

The other woman laughed and extended her hand. "Hi, I'm Tracey Faulk and this is my highly significant other, Pat Bishop. We're…"

"Late!" Jean exclaimed, sweeping through the living room. "I thought you gals were lost on Route Three!"

"We're so sorry," Tracey replied.

"Route Three wasn't the problem," Pat said. "There was an accident on Route Six. Everything is jammed up for a couple of miles."

The series of hugs and greetings that ensued in the dining room made it clear that both women were very well known to all of our neighbors.

Delaney and Gabriel played *Hungry Hungry Hippos*, followed by a game of *Operation*, followed by a game of *Battleship*. They snacked on popcorn and lemonade between each game. He even managed to smile and laugh a bit. The piece of poster board with Gabriel's depictions of Biscuit had been consigned to a corner of the kitchen, and he seemed to have momentarily forgotten about his missing pet.

As Gabriel poked a plastic peg into the *Battleship* display and read out the coordinates, Delaney's cell phone chimed. She took the call into the next room, but occasionally glanced into the kitchen. As she spoke in hushed tones, Gabriel picked up a blue dry-erase marker and began drawing on the poster board that was propped up against the wall. The lapse of his grieving memory was far more temporary than Delaney had hoped. Soon he was heading toward the doorway that led to the back stairway.

Delaney pulled the cell phone away from her ear and called out. "Hey, Buster Brown, where are you going?"

"To the bathroom."

"Why don't you just use the one down here?"

"My dad just painted it today. He told me not to use it until tomorrow."

"Okay," Delaney said. "But don't be long. You can finish sinking my ships when you get back."

He left the room, still holding the dry erase marker in his hand.

She quickly returned to her caller. "No, not yet," she whispered into the phone. "I told you: nine o'clock."

"Tracey and Pat used to rent an apartment over on Standish Street," Jean explained to Laine and me, "till I tracked down their dream home in Onset."

Pat overheard the comment. "We still can't believe you found just what we were looking for, right up to the widow's walk."

"Darlin', that's my mission in life," Jean smiled proudly, "finding the right home for the right people."

"Greetings everyone," Harry appeared through the kitchen door carrying a large tray of sliced salmon fillet on a bed of wilted spinach. He wore a light blue shirt that was neatly centered by a striped yellow tie.

"We were told this was going to be a casual affair," Fran protested.

"Didn't have time to change," Harry said, placing the tray in the middle of the table. He hugged Tracey and Pat. "You know how Jean's mission is putting the right people in the right homes? My mission is putting the wrong people in the big house. And no self-respecting public official will let you do that unless you're dressed for the occasion."

"Well," I added my voice said to Fran's protest, "you could at least loosen your tie."

Pam appraised both the platter and the chef. "You've got to like a man who cooks like Julia Child and dresses like Cary Grant."

"With the guys I used to meet it was the other way around," Tracey said.

Jean laid her head against Harry's shoulder. "Eat your hearts out, ladies."

"How long have you been out of Plymouth?" Laine asked Pat.

"Just over a year now," she said.

"But we miss it; we miss our friends," Tracey said as she leaned over and embraced Muriel.

"No Delaney and Samantha?" Pat asked.

"Delaney's baby sitting," Jean replied, ushering Pat into a chair. "Samantha's at a sleep-over in Marshfield."

"Is the clinic up and running?" Pam asked.

"It's been kind of slow," Pat said. But we're hanging in there. We pick up a couple of new patients a month."

"Patients?" Laine wondered. "Are you a doctor?"

"We're veterinarians," Pat replied. "I worked at the clinic on the other side of Plymouth Center for almost ten years. But I'd always wanted to run a place of my own. When Tracey came along, we discovered that we shared the same dream, so we hitched our wagons and went into business."

"Partners in crime, eh?" I said.

"And in everything else," Tracey added, smiling demurely. She was about to sit next to Pat when Beth took her by the hand and guided her along the table.

"Hunnee, you wanted to meet the couple with the plant-crazy basement..." Jean pulled out the chair at the end of the table. "... Well, meet Rick and Laine Delvecchio. You three have something to talk about."

"We do?" Laine asked.

"Jean told me about your basement," Tracey said. "I make my living as a vet but I'm a botanist in my free time," her eyebrows poked up slightly when she said "botanist."

Light brown hair flowed around her shoulders, framing reflective hazel eyes and soft facial features. "My specialty is tropical flora. When Jean told me about the subterranean garden at your new house, I couldn't believe my ears."

"I know the feeling," Laine nodded. "Every time I go into the basement I can't believe my eyes or my nose. The place stinks something awful."

"Well," Tracey continued, "if it's okay with you, I'd love to get a look at the layout; maybe take some measurements and shoot a few pictures or some video footage. I'd also like to check out the plants in your yard. I promise not to do any damage."

"That's fine with us," Laine shrugged. "But I'm not sure there's a whole lot to see in the basement. I think all of the plants there are dead."

"Oh, that's a pity," Tracey frowned. "Still, it would make a great presentation."

"Presentation?"

"I'm a member of a local horticultural association, but we're connected to other chapters across the country. Our next annual convention is in Atlanta. Most of the talks are kind of boring, especially for people who aren't interested in plants—"

"Uh-huh," Pat said, her eyes turning skyward.

"But," Tracey said, squinting at her companion, "for those of us who are interested in plants, I think that your unique garden would make for a remarkable show-and-tell."

"We're happy to oblige," I said. "But it isn't actually our garden. The previous owner—a guy by the name of Richard Hitchens—was the creator. Richard Heinrich Hitchens," I repeated his name in the hope that it might mean something to Tracey. "Have you heard of him? Maybe he's a member of your botanical association?"

She shook her head. "I know every member of the local chapter, but that name doesn't ring a bell."

I was disappointed. "If Hitchens was a member of your group, it would help explain things. Here's a guy who loves tropical flowers, and he has the money to indulge his passion. Case closed. But if he was a flower fanatic, it seems likely that he would've been a member of your group. As things stand, we have no idea why he went to so much trouble."

At precisely 8:30 Delaney led Gabriel upstairs to supervise his nighttime routine, but he seemed to know the drill well enough. Without her having to say a word, he changed into his pajamas, stepped into a pair of slippers, then padded down the hall to the bathroom. Delaney wandered behind him with folded arms, quietly admiring the Delvecchio's new home. Although cardboard boxes were piled about, and the walls weren't yet adorned with decorations, the elegance of the place showed through.

She then realized that no sound could be heard from the bathroom, even though the door was open. She expected to hear running water, or the chatter of an electric toothbrush, or the flush of a toilet. But there was no noise of any kind. Delaney quickly moved toward the door. "Gabriel?" she called as she walked into the spacious bathroom. She found him standing by a large vanity, staring at the wall. "What are you—" Then she saw the inky blue mess that held his attention. Scrawled on the wall were seven capital letters. The letters were disjointed, as if written in haste or composed by a child, but she could make out each one. Taken together, however, they formed a word or name that meant nothing to her: *LINDORM*. Above this series of letters was a crude rendering of a monstrous face, complete with ravenous eyes and an open mouth lined with fangs. Below the series of letters were two words that Delaney understood: *RUN AWAY*. On a gleaming porcelain surface next to this macabre artwork was the blue dry-erase marker, still uncapped.

"Oh, Gabriel!" Delaney cried. "How could you do—"

"I didn't do it!" he exclaimed, eyes wide.

"Oh please, Gabriel," Delaney said, pulling a length of toilet paper from the dispenser and wetting it at the sink. "This was *not* a nice thing to do. If I can't get this off you're mom and dad are going to be furious."

"But I didn't do it!" Gabriel pleaded again.

"Please don't lie to me. You're just making it worse." She vigorously rubbed the moist tissue against the wall and was relieved to see the blue lines begin to smear. "And why would you draw such an ugly picture of your dog? Biscuit wasn't mean, was he?"

"No!" he cried. "Biscuit is my best friend! That's not Biscuit!"

"Who is it supposed to be then?" she asked, toiling at the wall.

"I don't know! Honest!"

Jean circled the table, pouring champagne into everyone's glass.

"That jungle must have cost Hitchens a fortune," Laine agreed. "I just assumed he had a thing for tropical plants. Why else would he create such a huge garden?"

"I go back a long way with one of the building inspectors at town hall," Fran said.

"According to him, Hitchens wanted the garden for aesthetic

and recreational reasons. That's what he told the zoning board, at any rate."

"The board didn't question him?" Jean asked. She was on friendly terms with two of the five people on Plymouth's zoning board, and she knew them to be conscientious individuals. "It's not a rubber stamp committee," she added. "I'm surprised they didn't check it out more thoroughly."

"They did," Fran replied. "But Hitchens convinced them that the garden wasn't going to damage the local environment in any way. The fire inspector, health inspector, and building inspector separately toured the basement before and after the garden was constructed. But Hitchens satisfied whatever concerns they may have had."

"When did he do all this?"

"About ten years ago," Fran said.

"Closer to fifteen," Pam amended.

"Well," I shrugged, "maybe it is that simple: Hitchens just loves tropical plants."

"Maybe not," Muriel said. "My husband Gary would always wake up in the middle of the night to have a cigarette. Even when his doctor told him he had emphysema, Gary couldn't kick the habit. Late one night, while smoking on the front porch, he saw a truck pull up to Hitchen's house. Several workmen brought some large boxes through the bulkhead into the basement. Gary said they handled the boxes with great care and they worked very quietly. He just assumed they were special plants for Hitchens's garden. But on other nights he saw more special deliveries. More crates. He couldn't figure out why plants would be delivered in the wee hours of the night."

"What do you make of that?" Laine asked, turning to me.

I shook my head.

"Okay folks," Jean said, "let's not weird out Laine and Rick all at once. For tonight, let's just pretend this is a perfectly normal neighborhood." She lifted her champagne. "Now if you will all please raise your glasses…" Everyone obliged. Standing at the head of the table, she smiled down at Laine and me. "Here's to our old friends and new neighbors: May they have a lifetime of happiness on Bog Lane."

As she tucked Gabriel in, Delaney decided to give him a gentle lecture in place of a bedtime story. She explained that it was okay for him to be mad about Biscuit's disappearance. She explained that every person is different, and that people show their feelings in different ways. And she explained that if people don't talk about their feelings, those feelings can become mean and ugly. When she was done explaining, she leaned close and asked, "Do you understand?"

He didn't look away or even blink. He simply said, "I didn't do it."

She closed her eyes and sighed. "Okay," she said, "have it your way."

"What are you going to do?" he wondered.

She studied his small and remarkably innocent-looking face. "What do you think I should do?"

"I don't know," he said. "That's why I asked you."

"Well, we are both pretty lucky that you used a non-permanent marker. Otherwise we'd be in some trouble."

"But I didn't use a…" he tried to say "non-permanent" but could only pronounce an abbreviated clot of consonants. "I didn't use anything because I didn't do it."

Wow, Delaney thought as she peered into his clear, brown eyes, *you are good at this kiddo*. Then she came at it from a different angle. "Gabriel, do you remember bringing the blue marker upstairs?"

He nodded.

"Do you remember using the toilet?"

He nodded.

"And then what happened? What do you remember?"

"I washed my hands and I went back downstairs."

"What about the marker? What did you do with the marker?"

"I put it down before I peed. I musta' forgot about it when I washed my hands."

"You don't remember writing on the wall?"

"I didn't do it."

Delaney took a deep breath and glanced at her watch. "Okay, Buster Brown. I'm all done with this. You get some sleep."

"That was a scary face on the bathroom wall," Gabriel said.

"It was a *silly* face," she replied. "Maybe it was meant to be a mad face or a scared face, but it was just goofy, like a crazy cartoon." She crossed her eyes and contorted her lips and nose.

Gabriel laughed. "Do that again!"

She repeated the performance, but this time she used the fingers of one hand to widen her mouth while pushing the tip of her nose up with the index finger of the other hand.

Gabriel laughed even harder. "Do it again!" he cried.

"Hey! Just how many funny faces do you think I have?"

"One more?" he said hopefully.

She smiled. "Okay, but this is the last one. Now watch carefully…"

He looked intently at her but nothing changed. Suddenly he realized that the sides of her nose were rapidly flaring out and in, while the flaps of her ears were moving forward and backward just a tiny bit.

"Oh, boy!" he exclaimed, thoroughly awed, "how do you do that?"

"That's just one of many wonderful things they teach you in the honors program."

"Really? I wanna be honors, too!"

"Well, if you do your homework every night, read a lot, and pay attention to your teachers, you, too, can learn to make goofy faces."

Gabriel gazed at her with profound admiration. He already knew that Delaney was a nice person, and he knew she was really smart, but he had no idea she was so talented.

"Okay, Buster Brown, I'll leave the night light on," she said, caressing his cheek. "You have sweet dreams." She got up and flicked off the overhead light. But Gabriel's voice caught her as she was about to leave the room.

"Delaney, do you think Biscuit will ever come home?"

She understood that the dog would never be far from Gabriel's thoughts. Whether he was happy, or scared, or immersed in some challenge, some other part of his mind would always be wondering about Biscuit. She walked back to his bed. "I don't know, sweetheart," she answered, looking sympathetically into his eyes. "But I do know this: wherever Biscuit is, he feels your love—he knows that you love him."

"Really?"

"Really."

"How do you know?"

Delaney's lips formed into a pensive smile. "It's not something you *know*; it's something you *sense* deep down inside. It's the quietest thing of all, but it's the thing that matters most of all."

"But what if Biscuit is hurt or," the boy swallowed hard, "what if he died?"

Delaney was surprised that Gabriel, all of six years old, already seemed to grasp the reality of death. Then she remembered that he had been full of questions when his grandfather passed away last year. She chose her words carefully. "Gabriel, love can hurt; it can hurt really bad. Love can cry; it can cry really hard. And love can even close its eyes for a long, long time. But, in the end, love always finds a way. *Real love* always finds a way to make things work out for the best, even after our eyes have been closed for a long, long time."

"How?" the boy whispered earnestly.

"Because real love is bigger than us—it's bigger than all of us put together. It's bigger than the whole world. Real love is more alive, and more true, and more beautiful than anything else. So it can lift us up and become our home."

"You mean, like, heaven?"

"That's as good a word for it as any I've ever heard."

A moment passed in silence, and Delaney saw that Gabriel was lost in thought.

She allowed another moment to pass, then leaned over and kissed him on the cheek.

"Now you get some sleep, okay Buster Brown?"

"Okay," he said softly, still adrift somewhere within.

When Delaney returned to the first floor she went directly to the front door, opened it wide, and flicked on the porch light. Leaning against one of the porch's support beams, with his arms folded, was a tall, sandy-haired boy.

"You said nine o'clock." He glanced at his watch. "It's now quarter past."

"Well, if you're going to be like that," she cocked her head, "I guess you can just turn around and go home." She started to close the door but he quickly stepped forward and blocked it with his foot.

"Touchy! Touchy!" he exclaimed.

"Keep your voice down," Delaney said, crossing into the living room, "Gabriel isn't asleep yet."

The tall boy stepped into the house and quietly closed the door.

THIRTY

POTION

COTULKO REMEMBERED AN OLD INUCAN SAYING that equated the paws of a jaguar with the jungle's passage from dusk to night. Like the feet of all cats, a jaguar's paws were thickly padded so that it could prowl close to its quarry without being heard. By the time its prey detected the feline, it was often too late to escape its distinctive skull-crushing bite. Darkness in the Amazon seemed to pounce just as unexpectedly as a jaguar's paws.

Very little sunlight actually penetrated the jungle's canopy, so *a lesser form of night* pervaded the rainforest, making it difficult to keep track of the sinking sun beyond the layers of leaves and branches. But when the giver of daylight sank below the horizon, the jungle was no longer merely shrouded or gloomy—it became almost as black as one's closed eyelids. If the sun's radiance could barely find its way to the forest floor, moonlight had no chance at all. That's why Inucan parents warned their children to head home well before the sun set, or else they might find themselves suddenly sightless; stumbling through a wild domain where darkness equaled danger.

On this particular night, the whereabouts of every Inucan child was known, for they had all gathered around the fire-pit at *la recognus*—along with a good number of adults—to hear two hunters talk about an encounter with Surutas that had occurred earlier that day.

As the hunters told their story, Cotulko was at his cauldron on the far end of the village, ladling *ayahuasca* into a small wooden bowl. Lynn Lee accepted the bowl then held up an index finger with her free hand. "One more," she said in English. The shaman blinked at her. "Uno mas," she repeated in her flawed Spanish. The shaman shook his head and said something she didn't understand. She pointed to the cauldron. "Look," she reverted to English but hoped he would get the point anyway. "You've got a lot. One more bowl won't make any difference."

From under his brambly eyebrows, Cotulko watched Lynn.

"He not understand," said someone behind her. She turned to see Felipe, walking arm-in-arm with Mara. They stopped next to the shaman's cauldron.

"Well, can you make him understand?" Lynn said. "Tell him I just want one more bowl."

"No good," Felipe said in his broken English. "One...enough. Two hurt...will hurt you."

Lynn looked toward the center of the village where Pensador stood with a number of villagers. "Felipe, it's not for me. It's for Hitch."

"Who?"

"Pensador," she said. "It's for Pensador. But he doesn't want Cotulko to know it's for him." At the sound of his name, the shaman looked up but didn't say anything.

"Why?" asked Felipe.

"I don't know," Lynn shrugged. "Professional jealousy maybe? These two guys don't like each other. Maybe Hitch—ah, Pensador—doesn't want Cotulko to know that he has anything that's of interest to him."

Felipe frowned, then turned and looked at Pensador. He was standing behind a throng of Inucans who had gathered at *la recognus*. Cotulko followed Felipe's line of sight. When he saw Pensador a muted grin formed on the old man's face.

"Just tell him it's for one of the other villagers," Lynn said. "Better yet, tell him it's for you."

Felipe was about to explain that he didn't use *ayahuasca*, when he saw that the shaman was already ladling some from a pot next to the cauldron. Cotulko handed the small bowl to Lynn.

"Oh, great. What made him change his mind?"

Felipe shook his head. But he noticed that the bowl had been doled out of a separate batch of *ayahuasca*. He wondered what the difference was between the potion in the cauldron and the potion in the pot. He asked Cotulko, but the old man seemed not to hear the question. Instead, the shaman smiled at Lynn as she took the bowl with her free hand. He said something to her in Spanish, but Lynn didn't understand the words. She turned to the nurse.

"He wish you...how you say...walk inside," Felipe explained.

Lynn looked at the shaman, puzzled. "What does that mean?"

"Yourney," Felipe pointed to the bowls in Lynn's hands. "He want you go yourney inside."

"Yourney?" Lynn repeated, then laughed. "*Journey*; you mean *journey*. Long walk."

"Yes," Felipe nodded. "Long walk inside. Journey inside."

"Where inside?"

Felipe reached over and gently touched his finger to the side of her head. "Inside here."

Lynn laughed again and nodded at Cotulko. "You tell him if this stuff makes a good escort, I'll be back for more walks. More journeys. Okay?" She nodded at the shaman. Though he didn't understand a word she said, the self-educated chemist nodded agreeably.

Mara was looking at Cotulko and couldn't recall ever seeing him grin like that before. *If snakes could smile*, she thought, *that's what their smiles would look like.*

THIRTY-ONE

REVELATIONS

DINNER CONVERSATION RAN ITS COURSE: FROM the best and worst local shops, to the most dangerous intersections in town, to the varying quality of Plymouth's teachers, to the crimes and misdemeanors of state politicians. The food platters were almost empty when Jean announced that we would be having peach cobbler for dessert. As Laine helped her clear the table, I asked Fran when he planned to begin work on our back porch.

"Well," he replied, "now that you're the actual owners of the house, I can start Monday morning at eight, if that's not too early."

"That's perfect," I said. "But I'm curious: how do you approach this kind of job? I don't know anything about construction, so it all seems like Greek to me. How do you build a deck, connect it to a wrap-around porch, screen in the whole thing, and make it all look good?"

"Very carefully."

"Whoa there, honey," Pam cautioned as she cleared his plate from the table. "Don't overwhelm the poor man with details."

"Well, Pam," he said, "I'm not really sure if Rick wants to hear all the details."

He appraised me with a blasé expression. "Do you want to hear all the specific details?"

I read the look on his face. Unless a man finds his work endlessly fascinating, the last thing he wants to do in his free time is explain his work. "No," I replied. "I guess not."

Ever the gracious host, Harrison changed the subject. "Any sign of Biscuit?"

I shook my head, "No. No sign at all. Gabriel's taking it pretty hard."

"Who is Biscuit?" Tracey asked.

"Our Siberian husky. We'd had him for a few years, and Gabriel is quite attached to him."

"We all are," Laine added, walking out of the kitchen with a pot of freshly-brewed coffee. "But he and Gabriel are especially close."

"What happened to him?" Pat asked.

"That's the problem: we don't know what happened. I went out to dinner last Saturday and when I got home Biscuit was gone."

"Was he in the house when you left?"

"My memory of that evening is a bit foggy," I rubbed the bridge of my nose, trying to hide my embarrassment. "I remember Laine and Gabriel drove to Maynard; there was a thunder storm; and I fell asleep on the living room sofa. That's about it." I thought for a moment. "Actually, there was something else. During the night, I thought I felt Biscuit licking my arm. But it must have been a dream." I omitted the part about me being drunk, and Harry was good enough to leave it unmentioned.

Muriel turned toward me with inquisitive eyes. "Did you say Saturday night? The night we had that terrible storm?"

"Right," Laine recalled, "I drove through it on my way to Maynard. I actually had to pull over—I couldn't see five feet in front of me on the highway."

Muriel seemed lost in thought, but she was still looking at me. "My bedroom is on the side of the house that faces your place," she explained. "The storm had passed and I opened my windows open because it was hot. I fell asleep but the sound of barking woke me up. It was loud and very…angry or frantic. It went on for several minutes. Then there was a strange noise, like a whining sound, but it only lasted for a second or two."

Laine and I stared at Muriel.

"That was the last thing I heard," she added, answering our unspoken question. "I looked at my bedside clock and it was about nine-thirty or so. I fell asleep a short while later."

"The barking came from our house?"

"I'm pretty sure it did," she said. "It wasn't coming from the lane. The barks echoed a bit, like they were coming from a room or an enclosed space."

Laine and I looked at each other, mutually bewildered.

Delaney and her secret boyfriend had been kissing on the sofa for several minutes when he quietly undid the two top buttons of her blouse. She said "No," pushed his hand away, and re-buttoned her blouse.

The kisses and caresses continued for another minute. His hand slipped under her blouse and fingers probed upward toward her breasts. "No," she repeated, taking hold of his hand and pulling it out from under her shirt.

They wrangled on the sofa for a short while longer, until he slipped his hand between her abdomen and her blue-jeans; his fingers deftly unsnapped the top button. "No," she said again and yanked his hand away.

He sat up, exasperated. "Can you say anything but *no*?"

"Sure. How about *nein*?" she said with a stiff German accent.

"Jeez, that sounds even worse than *no*." He got up from the sofa and brushed his hair back. "You know, Dee, I thought we were going to do it tonight."

"Do what?" she blinked up at him.

"You know...*it*!" He gestured emphatically, as if "*it*" could only mean one thing.

"Oh, *it*. Jeff, we aren't going to do *it* anytime soon."

"Jeez. Baby, I can't wait forever!"

"You're fifteen," she reminded him.

"Yeah, okay, but how many times are we going to make out before we do *it*?"

"Hmmm," her face became that of an accountant brooding over some complex set of calculations. "Now let me see...how many times have we made out..." her fingers poked up and down as she spoke. "Give me just another moment...Oh yes, I have it now: *this is the first time we've ever made out*."

"Oh yeah? How many times did we roll around on the grass last Saturday?"

"Jeff, we were playing Frisbee Football with our friends, and you kept tackling me—which, by the way," she wagged her finger at him, "is against Frisbee Football rules."

"Still, it was sort of like making out. I was ready to do it right then and there."

"I'm pretty sure that's against Frisbee Football rules too," she said.

His lips formed into just enough of a pout for her to notice. "You know, Dee, I thought this was going to be a really special night."

"It is special, Jeff. We finally have some privacy, and my parents don't know we're together. We're having a secret rendezvous, like Romeo and Juliet. And my dad hates your guts, which makes it even more cool—like a 'forbidden love' kind of thing."

Jeff was dumbfounded. "Why does he hate my guts? We've only talked once for about five seconds. He doesn't know anything about me!"

"He knows you're packing a penis and two testicles. That's all the reason he needs."

"Jeez! I make honor roll every semester, and I'm going to apply to almost every school in the Ivy League. What the hell does he want?"

"A vow of celibacy."

"Oh, suck it all!"

"Look, Jeff, all I'm saying is that we're together in a nice, private place. There's a summer breeze coming through the windows, and we're kissing. Isn't this romantic? Isn't it fun?"

"Sure it's fun, but only up to a point. After that it becomes a kind of torture."

"Torture? Kissing me is a form of torture?"

"No, that's not what I'm saying. What I'm saying is…kissing you is like…it's like putting a piece of sirloin steak up to a starving guy's lips and saying, *'you can kiss but you can't eat'!*"

"You're comparing me to a dead cow?"

"That's not what I mean."

"That's what you said."

"Dee, there isn't a cow in the world that can compare to you."

Her eyes narrowed. "Is this your idea of sweet talk?"

"Look, do you know what we need right now?"

"We're not going to have sex."

"I'm not talking about sex. I'm talking about a nice, relaxing drink."

"Sure," she replied, "there's some lemonade in the fridge."

"I'm not talking about lemonade. I'm talking about something else…"

"Do you have something else?"

"No, but I bet these people do."

"What people?"

"The people who live here. I bet they've got a wine-cellar packed with all kinds of good stuff."

"Jeff, these people just moved in and they trust me. You're not going to raid their wine-cellar, or their cabinets, or anything else that belongs to them."

"They won't miss some sips of wine or a couple of cans of beer; they won't even notice. Trust me, Dee, it'll be fine."

"No."

He arched his head back and cried to the ceiling: "That word again!"

He sat next to her on the sofa and clasped both of her hands. "Dee, we've got to live for tonight. We've got to live for *the moment*. We can't worry about tomorrow."

"I'm not worried about tomorrow," Delaney replied. "I'm more concerned about next month when I don't get my period."

Jeff sat up straight. "That's not going to happen," he said confidently. "And if it does happen—" he rubbed his hands together as if washing them under an invisible stream of water—"we just get an abortion." He raised the palms of his hands to show her that they were clean. "See? No mess, no fuss."

"Oh, gee, I hadn't thought of that," she said with a dull grin. "Such a simple solution, too!"

"Right!" he exclaimed.

Her vacuous expression disappeared. "Jeff, I don't know how you keep making honor roll when you're such an idiot."

"What?"

"*We* get an abortion? *We?*" Delaney leaned forward and fixed her dwindling pupils on his widening eyes. "I've got news for you, Jeff. You will never have an abortion—*never*! No one will ever kill a child inside of your body—*ever*! You will never have to make that final decision, and you will never have to live with that choice. So you can take your 'live for today' attitude and stick it up your nose!"

Though startled by her outburst, Jeff scrambled to come up with something that might soften her stance. "Dee, lots of chicks get abortions."

The red-headed girl stood up and glared down at him. For a moment he thought she might pounce like a maddened tigress. But her smoldering eyes slowly cleared, and when she spoke it was in a strangely soothing voice. "That's really wonderful Jeff. I'm so happy for you, because you shouldn't have any trouble getting one of those *chicks* to give you some service." With that, Delaney turned and walked out of the room.

"Where are you going?"

"I'm going to check on the little boy sleeping upstairs. At least one of us has to take responsibility for *something!*"

Jeff followed her down a hallway to the back of the house. "Oh come on, Dee. Why do you have to be so pissed?" She ignored him and ascended the back stairway that Laine showed her earlier. He watched her climb the steps and disappear around a turn. He shook his head and looked down at his sandals. He sensed the evening was over, but decided to take one last shot. "Okay Dee. I'll go if you really want me to." She didn't reappear and ask him to stay. "Alright then Dee, I'm going to leave now."

Silence.

He made one last try: "I'll lock the door, okay?"

Nothing.

Jeff sullenly concluded that the evening really was over. "Suck it all," he muttered as he trudged toward a door at the end of the back hallway. But when he opened the door, he saw that it didn't lead outside or to another hallway.

It led to the cellar.

THIRTY-TWO

ORIGINS

THOUGH THE HOUR WAS LATE, scores of villagers—young and old—were mesmerized by the story that was being told. Two hunters talked about their encounter with an incarnation of Surutas. One of them, Destro, explained that they didn't actually see the creature's face, but they saw its body take hold of a large capybara and pull it under the surface of the river. They had already described how the doomed rodent had killed the newborn capybara pups.

Pensador leaned against one of *la recognus's* support beams and observed the gathering. As he studied the rapt faces, he smiled a secretive smile.

Long ago the Inucans worshipped Surutas. They'd even considered it blasphemous to refer to Surutas as a mere animal or by its animal name. But the bodies that Surutas inhabited always belonged to the same species of animal, and those bodies were always exceptionally sleek, powerful, and frighteningly inhuman. In seeking to somehow appease the dark side of nature, the Inucans focused on this creature whose sinuous movements and unblinking eyes embodied all that was unknowable and untamable in nature. So the tribe regularly offered Surutas something precious: a newborn infant. At the beginning of each rainy season, when the god seemed most voracious, they left a baby on the banks of the river, near one of Surutas's lairs. By giving nature something to quell its appetite for blood, the Inucans sought to lessen the suffering and death that might be inflicted upon the rest of the tribe during the remainder of the season.

But in the first decade of the previous century, Christian missionaries implored the Inucans to stop sacrificing their children. They told the tribespeople that there was a higher, living truth—a God who transcended the creatures and forces of nature. According to the missionaries, this ultimate reality sought compassion, not human or animal sacrifices. In time, their reasoning and persistence won over the Inucans, and the tribe stopped sacrificing its infants to the river god.

However, Surutas still commanded a sense of awe, and the villagers still spoke of its incarnations as if they possessed extraordinary powers. Perhaps it was a lesser god, but it remained a mysterious and ungovernable reality to the people of the jungle. So the Inucans continued to pass down stories about Surutas's epoch-defining incarnations.

And the first of these visitations—the most important incarnation of all—marked the origin of the Inucans themselves.

Five centuries earlier, a large chunk of the South American continent was ruled by the fabled Incas. Their civilization covered most of the Andes mountain range, stretching for thousands of miles along the Pacific Ocean. It was arguably the greatest of all empires in the New World—surpassing even Aztec and Mayan societies in wealth, size, and organizational structure. But though the Incas developed one of the most humane empires in history, it was still an *empire,* and was thus built upon the autonomy of other tribes. The "children of the sun," as the Incas called themselves, were generally gracious to clans that allowed themselves to be annexed. But they brooked no opposition: all rebellions and armed resistance were ruthlessly put down. If not killed in battle, captured rebel leaders were taken to Cuzco, the Inca capital, where they could behold the monuments and totems that reflected the glory of *Sapa Inca.* If the renegade leaders still refused to surrender and submit their clans to Inca rule, they were eventually executed or sacrificed to one of the many Inca deities.

One particularly defiant group of individuals became known by the Quechua phrase *Intip-Aucans,* which meant "children of rebellion." These men and women had been captured during military operations on the northern borders of the empire. But even in captivity they continued to wage a vigorous war of words against their captors. Inca royalty was alarmed by their eloquent appeals for freedom. The reasoned entreaties of these prisoners might spread beyond the Inca guards by word-of-mouth. If that were to happen, Inca control over already-assimilated tribes might be severely weakened. So the decision was made to move the Intip-Aucans outside the capital city, and to sacrifice them in a secret ceremony.

As these preparations were being made, word of an unprecedented sight reached Cuzco. On the outskirts of the jungle, at the easternmost boundary of the empire, a pure white incarnation of a powerful Inca river god had been seen by a group of sentinels. The deity had never donned such a color before, so the news caused great distress throughout the capital city. Inca soothsayers wondered if it was an omen of disaster. The emperor ordered one of his sons to lead an assemblage of priests to the place where the incarnation had been seen. Their task was to divine its meaning and, if necessary, offer a sacrifice that might win the river god's goodwill. The *Intip-Aucans*—the captive group of rebel leaders—were forced to accompany the Inca expedition into the jungle. If the god garbed in pure white desired a sacrifice, the blood of these defiant nobles would do nicely.

When the imperial host finally reached the riverbend where the incarnation had been seen, the prince ordered his warriors to search its banks and tributaries for miles around to determine the exact location of the white god. But while most of the soldiers were away, the *Intip-Aucans* overpowered the remaining guards and escaped into the jungle.

Though they had originally belonged to different clans, the renegades realized that they could only survive if they united to form a new tribe. They banded together and struck out in search of sanctuary.

In time, they took the name that the Incas had imposed on them—
Intip Aucans—and stripped it down to *Inucans*. They were proud to be
rebels, proud to have escaped Inca domination, and they pledged that
they would never again be taken alive by cruel overlords.

The group pushed deeper into the jungle and lived for years as
nomads. Eventually the renegades made contact with a group of heav-
ily-armed white men, some of whom wore silvery coats and hats of
metal. The Inucans sought to develop an alliance with these strange
invaders, but they proved to be even more domineering than the Incas.

The outsiders were far more interested in gold than any sort of
mutually-beneficial alliance. Indeed, it seemed to the Inucans that these
interlopers would destroy anything, kill anything, or pervert even the
most sacred truths, so long as they could acquire more gold.

The Inucans fought off these greedy warriors and moved in a south-
westerly direction until they came to a region of low hills that wasn't
occupied by any tribe. The area was a good distance from any large
river. The Inucans had already learned that outsiders who invaded the
Amazon jungle tended to travel on or along large rivers. The larger
the river, the larger the invasion force was likely to be. So the nomads
decided that this place—which was only served by some smaller tributaries of the Purus river—would be a good place to settle down.

Centuries passed and the Inucans flourished. But they never
stopped believing that they owed their existence to the pure white
river god whose appearance foreshadowed their own liberation. Thus,
they began to worship Surutas in all of its incarnations, and they waited
for the river deity to reappear in its pure white form. They believed that
such a visitation would mark the beginning of a golden age: a time of
unparalleled prosperity, freedom, and happiness for the Inucan people.

Pensador was thoroughly familiar with these legends. He had heard
them during his first stay with the Inucans fifteen years earlier. Now,
as he watched the two warriors conclude their story about the river
god, he was pleased to see that Surutas still held the Inucan imagination

firmly in its grip. This was one superstition that Pensador looked upon as useful, for it played to Lexel's talents and had become a crucial part of the company's larger plan. But the fact that the two hunters didn't kill the mother capybara pointed to the presence of a very different, and very troubling, superstition.

As Pensador mulled over this seemingly new wrinkle in the tribe's outlook, he felt a nudge in the small of his back. He turned to see Lynn Lee holding two small bowls of *ayahuasca*.

"Hey there, fella," she said with a whimsical smile, "wanna go for a ride?"

THIRTY-THREE

THE FACE

JEFF FLICKED ON THE LIGHT AND PEERED into the cellar; then he rubbed his chin and took a deep breath. "Sometimes a guy's gotta' do what a guy's gotta' do." With that, he slowly made his way down the steep, narrow steps. He was sure there was a wine-cellar in the basement, just as he was sure there would be wine in the wine-cellar. He told himself that Delaney would thank him when he actually handed her a glass of something tasty and alcoholic. It would put the romance back into their evening.

When he reached the bottom step he surveyed the dank area and saw the main stairway across the room. He then became aware of a fetid odor, but he knew that heavy humidity brought out all sorts of smells, especially in a cellar. A water heater and furnace squatted in the center of the room. On the side wall a set of cement steps led to the bulkhead. Cardboard boxes were piled on either side of the bulkhead doorway, and more boxes were neatly stacked along the far wall.

Then Jeff saw the stainless steel door on the opposite wall. This *had* to be the wine cellar because there was no other door in the basement. Its horizontal handle was long and functional—the sort of thing you would expect to find on the door of a walk-in freezer. He quickly moved toward it. The door was ajar and he could see that it was much thicker than an ordinary door.

Why would anyone put such a thing in the cellar of a house?

As he placed his hand on the edge of the door, he thought he saw a brief flash of light from the other side. But when he opened the door wider there was only darkness. The foul odor grew stronger. The room beyond didn't offer the slightest shade of color. The light-bulb dangling from the ceiling of the fieldstone cellar was positioned behind the door, so he opened the door as wide as possible to admit maximum light. With this additional illumination he saw that the door didn't lead to a room, but to a corridor formed by cinder-brick walls. He could see a few feet down this hallway, and he wondered at the barrenness of its walls. There was no light switch in sight. Seized by a mix of curiosity and determination, he stepped into the corridor. Its floor was smooth, unlike the pocked fieldstone cellar.

What the hell is that smell?

Jeff extended his left hand and placed it against the wall. His fingertips stretched toward the blackness, and the rest of his body slowly followed his hand into the shadow. The bad odor was getting heavier—he could taste it in his mouth.

He took another step.

This has to lead somewhere. He kept his hand stretched out against the wall, feeling for anything that might be a light switch.

He took another step.

The sound of footfalls filtered through the ceiling. Delaney was walking down to the first floor, but it sounded as if she was using the main stairway.

I can't turn back now. He took another step.

Suck it all. It's got to be here. His fingers, inching ahead, finally brushed against the edge of a smooth piece of plastic. He stepped forward and placed the palm of his hand over the rectangular light plate. Its protruding switch was angled downward. He stared into the blackness as his fingertips flicked the switch up. A blinding flash suddenly illuminated a haggard human face only inches from his face. Blue eyes—rimmed by bruised skin and centered by large black dots—stared straight into his eyes. Jeff yelled and stumbled backward. The light flickered again and again as he fell against the cement floor. Sharp pain tore through his back and the air vanished from his lungs in a swooping rush. He gasped as the corridor lit up a fourth time. But now the lights stayed on. Though still out of breath, Jeff scrambled to his feet and frantically looked up and down the hallway. He was alone.

An enormous, brightly lit room lay beyond the doorway at the end of the corridor. He stared into the room and saw what looked like a field of dead plants. But from his vantage point he couldn't see the entire room, and he had no desire to go any farther.

All he wanted to do was go home. He limped out of the hallway and up the main steps. Though he could barely breathe, he was too scared to stop moving.

Delaney heard the footfalls coming up the cellar steps and froze. Her first instinct was to grab a kitchen knife, but whoever was rushing up the steps would be on her before she could get her hand on a weapon. Suddenly the door burst open and she immediately struck a Bruce Lee-like pose, even though she didn't know anything about karate. She was about to kick wildly when she saw Jeff stumble through the door. "What the—what are you doing?! I can't believe you—"

He squeezed the words "I'm sorry" from his oxygen-starved body and pushed past her.

Her expression went from anger to concern when she saw how pale and shaken he was.

"What happened?"

"Nothing happened." He stopped in front of the refrigerator, put his hands on his knees and took a shallow breath. "Nothing," he said again in a strained voice. "I'll see you later." He moved toward the front door.

"Wait a sec! You can't just run out like this! What happened?"

"I've got to do my homework."

"It's summer—there is no homework."

"I've got to mow the lawn."

Delaney grabbed his shoulder just as he reached the door and forced him to face her. "Jeff, what happened? You look as if you've seen a ghost."

A nervous giggle escaped his lips.

"You're scaring me, Jeff."

He blinked at her and was finally able to take slow, even breaths. "I told you: nothing happened." He opened the front door and stepped onto the porch, but before closing it he looked back at Delaney: "You were right: there's no wine in the cellar."

He gently closed the door and filled his lungs with the moist night air.

Bog Lane was quiet except for the whir of air conditioners from a red house on the left. The smaller white house on the right had no air conditioners that he could see. But he noticed the silhouette of a child-sized face peering at him through the screen of a second floor window. *Good to be in your own home,* he thought, *good to be in a safe, familiar place.* The image of himself relaxing in his air conditioned bedroom, playing chess on his computer, gave him a deep sense of comfort.

But this mental picture dissolved and was replaced by the image of Delaney, sitting by herself. He knew that she was freaked out by his quick exit from the cellar. He shouldn't have allowed his nerves to run amok. Jeff was sure that his imagination had played a trick on him. The darkness of the cellar, the sudden flashing of the lights, his awareness that he was trespassing, and all of the horror movies that he had seen over the years—all of these things had conspired to dupe his senses. He was certain of that; and he was equally certain that Delaney was in no danger. Still, because of him, she was probably very frightened. And now he had deserted her. "Suck it all," he muttered.

Delaney stood on the other side of the door and wondered. *Something* had spooked Jeff, but she wasn't sure if she wanted to know what that *something* was. Should she check the cellar? She remembered that Jeff had left the door which led to the cellar wide open. Then another unwanted thought snaked into her mind: Could there be any possible connection between Jeff's fright and the blue mess in the bathroom? She was sure Gabriel had drawn the scary face on the wall upstairs. Had he also drawn or created something downstairs that rattled Jeff? She began to wonder if Gabriel's grief was twisting his mind in strange ways. She wanted the Delvecchio's to return, but she wasn't expecting them for at least another hour. Delaney was thinking about the open cellar door—and trying to scrape up enough courage to walk over and close it—when she heard three soft knocks on the front door. She slowly opened it to see Jeff leaning against the doorway with a sheepish grin on his face.

"Did you say there was some lemonade in the fridge?"

THIRTY-FOUR

INTIMO VIAGE

THE STUFF TASTED EVEN WORSE THAN HE REMEMBERED. Sitting at the edge of his cot, Pensador took a shot of tequila directly from the bottle. He never thought he would drink tequila to *relieve* a burning sensation in his mouth and throat, but the cactus-based liquor tasted far better than *ayahuasca*. He believed that one gulp of Cotulko's potion wouldn't be enough to beguile his brain-cells, so he clenched his eyes and took a second swig, followed by another mouthful of tequila.

When he opened his eyes, he saw that the bowl was still half full of the hallucinogenic brew. He was certain he would have to drink more to be transported to Timothy Leary land, but he didn't have stomach for another gulp just yet. He wondered how Lynn was faring in her tent. He guessed that after taking one sip of ayahuasca she would spit it out and take solace in the bottle of tequila he had given her.

Pensador set the bowl aside and lay back on his cot. An open flap just above him on the side of the tent revealed a rectangular section of sky through a mosquito screen. But clouds obscured his view of the heavens. If he could somehow wipe away this ceiling of water vapor, a breathtaking assortment of astral bodies would be exposed to anyone who was still awake in the village. On a clear night the Amazonian sky was an overwhelming tableau—a velvet dome encrusted by countless patterns of jewels. Celestial emeralds, sapphires, rubies, and diamonds glittered in such profusion that the mind was helpless to analyze the sight in any objective way. To reduce this *magnum opus* to mere numbers, masses, or velocities was to undercut its essential artistry. Perhaps the best that mere mortals could do was to behold the overall beauty of the masterpiece in subjective wonderment.

Pensador suddenly realized that his musings had veered too close to an untrustworthy sector of his mind. Such detours inevitably strayed into mystical quagmires of one kind or another, and he could not abide such muddy playpens, so he immediately obliterated his line of thought. As his father had taught him since boyhood, notions of a "creator spirit" had misguided the human race for far too long. The time had come to cleanse ourselves of such drivel once and for all. Beauty—even the crystalline majesty of the night sky—was a human invention. Beauty was created in our brains. It didn't actually exist in the night sky or anywhere else.

The lower part of Pensador's stomach cramped up and a wave of nausea rolled outward from his abdomen. But he fought down the pain and took solace, as he so often did, in dispassionate logic. He reasoned that without a human mind to fabricate the idea of beauty, the cosmos would be a random mass of particles, bouncing around in a pointless void. Therefore, to imbue the cosmos with beauty—or to imagine some sort of creative spirit at work in the universe—was to mislead oneself. But he knew that humans had an innate weakness for such falsehoods. So it was all the more imperative that such thoughts be consciously exposed as nonsensical. Similarly, any talk of "God" or "higher meaning" should be treated with polite contempt whenever it cropped up. Like persistently odious weeds, malignancies of the mind must be yanked out and cast aside. Of course, to keep from appearing close-minded, enlightened individuals must publicly concede *the remote possibility* of a truth or reality that transcended the human intellect. But such admissions were simply an academic nod to good form. They were not to be taken seriously by anyone above the level of a moron.

Pensador thought he heard someone vomiting in the village, but he was too tired to get up from his cot to see what was going on. His mind, however, required less energy to pursue its line of thought. It wasn't only "spiritual" people who got under his skin. Pensador was equally impatient with agnostics who, despite their agnosticism, took a sunny view of the cosmos. Such people maintained that nature could satisfy humanity's hunger for meaning, even though they admitted that nature was probably devoid of all inherent meaning. No one—not even the most amiable agnostic—could have it both ways. Either the cosmos had intrinsic meaning or it didn't. There was no in-between truth; no bifurcated philosophical platform that allowed people to logically hold contradictory beliefs. The rational mind couldn't celebrate the "wonderful mystery" of existence if existence was just a purposeless excretion of energy. But whenever the agnostic mind issued its "I don't know" motto, it unwittingly opened the door to spiritual concepts and convictions.

Beginning at his toes, Pensador's right foot slowly went numb.

He closed his eyes and surrendered to Cutolko's elixir. He yearned for a magical experience, and wished he had some *Pink Floyd* to soundtrack the excursion.

Pensador's left foot slowly went numb.

A luminous, life-sized image of a woman appeared in the tent. As the hologram congealed, her features became clearer and he winced at the familiar face. The woman was performing a macabre dance that consisted of violent spasms and awkward gyrations. At first he thought she was having a full blown seizure, but she didn't fall down. When she screamed, "Leave my baby alone!" Pensador realized that she was struggling against invisible hands that were attempting to restrain her.

"Damn it, Sonya, get a hold of yourself!" The voice boomed out of Pensador's memory and seemed to fill the tent.

But she continued to wail in Norwegian. "Take your hands off my baby!" Her arms stretched toward an invisible child. Pensador rolled over on his side and hunched his shoulders, trying to suppress waves of nausea.

"Stop this at once, Sonya," commanded the all-too-familiar voice.

"You're going to make it worse!" she cried. "You're going to make everything worse!"

"How can you possibly know that? Give me a chance!"

"A chance to do what? To kill him?"

"A chance to make him better."

"Better than what? Better than who?"

"This procedure might give him a healthy mind."

"He just needs to be loved," Sonya said. "That will make him good enough."

"Good enough for whom? Good enough for you, Sonya? Good enough for all the kids who will laugh at him? Good enough to become a village idiot?"

"He will find love in the world."

"Whose love, Sonya? Yours? You can't love him forever. What happens to him when you grow old and die? What happens when he's left all alone in the world?"

"Get your hands off my boy!"

"Damn you. I have the power to make him better. Why don't you trust me?"

Sonya suddenly froze in mid-struggle. Her apparition faded until only her exquisitely feminine voice lingered in the air: "Because you don't love him, Richard. You don't really care if he lives or dies."

Pensador tried to sit up on the edge of the cot, but a gleaming butcher's knife—held by a detached, albino hand—stabbed repeatedly into his abdomen. He managed to prop himself up on one arm. He tried to yell for Felipe, but his voice was enfeebled by the pain that knifed through his stomach. His feet dropped off the cot to the floor; his legs were as numb as chunks of wood.

Something sagged on the end of the cot where his feet had been a moment earlier. "Felipe?" he whispered. Pensador hoped that he had somehow called out through his delirium, and that the nurse was now in his tent. But when he looked over he saw a fat, naked ogre of a man sitting next to him. The strange visitor was looking straight ahead. Thatches of coarse, blond hair sprouted from his otherwise bald head. Pensador was about to speak, but he had to master another surge of nausea. During that moment, the man slowly turned and faced him.

Pensador realized that it wasn't a man at all. The stranger had the face of a small boy, encased within a massive skull. His eyes were dim and vacuous—utterly devoid of intelligence. Slabs of misshapen meat flopped off each side of his head, and a thick voice emerged from his rubbery lips: "I'm sorry, Dad."

The face and voice were brutally familiar to Pensador, but he couldn't speak through his mounting sense of dread.

"I had such high hopes," said a crisp, baritone voice from out of the past, "but this report makes a mockery of them. I could not be more ashamed."

"I'm sorry I let you down, Dad."

"You're not trying hard enough. You've got to work harder. You've got to devote more time and effort."

"I will, Dad. I will. I promise."

"You will remain here through the holiday, and you will prepare for the next semester. When I return, I expect to see a distinct improvement. Do you understand?"

"I understand," said the naked boy in the fat man's body, fighting back tears.

The phantom butcher knife—still gripped by a scaly, white hand—ripped through Pensador's internal organs. It tore indiscriminately through delicate nerve tissue as it sliced into fragile knobs of flesh. He doubled over in the corner of the tent, feeling as sick as he had ever felt in his life. Behind him he could still hear the plaintive, childish voice, saying the same thing, over and over: "I'm sorry I let you down, Dad."

THIRTY-FIVE

THE FEISTY NEIGHBOR

WE SAT AROUND THE DINNER TABLE and tried to make sense of Muriel's story. Pat Bishop asked the question that Laine and I hadn't wanted to consider. "Is it possible that someone attacked your dog inside your house?"

"I've heard that professional thieves sometimes look for recently sold homes," Tracey said. "The buyers have their stuff neatly boxed, ready to be picked up and whisked away. Sometimes the new home-owners aren't even staying at the place yet, which gives the thieves free reign. They pull up with a U-Haul truck so the neighbors think it's just moving men finishing the job. And they also come equipped with mace just in case there is a dog—"

"But we hadn't moved very much in at that point," Laine said. "There was really nothing for the burglars to burgle."

"And it still wouldn't explain Biscuit's disappearance," Harry added. "Even if he was maced or knifed, the thieves wouldn't have carried him away." He noticed that Laine winced when he said the word "knifed." He turned to her: "Sorry."

"Biscuit must have been barking for a reason," Jean said. "How else would you explain it?"

Harry shook his head. "There must be an explanation, but for the life of me I can't imagine what it might be."

Fran and Pam had been silent throughout this brainstorming

session. But when our ruminations hit a dead end, Fran cleared his throat. "You know, Hitchens supposedly had an attack dog. He told me that was the reason for the big fence."

Jean looked dubious. "You're thinking that Hitchens left his dog behind and it attacked Biscuit?"

"No," Fran said. "I just think it's very odd that in all the years Hitchens lived in that house, I never once saw the dog and never once heard it bark. But he had signs on his fence that read "Danger: Attack Dog," or something like that. The sign even had the face of a killer dog on it, like something out of *The Hound of the Baskervilles*."

"Maybe he just wanted people to think there was a big dog guarding the place," Pat suggested. "Maybe he wanted the protection of an attack dog without all the bother."

Harry looked at Fran. "Did you ever ask him about it?"

Fran nodded. "About a year ago." The carpenter tried to grin, but his lips gnarled into an uneven grimace. "Hitchens told me to mind my own business."

"What?" Jean said, wide eyed.

Fran nodded again. "That was the last time we ever spoke—not that we ever spoke very much. Hitchens was always in a hurry, whether he was coming or going. We were neighbors for years. But I think we talked a grand total of four or five times. And no conversation lasted more than a few minutes."

"That's no surprise," Muriel said. "Richard Hitchens had a lot to hide."

We were all a bit startled by Muriel's comment. Pat looked at Tracey, then back at her former neighbor. Once again, the veterinarian asked the question I was too timid to ask. "What was he hiding?"

Muriel's frailty seemed to vanish as she answered. "The fact that he mistreated his family. He had a loving wife whom he didn't deserve; and he has a loving son whom he doesn't deserve."

Two questions followed in quick succession from Jean and Laine:

"You saw a lot of them?"

"He HAS a loving son? I thought his son was..."

Muriel ignored the second question and answered the first. "Enough to know that he wasn't a good husband or a good father. Nothing changed after Sonya's funeral. He carried on as if nothing had really changed."

"Well," Tracey said, "sometimes grief is tricky. It's not always what it appears to be."

"Besides," Harry added, "what could he have done? Stop working? Stop living?"

Muriel looked directly at our host. "He could have treated his son like a son."

"What do you mean?"

"He could have kept him at home and cared for him," she replied emphatically.

Fran weighed in. "Wait a second. I know Jimmy attended a private school, but it was a day school. I'd see the limo pick him up in the morning. It's not as if Hitchens sent him away to a boarding school."

Muriel looked at the faces around the table as if peering at a jury. "He was planning to send him away," she said.

"How do you now that?" Harry asked, trying not to sound like an assistant district attorney.

"Jimmy told me."

Harry blinked and leaned forward. "When did he tell you?"

The old woman looked down at the barely touched serving of peach cobbler on her plate, then back up at Harry. "Shortly before he disappeared."

Several voices immediately converged:

"How long before he disappeared?"

"Did you tell the police?"

"The kid could talk? Wasn't he autistic?"

Muriel put her hands up to hold the torrent of questions at bay. "All I'm saying is that Hitchens doesn't deserve to have a family." The white-haired woman turned to Pam, who was the only person not staring at her. "Pamela knows that better than anyone."

All eyes turned toward the redhead. She had been a vivacious presence throughout the dinner party, but from the moment we began talking about #3 Bog Lane, her mood dimmed and she became conspicuously silent. Though she was looking down at her coffee cup, she knew that the group's attention was suddenly focused on her.

"Muriel's right," Pam said. "Hitchens is a cold-hearted bastard." She paused and looked up. "But that's the least of it."

"The least of it?" I said.

Pam took a deep breath, as if she was about to perform a swan dive. "I believe Hitchens had something to do with Sonya's death and Jimmy's disappearance."

The room became very still and Harry looked noticeably uncomfortable as he negotiated the line between friend and attorney. "Those are serious accusations, Pam."

Her voice was reduced to a whisper, but we heard her say, "I know."

"You also know that the police investigated Sonya's death," Harry said, "and they didn't find any evidence of foul play. Not even the private detectives could find anything to clearly implicate Hitchens."

"Private detectives?" Laine asked. "Who brought in private detectives?"

"Sonya's sister," Harry said. "I think her name was Helen—no, Helga; that was it, Helga. Right after Sonya died she flew over from Norway with a bunch of letters that Sonya had written to her. They described Hitchens as some sort of control freak. But that didn't prove anything, as far as the police were concerned. So she hired the best private eye on the South Shore to pursue the case. And when she couldn't afford his rates anymore, she hired a less expensive snoop. But neither of them could come up with anything solid. I think she went broke paying those guys."

"She was that sure that Hitchens had murdered Sonya?" Tracey asked.

"She was as sure as she was mad," Harry replied, "and she was pretty damned mad. According to the Plymouth detectives, every time Helga turned up at the station she was either enraged or in tears. Sometimes she was both. She came from a small fishing town in the northern part of Norway, so she didn't speak English very well, which didn't help matters. But she spoke just well enough to accuse Hitchens of murder. She claimed that he had found some way to poison her sister and make it look like an accidental overdose of sedatives and antidepressants. The more accusations she made, the wilder her claims became. One of the detectives told me that some of her claims seemed to involve monsters and hidden rooms and all kinds of crazy stuff.

Pretty soon the cops just tuned her out. In the end she ran out of money. "Accidental overdose"—that was the coroner's conclusion. Not suicide: not murder."

"What became of her?" Laine asked. "The sister, I mean."

"She became unhinged," Harry said. "She attacked Hitchens with a knife."

Tracey and Laine gasped.

"It happened in a restaurant in Quincy," Harry continued.

"Helga kept screaming she wanted justice. She screamed in broken English all through the court hearings. The judge had her moved to a separate room to keep her from interrupting. She was eventually deported back to Norway. Last I heard she was in a mental health facility in Oslo."

"What about the boy?" Tracey asked. "Hitchens's son?"

"It remains an open case. But there's no evidence to link Hitchens with whatever happened to the boy. He passed a lie detector test with flying colors."

"That's because he's a natural-born liar," Muriel said, her voice tinged with defiance.

Harry was bewildered. He had never known his elderly neighbor to be so combative. "Muriel, do you know the truth about what happened to Jimmy?"

She was silent.

"Because if you know something that would implicate Hitchens, I encourage you to share it with the police. If you like, I'll drive you to the station right now."

Muriel seemed to wilt in her chair. Her feistiness was gone.

"Still," Pam spoke up, "Hitchens was an emotionally brutal man."

"Okay," Harry replied, "so Richard Hitchens is a lousy S.O.B. But that doesn't make him guilty of murder or any other punishable crime."

All of us waited for Pam to respond, or to tell us what she knew about her former neighbors on Bog Lane, but no one wanted to prod the story out of her. Jean broke the silence with a comment and a question, both of which invited Pam to share her story. "I never met Sonya. She died—what was it—just a few years ago, right?"

"Five years ago," Pam said. "It's hard to…the whole thing was so horrible."

Fran placed a hand on hers and gently squeezed.

"It's okay," she said with a forlorn smile. "I know we're among friends." Pam looked at Harry, then at Laine, then at me. "I'll tell you about the Hitchens family, and it will bear out what Muriel said. But I don't think it will shed any light on Biscuit."

"Maybe not," Laine said, "but anything you can tell us would be much appreciated."

"And none of it will leave this room on our lips," I added.

Harry shook his head. "I'm not signing on to that."

"Oh, for crying out loud—" Jean admonished him, but he quickly cut her off.

"Honey, I'm an officer of the court, remember?" He turned to Pam with the concerned expression of a friend, but his voice was still that of a lawyer. "I'm sorry. I'm not trying to be a stick in the mud. But I work for the district attorney's office. You must understand that if you reveal some concrete evidence or a substantive line of inquiry, I'm legally obligated to pursue it."

Pam nodded. "I understand. And I wish I did have something concrete, because I'd drop it on Hitchens's head. But all I have are..." She sighed and briefly closed her eyes, "All I have are things that would never hold up in court."

Harry exhaled, plainly relieved.

Jean fixed an annoyed frown on her husband. "Satisfied? Now, your honor, if you have no further objections, may we continue?"

With a hint of magisterial dignity, Harry leaned back and folded his hands across his stomach. "Your witness, madam."

But before Jean could say anything, I turned to Pam. "Your daughter told me about a confrontation you had with Hitchens. You said something about him being the head of a troop of Boy Scouts. That sounds way out of character for him."

"I did?"

"That's what Sophie told me. She said that Sonya wanted to go shopping with you, but Hitchens wouldn't let her go. Apparently there was a scene in front of their house. At some point you alluded to his status as a trooper, or some special Boy Scout title. Why would a guy like Hitchens get involved with—"

Pam's burst of laughter took me and the others by surprise. Confused glances shot across the table as she slowly composed herself. "Hitchens had nothing to do with the Boy Scouts," she finally said. "When I had that argument with him, my daughters were with me. They heard me say something in anger, and they asked me about it later, so I made up a line about him being in charge of a special troop of Boy Scouts. I didn't want them to know what I'd said—they were too young."

"So he wasn't really a trooper?"

"Oh," Pam smiled, "he was a trooper and I'm sure he remains one to this day." Pronouncing each word very distinctly, she said, "He's a trooper ric."

First Fran started laughing, then Pat, and then everyone at the table, with the exception of Muriel and me.

"What is it?" I asked. "What am I missing?"

"Oh sweetie," Laine sighed. "Hitchens is a trooper ric. Get it?"

"What the hell is a trooper ric?"

"Say it three times fast."

THIRTY-SIX

THE SYMBOL

FELIPE SAT IN A CHAIR BY THE SCREENED WINDOW and looked out at the rain. It had been a long night and he yearned to take a nap, but he was determined to keep his vigil until his patient woke up. The gloomy morning and the patter of drops on the roof conspired against him.

Rain was a dismal reality of life in the Amazon. Jungles were created by rain, and the Amazon was the largest jungle in the world—larger than anything in Africa or Asia. The South American forest provides one-fifth of the Earth's oxygen: a natural bequest made possible by prodigious amounts of rain. Each year six to seven feet of water fell on Felipe's adopted home. He had visited London once, and he remembered that some of the people in that venerable city complained about the rain. But the Inucan village received nearly three times more rainfall than London.

Much of the rain that saturates the Amazon begins in the Atlantic, where atmospheric heat evaporates tons of ocean water and sends it westward on the tradewinds. This moisture periodically nourishes the roots, trunks, and branches of innumerable plants, and is then recycled skyward through countless leaves to continue its trek across South America. But when these masses of moisture approach the western edge of the continent, they encounter an obstacle they cannot overcome: the Andes mountain range. The snowmelt from these stony cathedrals adds tons of vapor to the thickening front. With nowhere else to go, the freighted clouds filter back eastward and finally pour their abundance out on the land.

Much of the resulting rainfall finds its way to streams and rivulets, where it flows along until it merges with the Amazon river, which returns the water to the Atlantic at the rate of seven million cubic feet per second—three times the volume of all the rivers in the United States. The Amazon's current is so strong that fresh water can be collected in the otherwise salty ocean over fifty miles from the river's massive mouth.

For protection from particularly intense downpours—which sometimes created lakes overnight—the Inucan village was located on a broad hill that was more-or-less flat at the top. The village also had numerous dug-out canoes. These sleek vessels turned encroaching flood waters into a navigable waterway or system of channels.

Felipe heard a groan. He turned to see Pensador stirring on a makeshift bed in the corner. The nurse walked over and checked the intravenous tube that was feeding a solution of dextrose and saline into his patient's bloodstream. Pensador tried to speak but could only manage another moan.

"Good morning," Felipe said in Spanish. "How do you feel?" He placed a hand on his forehead and checked his pulse. Pensador tried to get up, but Felipe's hand kept him on the bed. The outsider had no strength to overcome its gentle pressure.

"Just relax. You had quite a night."

"Is it over?" he whispered in Spanish.

"The worst is over. But you're still weak. You must rest."

"What happened?"

"The ayahuasca didn't agree with you. You had a bad journey."

Pensador remembered the night's bizarre sights and sounds. "How did I get here?"

"One of the villagers heard you vomiting inside your tent and called me. We carried you to my cabin. You've been here for almost ten hours."

"Ten hours?" He tried to complain, but could only manage a feeble cry.

"Don't get excited. Rest is the best medicine for you right now."

"The engineer is flying in...more supplies will be delivered—"

"When?"

"Very soon."

"Can't Moe, Larry, or Curly take care of that?"

"I have to be there."

"You're in no condition."

"Where is Lynn?" Pensador asked in a hoarse voice.

"She's in her tent. I let her go a couple of hours ago."

"Let her go? Was she—"

"Yes, but not as bad as you. She drank the ayahuasca all at once, and threw it up quickly. You weren't so lucky. I suspect that you took smaller sips, so more of it got into your bloodstream before your body threw the rest out."

"Did anyone else get sick?"

"No."

"Did anyone else drink the stuff?"

"Yes, several others."

Pensador thought for a moment, but even this motionless activity required some effort.

"Why only us? Why did only Lynn and I get sick?"

Felipe was checking the catheter, and Pensador didn't wait for his answer.

"Cotulko poisoned us. That lizard poisoned us." He tried to rise from the bed but Felipe gently pushed him down again.

"I know. I had it out with him this morning, and Yoro is dealing with him now."

"That maniac tried to murder me. So help me I'll crush him—"

"You're not in any position to crush anyone. Let Yoro and the village elders deal with him. And, just for the record, he wasn't trying to murder you."

"How do you know that?"

"If Cotulko wanted to kill you, you'd be dead. He admitted that he laced your ayahuasca, but not with anything lethal."

"With what then?"

"Cotulko's been experimenting with this stuff for decades," Felipe replied. "He knows how certain natural substances interact with the brain. The batch that he gave to you and Lynn contained chemicals that stimulate deep fears and painful thoughts. Last night, when he gave the special mix to Lynn, he said that he wanted her to have an 'intimate voyage.' I didn't realize what kind of *intimacy* he had in mind."

"That toad!"

"Yes. You had a bad journey. You were clinging to the big wooden box in your tent when we found you."

Pensador's head quickly craned up from the bed. "The box. Did anyone open it?"

"The only thing we touched was you," Felipe replied. "It took two of us to get you away from that thing."

"What thing?" A vein of panic throbbed through Pensador's voice as he arched his head toward the nurse. "What thing are you talking about?"

Felipe was mystified by his patient's distraught face and manner. "Calm yourself, Pensador. You're not—"

"*What thing are you talking about?*" Pensador cried.

Felipe stepped back and stared at his patient. "I told you," he said quietly, "the box in your tent: It took two of us to get you away from the box in your tent. What else would I be talking about?"

Pensador sighed as his head fell back onto the pillow. Felipe continued to stare at him, trying to make sense of his outburst. The patient took a couple of breaths, then raised his hand to look at his watch. He saw that his arm was attached to an intravenous line.

"I had to hook you up," Felipe said. "You were severely dehydrated. It's just a mixture of sugars and salt."

"I'm okay now," he said, trying to pull the line out of his arm.

Felipe stepped over and carefully removed the catheter. "Why are you so worried about that box?"

"Why do you want to know?"

"Just curious," Felipe said as he checked Pensador's arm for any discoloration.

"Let me worry about the box, okay?"

"As you wish," the nurse said. He turned to his desk and opened a notebook.

Pensador sat up on the edge of his bed as quietly as possible, but a grunt escaped his lips. Felipe shook his head without turning around. "That's not a good idea. You really should rest."

"I'm fine. Where's my shirt?"

"There was some regurgitated ayahuasca on it; Mara is washing it for you. Some of the women cleaned your tent. I hope that's okay. It smelled pretty bad after your sickness."

Pensador slowly stood up, keeping one hand on the bed, but he didn't say anything. His tank top T-shirt was still moist with sweat. Felipe poured a cup of water from an insulated container and handed it to him. "See if you can keep this down."

He took a sip, waited a moment, then gulped down the rest. "Thanks for everything," he said, handing the cup back to the nurse. "I'll be on my way."

Felipe opened his mouth to speak, but realized it would do no good. He sat back down at his desk and again turned his attention to the notebook.

Pensador took short, probing steps to the door. His body felt stiff and cramped, so he placed a hand on Felipe's desk and stretched. As his upper torso arched back, he noticed a small wooden cross over the doorway. It was a crude thing: a vertical, three-inch chunk of wood bisected by a thinner, shorter chunk of wood. They were bound together by a length of string that had been carefully wrapped round and round to hold the two pieces of wood in place.

"What the hell is that?"

Felipe glanced up. "It's a cross—the symbol of my faith."

"Faith?" The word was barbed with contempt as it left Pensador's mouth. "Faith in what? Lucky charms?"

Felipe took a breath and remembered the speech on Thursday night. "I don't have faith in the physical object on the wall," he said. "Its only purpose is to remind me of what I do believe in."

"And what might that be?" Pensador asked, his voice still coiled and edgy.

Felipe blinked up at him and took another breath. "The final triumph of love and hope over evil and despair."

Pensador laughed grimly. "The last time I looked around this demented world of ours, love and hope weren't winning in too many places."

"I know," Felipe said. "But the final act of our human story has yet to play out. In the end, I believe that all will become clear."

"Well, I don't," Pensador said. "In the end everyone will rot into nothingness, and there will be no meaning and no hope and no love."

Felipe pressed his lips together, forming a pensive frown. "Every thinking, feeling person is free to pursue whatever course they deem true. That includes me and you."

"Every thinking person is compelled to face the evidence," Pensador said, "and the evidence tells us that life is intrinsically meaningless."

"I think you're restricting yourself to a narrow field of evidence," Felipe replied.

"Am I supposed to accept love and conscience and spirit as some sort of evidence? How can you believe such nonsense?" He used the Spanish word *tonterias*.

The nurse laid down his pen and carefully considered the question, but he could feel Pensador's stare bearing down on him. Felipe sensed that his employer had fixed the same look—the same *attitude*—on many other people over the years. Coming from such a towering intellect, this scathing posture must have caused some individuals to abandon their personal beliefs. Felipe could imagine Pensador's colleagues offering him flustered disclaimers: "Me? I don't have a religious bone in my body!" But even though this man was his boss, the nurse refused to curry favor at the expense of his personal convictions.

Pensador assumed the nurse had nothing to say, so he turned to leave. He started to push open the cabin's screen door when Felipe's refined Spanish dialect caught him.

"Was that a rhetorical question or do you *really* want an answer?"

THIRTY-SEVEN

MEETING JIMMY

LAINE AND I WERE THE LAST TO LEAVE the Powell's home. Fran and Pam drove Muriel back to Bog Lane at about 10:30. Pat and Tracey returned to Onset half an hour later, but not before Tracey made a date with us to check out the arboretum in our cellar. We expected her visit on Monday morning, around the same time that Fran would begin work on our wrap-around porch.

During the ten-minute stroll back to our home, Laine and I discussed how we might clean out the basement after Tracey finished her study of its plants. We had no idea what to do with the subterranean trees. We considered hiring a landscaper to take care of the whole mess, but that would be very expensive. We also considered doing the job ourselves. If we cleaned out a bit each week, the task might take a couple of years to complete, but it would save us a bundle of cash.

Inevitably, our conversation turned to Pam's recollections. Earlier that evening, in the Powell's dining room, she spoke of her two run-ins with Richard Hitchens, both of which had turned ugly in short order. But we were surprised to find out that Pam had also conversed with Sonya Hitchens on a number of occasions. The immigrant's poor English, and Pam's inability to speak Norwegian, made such exchanges awkward. But, despite the language barrier, Pam learned that Sonya's husband exercised almost total control of her affairs. He kept track of her phone calls, opened her mail, and apparently counted the minutes whenever she went shopping or ran an errand. Sonya finally had to ask Pam if she could use her address as a P.O. Box so that she could safely receive letters from her sister in Norway. Even the immigrant's efforts to learn English had to be conducted in secret. It was all too clear that Hitchens wanted his wife to be as socially isolated as possible.

Sonya also worried about her son, who had been diagnosed with a type of autism known as "pervasive developmental disorder" at the age of two. Pam had seen the boy several times, and talked with him on a few of those occasions. Jimmy hadn't said very much, and he almost never looked at her face, but Pam described him as a cute little boy with blond hair and "sensitive" eyes. As far as she could tell, his autism hadn't affected his ability to think and learn. But it did seem to affect his ability to interact with others. Pam recalled that her twin daughters, Corinne and Paige, befriended Jimmy a few months before he disappeared. It was only after he was reported missing that they recounted the following incident to their parents.

The sisters had stepped outside on a chilly Saturday morning when they noticed Jimmy sitting in the backseat of his dad's Mercedes. His legs were dangling out of the open door and there was no one else in sight. Though they were several years older than the boy, Corinne and Paige were naturally sociable—and they were also very curious about their reclusive neighbor—so they walked over and introduced themselves. At first Jimmy didn't say anything to them, he just pulled his legs back into the car and looked down at the floor mat. But he didn't close the door. The sisters took this to mean that he wanted to make friends, but didn't know how.

Paige offered him a stick of peppermint gum. The boy looked up at her for a moment but his hands didn't move. Paige unwrapped the stick of gum and offered it to him again. Still, the boy didn't move or speak. Though Corinne already had a glob of gum in her mouth, she removed a packet from her own pocket and unwrapped a spearmint blade. "See," she held the gray rectangle in front of him, "like this." She placed it in her mouth and began to chew.

He watched her for a moment and then softly asked, "Why?"

Corinne shrugged. "Because it's fun. Try it."

Jimmy eyed the stick of gum that Paige held out and finally accepted it from her hand. He tentatively placed it in his mouth and looked at the girls.

"You've got to chew it," Paige giggled. Corinne modeled the procedure by mightily flexing her jaws. Once again Jimmy followed her example. A faint smile formed on his lips.

"Tasty, isn't it?" Paige asked.

The boy nodded and kept on chewing. He repeatedly glanced at the twin sisters. His shyness seemed to melt a bit with each passing second.

Corinne blew a bubble. As it expanded in front of her face, Jimmy stopped chewing and watched in amazement. The gray globe swelled until it finally popped, leaving a sticky film on Corinne's nose and cheeks. At first Jimmy was wide-eyed, uncertain how to react. But when he heard the sisters laugh, his eyes twinkled and he began laughing too. The girls noticed a dimple on his left cheek.

The sound of a car caused all three of them to look up. A tall man, with eyes that Paige later described as "intense," was emerging from the passenger seat of a black Mercedes SUV. An oriental woman was at the wheel. "What are you eating?" the man asked sternly.

Jimmy stopped chewing but didn't answer.

"I asked you a question," he said, slamming the car door.

"It's just a piece of gum," Paige said. "I gave it to him."

"Who are you?" Hitchens turned a withering look on Paige.

"She's my sister," Corinne replied. "Who are you?" She knew who the man was, but pretended otherwise.

"I'm that boy's father, and you must never give him anything to eat. He's on a very strict diet."

"It's just a piece of gum," Paige repeated. "It won't do him any harm."

"I'll make those decisions, if you don't mind. Now please go home. And you," he turned to his son, "get back in that house right now." Jimmy quickly got out of the car and ran up the front steps.

"We were just talking, that's all," Corinne said.

"Yeah," Paige added. "You don't have to be such a doofus."

"What did you call me?"

Corinne answered by blowing and popping another bubble.

Jimmy's dad was about to say something when a blond man—with what Paige described as "movie-star" looks—appeared at the front door. They had seen him before, but only for a few seconds at a time and always from a distance. Hitchens looked up at the man. "I told you to keep an eye on James."

"I was keeping an eye on him," the man said. "I knew exactly where he was."

"That's not good enough, Steven. Next time you make sure he either stays in the house or goes to the backyard. I don't want him out front."

The young man frowned and opened the door wide enough for Jimmy to slip inside.

As the boy passed by, head down and shoulders hunched, the blond man tweaked the boy's ear and smiled down at him. Jimmy looked up, stopped, and hugged the man's leg.

"I said get inside," growled the boy's father from the driveway.

Jimmy quickly disappeared indoors. The man in the doorway looked as if he was about to say something to Jimmy's dad, but he shook his head and followed the boy inside. Hitchens turned his attention back to the girls.

"You two: get off my property. And if I ever catch either one of you giving my son any more garbage to eat—"

"Yeah, yeah, yeah," Corinne sang as she and her sister sauntered away, arm-in-arm.

It was almost midnight when Laine and I turned down Bog Lane. As we approached our home, we traversed the same ground the twins had crossed on that chilly Saturday morning several months earlier. I imagined Hitchens standing there, glaring at the Sampson sisters as they traipsed out of his driveway. He was so protective of his property, and he controlled his son so thoroughly, that I found it very hard to believe that anyone could've snatched Jimmy from Bog Lane without being seen.

Laine and I had started to climb up our front steps when Delaney appeared at the door. A sandy-haired boy stood behind her, smiling nervously. "Hi," Delaney said as they stepped onto the porch. "Everything went fine. Gabriel is asleep."

Laine and I both looked at the boy.

"This is Jeff; he's a friend of mine from school."

"I live over on Bradford Road," he added quickly. "My dad has a pharmacy in town."

I reached for my wallet but Delaney told me not to bother. Then she turned to her friend.

"You go ahead, Jeff; I'll catch up."

"Nice meeting you both," he said, as he stepped by us.

Delaney waited until Jeff was a quarter of the way down Bog Lane before she turned to us. "Please don't tell my parents that he was here, that's all I ask."

Laine looked sympathetically at the girl, but didn't give her the answer she wanted. "I'm sorry, Delaney, but I can't lie to your mom."

"Oh, I know, Mrs. Delvecchio; I'm not asking you to lie," she said earnestly. "I'm just asking you to…" Delaney seemed unable to say what she wanted to say.

"To what?" Laine inquired gently.

The redhead clasped her hands in front of her, her fingers twisting as she struggled with each word: "To not answer any questions my mom doesn't ask."

Laine and I chuckled at the carefully worded plea.

"It would mean the world to me," Delaney continued. "I'll babysit for free for the next twenty years."

"That's a nice offer," my wife laughed, "but I'm hoping that Gabriel won't need a babysitter when he's twenty."

"Well, for as long as he needs one," Delaney offered again.

"You don't have to give us anything," Laine said. "And we insist on paying you for your time tonight. But if your parents ask if you were alone, I have to tell them the truth. I hope you understand."

"IF they ask," Delaney said hopefully.

Laine smiled. "*If.*"

"Thank you, thank you, thank you," she cried quietly.

I pressed some bills into her hand. She started to speak but I cut her off and pointed to Jeff, who was standing in front of the Sampson's house, more than halfway down the Lane. "Your friend is waiting."

Delaney walked down the steps but stopped and turned when she reached the last one.

"Does Gabriel have a nickname for Biscuit?"

"Not that I know of," I said, turning to Laine.

She shook her head. "Why?"

"Well, I know this is a hard time for Gabe so I don't want to get him into trouble."

"Trouble?" I said, suddenly alert despite the lateness of the hour. "What kind of trouble?"

"Well, he, ah, he kind of wrote on the wall with one of his markers—but don't worry," she quickly added, "I wiped it clean."

"He knows the walls are off-limits," Laine said. "He hasn't done anything like that for over a year."

"What did he write?" I asked.

"Well, that's just it: I'm not really sure. It was a word or a name that I've never seen or heard before." She spelled it and then pronounced it: "Lindorm. Do you know anyone by that name? Maybe he's the guy who sold Biscuit to you?"

I shook my head, but Laine looked off to the side, as if she had noticed something on one of the black, metal railings that flanked our front steps. "The vice-principal of Gabriel's school is named Lindurm—Eva Lindurm. Are you sure he spelled it with an 'o' and not a 'u'?"

"I'm pretty sure it was an 'o.' He also drew Biscuit's face on the wall, but it looked more like a Tyrannosaurus than a happy dog. He also wrote 'Run away.'"

"You must mean 'ran,'" Laine said, "as in 'Biscuit ran away from home.'"

Delaney shook her head. "I could be wrong, but I think it was 'Run away.'"

Laine looked at me. "Do you think Gabriel is blaming Biscuit for not being here?"

I was too tired to think clearly, so I shrugged. Laine answered her own question.

"He draws Biscuit with an ugly face and writes 'ran away.' What else could it mean?"

"That's what I was thinking," Delaney said. "Maybe he repressed his sadness or anger about Biscuit and now it's coming out in weird ways."

I looked at Delaney and recalled that she was shy of sixteen. "'Repressed'? That's a heady word for one so young."

Laine smiled. "Delaney has her sights on medical school. She wants to become a psychiatrist." Then she looked at the redhead, who seemed a bit embarrassed by this admission. "Your mom told me a couple of weeks ago. She talked about all the psychology books you've been soaking up. I hope you don't mind me mentioning it."

"No, no," she shook her head but avoided our eyes. "Well, I've got to go. I just want to say that that little boy of yours sure is a cutie, and he's got a lot of love in his heart. Please don't go too hard on him. I think he's just trying to work things out."

"We'll be gentle," Laine assured her.

When Delaney was a few steps away, I called to her. "What was that word Gabriel wrote on the wall?"

"Lindorm." She spelled it and pronounced it one more time: "Lindorm." Then she smiled and turned away.

Laine and I watched Delaney and Jeff walk down Bog Lane, hand in hand.

"You were pretty easy on her," I said. "Are you really not going to say anything about Jeff to Jean?"

"If she doesn't ask, I won't tell," Laine replied. "Delaney's a sweet kid, and Jeff seems like a good sort. Besides, I remember what it was like to be a teenager. It's a tough time. You need all the help you can get." She cast an appraising eye on me. "You haven't forgotten what was it was like to be in the throes of adolescent angst, have you?"

"Honey," I said through a tired yawn, "I barely remember what it was like to be forty."

THIRTY-EIGHT

REASON NUMBER
TWENTY-TWO

WHETHER THEY WERE IN THEIR HUTS, or at *la recognus*, or in the jungle, Inucans came out to watch the helicopter's aerial acrobatics. But this time the giant machine roared straight over the village.

Mara was on her way to Felipe's cabin when it glided overhead. Though she was holding a shirt in one hand, she covered both ears and hunched her head as the helicopter shot directly above her, moving east to west. Within seconds it arrived over Kalsulnak and circled the hill like a vulture ogling an earthborn carcass. She removed her hands from her ears and watched as the great metal bird hovered for a moment and then began its careful descent. Pensador's men had been using special tools and machines to clear an ever-widening patch of ground on the hill, and the bald spot on Kalsunak was now clearly visible from the village. Mara worried that the nearby hill—which had been one of her favorite retreats as a girl—would soon become a naked, ugly lump in the western sky.

As she watched the enormous machine settle on Kalsulnak, Felipe and Pensador emerged from the cabin. Pensador seemed troubled and Felipe looked very tired. She bowed her head silently toward the outsider and then handed him his shirt. Much to her surprise, he barely glanced at her.

Before leaving her hut to deliver the shirt to Pensador, Mara had donned her *cumpi*—a light vest woven from the most comfortable cloth spun by the Inucans. She often went about the village wearing nothing at all above her bellybutton. But this changed the day after Pensador's arrival in the village. His three male helpers seemed fascinated by her breasts. She also sensed that Pensador had taken a special interest in her, which made her feel even more uncomfortable. She had tried to tell herself that it was all in her mind, but the pearls he offered her yesterday swept away all doubt.

Now, as she handed him his shirt, she expected another of his long, searching looks. Instead, he said "thank you" absently while eyeing the helicopter on Kalsulnak. "I have to make sure things go well over there," he said in Spanish. A spirit of energetic purpose had always infused his words, but now his voice was strangely subdued. Felipe nodded at him but didn't say anything.

No sooner had Pensador begun to move toward the hill when he stopped and turned. He looked at Felipe and stuck out his hand. "Thanks for your time and help," he said. Felipe clasped the man's hand. *Something was different,* Mara thought; *something had happened.* Usually, Pensador's mind was like a hive of hornets: it was constantly buzzing with activity, and it didn't allow anyone to get a look inside. But now the hive seemed undefended.

"Since I've answered some of your questions," Felipe said, still holding on to the outsider's hand, "would you be willing to answer some of mine?"

"About what?"

"About your purpose here," Felipe replied. "I'd like to know how you intend to carry out the promises that you made to the Inucan people."

Pensador unclasped his hand. "Someone will be coming here tomorrow: a special visitor. You can ask *him* any questions you have about this…this mission."

Felipe's eyebrows furrowed. "Are you telling me that you're not in charge?"

"Tomorrow," Pensador said. "Ask your questions tomorrow." Before Felipe could speak again, the outsider turned and strode off toward Kalsulnak.

Mara moved closer to Felipe and put an arm around his waist; he wrapped an arm around her shoulders and squeezed softly. "What was that all about?" she asked as they watched Pensador walk away.

"We had a long talk," Felipe replied.

"About what?"

Felipe thought for a moment. "Reason…and hope," he said.

Mara was about to ask another question when a tall figure ran past them. It was Lynn Lee, moving swiftly through the center of the village. She turned to the couple as she jogged and cried out happily: "I'm going to get my smokes!" When she caught up to Pensador they talked for a moment, and then walked together toward Kalsulnak. Mara noticed that the helicopter in the distance wasn't clattering quite so loudly, and its spinning blades seemed to be slowing down.

"Well, I guess she made a full recovery," Felipe said.

"What are smokes?" Mara wondered out loud.

"Sticks that cause disease," he replied.

"Why would Lynn be happy about that?"

"Because," Felipe reflected, "before the smokes bring disease, they bring much pleasure and energy to the brain."

"Doesn't she know they bring disease?" Mara asked.

"She knows," Felipe said.

Mara was more confused than ever.

Felipe looked at her. "It's a trade that Lynn and a lot of other people are willing to make," he explained. "Or at least *they think* they are willing to make that trade."

Mara shook her head. "If I live to be a very old woman, I don't think I'll ever understand outsiders."

Felipe smiled. "That's reason number twenty-two why I love you."

She beamed at him, pleased and curious. "Because I don't understand outsiders?"

"Because you are so innocent of the world's ways."

The happiness that gleamed from her eyes softened to a contemplative gaze. "Do you want me to stay that way?"

He shook his head. "I don't know. There's a part of me that wants to take you all over the world and show you everything. Yet, by doing so, I would expose you to much..." he tried to think of just the right word, and settled on the Spanish *perversidad*. "You cannot experience the beauty and wonder of the wider world without experiencing its *wickedness* at the same time." As he spoke he realized that his anxiety for Mara's wellbeing revealed a certain degree of possessiveness. At that moment he was treating her almost as if she was his little sister rather than his sweetheart. He wasn't sure what to make of these feelings, and he was too tired to analyze them.

"But I would hate the wickedness," Mara said confidently. "I would reject it."

"Your innocence is showing."

She silently prodded him with a questioning look, and Felipe was reminded that Mara's face was nothing less—and perhaps much more—than a work of art. The glow in her eyes was unblemished by rank egotism or selfishness. A Michelangelo-like talent might be able to sculpt such a face, and a latter-day Rembrandt might be able to capture its hues and texture, but no human artist could accurately render the light and warmth that enlivened Mara's eyes.

A year earlier, when Felipe first realized how deeply he was drawn to her, he was struck by the extraordinary irony of his situation. He had traveled many miles into a savage jungle—far from civilization's beauty parlors and upscale boutiques—and here he encountered an exceptional incarnation of feminine loveliness. It was the last thing he expected to find in this wilderness. But the more he thought about it, the more it seemed to make sense in some roundabout way. Mara's innocence formed a vital layer of her beauty; the jungle was the natural guardian of her innocence. The rainforest kept odious influences at bay; it shielded her soul from all the glittering lures and cultivated addictions that might otherwise corrode her inner being.

"True wickedness doesn't seem evil on the surface," Felipe said. "That's what makes it wicked. If the truest form of evil appeared monstrous right from the start, no one would go near."

Mara was troubled. "You think I would be deceived?"

"Some very intelligent people have surrendered their consciences to evil."

"Why would anyone do such a thing?"

"Perhaps the evil offered them something they wanted very much, something they could only have by deadening their souls."

"What could someone want that much?"

"It's an old list," Felipe said wearily: "Power, wealth, pleasure, a sense of superiority..."

Mara knew that Felipe's answer would lead to several fertile fields of conversation. But she also knew they were standing in the middle of the village on a busy morning. This wasn't the time or place to continue such a talk. She would also have to put off a separate question that would surely lead to a far happier place: *What are the first twenty-one reasons why you love me?*

The fatigue she saw in his eyes kept her from asking that question. The only time she had ever seen him look so tired was when he remained awake for over two days, nursing an Inucan woman through a terribly difficult labor.

"You need some sleep," she said, gently pulling at his hand. "Come with me. Let me tuck you in for a nice nap."

"Mara," he said through a feeble smile, "I don't think I have enough energy to be tucked in by you."

THIRTY-NINE

THE AMBUSH PREDATOR

It was about midnight when I heard a splash in our backyard. I assumed the sound was made by a frog frolicking in the bog, so I went back to what I'd been doing: looking at Laine's face. She lay next to me in bed, and there was just enough illumination from a 2nd floor hallway light for me to discern her features. Her smoothly aligned lips, dainty nose, and serenely slumbering eyes formed a beatific vision in the night. Women in general, and my wife in particular, had a remarkable ability to appear genteel even when sleeping. I, on the other hand, was a slovenly, snoring mess while asleep. I knew this was true because I always woke up looking like the victim of a botched mugging. But what I envied even more than Laine's refinement in repose was her ability to fall so swiftly and easily into the realm of dreams.

Sleep seldom came swiftly to me, and on this particular night it came even less easily than usual. The word "Lindorm" kept snaking into my thoughts. Where or how could Gabriel have come up with a word that made no sense to me? Was it a character from a kid's program? Was it a furry, humanized homunculus from some fairy tale? Or was it an oblique reference to the vice-principal of his school? Eva Lindurm had cultivated a certain image among the students of Maynard's elementary school. In their eyes, she was a harsh disciplinarian who brooked no buffoonery or insolence of any kind. Stories about the punishments that she doled out were whispered in the school's corridors, lavatories, and recess yards. Of course, none of the stories were true, but Ms. Lindurm made no effort to clear her name before the student body. As a result of her legendary status, she could walk into an auditorium full of noisy, rambunctious kids and bring the entire room to a state of perfect silence within a matter of seconds. She didn't have to say anything or take any sort of action. All she had to do was stand where the kids could see her. Her fearsome reputation did the rest.

Laine had gotten to know Eva Lindurm and several of the teachers at Gabriel's school fairly well over the past year and a half. Though her square face and brunhilda physique made her a perfect fit for the role of drill sergeant, Eva Lindurm was actually the gentlest of souls. But could Gabriel's "Lindorm" have something to do with the vice-principal of Maynard legend? Was there some sort of connection in Gabriel's mind?

Snippets of conversation from the Powell's dining room also kept threading through my thoughts, and I wanted to somehow weave them all together so that Richard Hitchens, his strangely appointed house, and his tragic family history could all be tied into a coherent bundle. But no matter how many times I reassembled the strands of information in my mind, inexplicable gaps remained. I sensed that these crucial strings of missing data were just beyond my reach. My rational mind abhorred such vacuums, and an uncanny pessimism—which always seemed to be lurking in the shadows—now seeped into the empty spaces.

Then I heard it again: a splash sounded through the open bedroom window. It was as if a stone had been tossed into the marsh. Knowing that objects don't move unless someone or something moves them, I got out of bed and looked through the window.

I thought I saw ripples wave across the marsh. But when my

eyesight adjusted to the screen mesh and exterior shadows, the surface of the bog seemed to be in its naturally placid state. Still, the sounds I'd heard made me just curious enough to throw on a bathrobe and slip into my sandals.

The slimy, jumping animal had twice eluded the creature's grasp: first it hopped out of the bog; and then, with the predator in pursuit, it scampered in a wide circle and jumped back into the water. Both times the creature's snapping mouth had barely nipped the slimy thing's legs. Now the predator knew it had no chance of catching the little leaper, for the hunted animal knew it was being hunted, and it scurried away as fast as its limbs could kick. The predator slowly slid back into the bog.

The creature depended on the element of surprise to ensnare a meal because its metabolism and massive size didn't allow it to chase down speedy morsels over lengthy distances. So it had to wait patiently until something came close enough to be captured in one powerful lunge.

The predator had some awareness of these limitations. It didn't know how or why it possessed such consciousness, but it had bits of thought and memory that seemed foreign to its true nature. Having been endowed with such awareness, the creature couldn't make itself unaware. It had to somehow blend this alien mindfulness with its natural instincts so that it could continue to survive.

And the one instinct that dominated all of its other instincts was hunger. The predator's desire to eat often overpowered every spark in its brain, including its nascent thoughts. It yearned to enfold a living thing; to crush the vibrations out of an animal and to stretch its mouth around the thing's warm flesh. Toward that constant goal, its senses were attuned to the sight, scent, or movement of any edible creature.

A sharp pain suddenly sliced deep into the predator's body. It instinctively twisted over and looked for the thing that had bitten it, but nothing was there. The creature then writhed and thrashed in the bog until the pain became a dull ache. But the ache wouldn't go away. Is this hunger?

The predator glided deeper into the bog; it moved far more easily in water than on land. When it arrived at the other end of the marsh, it took up a position near the edge of the bog, just below the surface of the water. There it waited patiently for another meal to come along.

On my way out of the house I grabbed a flashlight and then slipped through the back door. The night was very warm and a blanket of humidity draped heavily over everything. This atmospheric moisture seemed to enrich every color, sharpen every smell, and deepen even the slightest sound. I stood on the back porch and peered out over the bog. The estate seemed unnaturally still. In the distance I could hear some bullfrogs croaking, but normally one or two of them could also be heard pleading for a mate from the nearby marsh. Had my presence on the porch frightened them into silence?

I flicked on the flashlight and padded down the steps. Off to the left, the incandescent beam revealed the lavender hues of some wild Bergamot, and a split second later the flowers' minty fragrance tickled my nose. Many other forms of plant-life sprouted within our vast yard, and it would take a considerable chunk of time for me to become familiar with all of them. I shined my flashlight on the ground a few feet ahead and slowly walked toward the bog.

Earlier that evening, Harry said that little Jimmy Hitchens used to play in this very yard. At least that's what the boy's father told the investigating detectives. After examining all other possibilities, the police speculated that a kidnapper climbed the fence and abducted

Jimmy while he was in the yard. If this scenario was accurate, the abductor would surely have had at least one accomplice on the other side of the fence. The police believed that the boy had been lured to the fence on one of the more rural sides of the estate, where there would've been fewer potential witnesses. Perhaps the bait was candy, a puppy, or some other eye-catching delight.

Jimmy seemed to be a prime target for such a crime. His father was one of the richest people in New England, and Jimmy's safe return would presumably bring a princely sum. But Hitchens told the police that he hadn't received any demand for ransom. As the days turned into weeks, the police could only assume that the kidnappers had less mercenary motives. That possibility sickened me.

I stood near the edge of the bog and imagined Jimmy wandering the grounds of the estate, in search of something—anything—that might brighten his lonely, six-acre world.

The predator hung effortlessly in liquid space, halfway between the pond's surface and its turbid floor. Nearby was an underwater tunnel, large enough for the creature to swim through. This long shaft led to the place that was once the predator's comfortable habitat—hot, watery, and full of plants. Some two-legged big-heads were usually in that place. Sometimes, from a distance, the big-heads would poke the predator with sharp objects, and it would quickly fall asleep. When it awoke it always felt strangely different: sometimes the predator felt as if something had grown inside of its belly while it slept. Sometimes, it felt as if something had grown inside of its head. The predator knew that the big-heads were the cause of these changes, and it yearned to grab and squeeze them to death. But they were always just out of reach, and they never turned their backs to the predator's jaws. The big-heads made up for their poking and prodding by occasionally letting a furry animal run loose. These four-legged creatures couldn't escape the predator for very long, and it enjoyed crushing them almost as much as it enjoyed eating them. With an abundance of warmth, water, plants, and living food, the predator had grown accustomed to its leafy world.

But then everything changed. For some reason, the big-heads attacked the predator and forced it to leave its home. As it escaped from their weapons, it swam through the tunnel and entered the cold water of the bog. The predator knew it would die if it didn't find warmth very quickly. On the side of the bog, just below the water line, it found another hole. This opening led to a crude but natural cavity which had once been the rooting place of a tree. The tree had died long ago, and its wood rotted over time, leaving behind a silt-filled abscess. The predator was freezing to death, but with its last burst of energy it prodded the rotting timber with its snout and exposed long veins of loose earth. The predator burrowed as the soil gave way, forming a long cavity that swarmed around its body. Instinctively, the creature curled into a ball and let the tepid mud envelope its flesh. Then it slipped into the deepest and longest sleep it had ever known.

When the predator finally awoke, it was terribly weak. It sensed that much time had passed; it also sensed that its den was slowly heating up, and with each passing moment it felt hidden stores of strength pulse through its body. Yet it somehow knew that this internal supply of energy wouldn't last. It had to find food as quickly as possible. Driven by the instinct to kill and eat, it broke through the silted wall of its lair and went on the prowl.

Little had changed since then. The predator's existence consisted of catching, killing, and eating small animals. But it yearned for something big and warm-blooded: something it could crush, something that would satiate its hunger for many days.

The beam of my flashlight dotted the marsh, illuminating lily pads that were strewn across its murky surface. Clumps of cranberries, along with the shrub's distinctive oval leaves, pocked the bog. Laine loved the tart fruit, and when the crop ripened in early autumn, she would no doubt spend many of her weekend afternoons thigh-deep in the marsh, scooping up berries.

Again I noticed the small holes that scored the perimeter of the bog at regular intervals, though dirt had covered some of them. These punctures seemed to be man-made, but for what purpose? I wondered how deep they went, so I stepped closer to the pond for a better look.

Barely perceptible vibrations rippled through the water and lapped against the predator's skin: something was approaching the pond. It walked on two legs, and judging by the tremors it created with each step, it was something big. Perhaps it was a big-head.

The predator remembered the first and only big-head it had ever killed. That big-head had actually stepped on its body. Big-heads were usually not so stupid. This warm-blooded feast virtually placed itself in the predator's jaws. The big-head was almost too big, but the predator managed to swallow its entire body. The prey's flesh was covered with strange materials and objects. These things made the predator sick, so it ejected the animal from its stomach and left the carcass to rot.

Now the predator inched closer to the shoreline and hoped that this newly-arrived big-head was covered with nothing but fur or skin.

I crouched down and shined my flashlight on the small holes. It was difficult to gauge their depth by sight alone, so I looked around for a twig that could serve as a measuring stick. I noticed a sprig jutting out of the pond, but when I reached over and picked it up, I saw that it was part of a larger branch. Still crouching, I placed the flashlight on the ground; its beam of light streaked horizontally over the pond. I tried to snap a twig from the branch.

The predator's eyes were positioned on either side of its head, which enabled it to see almost everything in its world. Its only blind spots were directly above and behind its head. Though the water was misty, it was close enough to clearly see the prey's shape. As the vibrations had indicated, it was big and two-legged. A sliver from the predator's face nimbly poked through the surface of the pond to gather more information. The resulting smells indicated that the predator had encountered this creature before.

Though it had been driven from its comfortable habitat, the predator had tried to reenter its home several times in the hope of finding some of the furry animals that it used to feed on. But it couldn't get through the door that sealed the end of the long tunnel. All of that changed one night when loud cracks ripped through the sky and water poured down over everything. In the midst of this commotion, the predator again tried to regain the comfort of its former home. This time, when it pushed against the hard door at the end of the tunnel, the barrier yielded. The creature crawled up into its former paradise, only to find it dark and deserted. All of the once fragrant plants were dead, and there were no large, plant-eating animals to satisfy the predator's hunger. Enraged, it moved through the area looking for anything that was still alive—anything it could unleash its fury upon. That's when it found the open door, which led to yet another open door.

The predator moved quietly through a series of rooms until it came upon a furry, four-legged animal that snapped its jaws and made loud noises with its mouth. Though the animal fought hard, the predator killed and swallowed the thing, which appeased its

hunger but not its rage. Later it came upon a big-head that had bur-
rowed into a large, soft object. The big-head seemed to be feigning
death, but the predator knew it wasn't dead. It could sense the thing's
breaths, and it yearned to crush the animal's lungs into the stillness
of true death. But a swarm of repugnant odors arose from the big-
head's body, which nearly sickened the predator. So, with its hunger
pacified, the creature left the big-head and returned to the bog to
digest the furry, warm-blooded meal in its belly.

Now the very same big-head was poised near the pond. But it
smelled better than before, and the predator's belly was no longer
full and pacified by warm flesh. Like all big-heads, the two-legged
animal's eyes were positioned in front of its face, which meant that its
side vision was poor. So the predator instinctively angled to one side
of its prey; it inched closer and prepared to strike.

When I finally broke off the tip of the branch, the palms of my
hands were smeared with some of the muck that caked its bark. I
was about to reach into the pond to wash the slime off my hands,
but at that moment I heard shrieks coming from my house.

Gabriel was screaming.

FORTY

COMMUNION

A DISTANT SHRIEK PIERCED the ephemeral folds of Pensador's sleep, and he slowly opened his eyes. Still groggy, it took a moment for his vision to adjust to the surroundings. His face lolled on a sheet which had been folded to serve as a pillow. His left arm dangled off the edge of his cot, and his half-open palm hovered near the floor of the tent. He turned his hand over to look at his watch. The digital dial read 8:22 AM, SUN, AUG-15. He slowly rolled over onto his back and peered up at the conical ceiling of the tent. Six evenly spaced steel rods radiated from its apex.

Pensador waited to hear another cry from the macaw, or whatever it was that had disturbed his slumber. Instead he heard someone speaking Inucan. It was a woman's voice, and though her tone implied some form of friendly intimacy, there was a mildly formal cadence to her words. He arose from the cot and the sound of his movement was followed by three faint knocks from the large box in the corner of the tent. Pensador ignored the knocks and peered through one of the tent's small screens.

An old woman was addressing a group of villagers at *la recognus*. He couldn't recall her name, but he knew she was one of the tribe's wisest elders. Several children circulated among the group, handing something to each individual. When they were done, they returned to the old woman and gathered around her. She held up a small object, and he barely heard the last four words of the sentence that she spoke to the assembled Inucans: "...in memory of me." She slowly lifted the small object higher in the air with both hands, and then spoke again: "Quickened by our humility and our love, we believe that Viro has placed a precious gift before our souls." She gazed at the object with reverential serenity. "We do this now to show that we accept the gift. In our tears and in our laughter; in our sins and virtues; in our hunger for peace, and in our hope, *we are one.*"

She placed the small object in her mouth and lowered her head. All the people in the group quietly followed her example. Pensador quickly realized that each person had consumed a bit of manioc. They seemed to be recreating an act of communion. For a long moment nothing could be heard but sporadic bird calls from the jungle. The Inucans who had gathered under the awning stood with bowed heads; many also had their eyes closed or hands clasped. Most of the villagers were sitting on the stools made of *chonta* hardwood, though some of the warriors stood on the outskirts of the group.

The old woman opened her eyes, looked out upon the assembled throng, and spoke again: "Like all the tribes of the Earth, we were once little different from the creatures around us. But, just as children learn to see beyond themselves, we are learning the Spirit truths that exist beyond our finite lives. Let us open our minds to that light; to understand as well as we can. Let us try to see a little better beyond ourselves; to be a little kinder, even to those who do not serve our desires. And let us never forget that above the law of the jungle, above the laws made by people, even above the laws of *pacha,* there is infinite-eternal truth: *Viro.* Peace to all."

Pensador had to search his memory before remembering that *pacha* was the Quechua word for *earth, time, and space.* These Inucans had evidently come to believe in a spiritual truth that transcended all of the brute laws of nature. This, he quickly realized, did not bode well for the Lexel project.

For a short while no one moved except for the old woman, who caressed the heads of the children within her reach. Then she stepped toward the gathering and many of the Inucans clustered around her. Knots of people slowly formed and unformed throughout la recognus. Though the Inucan adults seemed in no hurry to leave, several of the children quickly gave in to playful impulses and chased each other from the group, laughing as they went. A tranquil spirit pervaded the gathering. Pensador recalled the speech he gave on Friday night; he also remembered yesterday's conversation with Felipe. He winced. With each passing minute he regretted his speech ever more deeply. It had been a colossal misjudgment.

Pensador heard more knocks from the large box in the corner. Though they were a bit louder this time, he continued to ignore the sounds.

This was his third visit with the Inucans but, as he watched them socialize, he began to appreciate something to which he had previously paid scant attention: the Inucans were changing *from within*. As a trained anthropologist, he was accustomed to change triggered by technology. New instrumentality often generates cultural transformation. But the ritual he had just witnessed, and the words he had just heard, heralded an inner catalyst. Some of the villagers seemed to have internalized a set of beliefs that was silently re-molding their minds from within. Perhaps, he reasoned, this process began when the first Christian missionary visited the Inucans and learned just enough of their language to preach the gospel in their tongue.

Pensador had noticed the Sunday morning rituals at la recognus during his first two visits, but the groups were smaller then. Fifteen years ago it only numbered about twenty or thirty people; seven years ago there were perhaps forty or fifty people. Now he estimated that at least a hundred villagers were present. Though he didn't see Cotulko the shaman or Destro the warrior, he did see Yoro and Mara. He also noticed Felipe, smiling and conversing with various Inucans. The seeds of change may have been planted by a missionary many years ago, but

Pensador was certain that Felipe had done a bit of watering during the past three years.

This changing Inucan outlook hadn't been factored into Lexel's plans, and Pensador knew he would be blamed for this oversight. The Inucans seemed to increasingly believe in a moral-ethical truth that transcended the laws of nature. This transcendent truth encouraged the villagers to see the world in a new light. Such a lamp undoubtedly illuminated fresh priorities and values, all of which would surely ease Surutas's stranglehold on the tribe's pagan imagination. This, in turn, meant that Lexel's monster-in-the-box would have less impact on the Inucans.

Three knocks again sounded from the specially-designed container, but these were more distinct than the previous thumps. The thing inside the box seemed to sense that Pensador was up and about. He looked at the large wooden case and the series of air holes that dotted its upper end. A glob of pink, shiny flesh was dimly visible on the other side of the small openings. It probed and slid across the apertures, like a thick tongue poking into the air-holes of a harmonica. But it was far too large to squeeze through.

Next to the closed, wooden box was the steel cage with one remaining guinea pig. Pensador walked over, slid open the metal door and pulled out the rodent. Then he placed his left hand on the latch that sealed the pine container and slowly undid its hasp lock. As he stood there, holding the furry animal with one hand above its metal cage, he thought about the chimerical creature in the box. It had taken nearly fifteen years of hard work and tedious experimentation to put that ace up Lexel's sleeve. The final product of all that effort would certainly impress anyone. But in order for the creature to serve its purpose, it must do more than impress the Inucans: it must have a decisive influence on the entire tribe. If it was to achieve that goal, it would have to be unveiled soon, while the legend of Surutas still had an appreciable hold on the Inucan mind.

Pensador carefully mapped out a series of deductions in his mind.

Then he slowly slid the hasp lock back into its closed position with his left hand, and placed the guinea pig back into its cage with his right hand. Three angry thumps immediately sounded from the pine container, and which each jolt the sealed lid strained against the hasp lock. Though it could smell the guinea pig, the thing in the box seemed to sense that Pensador wasn't going to follow the usual routine. Maddened by the scent of prey, it again rammed three times against the locked lid.

Pensador ignored the noise and began getting dressed.

FORTY-ONE

VISITATION

GABRIEL'S SCREAMS BLASTED THROUGH MY LEGS. I tore out of the backyard and flew up the rear stairway at breakneck speed, but Laine had already plunged into his room and was flicking on the light when I stumbled through the second floor doorway. He was lying on his stomach, with his hands over his head. His face was turned to the side and he was still shrieking when Laine got on the bed and threw her arms around him. "Honey, what is it?" she cried.

"It's her! She's trying to get me! Keep her away!"

I quickly glanced at every corner of the room but didn't see anyone.

"The yellow-head lady!" Gabriel wailed. "She's trying to get me!"

I darted to the other side of the bed and threw open the closet door; then I fell to my knees and looked under the bed. No one was hiding anywhere in Gabriel's room.

"Oh, sweetheart," Laine said soothingly as she hugged him and kissed his forehead, "you had a bad dream."

"No!" he whimpered with his eyes still clenched tight. "She is here. She came here to get me."

"There is no one here, Gabriel," I said. "Open your eyes and look. We are the only people here."

Hugging Laine with all his might, he slowly opened his right eye, then his left.

From the safety of his mother's arms he scanned the entire room.

"You had a nightmare, sweetie," Laine said.

He seemed dazed and took a series of quick breaths. Then he looked pleadingly into his mother's eyes. "She was here. She told me to scream."

"What?" I said incredulously.

He turned toward me. "The yellow-haired lady told me to scream! She said 'scream'!"

Still holding him tightly, Laine smiled a reassuring mixture of doubt and amusement. "Now honey, don't you see how silly that is? Why on earth would the lady tell you to scream?"

"I don't know, but she did!" he exclaimed. "She woke me up and told me to scream."

"How did she wake you up?" I asked.

"I felt something here," he said, patting his chest. "When I opened my eyes, she was staring right into my face! Then she said: 'scream'."

"Gabriel," I said with a weary smile, "after she told you to scream, did she fly out the window? Did she melt into the floor? Did she just disappear?"

"I don't know," he said earnestly. "I tried to hide under my pillow. I didn't see where she went."

"Well," Laine said, "you can see for yourself that there is no one here but us."

Gabriel's brown eyes widened. "Maybe she did disappear! Maybe she's a ghost!"

"Oh honestly, Gabriel," Laine said with a chuckle. "How many times have we told you that there are no such things as ghosts?"

I nodded and thrust my hands into the pockets of my bath-robe. "I think someone has been watching too many episodes of

Scooby-Do."

Gabriel leaned his head on his mother's bosom. He was too tired
to argue but too frightened to be alone. "Can I sleep in your bed?"

"Of course you can, puppy pie," she lifted him up and carried
him into the master bedroom, singing one of his favorite lullabies
as she went.

> Blue horse, white horse, brown horse, gray;
> trotting down the paddy corner,
> bright, sunny day.

I turned off the overhead light but noticed that Gabriel's nightlight was still on. It was plugged into an outlet by the window that
looked out over the backyard. I walked over and peered out the
window. The bottom half was pushed up as far as it could go, and
a humid breeze flowed through. Through the screen I had a clear
view of the spot where I had been crouching minutes earlier. Then
I remembered that in my rush to get to Gabriel's room, I left my
flashlight by the bog. I carefully scanned the area where I'd positioned it, but it wasn't there. I must have kicked it when I ran into
the house.

Just as I was about to pull away from the window, a whitish
flicker of movement caught my eye. Something like a thick rope,
tapering to a point, undulated and disappeared into the depths of
the pond. Logic told me it was a split-second optical illusion. For
one thing, ropes aren't that thick; for another, ropes don't taper to
a point. Besides, if it was something real, it wouldn't have disappeared so quickly into the pond unless something in the water
pulled it down. This, I knew, could not be the case. So I told myself
that I'd seen a pale sliver of moonlight dancing on the bog.

Thus convinced, I yawned and turned off Gabriel's nightlight.

FORTY-TWO

INUCAN SABBATH

Y<small>ORO STUDIED THE SKY</small>. At various times throughout the day he liked to survey the heavens and predict the coming weather. Over the years his accuracy had improved considerably, though it seemed that nature always had fresh surprises in store. He speculated that today's weather would be reasonably fair. Stretching as far as he could see into the eastern horizon, a blanket of clouds moved majestically overhead. The feathery quilt augured light rain, but a gentle westerly breeze eased the air's damp grip.

Villagers came and went all around him: some carried tools of one kind or another; some, though empty handed, strode with a definite sense of purpose; a couple of women were immersed in conversation as they walked by. But no matter how distracted any of the villagers may have seemed, all who came close to the Sartum tilted their heads before moving off.

In the center of *la recognus* several children were playing a game that involved skipping over some strategically arranged sticks and stones. A few old men sat on the other end of the roofed communal area; they talked and sipped bowls of *a'qa*—a maize beer that the Inucans had been brewing since the days of the Incas. Nearby an array of fresh fruit had been laid out for anyone who desired a late morning snack. Every treat was free for the taking.

At the far end of the village, Yoro saw something that took his mind off the coming day. Lynn Lee was giving one of her white fire-sticks to a warrior. A few other Inucans stood near the young man and watched. The villagers were fascinated by these fire-sticks that seemed to give the outsider such happiness. Lynn placed one of the fire-sticks in her mouth and touched its tip with a flame. She inhaled deeply and then exhaled slowly. Yoro couldn't hear what was being said, but the young man tentatively placed a fire-stick into his mouth and mimicked the woman's action. She laughed, produced a flame with a flick of her hand, and touched it to the end of his fire-stick.

"Sartum."

Yoro looked up as the hair-cutter completed her *sumidad* and then gestured toward one of the *chonta* stools. She and another woman had set up work stations in la recognus, as they did every Sabbath. Anyone who needed a haircut could sit and have his or her hair clipped. Yoro walked under the huge awning and took a seat. An older boy was sitting on the next stool. Both the boy and the woman who was cutting his hair bowed their heads toward him. The woman then resumed snipping away at the boy's thick bangs with a bone-white implement which she held in the fingers of her right hand.

"Have you used your new fish-catching stick yet?" Yoro asked.

"Yes, Sartum," the boy beamed. "I caught a big tambaqui."

"Ahh," Yoro turned a satisfied grin on the boy. He could almost smell the plump fish roasting over a fire and hear the sizzle of its fat dripping into the flames. As far as he was concerned, the meat of a tambaqui was as tasty as anything that could be pulled out of the Amazon River or any of its tributaries—with the possible exception of a thick, juicy eel. "You have done well, my son." The Sartum referred to every boy in the village as his son, and every girl as his daughter.

"Indeed!" said a smooth, confident voice. The boy didn't know what the Anglo word meant, but he turned to see Pensador sitting on one of the stools off to his left, looking at him with an unmistakable smile of approval. "I'm glad you're putting the fish-catching stick to good use," the outsider explained in the Inucan tongue. "I'll get you some stronger line so that you can catch even bigger fish, though you might have to get one of your friends to help you reel it in. Before long, you'll be feeding half the tribe with your catches."

Having happily but nervously soaked up the Sartum's approval, the boy now had to absorb Pensador's compliment as well. Flanked by two of the greatest men he had ever known, he was too flustered to speak. Sensing his nervousness, Pensador turned his attention from the boy to the woman who was cutting his hair. She had stopped long enough to pay him the Inucan sign of respect, and he responded in kind.

"May I go next?" Pensador asked.

"Yes sir," she replied demurely, making eye contact for only an instant.

He noticed that she was using a set of piranha teeth to snip the boy's hair. Its jaws had been cut away from the rest of the skeleton, and every scrap of flesh had been boiled off. Now her fingers nimbly manipulated the intact white mandibles; its fangs were kept in razor sharp condition. "I thought you folks would be using scissors by now," Pensador said. "I saw some in Felipe's cabin. You can always order more if you need them. Perhaps we could even get some battery-operated clippers." He used the Spanish words for scissors and battery. The woman was familiar with the word *tijeras,* but not with *bateria.* Before she could say anything, Yoro spoke up.

"We sometimes prefer to keep our old ways."

Pensador was careful to lower his head to the Sartum before responding. "But surely scissors or clippers would be much more efficient, and your hair would probably look nicer afterwards."

"Faster and prettier are not always better," Yoro said.

"Faster and prettier not better?" Pensador flashed his gregarious smile. "How can faster and prettier *not* be better?"

"If they cost too much," the Sartum answered somberly.

"But Yoro," Pensador said, still smiling magnanimously, "it doesn't cost your people any land, gold, or labor."

The Sartum turned and looked at the outsider. "There are other ways to pay for some things, no?"

Pensador's expansive mood seemed to wither and his head slowly bowed, as if pulled down by the weight of his thoughts.

The woman touched the boy's ear, indicating that she had finished cutting his hair. He sprang off the stool and raced away. "Sir," she said to Pensador. But he continued to stare at the ground, lost in thought. She stepped beside him and began snipping his hair where he sat. He barely noticed.

"I wish we could start over," he said without looking up. The woman who had been cutting Yoro's hair touched his shoulder to let him know that she was done. But he remained on the stool, watching Pensador.

"Start over?" he asked. "From where? From when?"

"From fifteen years ago," Pensador said.

"Not even *Viro* can change the past," Yoro replied. "But Viro has allowed us to have the power to think about the future; and the future will turn into the past soon enough."

Pensador looked up at the Sartum. The old warrior-cum-philosopher was apparently branching into theology.

"If you *could* change your past," Yoro asked, "what would you change?"

"Oh my," Pensador said. He could have spent some time reflecting on that question, but a tribal elder approached. The man tilted his head and addressed the Sartum. "All is ready for *hiwaya*."

The woman who had been cutting Pensador's hair immediately stopped and stepped back. From his research on Inca civilization, he recognized *hiwaya* as a Quechua word which referred to a form of punishment that was practiced centuries ago. As he recalled, it involved dropping a heavy stone on the back of a wrongdoer. The punitive ritual sometimes cracked the malefactor's vertebra, leaving him or her crippled for life.

"Sarpay is getting the woman," the man said to Yoro.

"Good," Yoro replied. "The woman must be present." He turned to Pensador. "You, too, must be present."

"I'm free at the moment. But who is getting punished?"

"Ah, so you know of hiwaya?" The Inucan elder, and both of the hair-cutters, were surprised that Pensador was familiar with the ancient penalty. Yoro, however, seemed to take his awareness in stride. The Sartum had grown so accustomed to the outsider's remarkable range of knowledge that he was only surprised when Pensador *didn't* know something.

"I remember it from my readings," he said. "But I didn't realize hiwaya was still in use." Cotulko's face appeared in Pensador's mind, in answer to his own question. The Inucans were apparently treating the shaman's drink-spiking escapade very seriously.

"Our people kept some of the things that we learned from our keepers," Yoro replied. Pensador was struck by the fact that the Inucans always referred to the Incas as "their keepers." The Amerindians always wanted to remember that they had never been granted their freedom. They had to fight for every inch of their liberty. It seemed to Pensador that the Inucans were determined to view themselves not as victims, but as escapees from a treacherous world. Their outlook would only change when the pure white incarnation of *Surutas* inaugurated the dawn of a golden age.

Lynn Lee approached from the other end of la recognus, escorted by the gaunt woman who had led the morning worship service. Though she was much older and shorter than Lynn, the woman's movements were marked by a resolute sense of purpose, and she had no trouble keeping up with the geneticist's long strides.

"What's going on?" Lynn asked when she arrived at Pensador's side.

"It seems that we are to witness an archaic form of punishment," he said.

"You've got to be kidding," Lynn grimaced. "Is this going to be gruesome?"

"It might be unpleasant," Pensador replied.

Yoro extended a hand toward the elderly woman. "This is Sarpay; and this," he nodded toward the man who had interrupted Pensador's haircut, "is Hanoq." Both tilted their heads to the outsiders. "They are tribal elders and my two most-trusted advisors," Yoro added. "Please come with us." The trio set off for the southern end of the village.

Pensador and Lynn exchanged bemused glances, then followed.

FORTY-THREE

SKY PALACE

GABRIEL'S VOICE CRACKED AS HE TALKED about his faithful companion. "Biscuit always waited for me. He waited for me outside school; he waited for me at my aunt's pool; he waited for me at the Boys and Girls Club. No matter where I was, he always waited for me." The boy sniffed, gulped, and peered at his hostess; it was a plea for understanding. "One time Sammy Sullo tried to take my lunch money from me—he pushed me down and laughed at me. But Biscuit growled and chased him away. Sammy never came near me after that, cause he knew Biscuit would get 'im." Gabriel pulled up the front of his green tee shirt and wiped the thin streams that ran down his cheeks. Though his voice, too, seemed drenched with sadness, the words, "I miss Biscuit so much," somehow squeaked through.

Sophie sat across from Gabriel and fought back her own tears.

The day had started like any other sleepy summer Sunday: her dad made blueberry pancakes for breakfast; she daydreamed through Reverend Sewell's sermon; then she fed both of her pets—Swifty, her box turtle, and Twiggy, her teddy-bear hamster—as soon as she got home from church. But this day was supposed to be different from a normal Sunday. Earlier in the week Sophie's dad had finished building a treehouse in the back yard, so she invited her three closest friends to a special housewarming party, complete with tea and cookies. The tea was imaginary; the cookies were real. But Alison's parents were taking her to visit her grandmother; Amy had gone to Storyland for the weekend with her family; and Rita had been grounded for letting her pet parakeet out of its cage. It swooped into the living room just as Rita's brother unwittingly slid open the patio door. The bird was last seen heading in the general direction of Cape Cod.

Sophie's housewarming party, it seemed, would have to be populated by friends who were no less imaginary than the tea that was being served. But as she arranged the server, cups, and the platter of cookies in the one-room abode, she heard a boy's voice calling out from the sidewalk. "Biscuit! Come here boy! Biscuit! Come home!" Peering through one of the small windows of the treehouse, she saw Gabriel walking down the lane toward the street. He had an *Indiana Jones* explorer hat on his head and a set of small binoculars in hand.

"Where are you going?" she called.

"I'm searching for my dog," he said.

"Why don't you come up and have some tea and cookies first?"

Moments later he had scaled the bottom-most boughs of the massive oak tree and entered Sophie's new home-away-from-home. She smiled proudly as he gasped at the branch-borne apartment. The room was big enough for them to play a game of hop-scotch. Sophie's mom had made a pair of red curtains for each of the twelve-inch square openings that served as windows. Her sisters had even given Sophie their play table, with matching chairs, which had been the centerpiece of their own tea parties when they were Sophie's age. The plastic furniture fit perfectly in the pine-scented room.

"I never had a friend who had a house," Gabriel said.

"Yes, this is a very special occasion," Sophie said with a regal flourish. "And since you are the very first guest to *Sky Palace*, you can visit any time you want. You just have to get permission from me first."

"Sky Palace—what's that?"

"It is a mansion in the clouds," Sophie said as she lifted an elegant silver vessel from the table. "It is the name of this…," she paused to remember the word her dad had used, "this dwelling." Then she turned to Gabriel and momentarily put aside her royal accent. "My mom thought of it."

"Sky Palace," Gabriel echoed thoughtfully. "That's a cool name."

"Yeah," Sophie giggled, "it really is." She quickly recovered her regal manner and tipped the swan-necked server over a porcelain cup. The tea service had once belonged to her grandmother. Sophie's mom said she could keep it in Sky Palace as long as she didn't damage any part of the set. She poured an imaginary stream of tea into Gabriel's cup, then lifted an ornate creamer. "Would you like some milk and sugar with that?"

Gabriel studied the inside of his cup.

"You have to make believe," Sophie said confidentially.

"Oh." Gabriel reappraised the empty cup then lifted it to his lips and sipped loudly. "Wow! This is the best cocoa I ever had!"

"It's tea," Sophie frowned.

Gabriel nodded, took another sip and exclaimed: "This is the best make-believe tea I ever had."

But his satisfied gleam quickly faded. Sophie offered him the platter of cookies but he shook his head. "What's wrong?" she asked.

"I wish it was just as easy to make believe Biscuit was here," he said. With no further encouragement from his hostess, Gabriel began talking about all the nice times with his Husky. Biscuit had been a loyal friend through thick and thin, and the dog's disappearance had plunged the boy into a cold, dark place that existed alongside his warm, sunny memories. At first Sophie was annoyed that her housewarming party seemed to be turning into a funeral. But each sentence Gabriel uttered formed a strand of tender memory, and she quickly became entwined by the web of affection and longing.

Sophia Sampson, however, was not one to wallow helplessly in such entanglements. Deeply empathetic by nature, she experienced other peoples' sorrows as if they were her own, so it gave her great happiness to relieve people of painful burdens. When a friend or relative was vexed by a problem, her first instinct was to think and act her way toward a solution.

"Do you now what we're going to do, Gabriel?" she asked as she stood up.

The boy blinked at her through his tears.

"We're going to find Biscuit," she said boldly.

"How are we gonna do that?"

"I've got a plan."

As Sophie and Gabriel combed through the eastern side of the Delvecchio's enormous yard, she wished she had remembered to bring her *Hannah Montana* sunglasses. It was a glistening summer day: the kind she dreamed about on bleak winter nights when it seemed that the sun might never show its face again. Though the leaves of the trees were like countless little visors, beams of light still filtered through the canopy and bounced off every surface, filling her head with their summery radiance. As she squinted and pressed onward, she could hear an occasional car cruise down the road that ran beyond the back fence. Whenever a set of tires whooshed up the street toward Kingston, she thought: *Someone's going to the city.* And whenever a set of tires whooshed in the other direction she thought: *Someone's going to the beach.*

In accordance with her plan, Sophie and Gabriel stayed close enough to hear each other speak, but far enough away to examine a good swath of land as they walked.

"Maybe Biscuit fell into a hole, or got trapped between some rocks or something," Sophie said. "If something like that happened, then this is the best way to find him."

"Yeah, you're right!"

Sophie imagined Gabriel's hopes fluttering and rising like a big, colorful balloon.

By lunchtime the pair had covered two strips of property, carefully checking around big trees, stone outcroppings, and occasionally calling Biscuit's name. But there was no sign of the dog. As they made their way through the center swath of the estate, Sophie heard Gabriel's weary sighs from twenty feet away. She sensed the billowy balloon was sinking back to earth.

"We've still got a lot of land to search," she said as she hopped over a stream. "Let's not give up now."

Gabriel took her words to heart and moved on. As they kept abreast of each other, he looked over at Sophie. He would see her for a moment as she surveyed the landscape around her, then she would disappear behind a tree or some bushes, and then reappear a second or two later. It occurred to him that this girl, whom he had known for a very short time, had left her special party to help him search for his dog. He couldn't think of many people who would do that for him. Somewhere within that cold, dark, private place where he cried for Biscuit, Sophie's spirit had appeared as a glowing ball of warmth and light, like Glinda in *The Wizard of Oz*.

"I always wanted a big brother," he said as they stepped steadily through the woodland. "But a big sister is just as good."

From across a grassy clearing he thought he saw Sophie smile. She then passed behind a cluster of trees. He waited for her to reappear so that he could tell her how lucky he felt to have met her.

But she didn't reappear.

He stopped and tried to peer through the branches and leaves that separated them, but he couldn't see her.

"Sophie?"

When he didn't get an answer he began to worry.

"Sophie?" he called out again, a bit louder this time.

In the seconds of silence that followed, his worry turned into fear. He charged through the layers of foliage that divided them, calling her name as he went. All at once he came to a sliding stop to avoid tumbling over her. She was crouching at the edge of a small bog, staring down.

"Why didn't you say anything?" he cried. "You scared the willies outta' me!"

But instead of answering him, Sophie stretched out her arm and pointed at something.

Gabriel followed her finger and noticed that there was no water in the shallow, earthy bowl, just a layer of mud strewn with shrubbery.

"What's the big—" then Gabriel saw him. Sitting in the small crater, half covered by leaves and twigs, was a boy. His face was smudged with dirt and his blue eyes stared back at them from under thick, yellow bangs.

"Who are you?" Gabriel asked.

"I already asked him," Sophie said, "but he won't say anything."

"What should we do now?" Gabriel wondered.

Sophie was about to tell him to fetch his parents, but before she could put her thought into words, a desperate whisper came from the hollow. She thought it sounded like the strained bleats from one of her clarinet sessions.

"My name is Jimmy."

Through the smudges of grime that obscured his features,

Sophie suddenly recognized the boy. "You're Jimmy Hitchens!" she cried, the pitch of her voice rising with each word. "You're the boy everyone is looking for!"

His eyes opened wide at the sound of his own name and he thrust his mud-stained hands out, as if to keep her from yelling or moving. "Please, please, *please*," he whispered frantically, "don't tell!"

FORTY-FOUR

THE SHAMAN AND
THE STONE

WALKING AT A BRISK PACE, Yoro, Sarpay, and Hanoq led Pensador and Lynn past two storage sheds on the edge of the hill. They proceeded down a meandering path that eventually emptied out to a shorter hill. Long rows of crops lined the broad mount, which was centered by another storage shed.

The quintet walked behind the wooden structure, where six older Inucans—five men and one woman—waited in an open area. Pensador and Lynn immediately recognized Cotulko. His arms were folded across his chest and his eyes were unrepentant. Barely touching his toes was an oval-shaped stone. Pensador estimated that it weighed at least forty pounds.

"These are the other council elders of the tribe," Yoro said. He introduced each one by name, and as he did this, the elders formed a semicircle in front of the shaman and the stone. Then Yoro gestured toward Cotulko. "I believe you know this man." Lynn and Pensador, standing behind the elders, both nodded.

"Is there a *statement of justice* you want Cotulko to hear?" Yoro asked Lynn.

Pensador paraphrased the question in English: "He wants to know if you have anything to say to the shaman about the spiked *ayahuasca*."

"Yes," she said, looking at Cotulko. "You suck."

Yoro and the seven elders waited for Pensador's translation. Against his better judgment, he recited Lynn's comment verbatim in Spanish. The elders looked confused; Cotulko met Lynn's eyes and shrugged, unfazed.

"Lynn," Pensador said quietly, "the concept of 'sucking' doesn't mean anything bad to the Inucans. The idiom is alien to them."

"Don't they have some equivalent term?"

"The Inucans aren't real big on insults," Pensador said. "To them, someone is either basically selfish, basically unselfish, or somewhere in between."

Lynn pulled a pack from her pocket, tamped out a cigarette, and placed its butt between her lips. Then she took a lighter from another pocket and flicked open its cap. The Inucans stepped back when a flame suddenly popped out of the device. She took a deep drag on the cigarette and looked at the shaman. "Cotulko, you are a very bad man."

When Pensador translated her statement, the silver-haired man stared at her and asked: "How would you know what bad is?"

"What did he say?" Lynn asked.

But Yoro turned from Lynn to Pensador. "Is there a *statement of justice* you want Cotulko to hear?"

Pensador glanced at his watch and shook his head. "Will this take long, Yoro?"

"No," the Sartum replied. Then he stepped forward and looked directly at Cotulko, his face as hard as the stone which lay at their feet. But the shaman stared back at the Sartum, his arms still folded defiantly across his chest. "You have dishonored your people," Yoro intoned gravely. "You know what you must do."

Cotulko grunted, stepped back, and got down one knee. He paused for a moment before folding his other leg beneath him. From his kneeling position he looked at each member of the council then slowly laid face down on the ground, arms outstretched.

Yoro stepped forward and firmly grabbed each end of the stone with his hands. With some effort he lifted it up, hoisted it to his chest, and let it press against his torso while he took a deep breath. Then, with a snort of exertion, he pushed the stone high above his head and held it there, standing directly over Cotulko's prostrate form.

Lynn flinched and moved behind Pensador. She feared Yoro might drop the heavy rock directly on Cotulko's silvery mane, and she prepared to turn away from what would surely be a gooey mess. "Do we really have to be here for this?" she asked. Without waiting for her boss to answer, she dropped her cigarette and cupped her hands over her ears, anticipating the grisly sound of a cracking skull.

"Sartum, this isn't necessary," Pensador said. "Don't do this for our sake."

It was Hanoq, not Yoro, who answered. "This is our way. This must be done to address the shaman's wrong."

Yoro held the stone in the air, his sinewy muscles strained under ocher skin until his arms trembled. Then he slowly began to sink down to his knees. With the heavy rock still held aloft, he knelt over the shaman, lowered the stone, and gently touched it to the soft tissue between his shoulder blades. He then placed the stone on the ground next to Cotulko's head.

Silence and stillness reigned over the scene until Lynn stepped out from behind her boss and placed her hands on her hips. "That's it?" she frowned. "That's all?"

As Yoro slowly got to his feet, Sarpay sensed Lynn's dissatisfaction. She asked Pensador to translate and then she turned toward the geneticist: "Unless a wrongdoer has destroyed a life or done irreparable harm, our wish is to change the wrongdoer's heart, not to destroy him." Pensador interpreted her words as quickly as he could, and spoke just loud enough for Lynn to hear him over Sarpay's voice. The elder continued: "In *Viro's* spirit, which becomes clearer to us through prayer and careful thought, we have come to believe that—if possible—justice should be tempered by mercy." She pointed to Cotulko, who was rising to his feet. "This man must live with the shame of what he has done, knowing that he must earn back the respect of his people. As part of this lesson, he must work as your personal servant for seven days. He must then work as Pensador's servant for seven days."

"Personal servant?" Lynn asked, suddenly curious.

"He must carry out any task that is within his power," she explained. "He must clean, carry, fix, fetch, and cook as you direct."

"I don't think I want to eat anything he cooks," Lynn said, lighting up another cigarette. "But the rest of it sounds promising." She exhaled a cone of smoke at the shaman. "How are you at giving foot massages?"

Though he didn't understand Lynn's words, Cotulko had heard Sarpay clearly enough. He shook his head. "I will not serve these people."

"What did you say?" Yoro asked grimly.

The shaman bowed to the Sartum before addressing all of the elders. "I have submitted to the shame of *hiwaya* because I am Inucan and I honor our ways. But I refuse to honor these outsiders," he glanced at Pensador and Lynn. Though Cotulko addressed himself to the elders, Pensador sensed that his comments were more for his benefit than theirs. "As I have already told you, I did not seek to kill them, or to do irreparable harm. But I wanted to make them sick. *My purpose was to make them sick enough so that they would leave us.* But Felipe's medicine proved more powerful than my potion. You may think that is a good thing, but you will live to regret their presence among us."

"What's he saying?" Lynn asked. "Is he talking about us?"

Pensador looked intently at the shaman and didn't answer.

"I will leave the tribe rather than serve these outsiders," Cotulko said. "I will walk to the mountains, come what may. I am not afraid of death or life. But I am afraid for the people." His ponderous green eyes perused the faces of the elders, then settled on Yoro. "Your duty, Sartum, is to protect the people. In this, you are failing; for you are allowing these..." he turned towards Pensador and Lynn, his voice bristling with contempt "...*these parasites* to dig into our flesh."

"This is not the place to say such things," Sarpay said. "You can meet with the elders in private—"

"Hear me well," Cotulko said, ignoring her suggestion as he turned back to Yoro. "More outsiders will come. They will bring smiles and gifts and fine words. Then they will *use us* for *their* purposes. And when they have no further use for us, they will leave us, just as a fat mosquito flies from a sick, dying body."

Yoro was stung by the shaman's words; but he tried to reach his old friend without causing any more pain. "Cotulko, I don't blame you for not knowing my thoughts on these outsiders. But surely you know me well enough to know that I will not allow *anyone* to prey upon our people. You, of all my kinsmen, must know that I would die before inviting an evil presence into the village."

"I know that your devotion to the people is true and pure," Cotulko said. "I do not question your dedication, old friend. But I do question your memory."

"My memory?"

"Yes, Sartum, your memory." The shaman's face became a sardonic mask as he spoke his final words to Yoro. "In all your years as a warrior, you have tracked many kinds of beasts and set your face against many kinds of enemies. You have smelled the stench of evil. Unlike these outsiders, you know that evil exists. But you have forgotten what its tracks look like."

With that, Cotulko turned and bowed once last time to the elders. "I will say farewell to my people in the village; then you will see me no more." He strode off toward the path that led back up the hill. No one spoke until he had disappeared into the jungle.

Lynn broke the silence: "What was that all about?"

Pensador stared at the stone and said nothing.

"Hitch, talk to me," she pleaded. "What did the witch-doctor say?"

But Pensador seemed to be listening to the unheard voices of an internal debate.

The now-familiar sound of thudding rotor blades became dimly audible in the distance. The group turned and peered eastward, where two dark moles appeared against the layer of clouds that hung from the sky. The dots grew larger by the second.

"Damn," Pensador muttered. "Talk about bad timing."

FORTY-FIVE

THE GOOD NEIGHBOR

WITH SOPHIE IN THE LEAD, THE trio moved quietly through the wooded area. She was careful to avoid clearings where they might be seen by anyone who happened to be watching from the Delvecchio house. When they arrived at the border of the Sampson yard, Sophie showed the boys a teepee shaped opening at the bottom of the fence. It was just large enough for her to squeeze through, and the boys had no problem crawling after her.

Once they were on the Sampson side of the fence, Sophie told the boys to hide behind a row of bushes off to one side. The massive oak tree that held Sky Palace stood between them and the windows of the Sampson house, but she didn't want to take any chances.

"You both wait here," she whispered.

"Where are you going?" Gabriel asked.

"I want to make sure the coast is clear. Keep watching those three windows," she said, pointing to a set of bay windows on the first floor. "When you see me wave, bring Jimmy to Sky Palace and climb up as fast as you can."

"I'm thirsty," the other boy's reedy voice pleaded. "Can you get some water?" Jimmy's soulful eyes aroused her sisterly concern.

"Don't worry," she assured him, "I'll get some food, too." Before leaving, she looked at both boys. Jimmy's blond hair shimmered in the sunlight. She removed Gabriel's wide-brimmed *Indiana*

Jones hat from his head and placed it on Jimmy's head. "Just in case someone sees you," she whispered. "This should hide your hair."

Minutes later Sophie was taking stock of everyone's whereabouts in her home. Her dad was sitting in the den, reading the Sunday paper.

"What's going on, honey-bee?" he asked without looking up.

"Nothin'," she said as she moved into the living room. Paige was lying sideways across an arm chair, talking on the phone to one of her friends. As she chatted, her pony tail bobbed in the direction of the glass door which led out to the patio. Paige was in a perfect position to *not* see what was going on in the backyard.

Two down, Sophie thought, *two to go.*

She passed into the hallway where she heard a gurgling spurt of water from upstairs, followed by a full-throated gush. Someone had just turned on the shower. She hoped it was her mom, but a second later she heard the ding of a pan from the next room. She moved into the kitchen just as her mom slid a skillet onto one of the stove's back burners and placed a pot on the front right burner. Sophie deduced that Corinne must be in the shower. *Three down; one to go.*

"Is the housewarming party already over?" her mom asked, peering into the oven to check on a large tray of turkey tetrazzini.

"No," Sophie said, cracking open the refrigerator.

She heard her mom close the oven door. "What are you doing Sophie?"

"Just getting a few things."

"Why? We're going to have lunch in just a bit."

"Well..." Sophie said, still probing through the fridge, "I have a...a guest at Sky Palace. You always taught me to make guests feel special, right?"

"Who's your guest? I thought you told me your friends couldn't come over?"

"Its…Gabriel came over," she said, scanning the contents of the fridge. "He's hungry."

"Oh, you don't want to ruin *his* lunch, honey."

"They aren't having lunch today."

"Why not?"

"They had a really big breakfast." *It isn't bad to lie for a good cause,* she told herself. She imagined a gopher slipping into a tunnel to escape a fox.

"Not having lunch? That's strange…"

"Yep," Sophie said, "it is, isn't it?" She continued to forage through the fridge's compartments. Her mom turned and watched her stack up a package of bologna, several slices of cheese, half-a-loaf of bread, pieces of fruit, and three bottles of water.

"Sophie, if Gabriel is *that* hungry just invite him over for lunch. Scott and Eliza are coming over, so I made extra. There's enough for everyone."

"Um, he probably won't want to come over."

"Why not?" Her mom asked as she resumed tinkering at the stove.

"He's kinda' shy."

"He is? A couple of days ago you told me he was very friendly."

"He's friendly," she said, "but he doesn't like being cooped up with a lot of people in one room." Sophie sensed that her escape tunnel was getting longer by the second. She had to get out of the kitchen before her mom's curiosity turned into an unhappy game of *Twenty-One Questions*.

"Well then, you and Gabriel can have lunch in the living room. I'll call his mom to make sure it's okay with her."

"No!" Sophie exclaimed, then quickly regained her composure.

"I'll ask him. You don't have to call Mrs. Delvecchio." Sophie quickly stuffed everything back into the fridge. Jimmy would have to go thirsty and hungry a bit longer. She moved toward the kitchen door.

"Sophia Sampson."

Oh, oh. Whenever her mother said her full name, it sounded like the call from the witness stand of a courtroom. She stopped and turned. "Yes, Mom?"

"What's going on?" she inquired, arms akimbo.

Sophie knew she had little hope of outwitting her mom, who could read her thoughts as if they were printed above her head like the blurbs in a comic book.

But she was determined to try.

"What do you mean, Mom?"

"Why don't you want me to call Mrs. Delvecchio?"

"She's having a problem with her phone. It's not working."

"Their home phone isn't working?"

"That's right. It's not working."

"Then I'll walk over and ask her."

"But…" Sophie sensed that her tunnel was collapsing. "…I think she's putting stuff away. They still have a ton of boxes in the house."

"You're right, Sophie. Gabriel's parents are probably too busy unpacking to make lunch. So do you know what I'm going to do? I'm going to invite them over, too." She started to undo her apron, and Sophie was about to make a full confession, when Paige entered the kitchen and extended the cordless telephone to her mom.

"Someone kept beeping in, so I took the call. It's some guy for Mrs. Gray. He says it's an emergency."

"An emergency?" her mom frowned. Sophie watched her take the phone. "Hello?... Yes, this Pamela Sampson…"

Paige leaned against the counter and looked at Sophie. "Well, well," she quipped, "you didn't by any chance swallow Rita's bird, did you?"

Sophie flashed a look—part confused and part annoyed—at her big sister.

"You look just like the cat that swallowed the canary," Paige explained.

"Rita's bird was a parakeet." Sophie was only too happy to point out her sister's error.

"Same difference."

"Is not."

"Okay. So you look like the cat that swallowed the parakeet."

"You think I *always* look that way," Sophie muttered.

"That's because you're *always* up to something."

"Am not."

Paige's response was cut off by her mom, whose voice was suddenly fraught with worry: "I'll go over right now." She hurried into the living room, calling out to their dad as she went. "Honey, there's a problem at Muriel's. Where do we keep the key?"

"Did something happen to Mrs. Gray?" Paige asked as she followed her mother out of the kitchen.

Anxious words were exchanged in the next room. From the study came the sound of desk drawers rapidly opening and closing; then there was a flurry of footfalls in the hallway, followed by the thwack of the front screen door. The anxious voices faded across the street.

Sophie could not believe her luck. She was left all alone in the kitchen, with a well-stocked refrigerator at her disposal. She felt like a bank robber standing in front of an open vault while the entire police force rushed off to some bigger emergency across town.

Minutes later Sophie settled into Sky Palace with Gabriel and Jimmy. She opened a large, green shopping bag and placed a variety of foods on the small table: fruit, nuts, bologna, cheese, a half-filled box of corn flakes, and three bottles of spring water. Jimmy quickly opened one of the bottles and took a long swallow. Then he lowered the bottle, took a deep breath, followed by another long swallow. When Jimmy had his fill of water, he ran the back of his hand across his mouth and glanced nervously at his two rescuers. Sophie thought he looked small, skinny, and scared, like a cornered, underfed gerbil.

"Don't be afraid," she said. "We're your friends."

"Yeah," Gabriel confirmed with a vigorous nod, "we're your friends."

"My name is Sophia, but you can call me Sophie. And this is Gabriel."

"Yeah, you can call me Gabriel."

Jimmy lowered his gaze so that the brim of the hat hid his face from them.

"Where have you been all this time?" she asked.

The boy didn't answer. A siren blared in the distance.

"If you want us to help you," Sophie continued, "you have to talk to us."

"Yeah," Gabriel said earnestly, "you have to talk to us."

But Jimmy didn't talk or move.

Sophie reached over and started to remove his hat so they could see his face, but he dropped the plastic bottle, grabbed the hat with both hands, and crammed it back on his head. "What's wrong with you?" Sophie asked. "You don't have to be afraid of us."

"I'm not afraid," said a thin voice from beneath the hat.

"Then why don't you look at us?"

The boy's shoulders hunched up for a second.

Sophie frowned. "If you don't talk to us, I'll have to tell my parents about you."

The boy immediately looked up at Sophie. "No!" She was unmoved by his cry, but she couldn't turn away from his sad, blue eyes.

"Then talk to us," she pleaded, as the siren in the background grew steadily louder. "We're trying to help you."

The boy's hunched shoulders slowly sagged. "Okay," he sighed. "I'll talk to you."

The siren's wail blared over his final word.

Sophie turned and looked through the small window that faced the lane. An ambulance stopped in front of Mrs. Gray's house and a police car pulled up beside it a second later.

"What's goin' on?" Gabriel asked.

"Something must've happened to Mrs. Gray," Sophie said.

Jimmy scrambled over and peered out the small window. Cheek-to-cheek with Sophie, he watched what was happening on Bog Lane.

FORTY-SIX

LEX

THE SIKORSKY PERSONNEL HELICOPTER touched down on the far end of the village, which became the epicenter of a short-lived storm of dust and leaves. Pensador, who had guided the chopper's descent with arm signals, stepped back and pressed his red and white handkerchief to his mouth. Lynn used his broad shoulders to shield herself from the tempest. About ten feet behind her stood Yoro and the seven elders of the tribe. Over their heads another helicopter—a large cargo carrier—continued on its mission toward Kalsulnak.

The pilot of the smaller Sikorsky cut its engines and the whirling rotor blades became more distinct as they beat less furiously. With the diminishing updraft, the aircraft's shock absorbers compressed and its fuselage sank several inches toward the ground. Emboldened by the quieting engines, Inucans streamed toward the scene from all over the village. Soon most of the tribe had gathered behind its leaders. Felipe also emerged from his cabin and joined Mara on one side of the crowd just as the helicopter emitted its final mechanical growl.

Through its side windows the Inucans could see some movement inside the machine, but they couldn't hear anything except for the staccato thwacks from the helicopter that was descending on Kalsulnak. Pensador turned and appraised the gathering of villagers. He tried to smile reassuringly, but to Felipe it looked more like a nervous grin.

A loud click drew everyone's attention back to the helicopter. The large side door slid open to reveal a bald, pudgy man wearing Bermuda shorts, black socks, and a festive, short-sleeve shirt covered with floral designs. Felipe knew this was the engineer who had visited Kalsulnak two days earlier, but he looked more like a tourist than anything else. Though sunglasses hid the man's eyes, Felipe could sense his discomfort. A sea of faces focused on the visitor.

After an awkward moment the engineer said hello to the villagers. The ensuing silence reminded him that the Inucans didn't speak English, so he doffed an invisible hat. But the meaning of this gesture was as obscure as the Anglo word for "hello." Not knowing what else to do, the man simply smiled at the Amerinidians. This greeting the villagers understood, and some smiled back at him.

The engineer poked at something with his foot until a small set of steps swung into place under the chopper's doorway. He grabbed a backpack and began to debark from the aircraft. But when he took his eyes off the steps to remove the sunglasses, the heel of his foot glanced off the bottom tread. Suddenly he was stumbling forward as the glasses and backpack flew out of his flailing hands. Pensador instantly crouched down and almost caught him, but it was like catching a massive bowling ball. The stout, plunging figure clipped Pensador's shoulder and fell heavily onto his side, scraping his forehead on the ground as his body slid to a stop. The crowd erupted in laughter. In a moment Felipe was at the man's side, examining a jagged wound on his right temple. He also noticed a less-serious gash on his right knee.

The engineer looked up to see two olive-complexioned faces peering down at him; the worried expressions that met his eyes were out of sync with the waves of laughter that had flooded his ears. One of the two faces was smooth and youthful, the other craggy and weathered. They exchanged words he didn't understand.

"Is he badly injured?" Yoro asked the nurse.

"I don't think so, but I should clean and suture this cut."

The engineer felt something being pressed against his forehead.

"You hurt?" the younger man asked in a heavy Hispanic accent. "You legs hurt?"

"No, only my pride," the engineer said, his face flushed with embarrassment.

Then he heard a familiar voice. "Do you think you can walk, Tom?" He saw Pensador crouch next to him.

"Yes, I'm okay."

The other man said something in Spanish and placed a handkerchief in the engineer's hand.

"The nurse wants you to press that against the cut on your forehead," Pensador said. "We're going to get you over to his clinic so he can sew you up."

Pensador took hold of the engineer's right side, the young Hispanic man took hold of his left side, and together they slowly lifted him to his feet. When the crowd saw the dazed man rise up, they erupted into whoops and cheers. Lynn Lee stepped toward him and kept time with the din by clapping her hands.

"You're a hit, Tom," she said.

"I'm a hit alright," he snorted. "Six years at Cal Tech just to learn how to be a clown." But when he turned and saw all of the smiling faces, he was dumbfounded. The Amerindians clearly liked his antics, intentional or not, and they responded like an entertainment-starved audience at a backwoods circus. Still pressing the increasingly saturated cloth to his temple, he again removed an unseen hat with his other hand and bowed slightly. The Inucans interpreted this as *sumidad*, and they were delighted that this stranger had displayed such deference to the entire tribe. They roared their approval, and the engineer beamed from ear to ear. "Heck," he said, "I could get used to this kind of treatment." But the clamor subsided as the crowd's attention shifted to something above and behind the engineer. Along with Lynn, Pensador, the nurse, and the craggy-faced Amerindian, he turned and looked at the chopper.

The figure that slowly emerged from the aircraft had to stoop to fit through its doorway; then the man stood to his full height on the top tread of the helicopter's steps. Felipe estimated that he was at least as tall as Pensador, and though his salt-and-pepper hair marked him as an older man, he had the broad shoulders and trim waist of a younger man. His face, too, retained the angular contours of youth. His straight, hawkish nose was perfectly aligned above thin lips, and his sharply-defined eyebrows were matched by a jutting chin, all of which might have been chiseled out of granite. But the man's unwavering, widely-spaced eyes were his most striking features. They radiated a powerful blend of intelligence, knowledge, and self-confidence which must have induced some self-doubt in any person who came near. It seemed to Felipe that this man's eyes had never looked up to anyone or away from anything. His steady gaze promised hard answers to hard questions, and each infrequent blink might have been a snapshot of the world's evolving possibilities. If one word could ever sum up a human face, the word that best summed up this man's face was *certainty.* He seemed to have the overpowering certainty that he was the right man at the right time in the right place.

As he stood there, staring down at the crowd, the helicopter on Kalsulnak stopped chopping the air and all was silent. Scanning from left to right, the mysterious visitor seemed to sort through the faces arrayed before him. When he spotted Yoro's grizzled visage, an enigmatic half-smile formed on his lips.

Felipe heard Pensador take a breath, then watched him step forward and turn toward the Sartum. "Yoro, I would like to introduce you—and all of the Inucan people—to my father: Richard Heinrich Hitchens."

PART THREE

We believe no evil till the evil's done.
—Jean de La Fontaine, *Fables*

FORTY-SEVEN

EMERGENCY

As we jogged along the side of the road, I noticed that Harry's breathing wasn't as labored as mine—a reminder that he was several years younger than me. He also provided a visual reminder by kicking his knees higher with each stride.

"Show-off," I panted.

He grinned and began swinging his arms up and down with exaggerated thrusts, like one of the *Rock 'em Sock 'em Robots* in my son's game.

Though I had officially resided in Plymouth only four days, I'd already mapped out two good jogging routes in and around my neighborhood. One was just over a mile long: good for early morning jump-starts before I headed off for work. The other circuitous route was nearly triple that length: good for weekends or days when I worked at home and didn't have to worry about punctuality.

Earlier that morning, however, I hadn't given any thought to running. My thoughts were consumed by last night's events—especially the cryptic message on the bathroom wall. Over a Sunday morning breakfast of scrambled eggs and toast, I asked Gabriel about the seven letters that Delaney reported: Why had he written LINDORM? Was it a word? Someone's name? I didn't ask Gabriel *if* he had done it; I thought it would be easier for him to fess up if he knew I was on to him, so I didn't give him a platform on which to plead innocent.

But he pleaded innocent nonetheless. He insisted he knew nothing about LINDORM or any of the writing on the bathroom wall. Laine was washing the fry pan as I pressed my questions, but I knew she was listening to every word that passed between Gabriel and me. At some point she quietly picked up the cordless phone from its re-charge unit in the kitchen and left the room. Meanwhile, Gabriel confessed to accidentally leaving his marker in the bathroom, and he said that he found the writing on the bathroom wall, but he looked straight at me and insisted that he didn't do any of the writing.

Though I didn't say so, I was increasingly inclined to believe him. Gabriel was a creative boy, but he wasn't in the habit of leaving bizarre messages on walls or anywhere else. And he simply wasn't that good of a liar. So a new culprit slowly came into focus: Jeff, Delaney's secret boyfriend. He was the only other person in the house at the time. He certainly had the opportunity to indulge his adolescent impulses, and he probably knew that Gabriel would be blamed. As for motive, Jeff was probably trying to scare Delaney into his arms. Teenage boys have been known to play crazier angles than that.

The more I thought about it, the more I suspected that LINDORM was some sort of codeword currently used by boys in heat. Or maybe the term was invented by Jeff and had meaning for him only. Maybe it signaled a sexual conquest. Maybe it was a sorcerous invocation, intended to magically reduce the resistance of teenage girls. After dismissing Gabriel I glimpsed through the dictionary but there was no listing for LINDORM. Then I looked it up online and eventually came across a book entitled: *Lindorm, The Cry of the Serpent: Writing and the Demonic...* As far as I could tell, the book's purpose was to shed light on the phenomena of evil by analyzing the works of Soren Kierkegaard and Franz Kafka. I convinced myself that this vaguely fit my suspicions about LINDORM being some sort of talismanic utterance. But as I mulled over this information and debated what to do next, Laine walked into my office and thumped the cordless phone on my desk.

"Guess who just had a nice chat with Eva Lindurm?"

"You gotta' be kidding... Isn't there a law against calling public school officials during summer vacation?"

She ignored my comment. "Eva doesn't know what Lindorm means. But she told me that her family name in Germany was 'Lindwurm.' Her grandfather changed it to Lindurm after emigrating to the U.S. because Americans kept pronouncing the name 'LindWorm,' rather than the Germanic 'LindVurm.' "

"What are you telling me? Lindorm is a kind of worm?"

She shook her head. "No. According to Eva, 'Lindwurm' is an old German word for 'dragon.'"

I looked at her as if she had said a word I didn't understand.

"You know: 'dragon'—as in 'mythical, serpentine monster'."

Now, as I struggled to keep up with Harry, I wondered if I should say anything about his daughter's secret beau. I was mindful of the promise Laine had made to Delaney, but if my suspicions were correct, Delaney might be dating the future founder of some weird, dragon-worshiping cult. But how could I say that to Harry? How do you tell a father that his daughter might be dating the next Aleister Crowley or Charles Manson? And what if my suspicions about Jeff were wrong? What if LINDORM had no sinister meaning at all? What if it was just the mischievous but benign offshoot of an adolescent mind?

Harry and I finally approached the street that would take us back to Bog Lane. With my last reserves of energy, I broke into a sprint—or as much of a sprint as I could manage. But I had only put about ten feet between us before Harry charged. He quickly passed me, laughing as he went.

That's when the ambulance screeched by us.

"Do you want me to flag it down for you?" Harry shouted, still laughing. The van turned the corner that would take us back to my house. Harry slowed to a trot just as a police car veered down the same street. We reached the intersection in time to see the ambulance and the police car take another left turn into Bog Lane. They could only be going to one of three houses—and one of those houses belonged to me. Harry and I simultaneously broke into a full sprint.

The moment we turned the corner and saw the emergency vehicles parked in front of Muriel's house, a wave of relief flowed through me, immediately followed by a wave of shame. For a moment it felt as if I'd wished something bad on our elderly neighbor. But this thought made no sense at all, so I quickly banished it from my mind.

Paige Sampson stood on the sidewalk next to the ambulance; Laine and Jean were hurriedly pushing through the front screen door of my house. Below their worried expressions they wore billowy, untucked white shirts. These frayed garments had once belonged to me, but—like all of my old shirts—Laine used them as smocks for projects around the house. When Harry and I had taken off on our jog earlier that morning, our wives were scraping wallpaper in the guest room on the third floor. The tell-tale smudges of gray paint on each of my old shirts, which covered the women down to the knees of their blue jeans, told me that the scraping part of the job was over, and the painting had begun.

"What happened?" Harry asked through quick breaths.

"I don't know," Paige said. "I think maybe Mrs. Gray had an accident. My parents told me to wait out here."

Jean and Laine joined us in time to hear Paige's answer.

"I'll check it out," Jean said.

Just as she swung open the screen door to Muriel's house, Fran stepped out. "Muriel's had a heart attack," he said. Paige gasped and cupped her hands over her mouth.

"Is she conscious?" Laine asked.

"Just barely," Fran said. "They are getting her on the stretcher. Pam will go with her in the ambulance."

"I'll follow in my car," Jean said.

"Let's take mine; it's closer," Laine said, scanning the street. "Gabriel?" she called out. "Gabriel!"

"I'm over here, mom!" Our son's voice wafted out of the Sampson's backyard.

"He promised he wouldn't leave the front porch," Laine huffed angrily in my direction. "Rick, you give him a good tongue-lashing. I'll call from the hospital."

I was still too winded to speak. But, with my hands on my knees, I managed to nod.

FORTY-EIGHT

COUNCIL

"A DIFFERENT STRATEGY?" Even when asking a simple question, his father's deep voice and penetrating eyes gave the impression that he was about to reprimand someone.

"I'm not suggesting a major change," Pensador said. "But I think we should postpone some of our target dates."

"Steven, why is that necessary? Has something gone wrong? What has suddenly changed?"

Pensador and Lynn shared a furtive glance. He thought she might tell his father about the Inucans' chilly response to the "four great truths" that he ad-libbed during his speech on Thursday night. But, to his relief, Lynn tamped an unlit cigarette against the back of her hand and said nothing.

"Well, I wouldn't call it 'sudden,'" Pensador replied. "I suspect the Inucans have been slowly changing for decades. This third visit has given me some perspective, and it has become apparent to me that a particular mindset is emerging among them." His father was about to ask an obvious question but Pensador tried to get beyond it without having to provide an answer. "The bottom line is that the Inucans might not be so eager to cooperate with our project."

His father's face turned into stone. It was a transformation Pensador had seen many times before, though the visage had never looked quite so hard.

"This is not a fatal problem," he added quickly. "We can proceed with our mission. I just think we ought to relax our timetable and move at a slower pace. We shouldn't try to take any genetic samples until at least October."

"October?" His father spat the word out of his mouth as if it was toxic. The founder and Chief Executive Officer of Lexel Corporation— who was known simply as *Lex* to his employees—fumed at his son's suggestion. The six people who watched Lex waited for the verbal explosion that was sure to follow. Lynn was sitting cross-legged on one of a number of large plastic containers that were stamped with the Spanish word *CONSTRUCCION*. Tom Fester, the project engineer, sat halfway up a pile of cinder blocks that vaguely resembled a miniature Mayan pyramid. A freshly-knotted series of stitches laced the side of his head, making him look like the victim of a temporal lobe lobotomy. Moe, Larry, and Curly—who had been constructing two large tents at the edge of the clearing—looked up whenever Lex raised his voice. Though he was speaking a language they didn't understand, they were attuned to anything that might be a command. And in the center of the clearing, standing several feet apart, were Richard and Steven Hitchens, father and son.

Earlier that day Pensador had introduced Lex and Tom to the Inucans. This was followed by an impromptu reception at *la recognus*, but the atmosphere wasn't nearly as festive as it had been when Pensador arrived three days ago. Cotulko's self-imposed exile had left the tribe in a somber mood, and the daily helicopter deliveries on Kalsulnak made villagers wonder if some sort of invasion force was gathering strength on the nearby hill. Still, the Amerindians made an effort to be hospitable to Pensador's kinsmen.

In Tom's case this was easily done. The engineer was a jovial, down-to-earth man whom the villagers found impossible to dislike. Although they had never seen even a mildly obese person, smiles came gracefully to the man's round face, and his eyes saw gentle humor in almost everything. His spirit spoke not of hard judgment but of kindly acceptance.

Pensador's father, on the other hand, exuded silent verdicts even as he tried to act friendly. His *sumidads* seemed stiff and grudging, and the look in his eyes betrayed a mind that was constantly assessing everyone's relevance to some secret problem. But his fluency in their language astonished the Inucans. No stranger had ever arrived *already knowing* their tongue. For some of the Amerindians, this feat hinted at almost supernatural powers. But others remembered that this man was Pensador's father. They reasoned that if the son was immensely gifted, how talented must be the man who sired and molded him?

The celebration ended along with the rain, and at Pensador's suggestion the Lexel group walked to Kalsulnak. Now, as all of them sat or stood in the man-made glade, the only sound that could be heard was the wind rustling through the rainforest. Though Moe, Larry, and Curly had worked hard to clear the area of trees, the jungle already seemed to be closing back in on them. Gnarly vines weaved through the surrounding wall of vegetation like resinous serpents waiting for the right moment to strike.

"October is out of the question," Lex snapped.

"But the extra time will help the Inucans adjust to our presence," Pensador said. "And I suggest we minimize that presence as much as possible. Other than the seven people who are here right now, no other Lexel employees or construction workers should ever enter the village."

"We can manage that," his father said. "But we've got to start work on the Inucans by early September. Tucker's expecting the first samples in Crestview by the end of *this* month." Lynn looked up at him and opened her mouth to speak, but he continued. "The Crays are already in place and a complete inspection matrix is on the—"

"Crestview?" Lynn finally asked. "What's wrong with Plymouth?"

The man looked at Lynn, then at his son. "I had to sell the house."

"What?" Lynn blurted.

"Why?" Pensador asked.

Lex thought his son's face and voice seemed nonchalant compared to Lynn's. If he didn't know any better, he would've assumed that Steven already knew about the sale of the Plymouth house. Lex stroked his chin as he looked from Lynn's face back to his son. "I got an inside tip from Tessler last month," he said. "It seems that someone at M.I.T. passed information to the feds. Fortunately, the info amounted to little more than suspicions. But Tessler had reason to believe the E.P.A. was preparing to check us out. We had to clear out the Plymouth lab as quickly as possible."

It took Lynn a moment to digest this news. "Was it necessary to sell the house? Wasn't it enough to clear out the lab?"

Lex shook his head. "The E.P.A. is full of caped crusaders who would love to crash an operation like mine. The only thing that might put them off my trail is if they get to Bog Lane and find a wholesome family living in the place—a family that has no connection to me. In that case, the feds might assume they were given a bad lead and just go away. But if the E.P.A. agents get to Bog Lane and find my name on the deed of a perfectly inhabitable yet strangely empty house, they will keep sniffing around and asking questions. They might even somehow stumble into the lab itself. My only hope was to cut all ties to the place."

"What if that doesn't put them off?" Pensador asked.

"The Crestview house is still listed under Sonya's maiden name," Lex replied, "so it won't come up if someone does a cursory computer check of my holdings. Also, Crestview is about fifteen hundred miles closer to the Amazon than Plymouth, and about two thousand miles closer than the Prescott lab. From here we get to Crestview in just three hops: from Codajas to Caracas; from Caracas to Miami; from Miami to Pensacola. Then it's just a thirty minute drive to the lab. Crestview was the logical fall-back position."

Lex waited for more questions, but when none were raised he

voiced the question his son had hoped to avoid. "Steven, in what ways have the Inucans changed?"

"Well, it's a very subtle change," Pensador replied. "The bottom line—"

"Let me worry about the bottom line," Lex said. "Tell me about this change."

Pensador exhaled, resigning himself to a potentially miserable exchange. "Rather than sort through my perceptions, let me give one concrete example. Just a few days ago some Inucan hunters in search of fresh meat came upon a female capybara that had just given birth to a litter of pups. The hunters refused to kill the capybara. They said such an act would be terribly unjust—*atola,* in their tongue. They believed that if they killed the capybara mother or its newborns, the injustice of their act would have somehow come back to them, sooner or later." Pensador scanned the faces around him. "That belief is the tip of an iceberg; it presages a much deeper change in the tribe's ethos that will complicate our mission."

"I think I see your point," Lex brooded, his knuckles stroking his jaw.

"I don't see it at all," Tom shrugged. "What's so bad about not wanting to kill an animal that just gave birth to some pups?"

"It's unnatural," Pensador said, turning to the engineer. "Those hunters refrained from getting fresh meat from a wild animal because of some purely moral or religious consideration. That means the tribe's relationship to nature has been, or is in the process of being, fundamentally altered."

Tom's pudgy face screwed up in thought. "Is that a bad thing?"

Pensador removed his hat and used it to swat away a cluster of bugs that hovered around his face. "Let me explain: Like all people living in a primeval state of nature, the Inucans saw themselves as just another type of animal struggling to survive. All that mattered were the brute forces of nature that had to be overcome or placated. But now they see themselves as being in some sort of a relationship with a *higher truth*—not an intellectual abstraction or a nature deity, but a purposeful, moral, living truth. This imposes an ethical responsibility on them to behave differently, and it causes them to see themselves not simply as intelligent animals struggling to survive, but as moral beings in a cosmos that has spiritual meaning."

Tom nodded to show that he understood, so Pensador continued: "We were fully prepared to deal with a tribe that worshipped nature gods or nature itself. We were prepared to use their religion to our advantage. But, as I've explained, many of the Inucans now seem to believe in something higher than the laws of nature. According to the Inucans, this *something* is the ultimate reality. They call it 'the infinite eternal.' They believe that this creator Spirit—which they call *Viro*— brought the cosmos into being."

"Sounds like they're talking about God," Tom said.

Pensador nodded. "Yes: a God who transcends physics and our human powers."

"If this Inucan deity transcends physics, what is the nature of their relationship with it?" Lex asked. "How do they connect with it?"

"They seem to discern its presence primarily on a moral plane," Pensador said. "That's why they increasingly judge their own actions by some spiritually sanctioned sense of ethical right and wrong. Even their ritualism seems more symbolic than it did fifteen years ago. Now their rituals serve mainly to remind *them* that they must try to adhere to a higher ethical standard."

Lex looked like a man who was swallowing something sour. "What is the nature of their moral code?"

"As far as I can tell, it's some version of the golden rule: 'Do unto others—' "

"I know how it goes," Lex grimaced. "Damn missionaries."

"I don't think missionaries are to blame—at least not entirely," Pensador said. "The Inucans inherited the raw concept of *Viro* from the

Incas centuries ago, and it's been evolving in their minds ever since."

"Viro," Tom mused, "sounds like a pill for erectile dysfunction."

"It's not," Pensador said. "Viro is the highest and most abstract deity of the Inca pantheon. The ancients considered Viro to be the unseen creator of the entire cosmos. Viro is the rough Inca equivalent of the Judeo-Christian God."

"I still don't see how this will interfere with your project," Tom said. "Whether the Inucans worship an invisible, moral God, or a nature idol, or a thousand different gods, what difference does it make to Lexel Corporation?"

"The corporation can manipulate idols," Pensador said. "We can tinker with nature to a considerable extent; but we cannot usurp an intangible, moral God."

"You're wrong," Lex said firmly. He was adept at finding fresh opportunities in every obstacle, and he had already latched onto a solution to their problem. "We will simply use their emerging belief-system to our advantage. All we have to do is convince them that this project has a very spiritual dimension. We will present ourselves as meek souls doing gentle science in the service of God."

Lynn winced and Pensador averted his father's gaze.

The C.E.O. was bewildered at their reactions. "You needn't be so squeamish about it. I had to tell a pack of lies in Brasilia to get permission to build this lab. The Indian Protection Bureau thinks we're investigating new ways to control malaria out here. Even that wasn't enough. I had to fill a few pockets to get certain people to look the other way when we flew all the new lab equipment into Codajas. Where the hell do you think this mission would be if we weren't willing to play outside the lines? We've been doing it all along. What's one more lie to a tribe of cultural pygmies?"

Tom stirred uncomfortably on his perch. Lynn stood up and turned her back to Lex as she lit a cigarette. But Pensador squarely faced his father. "The Inucans are not cultural pygmies," he said. His voice wasn't as deep as Lex's, but his words carried the same authoritative punch.

A mildly-amused look softened Lex's eyes. "What's this? Has the detached anthropologist left the building?"

"I know the Inucans well enough to realize they've come a long way," Pensador said, trying to sound impassive while still driving his point home. "They've found life and hope in an environment that probably would have destroyed us."

"*Hope?* Did I hear you right?" A grimmer shade of amusement darkened Lex's eyes. "What's going on here, Steven? You're not flailing in the deep, are you?"

FORTY-NINE

THE NUMBER

HARRY, FRAN, AND I WATCHED THE AMBULANCE pull out of the dead-end street; Laine and Jean followed in my wife's Honda CRV. The policeman had left a minute earlier in response to another emergency call, and Paige returned home to tell Corrine what happened.

Harry turned to Fran. "How did you know something was wrong with Muriel?"

"She's on a life-line system," he said. "Lots of old folks have them."

"A what?" I asked.

Fran held up a looped cord with a small metal device attached. "Muriel wears this thing around her neck. If there's an emergency of some kind, she presses this button. A signal goes to the life-line headquarters, and they immediately notify us to check on her."

"What if you're not home?"

"Then the next two names on her list of emergency responders are notified. If neither of them answers, the life-line people call the cops."

"You have a key to Muriel's place?"

Fran nodded. "All responders have keys."

Harry's eyebrows angled upward. "So Muriel put you and Pam at the top of her list? Ahead of her own kids?"

"Her kids don't live in the neighborhood," Fran said as the

ambulance's siren faded in the distance. "The idea is to have people who can respond right away."

"That takes some kind of trust," I said. "It says a lot about you and Pam."

"It says a lot about Muriel," Fran replied. "She's been like a grandmother to all of our children. She loves kids; would do anything for them."

"Speaking of the little buggers," I said, "I'd better find out what mine is doing in your backyard."

The ambulance plunged through intersections and veered around corners on its way to Jordan Hospital. Its blaring siren and roof-top rack of flashing lights would normally have cleared a path through traffic, but this was a sleepy Sunday morning and there weren't many cars or trucks on the road. Inside the emergency van, Pam held Muriel's clenched left hand and mopped the perspiration off her forehead with a clean cloth. When she had found the old woman on the kitchen floor just twenty minutes earlier, her right hand was clutching the telephone and her left hand was balled into a knot. Though her fingers were withered by age, it took some effort to extricate the phone from her grasp.

Now, though Muriel was barely conscious, her left hand was still clenched. She moaned softly as her face turned stiffly from side to side. Pam glanced through the vehicle's rear windows and saw the black Honda following about thirty feet behind. When she recognized the two faces in its front seat, a wave of relief coursed through her. Laine was a newcomer to the area and barely knew Muriel; Jean lived over a block away and only knew Muriel through the Sampsons. Yet both women had apparently dropped everything to help out. It meant the world to Pam, and she knew it would mean at least as much to Muriel.

"Everything is going to be okay," Pam whispered to her old friend. "We're going to take good care of you." She didn't expect a response, but she heard the elderly woman murmur something. As the attending EMT took Muriel's vital signs, Pam leaned close, still holding her neighbor's fisted hand. Her lips moved but only jibberish emerged. Then Pam felt the woman's frail fingers open up like the petals of a desiccated flower. She sat back and looked at Muriel's hand. There, in her pale palm, was a slip of crumpled paper. Pam examined it more closely and saw a name and telephone number penned in blue ink. It was bold, masculine print, very unlike Muriel's scrawl. Pam didn't recognize the phone number's area code, but the name on the paper was familiar to her: *Steven Hitchens.*

The large oak tree, and the house that it held, caught my eye the moment I stepped into the Sampson's backyard. The ancient tree had sprouted massive branches, one of which was unusually close to the ground. This made the tree easy to climb and a perfect place for a treehouse. It quickly became clear to me that Francis Sampson must be a first-rate carpenter. This wasn't the sort of ramshackle contraption that people usually think of when they think of treehouses. Its floor was about eight feet off the ground, and the house was almost big enough to fit a Volvo. It was fully enclosed, with a small screened window on each wall, complete with shutters and a sloped roof of slate shingles. Every corner of this home-away-from-home was solidly supported by the oak tree's muscular branches, and the structure looked sturdy enough to withstand hurricane-force winds. If this was Fran's idea of a whimsical project, I couldn't wait to see the job he'd do on our deck and porch.

As I approached the tree I called out: "Gabriel, are you in there?" From inside Sophie's house came the rustle of movement and excited murmurings. Then my son's face appeared at the window that overlooked the lane. "Hi dad! I'm in here. Me and Sophie are playing."

"Alright, I just wanted to make sure everything is okay," I said.

"Everything's okay," he assured me.

"I'll be working in my office," I said, pointing to the third floor of our home. "When you leave the treehouse, come straight home. Understand?"

"Got it, dad."

I was about to leave when I took another admiring look at Fran's handiwork. I decided then and there that I wanted to see the interior of the treehouse. "Hold on a sec," I called out. "I'd like to come up and take a look at the inside."

As I approached, I heard more furtive voices. Then Sophie's face appeared at the window.

"I'm sorry Mr. D., but no commoners are allowed in Sky Palace."

I looked up at her. "I'm a commoner?" I said, feeling somewhat diminished.

"Yeah. You know, there is royalty, then there are knights and damsels, then there are commoners."

"Can't I be a knight?"

"Well, you're a grown-up, and grown-ups are the most common form of commoner."

"Oh," I said.

FIFTY

FLAILING IN THE DEEP

ON MORE THAN ONE OCCASION LEX had compared the ocean to spiritual beliefs. Some people, he had noticed, were wary of the inscrutable depths: they dipped their toes into the tide but that was about as far as they went. Others allowed their ankles to get wet; some walked in up to their knees and a few wandered in all the way up to their bellybuttons. And then there were the rest—the desperate or the hopeful—who ventured up to their necks and were inexorably swept off their feet. These were the ones who found themselves in over their heads and thrashing away for dear life. Sometimes, in their struggle to stay afloat, they latched onto other people and pulled them down too. So when Lex talked about "flailing in the deep," Pensador knew exactly what he meant. Like most people, Lex enjoyed walking on a sandy beach. But the thought entering that greenish-blue porridge, with all of its slimy parasites and unseen monstrosities, sickened him.

"Well?" he asked. "Should I worry? Are your knees wet?"

Pensador ignored these questions. "Even if the object of one's hope isn't real, that doesn't make its effect on the believer any less real."

"Don't be stupid," Lex said. "If something isn't real, it isn't real. Enlightened eyes see the illusion for what it is, and the fairy tale becomes a fairy tale, period."

"Fairy tale or not, it gives them hope; and hope gives the sincere

293

believer a considerable degree of inner strength—far more than they would have otherwise."

"The kind of hope you're talking about is a prop for weaklings," Lex said.

"That's the point, Dad. Whatever their human flaws may be, spiritual hope gives them inner strength, as well as a goal to move toward. It makes them more than weaklings."

"I can't believe you're spouting this crap to me," Lex huffed. "Are you an enlightened man or not? Are you a member of the smart, rational crowd or not?" Lex's questions were firm and clear, and his eyes radiated a wave of certainty that swarmed through Pensador's train of thought, causing him to lose track of his deliberations. Lex took advantage of his son's silence to answer his own questions: "Take pride in the strength that comes through logic and science. Everything else is a crutch for sentimental runts."

For several seconds nothing could be heard except the hum of insects and the occasional squawk of a macaw. The words of a response slowly took shape in Pensador's mind, but he hesitated before finally airing them. "Perhaps humility requires the rarest kind of inner strength. *Real* humility, I mean."

"What the hell does humility have to do with this?" Lex said. "Some of the greatest scientists in history had egos the size of battleships. Logic is logic; science is science. Everything else is tiny print in the margins."

Pensador shook his head. "It's not that simple. It takes humility to really believe in an *intrinsic* moral truth that is bigger than one's ego or ambitions. The Inucans have that kind of humility. We don't."

Lynn had been listening to the impromptu debate as she scanned the jungle and finished her cigarette. Now she turned and looked at Pensador. She was surprised to hear him defend the tribe's religious ethos, and she wondered if he was simply in an argumentative mood, or if he had somehow experienced a genuine change of mind.

Lex studied his son's face. "I'm glad you said 'we.' But you seem to have some reservations about being a member of the enlightened group."

Pensador locked eyes with his father but said nothing.

"Come on, let's hear it," Lex continued. "Are you just sticking up for the Inucans' right to be delusional, or do you think you're missing out on something? Would it make you feel better to scrape your knees to a big, gooey moral truth?"

Pensador remained silent but didn't look away from his father's stare.

Tom sat on the cinder-block pyramid and warily eyed father and son. He hadn't been sure what to expect on his first night in the Amazon. He had imagined fighting off reptiles, or running from cannibals, or dodging poisoned arrows, or being seized by the vines of gigantic man-eating plants. The one thing he hadn't foreseen was a philosophical *tête-à-tête* on the possibility of intrinsic meaning.

Lex was confident that he could defeat anyone in an intellectual duel. But his son's momentary silence stymied him. Realizing that their talk had taken an unexpectedly contentious turn, and that Lynn and Tom were paying close attention to every word, the C.E.O. did his best to smooth things over. "Look, Steven," he said, reverting to his most reasonable tone, "if you want to see yourself as an ethical being, that's fine. I see myself as an ethical being, too. But never forget that there is no moral truth *out there* beyond the rainbow. We construct moral truths for ourselves. Moral truth only resides in one place," he said as he reached up and tapped the side of his head, "in here."

"If it's all in our heads, then it's really just a phony truth," Pensador said, "like one of those fairy tales you despise so much."

"Steven," Lex said, parrying his son's words with a gentle voice, "you don't have to believe in anything except yourself to be an ethical individual."

"Then we're lying to ourselves; we're doing the very thing you taught me to never do."

His son's obstinate attitude was bending Lex's patience. "What is this about, Steven? What are you doing?"

"I'm using reason, like you've always recommended," Pensador said. "According to reason, *a stream in nature cannot rise above its source*. The human race is a species or stream in nature. So if our notions about moral-ethical goodness are true, they must derive from something *higher* than us. But if there is no meaning in nature—or in whatever created nature—then all our ideas about moral-ethical truth are just another kind of lie, another kind of ultimately empty spirituality."

Lex's lips formed something between a smile and a smirk. It was a look he usually reserved for the final stroke of a chess match, when he checkmated his opponent. "It's all too clear, isn't it Steven? What we call *ethical truth* is really a purely relative and subjective thing. Ethics change from person to person, moment to moment, culture to culture, generation to generation. This can only mean one thing: *there is no higher truth*. The only moral truths aren't *truths* at all—they're just temporary agreements to suit a particular situation for a particular individual at a particular moment. The idea of objective ethical truth, just like the idea of spiritual truth, is a big, empty delusion. But do you know what? That's perfectly okay. Look at me. I've been living with that knowledge for about half a century, and it hasn't prevented me from being happy." Lex stretched out his arms. "The man who stands before you is a fulfilled being in a meaningless universe."

"He's also a liar," Pensador said.

Lynn closed her eyes and put her fingers up to the sides of her head. Tom's lips puckered as if he was about to whistle, but no sound emerged.

Lex's arms returned to his sides as his proud smile faded. "What are you talking about?"

"A moment ago you said that you see yourself as an ethical being. But now you say that all ethics are just a matter of opinion. So *anyone* who has an opinion is an ethical being. It doesn't matter what the opinion is, because all opinions are valid. According to your way of thinking, the ethics of a saint are no truer than the ethics of a Hun."

Lex glanced at Tom and Lynn, then he nodded gravely. "Yes. But one opinion may better aid the survival of our species than another opinion. Genetic survival and genetic improvement: that's what *really* matters. That's the true bottom line. When you get right down to it, everything in life—love, law, art, relationships, philosophy, sex, competition, cooperation, war, morality—it all boils down to our genes. *Genetic adaptation is the one and only true meaning of life*; all other meanings are hopelessly subjective…they're all psychological inventions and fantasies."

Though he appeared to be lost in thought, Pensador slowly nodded. "So according to your bottom line, nations that prevent misfits and oddballs from breeding—or societies that take resources from disabled kids and give them to genetically healthy children—could argue that they are ethical because they are suppressing bad genes and promoting good genes. Right?"

"Of course, but when you put it in those terms it sounds…well, it sounds rather cold. When you say such things in public, your statements should be worded a bit less clearly." Lex realized that Tom and Lynn were taking in each word, and for their sake he struck a more affirmative note: "Let's not lose sight of the goal here. Let's all remember that we are engaged in a supremely ethical quest. We are here in this rainforest not only to improve the genetic health of the Inucans, but the genetic health of our entire species. Nothing—absolutely nothing—is more important that that. While millions of people around the world mindlessly pound at every little problem, trying to build an ill-conceived contraption called 'progress,' we will use solid scientific principles to construct a genetic temple that will rise higher, and do far more good, than anything the world has ever seen. This will be *our* monumental legacy to humankind."

Pensador continued to stare at his father. "Whatever happens, then, we will know that we did the right thing. If we destroy the Inucans while trying to improve human genes, we can still see ourselves as ethical beings. We can make decisions about the Inucans' destiny, we can experiment with their DNA, we can lie to them; and through it all we can tell ourselves that we are perfectly ethical beings."

"That's what it means to be a truly enlightened leader," Lex said. "Those of us who have liberated ourselves from all superstition bear a heavy socio-biological responsibility. Son, you must understand that the human race is essentially ignorant. Whether people know it or not, they need scientifically-literate leaders to make important decisions on their behalf, because people are just too ignorant to make the correct choices for themselves. Mark my words: someday the world will thank us for our courageous and far-sighted decisions."

Tom Fester looked down and swallowed hard. He didn't know much about genetics and he didn't philosophize very often, but he was beginning to wonder what he had gotten himself into. He had worked for Lexel Corporation before, and he knew the company was involved in cutting-edge genetic research. He also knew that Lex always paid top dollar. For this job, in fact, he was being paid in untaxed dollars. That was all he really needed to know. Everything else was a matter of practical technicalities. He had viewed this as a job, pure and simple. The engineer would study the topography of the hill, take soil samples, draw up his blueprints, and supervise their construction. Then he would collect his pay and walk away, as he had done many times before. All unnecessary inquiries would remain unasked. But Pensador's comments were forcing Tom to ask himself some uncomfortable questions. The engineer glanced over at Lynn and saw that she was fumbling to light another cigarette.

Pensador took one step back and clasped his hands together. He pressed his bundled knuckles against his lips and seemed to focus on an invisible point in the space between his eyes and Lex's chest. Then he slowly looked up and met his father's gaze.

"What if we are wrong?"

"What do you mean?"

"What if those illiterate Inucans are right? What if there is an ultimate reality that visits moral justice upon sane, rational beings like us?"

"Oh, *please,*" Lex snapped, "spare me this claptrap. It's repulsive to think that anything could pass moral judgment on me—" he abruptly turned to Tom and Lynn; "—on us, I mean. It's nauseating to think that there is anything more ethical than brave humans who are trying to better themselves." The C.E.O. struggled to compose himself, and he quickly hit on a point that would put an end to this discussion. "Steven, ask yourself a simple question: how can there be one higher truth—one God—when people around the world see that truth differently? Don't you see how ridiculous that is?"

Tom and Lynn looked expectantly at Pensador.

"*People around the world,*" he repeated slowly, as if reciting a verse of poetry. Then he paused and imagined his father's question in the form of three dimensional letters, suspended in space. He saw the words from above and below, from the front and back. As he gazed at the question, the answer slowly formed in his mind. "People around the world see the sun at different points in the sky. A person in western Africa sees a rising sun; a person in eastern Asia sees a setting sun; and a person in southern Europe sees the sun in the middle of the sky—yet they are all seeing the exact same sun at the exact same moment." He looked at his father. "Perhaps the same basic principle applies to God. Maybe people see God differently because of their different cultural circumstances and different levels of personal growth. But they are seeing the same reality from different places."

Lex's face angled down but his eyes remained fixed on his son's face. When he spoke his carefully modulated voice was replaced by a series of ominous sounds, like the simmer of a fuse. "That still leaves us with a lot of different perceptions. Even if something *like* God exists, there is no way of telling which of those perceptions is the most accurate. There's no way telling which of those people has the best understanding of God. Maybe Hitler was right—maybe God is a warlord who wants us to fight and kill. Maybe God wants the strong to triumph over the weak. Maybe God wants to be entertained by our struggle for supremacy."

Pensador thought back to his long conversation with Felipe the previous morning. "Then again, maybe the people who have the truest understanding of God are the ones who want everyone to find peace. Maybe the people who have the truest understanding of God are the humblest...the most compassionate...the most willing to put peaceful goodness above pride. Maybe that's the truest expression of God in human lives."

Lex's eyes hardened until they became bulging blue marbles, half sunk into his face.

"Goodness? Did you say *goodness?* What the hell is that? Goodness is a mirage, don't you understand that yet? Good and evil are for dim-witted primitives, not for us. *We're way beyond good and evil. We make our own rules.* If we say kill, we kill. The logical reasoning behind our choices *makes* our choices right."

Pensador's flow of thought was dammed by the sight of his father's face, bathed in the hypnotic glow of intellectual certainty. He wondered what this man might be capable of if enough power were placed in his hands. "I'm not so sure, Dad. Christ never killed anyone, never ordered anyone to be killed, never ordered any deadly attacks to convince anyone of his truth. Maybe he was on to something."

"Christ? You talking to me about Jesus Christ? Are you shittin' me? You're not just flailing in the deep—you're taking a goddamn swan dive! I cannot believe this: *my own son!*" He spun around and glared at Tom as if to extract a guilty verdict from him. But the engineer quickly looked down at the massive pile of cinder blocks. Lex turned toward Lynn, but she dropped her cigarette and crouched to pick it up. When she stood up she made sure to face the jungle.

With no one else to appeal to, the C.E.O. turned toward the three muscular men who sat at the far edge of the clearing. All three immediately stood up like trained attack hounds, waiting for a command. Their reflexive reaction reminded Lex of the power at his disposal. Soothed by this assurance, he faced his son and issued his own verdict: "Steven, if you are going to carry on as an enlightened individual in this world, you had better divest yourself of this nonsense once and for all. There is no *higher* truth; there is no *intrinsically* meaningful golden rule; there is no God."

One corner of Pensador's mouth curled upward. "Well, Dad," he said, "I'm relieved to hear you say that. Because that's exactly what I told the Inucans."

FIFTY-ONE

MURIEL'S SECRET

MURIEL FELT A JOLT AS THE GURNEY's wheel-footed legs were snapped into position in the hospital's ambulance bay. There was a sudden rush of movement. She was lying down and gliding backward. It felt strange to move so briskly in that position. Muriel slowly opened her eyes and saw lights passing above her like a series of glowing comets.

"My glasses," she murmured softly, "my glasses..."

Someone slipped her eyeglasses on her face and two people slowly came into focus at her feet: she recognized Jean Powell and Laine Delvecchio. Both were moving just as swiftly as she was. Muriel felt a hand gently press her arm, and she looked over to see Pamela moving by her side. All three faces looked worried. Muriel whispered the word "Hi," and her three friends seemed to take a collective breath when they heard her speak. They continued to move with the gurney until an arm thrust out from one side barred the trio from going any farther. Muriel watched their concerned faces and tried to unburden them with a smile, but the doors of the emergency room slid shut. Then her ponderous eye-lids also closed.

When they opened again she was looking at an off-white sky, streaked by soft cones of light that angled in from the corners. She heard a man's voice, punctuated by a rhythmic beep. At first it sounded as if the man was humming to the tinny pulse, but words gradually formed in her ears: "—seem as if any serious damage was done, but we won't know until we run more tests. For now—"

"She's awake," said a familiar female voice. "Look, she's awake."

Muriel turned her head slowly toward the voice and saw four blurry figures standing around her. As the quartet hovered closer, she wondered: *Where am I? What is this place?* Then she remembered: she had gone to the kitchen and picked up the telephone to make an urgent call; that's when the pain tore through her chest and shoulder. She bent over on her left side, trying to somehow smother the terrible ache and then grasped for her emergency necklace to call for help. The last thing she remembered was her kitchen floor rushing up at her.

"My glasses," she said feebly.

"She wants her glasses. Get her glasses."

There was a slight commotion and someone said, "Here they are." She felt the bows of her eyeglasses slide over her ears and two faces came into focus on her left side: Jean and Laine. On her right stood Pamela and a young man wearing a white lab coat.

"Oh my soul," Muriel whimpered. "Oh my dears, you are such good neighbors."

"Neighbors?" the man said, turning to Pam. "I thought you told me you're her daughters. Only close relatives are allowed in the ICU."

"We are her daughters," Pam said firmly. "She sometimes calls us her neighbors because we live in the same neighborhood."

Jean and Laine glimpsed doubtfully at each other, and the doctor gave Pam an even more skeptical look. But Muriel had been listening, and she spoke just as the man was about to say something to Pam. "My beautiful, beautiful daughters," she said faintly.

Pam beamed and turned to the doctor: "See!"

Jean and Laine again glanced at each other.

"Well, okay," the man said. "But she needs to get some rest. You can stay for a few more seconds but—"

"Please let me talk to my daughters," Muriel said to the doctor. "Just for a little bit."

The man looked at her, then at the three women, then back at Muriel. The electronic beep continued to pulse in the background as he made his decision. "Okay, but just for a bit. You need your rest, young lady," he said as he tapped the blanket over her knee. "I'll be back in a few minutes." The doctor turned and disappeared through a cloth partition, and Muriel realized that the area around her bed was almost fully encircled by light blue curtains that hung from the ceiling.

"Where am I?" she asked.

"You're in the Intensive Care Unit at Jordan Hospital," Pam said.

"You had a heart attack, hunnee" Jean added, "but it wasn't too severe."

"You're going to be fine," Laine nodded reassuringly.

Muriel tried to reach up with both her hands, but the blanket covered her entire body up to her neck. "No need, honey, no need," Pam said as she caressed her neighbor's face. "Just relax for now. There'll be lots of hugs later."

"We called your children—I mean your *real* children," Jean added confidentially.

"All the ones we could reach are on their way here," Laine said.

"I feel as if you are my children," Muriel replied weakly. "I couldn't have wished for better." Her face slowly turned toward the redhead. "You saved my life, Pamela."

She shook her head. "No need to talk, just rest."

"No. There is a need..." Muriel's voice was thin and frayed, but just loud enough for all three women to hear. "...I must tell you something. You must listen."

Jean flashed a mystified look at Laine and then smiled at the old woman. "We'll just step out, darlin', so you two can talk."

"No," Muriel said. "Please stay. You can both help Pamela."

"Help *me*? Help me with what?"

Muriel peered intently at her friend. "Find Jimmy."

Pam's head and shoulders jutted back in surprise. "Jimmy? You mean Jimmy Hitchens? Muriel," she said, shaking her head, "no one knows where Jimmy is or what happ—"

"I do." Immediately after she spoke, the blanket on Muriel's chest swelled briefly but noticeably outward.

"You do what?" Jean wondered out loud.

"I know where Jimmy is."

The three women looked at each other, perplexed.

"Muriel, honey," Pam began softly, "you had a heart attack. Maybe with everything that's happened you've become...you know, a little bit confused about things. That happens sometimes." Laine and Jean nodded in agreement.

The woman's stiffly-matted white hair shifted from side to side as she slowly shook her head. When she spoke, her eyes pleaded for understanding. "I'm not confused. You see," her voice dropped a decibel, and none of the women around her could make out her next sentence.

"What?" Laine asked.

The old woman again opened her mouth to speak, and the three younger women leaned in to hear her. The voice was as withered and delicate as the crackle of rice paper, but they could now make out each distinct word: "Jimmy has been living with me since February."

The statement hung in the air like the syllables of an unknown language. But their meaning soon filtered down into the minds of all three women.

"Ohh—myy—Gawd…" Jean's exclamation was as frozen and trance-like as the expression on her face. Pam and Laine were just as stunned, but unlike Jean they couldn't bring themselves to say anything at all.

Muriel arched her head up as much as her weakened state would allow. "You mustn't tell anyone. Not now. But this is what you must—"

"Muriel!" Pam's voice burst through the chaos of her own emotions. Laine quickly grabbed the redhead's arm: "Shhh! They'll hear us," she said, glancing at the light blue curtain and the unseen ICU desk beyond. Pam took a breath and lowered her voice, but she couldn't hide her astonishment or anger. "Jimmy's been living with you all this time? Are you serious? Are you freakin' serious?"

The old woman closed her eyes with a pained look that could only mean *yes*.

Pam could barely contain her shock and disbelief. "Oh Muriel! Muriel! Muriel!"

For a moment Laine feared that she might fall over into a dead faint.

"Hunnee," Jean said in her most restrained voice, pawing nervously at a bracelet on her left hand. "Why didn't ya' say anything to anyone?"

"Please listen," the old woman whispered. "I know this is hard, but hear me out—just hear me out. That's all I ask…"

Pam managed to take several even breaths. She then folded her arms but never took her eyes off Muriel. Jean and Laine stepped back from the bed but, like Pam, continued to stare at the sallow, contrite face.

"Last winter," Muriel began, "Steven Hitchens brought Jimmy to my house. He said that their—"

"Who?" Laine asked. "Steven?"

"Jimmy's older brother," Pam said, still staring at Muriel.

"Jimmy's half-brother," the old woman amended. "He told me he was about to go to Brazil for a year, but he was very worried about Jimmy. He was afraid that their father might send the boy to live in a boarding school. He said this would be unbearable for Jimmy, but that their father might send the boy away no matter how much it hurt him. Steven asked me: If his father made plans to send Jimmy away, could the boy take shelter in my house? I know their father to be a cold-hearted man, so I told Steven I would do whatever I could to help. Right there in front of me, he told Jimmy to come to my house if he ever needed help or a place to stay."

Muriel paused but her eyes continued to plead for understanding.

"About a month later I heard someone crying in my back porch in the middle of the night. It was Jimmy; he told me his father hated him, and was planning to send him to a special school, far away. He held on to me and cried in my arms; that little boy *clung to me* for protection. What could I have done? What would you have done?"

All three women were transfixed by Muriel's words, and as she told her story their frozen state of shock gradually thawed into streams of thought. "I've done my best to keep my promise to Steven and Jimmy. I've done my best..."

"Do you still talk to Steven?" Laine asked

"He sends money every week, and he calls every few days to talk to Jimmy. The boy is always so happy to hear his big brother's voice. After Sonya died, Steven was the only person left who really cared about that little boy."

"Except for you, it seems." Respect and exasperation tugged for control of Pam's voice. Her anger had splintered into a mass of thorny, half-formed questions that poked at her thoughts. But before she could ask any of them, Muriel pressed on.

"I've been feeling poorly these past several days. It got me to thinking: what would happen to Jimmy if something happened to me? I'll be seventy-eight years old in a few weeks. I almost feel as if a little part of me dies every day. What would Jimmy do if I fell down, or got sick, or something worse? He would be all alone and lost... So I called Steven last night and told him that I might have to bring Jimmy to someone who can take care of him until Steven returns from Brazil. I was thinking of my son's family in New Bedford." Muriel's white mane sunk down and a sob punctuated her story. "Jimmy must have been listening in the next room, because when I returned from church this morning he was gone. He must have been terrified at the thought of being sent to live with strangers in a new home far away. I tried to call Steven to tell him what happened, but my heart..." The old woman began to weep quietly. Pam sighed as she watched tears meander down the furrows of those ancient cheeks. "It's going to be okay," she said, rubbing the blanket over Muriel's arm. "Don't worry; everything's going to be okay."

Laine shot a bewildered look at Pam, as if to say: *It is?*

Jean leaned forward: "Muriel, do you have any idea where Jimmy is right now?"

As she peered up at Jean, the droplets in the corners of Muriel's eyes were magnified by her glasses. "Jimmy's frightened of any person or place he doesn't know. He wouldn't have gone very far. The place he knows best, apart from his own home, is his backyard. He must be hiding somewhere in the woods at the end of Bog Lane. That's where he must be: somewhere in those woods."

"Okay, then," Jean turned to Laine and Pam, "I'll notify the police—"

"No!" Muriel cried. "No police. They'll call Richard Hitchens and he'll just send Jimmy away to some God-forsaken institution."

"Well what do you want us to do?" Laine asked.

"*Find him,*" Muriel implored in a hushed tone. "Find him and tell him that you're not going to send him away. Tell him that you're going to take care of him in his old house, or in my house, or in Pamela's house. *Tell him he will stay on Bog Lane until his brother returns.* Jimmy has met you, Pamela. He knows you; he will come with you. But you three must find him yourselves. You mustn't tell anyone else!"

As the old woman spoke, her three listeners were staggered by the scope and weight of her request, but none of them spoke.

"I'm sorry to give you this terrible responsibility," Muriel said in a quavering voice. "But I know I can trust all three of you. You're not ordinary people."

"We're not?" Laine asked, her fingers rubbing the side of her head.

"You are moms," Muriel said. "You are good, caring mothers. You know what it is to suffer to bring life into the world. You've given other lives a chance by giving up parts of your own lives and bodies and hearts."

The three women looked away from Muriel's distraught face, but they couldn't deafen themselves to her desperate appeal. As the electronic beep in the background pulsed more rapidly, the frail voice continued to plead. "Please, for that child's sake, go into Hitchens's estate and find him. You know in your heart that it's the right thing to do; you know that it's—"

The blue curtains suddenly parted with a metallic *shllling* and the young doctor stepped into the makeshift room. He was stunned at the sight of Muriel's tear-streaked face. "What the hell is going on here? What are you doing—trying to finish her off?"

Jean tried to explain but the doctor called for nursing assistance and then ordered Muriel's daughters out of the ICU. They were quickly escorted to the door as a nurse and an intern arrived at Muriel's bedside. The intern began checking the old woman's vital signs while the nurse tried to calm her down. The last thing Pam, Jean, and Laine heard as they were ushered out of the ICU were Muriel's anguished cries: "Find Jimmy! Save Jimmy!"

FIFTY-TWO

EXECUTIVE DECISIONS

RICHARD HITCHENS STRODE DOWN Kalsulnak's eastern slope, his limbs thrusting in wide arcs of barely-controlled fury. Just enough daylight lingered for him to see the yard-wide path that led to the Inucan village. His son was on his heels every step of the way. "Don't do this," Pensador said. "It won't work; this is going to backfire."

"Lex! Stop!" Lynn called out from behind Pensador. Tall as she was, she had difficulty keeping up with the two men. "Don't act rashly. Whatever you're going to do, stop and think first! Damn it, Lex, stop and think!"

"Dad," Pensador tried again. "Please stop. This is going to backfire."

Lex suddenly turned and confronted his son. "*Backfire?*" He growled between snorts of air. "Did you say *backfire?* Don't you realize that this whole mission started to backfire the moment you made your editorial comments to the Inucans?"

Lynn brushed strands of hair from her face and caught her breath. "We can recover from this; there's no—"

"You of all people!" Lex continued to glare at his son. "You're a god-damned anthropologist! These Neanderthals are living in a raw state of nature; did you really think they were going to accept a secular view of life? In a matter of minutes you threw away all the trust we built up—all the trust that it took *fifteen years and millions of my dollars* to build up. Of all the stupid-ass things you've ever done—"

"Lex!" Lynn's cry pierced her employer's bitter stream of words. "This won't solve anything! Let's go back up the hill and plot out an alternative strategy. We can do this. We've overcome bigger problems than this."

He turned to Lynn and shook his head. "The damage is done. There's nothing left for us to do but make the Inucan prophecy come true. It's our last hope."

Pensador already knew what his father intended, so he spoke out again: "It won't work. We should reconsider this whole thing."

Lex fixed his eyes on Pensador. "Advice from you? Do you think I'm going to stand here and take advice from the idiot who senselessly screwed this entire project?"

Pensador drew a deep breath. "Please try to understand. It would've been such an advantage for the company—for our project—if the Inucans could've joined with us." Lex opened his mouth to speak but his son cut him off. "You may think it's crazy, but it didn't seem crazy at all last Thursday." Pensador fell back a step and the pace of his words slowed. "Dad, I was so close. The Inucans seemed ready to go along with anything I said. You would've been amazed at how they reacted to me that night…how *they trusted me*. I was sure I could get them to believe. And if I could've capitalized on that trust, it would've guaranteed our success. You would have been so proud… And it would've made everything so clear, so good, *so honest*. There would have been no more hidden agendas, no more skulking around in the dark…" he paused and took another breath…"no more lies."

Lex's eyes narrowed. "Is that what this is really all about? Were you having a crisis of conscience? Were you trying to absolve yourself of your role in this project?"

"No," Pensador replied quickly. "I was just trying to find a better way…a better way for *all* of us. Don't you see?"

"Yes, I do see…" But the twin coals that stared back at Pensador did not cool in the twilight. "…I see that you're full of shit. I see that you jeopardized this entire mission just to ease your tender concerns over some antiquated sense of right and wrong. I see that you betrayed all of your colleagues just to relieve yourself of some uncomfortable fantasies."

As Pensador grasped the depth of his father's rage, the gravity of regret slowly wrenched his face downward until he was staring at his own mud-spattered boots.

"I'm sorry it didn't work. I'd give my life to have that moment...that speech...back again."

Lex's voice—baritone deep yet razor sharp—cleaved the air: "Unfortunately, it doesn't work that way."

Lynn had remained silent for as long as she dared. "Lex, let's shift our focus. We can all make this better; all of us can pull together and—"

"Lynn," the C.E.O. said without looking away from his son, "shut up."

The geneticist threw up her hands and emitted a cry of exasperation. She was about to unleash a volley of words in Lex's direction, but after a moment's thought she spun around and retraced her steps to the top of the hill, mumbling to herself as she went.

She barely noticed Moe, Larry, and Curly, who stepped aside to let her storm past.

All three men were focused on Lex, standing farther down the path.

Though Pensador stood with his father on the trail, his mind's eye was momentarily back in the book-lined library of an elite boarding school. A boy stood in the middle of the empty room: his body swollen by every poisonous word it had ever swallowed. Steven Hitchens was once again the son of his dreadful imaginings. Thatches of blond hair sprouted from an otherwise bald scalp, his tongue was thick and coarse, his face pulpy and misshapen, and his eyes dull and vacant.

I'm sorry I let you down, Dad.

"Do you have any idea what this has cost me?" Lex fumed. "The time, the work, the money...You risked it all just to ease your own feeble conscience. Do you really think I'm going to go on carrying your failures on my back like a dumb donkey?"

I'll try harder; I promise.

"At least your brother had a biological excuse for his failings. But you have no excuse. You had all of my genetic gifts, every one of them. I poured myself into you!"

I'll do better, Dad, you'll see...

"No son has ever had a better chance for real greatness. You could have been an authentic superman—a true *ubermensch*. But this latest failure reveals an unredeemable deficiency: not just a defect of intellect but a want of inner strength. You let a weak-kneed conscience goad you into making an appallingly stupid decision. All those years I was so concerned about the brilliance of your brain when I should have been more concerned about the straightness of your spine and the thickness of your balls!"

With each word a drop of acid stung Pensador's eyes. He slowly lifted his head and met his father's glare.

"Oh, you've got to be kidding," Lex snorted. "Are you going to have another breakdown, Steven? Am I going to have to put you in fairyland for another six months?"

Pensador was silent. The rain of contrition that had been drenching his thoughts slowly chilled into something glacial and jagged. The C.E.O. saw his son's face harden.

"Well that's a big relief, isn't it?" Lex said. "Let me tell you what you *are* going to do now. You are going to walk back to the village as if everything is just fine. There you will immediately confine yourself to your tent. And you won't come out of your tent until I tell you to come out. Do you understand these instructions?"

In that instant Pensador made a decision. He knew that this decision would alter the course of his life more than any other choice he had ever made. Yet nothing changed or moved at that moment, except for the corner of his mouth, which curled upward by increments that were too miniscule to measure.

Lex stilled his own anger just long enough to read his son's mind. But Steven's face was as cryptic as his silence. Lex wondered if some vital synaptic trestle had crumbled in his son's brain. For a brief moment he even wondered if Steven was capable of taking some sort of action against him. But as the two men faced each other, Pensador sensed movement over his shoulder. Lex breathed more easily as a familiar trio took up position behind his son.

"I won't have to repeat my instructions, will I, Steven?"

Pensador lingered several more seconds, glanced over his shoulder at the three figures, then faced Lex again. In that instant he quietly leaned forward. The ease and grace of his movement beguiled the hair-trigger instincts of the four men who surrounded him, so they stood motionless as Pensador gently kissed his father on the cheek.

Lex was too surprised and confused to speak; he could only stare at his son. Pensador then stepped around his father and made his way down the path that led to the Inucan village.

Lex silently collected his thoughts and averted the stares of his three workers. When his son disappeared beyond the shadows at the bottom of the trail, Lex turned his attention to the three men. He knew them not by the nicknames Pensador had bestowed, but by their real names: Duarte Cabral, Jorge Correia, and Sinchenzo de Sousa. They had a few things in common: they were Brazilian by birth; they were functionally illiterate; and they had been drawn into Lex's orbit when they were just teenagers...

A decade earlier Lexel Corporation began operating a clandestine program in some of Brazil's largest cities. These urban areas swarmed with runaway children who would do almost anything for a meal or a pack of cigarettes. Lexel's genetic teams, operating on the margins of daily life in places like Sao Paolo, Belo Horizonte, and Rio De Janeiro, had been able to run valuable DNA tests on these youthful "cast offs" at an absurdly low price and with no legal complications.

Duarte, Jorge, and Sinchenzo had been among the thousands of adolescents who had been screened. Their personal and genetic profiles were fed into a database to which only a handful of Lexel employees had access. Boys and girls with desired genetic traits were kept on a short leash and often called back so that additional specimens could be culled or various theories tested. In some cases, risky procedures were carried out for the price of a pair of shoes.

But Lex's interest in Duarte, Jorge, and Sinchenzo had nothing to do with their genetic make-up. What caught his eye was a computer analysis that identified these three boys as having certain personal characteristics: they were physically strong, intellectually slow but teachable, and they had low expectations of themselves and of life. Perhaps most important of all, the psychological profile indicated that all three boys would be extremely devoted to anyone who met their simplest needs and gave them a sense of belonging.

Lex stepped into the void that plagued their lives. He gave them a steady stream of *reals* and guaranteed them a lifetime of material security. He gave them girls, and when the boys matured into men, he gave them women. He gave them a welcoming tribe—Lexel Corporation— to feed their hunger for acceptance. And, most important of all, he gave them crumbs of power and purpose, which tasted like a feast in their famished mouths.

All they had to do in return was pledge a lifetime of obedience to Lex.

The C.E.O. had put their devotion to the test many times over the ensuing years.

And now he was about to test their obedience again.

FIFTY-THREE

THE SEARCHERS

LAINE SWERVED AROUND A CORNER AND hit the gas pedal.

"Take it easy, there, hunnee," Jean said over Laine's shoulder. "It won't do Jimmy a lick o' good if we plow into something."

Pam sat in the passenger seat, her head down, eyes clenched, and fingers massaging the temples under her red curls.

"Sweetie," Laine said, glancing over, "you sure look like your hurting."

"Migraine," Pam replied without looking up. "Why do these things hit at the worst possible times?"

"Your question answers itself," Jean said from the backseat. She leaned on the middle armrest watched a traffic light flash from green to yellow. "You know, girls, after Muriel told us about Jimmy, I didn't know what was comin' next. When she said we weren't ordinary people, I thought she was fixin' to tell us we were the off-spring of interstellar aliens or something like that."

"If you're trying to lighten the mood," Pam murmured, "it's not working."

"Shit!" Laine exclaimed. She tried to beat the red light but, at the last moment, noticed that the only other vehicle at the intersec-tion was a police cruiser. She braked and the Honda's tires slid for an instant—hard rubber grating against even harder asphalt—until the car came to stop.

"Maybe you shoulda' blazed right on through, Lainey," Jean quipped. "Then the cop coulda' just followed us all the way to Jimmy."

"No," Pam said. "Muriel was right: we've got to find him ourselves. We've got to protect him from Hitchens."

Jean sighed. "You have any idea how long it's gonna take to scour all six of those acres? Must be a thousand trees and bushes in that place. And then you gotta' figure Jimmy's not gonna make it any easier for us...."

"Even if it takes all day," Pam said, "even if we're out there with flashlights tonight, we'll keep searching until we find him."

"What if he's not even there?" Laine asked as the light turned green. She accelerated slowly until she could no longer see the police cruiser in the rear view mirror, then she pressed down on the gas pedal until the Honda was moving well over the speed limit. "What if Jimmy is getting lost in some other part of town while we're searching the wrong place?"

"I got an even worse vision," Jean said. "What if he gets badly hurt while we're lookin' for him? We'll be asking ourselves 'why didn't we call in the cops when we had the chance?' Not that it matters, but it'll come out that the wife of the assistant district attorney didn't bother notifying the police when it might have made a difference."

Pam's left hand stopped rubbing the side of her head and reached over to manipulate the rearview mirror. She readjusted it until her eyes were looking directly into Jean's eyes. The migraine was still knifing into her forehead, but the pain didn't restrain her words. It propelled them. "I wouldn't worry too much. I really don't think this will damage your husband's career."

Jean took in Pam's tone and look. "What's that supposed to mean?"

"It means a child's wellbeing is more important than anyone's reputation."

"Whoaa there, missy," Jean put her hands up as if trying to stop a runaway stallion. "You better just keep a tight hold on those critters."

"What critters?"

"Those snap judgments of yours."

Laine glanced over her shoulder and tried to dampen the smoldering fray. "Ah, ladies—"

"Look," Pam said through gritted teeth, "that bastard already made Sonya suffer. He made her suffer right into her grave. If you think I'm going to sit by while he makes her only child suffer into his grave—"

"Maybe we're not doin' her only child any favors!" Jean snarled back at the eyes in the rearview mirror. "Maybe the best favor we could do Jimmy is to get a hundred cops out there lookin' for him as soon as possible—*before* something horrible happens."

"Don't you get it, Jean? One of the most horrible things that could happen is for him to be handed back to that prick of a father!"

Laine again cast a worried look at her passengers. "Ah, ladies—"

"Oh, missy, I can think of a couple of things even more horrible than—"

"Stop calling me 'missy'!"

"Damn!" Laine blurted.

The sound of screeching rubber suddenly ripped the air. Laine's foot was crammed down on the brake and the Honda was careening sideways. Anything that wasn't bolted down rushed off its surface and clattered to the floor of the car. The centrifugal force threw Pam and Jean against the passenger-side doors. When the Honda finally jolted to a halt, their heads were pressed against the windows.

Hearts pounding, all three women slowly looked up. Standing in the middle of the road, less than two feet away from them, was a young girl astride a bike with training wheels. The softly-rounded edge of a silver helmet framed her head like a halo. Her face was bloodless white, her eyes were bulging orbs, and her mouth gaped.

There were no other cars on the road, and the only other pedestrian was an angry dad. He rushed to the scene and steered his daughter's bike off the road while glaring at Laine. "What the hell is wrong with you?" he growled. "Slow down!"

The pair disappeared around some hedges, and for several seconds the only sound that Laine, Jean, and Pam could hear was the labored heaving and hissing of their own lungs. But then delicate chimes filled the Honda and formed into a playfully exotic melody. It was *La Macarena*, and it was coming from the floor of the car. By sheer force of habit, Laine slowly reached down and picked up her cell phone.

"Hello?" The voice sounded numb and tentative.

"Laine? Is that you?"

There was a pause. "I think so."

I was suddenly worried. "What happened? What's going on?"

I heard a deep breath. "I just came within a few inches of flattening a five-year-old."

"What?"

In the background I heard Jean's dazed but mellifluous voice: "Ain't life exciting?"

"Laine, where are you?"

"Somewhere between Jordan Hospital and Bog Lane."

"Do you need help? Is everyone okay?"

"We all seem to be in one piece. Let me pull over."

I heard movement, then Laine's voice came back on the line,

sounding a bit more grounded. "Oh sweetie, you wouldn't believe how close I just came to...oh God."

In the background I heard car doors opening and closing. I imagined that Jean and Pam had gotten out of the Honda to collect their wits and stretch their legs. Laine proceeded to explain the near-accident in detail. When she was done, I asked the obvious question.

"Why were you going so fast? That's not like you, honey."

"Ah, well," she seemed to be groping for an answer. "You know how it is; I just wanted to get back home."

"If you stay within the speed limit you'll get here in one piece. How's Muriel?"

"She had a mild heart attack. It looks like she's going to be okay, but she'll probably be in the hospital for a little while."

"Does she need anything? Is there anything I can do?"

There was another pause, followed by a flat "No." Car doors again opened and closed. I assumed Jean and Pam were back in the Honda.

"Look," Laine said, "I'll be home in just a bit. But there's something I have to do, so order out tonight. I won't have time to cook."

"What do you have to do?"

Yet another pause. "You know," she began in a way that made me think she was trying to change the subject, "Gabriel had a big lunch, so we won't have to order until—"

Another voice, which sounded like Pam's, spoke up: "Gabriel had a big lunch?"

"Yeah," Laine said.

"How much did he have?"

Laine chuckled. "Well, let me see; he had a grilled cheese sandwich, tater tots, and a sliced apple—all his favorites. Why?"

The other voice spoke a bit louder now, and it was clearly Pam's.

"Is that Rick?"

"Yeah. Why?"

"What phone is he on?"

Laine's voice filled the line. "What phone are you on honey?"

Now I couldn't help but chuckle. "Why? What difference does it make?"

"Is your home phone working?" I heard Pam ask.

I answered before Laine could relay the question. "If it's not working, we must be communicating telepathically."

"He's on it right now," Laine said to Pam.

I heard Pam say something, but couldn't make out the words. "What's she saying?"

"She's wondering why Sophie lied to her," Laine replied. I overheard more snippets of talk: something about food, refrigerators, and a hungry guest.

There was a brief silence, and for a moment I felt like a safecracker listening to a code click into place. Then Jean's worried drawl pierced the quiet: "You okay, darlin'? You're lookin' a bit peaked all of a sudden."

Laine's voice, unexpectedly low and tense, whispered through my earpiece: "Honey, I could be wrong about this, but I think Pam's having a stroke…"

From somewhere in the Honda, the redhead's voice surged over the phone line with escalating intensity: "Sophie. Sophia! Sophia Sampson!"

FIFTY-FOUR

SOLE SURVIVOR

THERE WAS A THUMP FROM INSIDE the large box. The three hulking figures quickly stepped back and trained their flashlights on the varnished, pine container. Then they approached it with tense, tentative movements, as if an enraged jack-in-the-box might burst out at any moment.

In the shadows of the tent, Pensador lay on his cot and pretended to be asleep. Through half-open eyelids he watched Moe, Larry, and Curly as they stood around the box and whispered to each other in Portuguese. Their heads craned this way and that, and it seemed to Pensador that they were angling for a view that might magically reveal the contents of the closed crate. He overheard Moe say, "It's making noise. It must be alive." In the radiant shafts emitted by their flashlights, Pensador could see that all three men now carried holstered weapons. They would never have unpacked their firearms unless Lex had ordered them to do so.

A muffled *squeak* came from the cot, and all three men turned toward Pensador, but his recumbent body didn't move. One by one, Moe, Larry, and Curly turned their attention back to the mysterious container. Moe slowly reached out his hand and fingered the metal hasp that held its lid down.

Another *squeak* came from the cot, but it was more distinct this time.

All three men again turned toward Pensador, who remained

stretched out on his back, hands folded over his stomach. "Are you awake?" Moe asked in Portuguese.

"Would you believe me if I said *no?*" Pensador replied, also in Portuguese.

"*El lider* told us not to talk to you," Larry said. The three stooges always referred to Lex by the Spanish title "the leader."

"So why are you talking to me?"

"Is the thing in the box okay?" Moe asked.

"Did Lex send you to find out?"

"Yes."

"Then find out."

The three men looked at each other, silently debating who would open the lid.

Another *squeak* came from the cot.

"What is that? What is making that noise?"

Before Pensador could answer, a loud thump resonated from the box. All three men jumped back. A surge of movement—flesh sliding against wood—filled the tent. Larry reached for his pistol.

"It sounds mad," Moe said, glancing nervously over his shoulder at Pensador.

The rubbing noise stopped.

"Exactly what did Lex tell you to do?" Pensador asked without moving from the cot.

Curly spoke up: "To bring the box to the center of the village."

"To place it in *la recognus*," Larry added, "and to guard it until morning."

"But first," Moe said, "we are supposed to make sure it's okay." He turned to Pensador. "Is it okay?"

"Open the lid and find out," Pensador suggested.

The three men again peered at the box from their safe vantage points.

"It will like being moved," Pensador reassured them. "Once you pick up the box, it will quiet down—it won't shift around so much."

"Why?" Moe asked.

"I don't know," Pensador said. "But I know that it is calmed by the sensation of movement."

The beam of Larry's flashlight slowly swept to the side of the large box until it revealed an empty cage. "Its food is gone," he said.

"The thing must have eaten it," Curly said.

"There were three in Codajas," Larry said. "Now there's none."

"So it must be well fed. It must be okay," Moe concluded.

"Yes," Curly agreed, "it must be."

Moe rubbed his jaw thoughtfully. "Then that's what we'll tell *el líder*, okay?"

Curly and Larry nodded.

In the darkness, an unseen half-grin formed on Pensador's face. Moe turned to him. "Your father told us to get the clicker from you. Do you have the clicker?"

"How are you supposed to ask for the clicker if you're not supposed to talk to me?"

"You know what the leader meant."

Pensador reached into his breast pocket as if he had been anticipating this request. He pulled out a silver, rectangular device that gleamed in the cone of illumination from Moe's flashlight. He held it up so that the stooges could clearly see it, then said: "Don't click it. Don't press it, or else the thing in the box…"

Larry, who was closest to the cot, took the device from Pensador's hand and eyed it suspiciously. Moe took it from him and studied it under his flashlight. "Why is this so important? What does it do?"

"I suspect you'll find out in the morning."

Moe shot an unsatisfied look at Pensador but he didn't elaborate.

Realizing the man on the cot would be of no further use, Moe slid the clicker into his own breast pocket and barked at his companions. "Let's get this done. We still have other things to do." The three men slid their flashlights into the side pockets of their khakis so that the torches were pointed upward, throwing balls of light against the tent's conical ceiling. Moe and Larry each took hold of a corner on one side of the box while Curly—who was the most muscular of the three—put a hand around each corner on the opposite side. Moe gave the count: "*Um, dois, tres…*" The men lifted the large box and began moving toward the flap of the tent. With each short, probing step, the cones of light that shot up from their side-pockets swung to and fro like frantic searchbeams. Although the box was bulky and heavy, the men managed to lug it out of the tent.

Pensador listened to their feet slide as they shuffled off toward la recognus. He then pressed a tiny button on his watch and its digital face lit up. *1:52 AM.* Though the first rays of daylight were only a few hours away, he knew it would seem much longer. He also knew that he wouldn't get much sleep.

Pensador reached under the cot and pushed aside various objects until his fingers felt a mass of fur that feebly tried to resist his grasp. Taking hold of the animal with one hand, he pulled it out and lifted it onto his chest. The guinea pig sniffed suspiciously and then made the only sound it was capable of making: *squeak.*

"You almost gave yourself away," Pensador murmured, patting the rodent's fur, "you wouldn't have outlived your cousins by very long." One dark eye on the side of the *cuy's* head peered back at him as its nose probed the button on his breast pocket. It quickly concluded the button was not edible, and continued to sniff around his chest. Pensador stroked the creature's mane and estimated that it weighed at least five pounds. Just enough flesh to appease a large predator's carefully honed hunger for a day or so.

The quiet of the night was suddenly pierced by the sound of steel pounding on wood. Pensador got up and looked through the furled door of the tent, the folds of which were parted just enough to give him a clear view of the center of the village. There, at one end of *la recognus*, Moe shined two flashlights on Larry and Curly, who were arranging sheets of plywood and hammering them into place. Within a few minutes Pensador realized that they were constructing a small, simple stage—just large enough to hold two or three people. As he watched the men work, the *cuy* waddled off the cot, slipped between his feet, and escaped through the fold of the tent. The stooges, busy with their task, didn't see the guinea pig ambling off into the Amazonian night.

FIFTY-FIVE

SANCTUARY

HAVING PRESSED HIS BACK INTO A CORNER of the treehouse, Jimmy ate a cheese sandwich. He kept his head down as he chewed, but his eyes occasionally darted at his two rescuers. Gabriel sat at the little table while Sophie arranged the remaining cookies on the platter and tried to think of new ways to befriend Jimmy. She tried not to stare, for she sensed that this frightened him. But she noticed that each of *his* glances lingered slightly longer than the one before.

To help him feel more at home, she had brought her two pets into Sky Palace: Twiggy the teddy-bear hamster, whose legs were just long enough to keep her plump belly off the floor; and Swifty the box turtle, who refused to come out of his shell no matter how much Sophie coaxed and pleaded. She finally gave up and turned to Jimmy: "See: he's kinda' like you."

Gabriel chuckled, but Jimmy looked down and nibbled nervously on the sandwich.

Twiggy explored the small room, sniffing along the seam where the wall met the tiled floor. Gabriel touched the hamster with iffy finger swipes, as if checking a hot stove. "You can hold her," Sophie said. "You just have to be gentle." She picked it up and caressed its soft, coffee-colored fur that was punctuated with cream-colored spots. "She's almost one year old," Sophie said proudly.

328

Emboldened by the demonstration, Gabriel eagerly held out his hands. "Okay, okay; let me try..."

Just as Sophie carefully held out the hamster, the sound of slamming car doors startled both Jimmy and Twiggy. She placed the rodent into Gabriel's hands and looked out of the window that faced the lane. Her mom, Ms. D., and Ms. P. were walking into the Sampson's backyard. All three women were staring straight at Sky Palace as they strode, and her mom quickly spotted Sophie's face in the window.

"Sophia Sampson!" she called out in the most peeved voice Sophie had ever heard her use.

"Oh, crap!" she exclaimed.

Hearing a word that sounded vaguely forbidden, Gabriel and Jimmy looked at each other with surprised expressions. Gabriel giggled.

Still spying out the window, Sophie considered announcing—in her most royal highness-like accent—that Sky Palace was off-limits to grown-ups. But as her mother rapidly approached, Sophie got a clearer look at her eyes and realized the royal decree would be useless. She scrambled to the door of Sky Palace just as the women reached the trunk of the tree.

"Sophia, you come out of there right now," Pam ordered.

I was on the third floor, trying to arrange the room that would become my study, when I heard the distinct slam of a car door from the lane, followed by another, then another. From the window that overlooked the front of the house I saw Laine, Pam, and Jean marching into the Sampson's backyard. Their pace and bearing indicated a definite sense of purpose.

By the time I walked downstairs and entered the gate of our neighbor's yard, something like a standoff had taken shape: Pam was ordering Sophie to come down from her treehouse, but Sophie was kneeling in the doorway and explaining that she had to look after her "guests."

Laine saw me approaching and quickly walked out to meet me. "What's going on?" I asked.

She slipped her arm around my arm and led me away from the treehouse. "It's a family thing," she said.

"What sort of family thing?" I asked, looking over my shoulder.

"Sophie lied to her mom, and—well, you know how these things can get…"

In the background I heard Sophie pleading: "—I can't tell him to do that. He's scared, Mom. He's really, really scared."

Mindful that Gabriel was in the treehouse, I turned to Laine: "Who is she talking about?"

"Oh, one of her friends," Laine said, still trying to guide me away from the scene. But the more I overheard, the more I resisted her pull.

"I have to take care of him," Pam said. "Now bring him out here."

"But he's fine, Mom," Sophie replied, "I'm taking care of him. You know how you always taught us to never mistreat a guest? Well, he's my guest."

Pam was about to say something when she looked over at me. I could sense a sudden effort to still a rising tide of anger. Laine gave another tug at my arm, but I gently pulled away and walked toward the treehouse. "Gabriel's in there," I said to Pam. "He told me that he and Sophie were alone."

"It's a day of fibs and revelations," Jean drawled as I strode past her.

"What's going on?" I asked Pam.

She opened her mouth to speak, but her effort dissolved into a sigh of resignation.

"What's going on here?" I asked again, looking at all four faces, but no one answered.

My temper flared. "Gabriel," I growled, "are you in there?"

"Yes, Dad."

"Show yourself, right now!"

He squeezed his body into the doorway next to Sophie. "Hi, Dad," he said, smiling sheepishly.

"Who else is in there?"

"Sophie."

"I know that," I snarled, "I can see her. Who else is in there?"

Gabriel looked at Sophie as if for guidance, which sparked another eruption from me.

"Who else is in there?" I yelled loud enough to be heard at the end of Bog Lane.

"Jimmy." As Gabriel said the name, a voice whimpered from inside the treehouse.

"You're scaring him to death," Sophie said, scolding me with her eyes. "Keep your voice down."

I had no intention of being shushed. I looked at Pam and Jean but they each glanced away. The piteous sound of weeping grew more distinct and Sophie disappeared inside the treehouse, leaving Gabriel in the small doorway.

"Jimmy who?" I demanded in my sternest voice.

"You know," he said, as if the answer was perfectly obvious, "the boy who used to live in our house."

FIFTY-SIX

TEQUILA SUNRISE

SOMEONE WAS TOUCHING HIS SHOULDER. Pensador awoke to see Tom Fester's round, jowly face looming over him. "Sorry," the engineer said, "but where does a guy have to go to get a decent cup of coffee around here?" He was still wearing the floral beach shirt from last night.

Pensador checked his watch: 6:37AM. "Depends on what you mean by decent," he replied groggily. "If you mean tasty, you'll have to walk a few hundred miles."

"At this point I'll drink anything that tastes remotely like coffee," Tom said as he sagged into a canvas chair and fanned his face with a straw sun hat. "I thought I knew what humidity was," he wheezed. "Ignorance really is bliss…"

"Welcome to the Amazon," Pensador said, sitting up on the edge of the cot.

"Did you get any sleep?"

"Off and on. In and out," Pensador replied as he stood up and stretched. "How about you?"

"The same. Your father kept those three workers busy most of the night. Two of them were trying to make some campfire coffee on the hill a little while ago, but Lex was teaching them to say something in the Inucan language. He had them repeat the phrase about a thousand times. I was in my tent but I couldn't shut out their voices. Now I can't get them out of my head. I only understand the first word of the phrase that Lex taught them: *Pensador*. That's what they call you around here, right? The rest of the words were gibberish. But they keep playing in my head, like a bad TV jingle."

Pensador had turned on his battery-operated hot plate and began heating enough water for one mug of instant coffee. "What were the sounds? Repeat the sentence for me."

Tom did his best to duplicate the syllables and consonants, but his tongue had difficulty with the pronunciations. Still, Pensador was able to make out each word. "What does it mean?" Tom asked.

Pensador translated the statement into English: "*Pensador said please come now to the gathering place. Very important.*" The fact that his father had used his name without his permission was bothersome, yet it was the least of Pensador's worries. He went to the flap of the tent and peered out. The sky was completely covered by a patchwork of clouds, but he could see the indistinct disc that had crested in the east. Its light, though filtered by layers of atmospheric gauze, burnished the narrow range of colors that draped the landscape. From the sandy brown soil, to the terra cotta huts, up to the virescent hues of the trees—the Amazonian tableau was unadorned by artificial surfaces or colors.

Inucans were streaming across this primeval vista to *la recognus*. Yoro was already there, standing by himself under one end of the massive awning. He had positioned himself in front of the stage that the stooges had built during the night. But the only thing on the platform was the large pine box. Pensador wanted Yoro to stand a bit farther from the box, but he persuaded himself that there was enough distance between the Sartum and the stage. Two of the stooges had apparently gone from hut to hut repeating Lex's sentence and usurping Pensador's name. Now it seemed as if the entire tribe was responding to the request.

"Where is Lynn?" Pensador asked.

"She had just come up the hill when I was getting ready to come down here," Tom said. "As I was leaving, she and Lex started to argue about something. What the hell is happening here, Hitch? Seems like everyone is tensed up or arguing or hiding something. What the hell is going on?"

"You're in luck," Pensador said, sitting back on the cot, "because at the moment I have nothing else to do but explain." He reached over and pulled a half-full bottle of tequila out of a knapsack.

"You're drinking at this hour?" Tom asked, staring in disbelief.

"I've got a feeling it's going to be one of those mornings," he said.

Richard Hitchens strode down the path from *Kalsulnak* to the Inucan village. As he drew closer to his appointment with destiny, he wanted to preserve the scene for posterity. He wanted to memorize every sight and sound as clearly as possible so that he could give an accurate account of this day in his autobiography.

It had occurred to him that individuals who changed the course of history often didn't realize they were doing so. A twenty-three year old Albert Einstein served as a junior clerk in the Swiss Patent Office. He sat at his desk, day after day, imagining things about space and time that no one had ever imagined before. All the while, his bosses were telling him to spend his time examining things like horse harnesses and mechanical nose-pickers. As young Einstein tried to confine his mind to that miniscule job, did he suspect that his fantastic but still private notions were going to change the course of physics and our understanding of the universe? Probably not, Hitchens concluded.

And what of the cranky but little-known teacher at the University of Padua who decided to check Aristotle's teachings on motion and mechanics? On the day when the professor measured the velocity of falling objects, some of his colleagues smirked at him. It was perfectly silly to go to all this trouble, they quipped. Of course heavier objects fall at faster speeds—it was a matter of common sense! But the crusty pedagogue was determined to put common sense to the test. Hitchens would have loved to see the faces of those critics when their presumptions plummeted and collapsed before their eyes. The professor's modest experiment helped give scientific methodology a central place at the table of Western Civilization, and it also launched one of the most spectacularly productive careers in the history of science. Yet, as that tradesman's son quietly gauged the rates at which various objects fell, he didn't realize that four centuries later his name—Galileo Galilei—would be known by every educated person on earth.

And what of the tanner's son who was rated "mediocre" in chemistry when he took the entrance exam to *Ecole Normale Superieure* in Paris? How could his professors have known that this mediocrity would devise chemical experiments that would eventually save countless lives? How could they have deduced that this nobody would someday be ranked as the greatest scientist of medicine *ever*? Indeed, on that day when he had to contend with the disdainful eyes of his superiors, how could a nineteen year-old Louis Pasteur have known what the future had in store for him?

Unlike those gifted men at those auspicious moments, Richard Heinrich Hitchens had no intention of letting his own "threshold instant" pass unnoticed. Someday, when journalists asked him, *"Was there a moment when everything was about to go wrong, and you took action to save the entire project?"* Hitchens would be ready with the answer, complete with vivid descriptions and step-by-step narrative. Even the geography was symbolic: he was walking down a mount to educate a group of people who were waiting down below. He had scaled the heights of scientific knowledge and was now descending to share his self-attained enlightenment with the human race.

The setting was mythic, yet perfectly real.

Hitchens stopped at the outskirts of the village. Beyond a cluster of huts he could see the towering roof of la recognus. He imagined a beam of radiant sunlight bursting through the clouds and illuminating its weather-beaten shingles. But there were no symbolic shafts of light from the cosmos on this day, so Hitchens would have to supply his own light for the occasion. This did not disturb him in the least.

He strode into the village.

FIFTY-SEVEN

PLYMOUTH MONDAY

Though it felt as if much of my brain was still asleep, I could hear the sound of cardboard sliding against cardboard, followed by the occasional thud of a box landing on the floor. The sounds traveled up the basement steps, through the open door that led to the kitchen, to my chair at the table. Laine's voice followed the same course: "Rick! Did you see the box with the rain gear? You didn't unpack it, did you?"

"There's no rain in sight, honey," I said wearily.

"I'm looking for your waders," she called out. "I'm gonna need them to get into the bog." I heard more rummaging sounds, followed by a happy "Ah-ha! Got 'em!"

"Cranberries aren't ripe yet, honey. It's gonna take another month, I think."

"Some always ripen prematurely. Plus I want to check out the rest of the estate while Tracey checks out the garden."

"Tracey?"

"Tracey Faulk, from Jean's party—remember? She's gonna be here in just a bit."

"Oh, right." Sunday's crises had driven that plan out of my head.

"I'm hoping she'll give me some pointers about growing different plants or maybe even harvesting different kinds of berries. She knows all about that kind of stuff."

"Sounds lovely," I muttered to myself as I brooded over my morning mug of tea.

I wondered if I should be drinking a cup of Laine's brain-blitzing coffee instead. She drank half a pot earlier and the effect was plain to see: she was powering her way from task to task, and searching for other worthy purposes on which to unleash her boundless energy. Meanwhile, I was barely able to finagle my legs into a pair of Bermuda shorts and stagger downstairs.

Along with Jean, Pam, Fran, and Laine, I'd spent half the previous night in the Sampson's kitchen, trying to figure out what to do about Jimmy Hitchens. Now that his immediate physical safety was assured, we had to decide on the next step. Harry had been pointedly excluded from our hand-wringing session. As an assistant D.A. for Plymouth County, he would've been compelled to immediately report the boy's whereabouts to the police, so we kept him in the dark. Jean phoned him to say that she'd be home later; she gave some excuse about hobnobbing with friends. Pam and Laine brought Fran and me up to speed. They explained that Jimmy Hitchens was a mildly autistic and chronically anxious boy, and nothing made him more anxious than his father. Somehow we had to protect him while also protecting our own status as law-abiding citizens. We had to figure out a way to do "the legal thing" while also doing "the right thing."

Around 2AM, after much brain-storming and speculation, we settled on a plan of action: Over breakfast Jean would carefully lay out the situation for her husband. She would inform Harry of the boy's diagnosis. She would tell him about Muriel's involvement. She would explain that Richard Hitchens was a psychologically abusive father whose son had run away from him, and she would also explain that we were acting on the boy's behalf. Jean would tell Harry that the Sampson's were willing to act as the boy's foster parents until his brother returned from South America. She would ask her husband—and, by extension, the Plymouth Police—to take these extraordinary factors into consideration as they set about doing their duty.

It sounded like a good plan at 2AM. But after six hours of restless sleep, I had my doubts. Now, as I sat at my own kitchen table, I wondered how things were going at the Powell's breakfast nook.

With our permission, Sophie, Gabriel, and Jimmy had spent the night in Sky Palace, along with Sophie's hamster and box turtle. Sleeping pads, blankets, and sheets were provided, and Gabriel was delighted to be camping out with his new friends. If nothing else, this novel experience distracted him from Biscuit's absence.

As the brilliant summer morning settled over our seaside town, Gabriel came into the kitchen through the back door and announced that he and Jimmy had to use the bathroom. I had yet to lay eyes on the lad, so I waited for him to appear behind my son. He had been the subject of so much concern and conjecture that I was eager to get a look at him. But Gabriel lingered in the doorway and stared at me.

"Well?" I said, knowing they would have to go through the kitchen to get to the first floor bathroom.

Gabriel stepped back outside and I heard a flurry of garbled words. Then he stepped back in. "Could you go to another room, Dad?"

"Why?"

Gabriel frowned. "Jimmy's kinda' scared of you. He says you're like his dad."

I was wounded. I'd never thought of myself as a tyrant, yet here I was being unfavorably compared to a blatantly oppressive father. I wanted my son to be indignant on my behalf; I wanted him to argue with Jimmy... 'Hey, my dad is a great guy! You won't find a better father anywhere!'

Instead, Gabriel just stood in the doorway, blinking at me. So I grabbed my mug of tea and stood up. "Have it your way," I said sulkily. As I left the room and walked down the main hallway I called over my shoulder, "Mom made French toast—it's in the microwave. You guys can share them. Syrup's on the counter and juice is in the fridge." Behind me I could hear two pairs of little feet pattering through the kitchen.

I swung open the front door and stepped out onto the wraparound porch just as Fran Sampson approached the steps. He lugged a tool-box with his right hand while a military brown duffel bag hung from his left shoulder.

"Morning neighbor," I called out.

He nodded his greeting. "In all my years as a carpenter," he said as he climbed the steps, "this is the first time I've ever walked to work."

I held open the screen door for him. "Is it all it's cracked up to be?"

"It sure is." He stopped on the threshold of my home and added: "Distance matters, but I don't think this job will last long enough for me to get spoiled."

"Let's hope not," I grinned, wondering how many days it would take him to finish the job. Jean's comment about his meticulous work ethic echoed somewhere within: "Perfection takes time, darlin'..."

"The kitchen is straight ahead," I told him, "the back porch is just beyond. I suppose you'll want to start there."

"I'm going to take some measurements and case things out first. Then I'll drive to the lumber yard and see if I can find any good stuff cheap."

"You're the expert." I ushered him indoors, but instead of

following I lingered on the porch, savoring the last few sips of my tea and sizing up the morning. Plymouth seemed to be in store for another perfect summer day. The only blemishes on an azure sky were some milky streaks high in the atmosphere, in that ethereal realm occupied only by supersonic jets and ozone-eating hydrocarbons. Happily, this would be a work-at-home morning for me, and I planned to spend it finishing up some project drafts. I was scheduled to show my designs to a client in Quincy at three o'clock. But Laine and I had planned a barbeque lunch—the first in our new home—to which we invited Jean and the Sampsons. The gas grill was ready for duty in the backyard, and we were all anxious to hear about Jean's talk with Harry.

I swallowed the last drop of tea just as a blue Toyota Corolla hatchback pulled down Bog Lane and stopped in front of my steps. Through its open windows I could hear two familiar but irritated voices trade the parting shots of a quarrel.

"It's not your decision; just let me handle it my way."

"I'm just giving you a better way to deal with it."

"You're micro-managing again, that's what you're doing." Tracey Faulk, wearing blue jeans and a pink short-sleeve shirt, stepped out of the car and slammed the door shut. A light blue shoulder bag clapped gently against her back as she hiked up my front steps.

"Then do it your way," Pat Bishop snapped from the driver's seat.

"I intend to," Tracey retorted without breaking stride.

"Fine."

Tracey bounded to the top step of the porch and almost bumped into me. "Oh! Sorry!" She unslung the backpack with one hand and brushed a few strands of brown hair from her face with the other.

"Good morning," I smiled.

"Yeah," she said, trying to collect herself. "I hope I'm not too early."

"Not at all. Pinball girl is rushing around somewhere inside. She loves to give people the tour. She'll show you the basement, too."

"Pinball girl?"

"Laine. After she's had a quart of her coffee she bounces from one job to another like a pinball in an arcade game."

"Oh, my."

"Speaking of her coffee, would you like a cup? Gauranteed to keep you going for three or four days..."

"No, thanks," Tracey said. "I'd like to get right to the garden, if that's okay..."

"Sure thing." I opened the screen door for her. "Is Pat coming in?"

"Oh, God," Tracey moaned as she entered the house, "I hope not."

I walked down to Pat's car and found her sitting at the driver's seat with her forehead resting against the steering wheel.

"Ahh," I commiserated, "I wish I had a nickel for everytime I've used my steering wheel as a head massager."

Pat peered up. She had that pained look of exasperation that can only be inflicted on us by our loved ones. "Women," she muttered, "what the hell do they really want?"

I shook my head. "It's one of life's greatest mysteries. Just when you think you know the answer, the answer changes."

Pat nodded glumly. "Ain't that the truth."

FIFTY-EIGHT

BUILDING BLOCKS

PENSADOR TOOK A SWIG OF TEQUILA straight from the bottle. He closed his eyes as the liquid seared the soft tissue of his mouth, throat, and finally his brain. The mildly-pleasurable burn leached across the barrier between flesh and consciousness. This was precisely the effect he craved. He savored the feeling a moment longer, then turned to the engineer. "Do you know what a transgenic organism is?"

"Trans-genic organism," Tom repeated and considered the phrase as if it were a mathematical equation. "Cross-over animal?"

"You're onto it," Pensador said. "A transgenic organism is created when one animal's genes are effectively inserted into another animal."

"You mean like interbreeding?"

"Sort of. Except that the transference may occur between animals that could never breed in nature."

"So how can it happen?"

"Scientists have been genetically engineering organisms since the early seventies. They started with tiny things like viruses and bacteria, and gradually worked their way up the chain of life. But within the past fifteen years Lexel Corporation has excelled in this area. We've used the methods and technologies developed by other labs and gone full throttle." Pensador took another shot of tequila then ran a hand under his lip. "Of course, we've had to do much of our work in secret. But even with that limitation, we've done things no one else has dreamed of, except for a few science-fiction writers."

Tom looked skeptically at his host. "You're not going to tell me that you've created new lifeforms?"

Pensador grinned at his guest. "As a matter of fact..."

"You mean microscopic life?"

"Oh, no," Pensador said, stretching the syllables of each word. "We're way beyond microbes and molecules. I'm talking about highly-evolved mammals: chimpanzees, dolphins, dogs, and—in the not-so-highly evolved category—certain reptiles."

Tom stared back at Pensador. "Wait a sec. You're telling me that you've taken parts of different animals and stitched them all together, sort of like a Frankenstein thing?"

Pensador laughed. "It's not quite so crude. We took the microscopic building blocks of various organisms—their genes—and spliced them into other animals."

"How is that possible?"

"It's possible because—except for some viruses made of RNA instead of DNA—the genes of all animals have the same basic structure and function in the same basic ways."

"You mean my genes and a worm's genes are the same?"

"The arrangement of the genetic bases is different, which makes a huge difference in the resulting organism. But the raw materials are the same. A mansion and a barn look completely different, yet they are made of the same fundamental substances, and those substances work in the same fundamental ways."

"So these 'building blocks' are interchangeable?"

"Right. Now don't misunderstand—this sort of thing is *not* easily done. But when a foreign gene is successfully spliced into an organism's cellular system, that animal's body begins to produce the proteins for which the spliced gene codes. In this way one species may take on some of the characteristics of a different species."

Tom shook his head. "But how do you know which genes will have what effect?"

"We don't," Pensador replied, but added with a sardonic smile: "at least *we didn't*. A lot of our successes were dicey affairs, to put it mildly. We often implanted genes without really knowing what sort of effect they would have. We learned through innumerable trials and almost as many errors. Lexel has had about forty talented researchers working in three different labs for well over ten years. I won't tell you about the countless disappointments; all the grisly failures—all the times when we came this close to quitting. But we kept going because people like Lex and Lynn just refused to give up."

"Lynn?" Tom pointed the direction of Kalsulnak. "Our Lynn Lee?"

"The same," Pensador said. "Don't let her quiet disposition fool you. She's a driven, chain-smoking bitch. You won't find five people on this planet who know more about genetics than our Miss Lee. She eats, drinks, and breathes this stuff. It's the only thing in life that really matters to her. More than any other person, she's the brains behind Lexel's breakthroughs."

"I thought Lex was the brains of the outfit."

"Lex is the grand strategist behind Lexel. He gives us our sailing orders and plots our destinations. He also writes all the checks. But without Lynn's genius, Lexel could never have created the menagerie it has created."

"Menagerie?" The questions seemed so ridiculous that Tom couldn't suppress a chuckle. "You mean like a zoo full of weird new animals?"

Pensador nodded.

"Where do you keep these animals?"

"Most of them are dead. We killed them ourselves."

A perplexed look sagged over the engineer's face.

"It wasn't the animals we were interested in," Pensador explained, "it was the knowledge and the technology that created them—that's what we were after." He took another sip, but didn't take his eyes off his guest until he lowered the bottle. "However, there was one particular creature we were very interested in creating."

"What creature?"

"Our lab name for it was Surutas."

"Surutas. What is it?"

The pot of water on the hot plate simmered loud enough to distract Pensador from his answer. As he got up and mixed a cup of instant coffee for the engineer, he explained the legend of Surutas and its crucial place in Inucan culture.

Richard Hitchens stood next to the large pine box on the newly-constructed platform and smiled down at Yoro. Dozens of other Inucans had also gathered at la recognus, but none of them came as close to the stage as their Sartum. More Amerindians streamed from their huts toward the capacious shelter in the center of the village, though some stopped and waited just beyond the structure. Hitchens scanned the gathering crowd, then raised both arms and gestured for the Inucans to draw closer. "Come, my friends," he called out. "Don't be…" he couldn't think of the Inucan word for "timid," so he settled for the Spanish timido. But he quickly realized that the Inucans might not be familiar with this word, so he repeated his call, using the Inucan word for 'afraid' in place of 'timid.'

"Where is Pensador?" Yoro asked. His voice sounded as if it was layered with pebbles.

"He will join us later," Hitchens replied. He could sense some annoyance and anxiety in many of the faces in the crowd, starting with Yoro's. The Inucans were probably irked that the normal rhythms of their daily lives had been disrupted.

No matter how culturally primitive the Amerindians might be, Lex viewed the tribe as a microcosm of the human race. Like the rest of humanity, the Inucans substituted subjective perceptions for genuine truth. Like the rest of humanity, the Inucans were swayed by their spiritual beliefs. And, like the rest of humanity, the Inucans shrank away from the vigorous pursuit of real progress and settled for cozy mediocrity. Fearful of suffering and failure, they huddled in their psychological caves and let precious time slip away. They didn't realize that advancement has never occurred without jeopardy, pain, and hardship. Great progress always involves great risk. So it remained for one visionary individual to push the human race out of its cloistered cave of superstition onto the broad, sunlit plains of scientific understanding.

Of course, people around the world wouldn't immediately realize that Hitchens was performing an unprecedented service to the species. When finally faced with Lexel's *fait accompli*—a group of genetically advanced humans—Hitchens and his corporation would be denounced by commentators of all stripes. He had no illusions about the world's knee-jerk reaction. But when journalists actually met Lexel's creations, they would gradually realize there was nothing to fear. The new race would look much like the old race, except that it would be a blend of humanity's current colors and facial traits. No members of the new race would have a propensity for chubbiness or skinniness, and they would all be of roughly medium build and medium height. More importantly, humanity's current susceptibility to genetic defect and physical disease would be abolished. But the crowning achievement would be the new race's capacity for critical thought. Hitchens's Homo sapiens would be uniformly intelligent; although they would be capable of experiencing subjective perceptions and emotion, their minds would be ruled by objective thought and pure logic.

The details of Lexel's revolutionary work would then be made available to the international scientific community. Researchers in all nations would thus be free to use Lexel's methods and designs to improve their own societies. In this way, Hitchens would rewrite the script of human destiny. In return for a period of unrestricted research, countless generations of human frailty and despair would be derailed. For the first time in their long, sad history, Homo sapiens would gaze out upon a bright and breathtakingly clear horizon. Hitchens knew that this extraordinary achievement was within his reach. He only needed three things: time, human subjects, and freedom from government agencies and watchdog groups.

As he thought about the second item on his list, he looked down at Yoro and smiled again. The Sartum looked up at him but didn't smile. Hitchens turned his attention back to the gathering villagers. It seemed that the entire tribe was now within the sound of his voice, so he began: "My dear friends…"

FIFTY-NINE

THE LESSON

"No!" Fran's voice resounded from inside my house. "Put that down!"

I said a hasty goodbye to Pat and went inside to find Fran on one knee in front of Gabriel, holding a nail gun in his hands. Jimmy disappeared out the back door just as I entered the room.

"This is a tool," Fran explained, "but it can hurt you if you don't use it the right way."

"What does it do?" Gabriel asked, staring at the yellow and black device. He'd probably been drawn to it because it looked like a big, colorful water pistol. Laine and Tracey appeared in the doorway that led to the cellar steps as Fran held out the nail gun.

In a glance they understood why Fran had shouted.

"Not to worry," he said to Laine, "I forgot that the battery pack wasn't even attached. The boys weren't in any danger."

"You'll have to be extra careful with those kinds of tools," she said. "Gabriel hones in on anything dangerous." She and Tracey walked across the kitchen, and I noticed that Laine held the thigh-high pair of wading boots in one hand and a shopping bag in the other.

"You're already done in the basement?" I asked Tracey as she walked by me.

"No way," she said. "I want to get a look at the flowers in the yard first. I'm saving the underground garden for last. But I saw enough to figure out one thing: those organic support beams aren't organic at all. They are reinforced cement pillars with steel attachments and lots of moss or lichen crawling over them. Someone wanted them to look like trees, but they're not trees. And I'm thinking there are more surprises in store down there. Based on what I just saw, it's going to take me at least a couple of hours to get the whole garden on film."

"Great," I said. "You can join us for lunch and clue us in on what's going on down there. We're gonna have a little barbeque in the backyard."

"You've got a deal," she smiled.

Fran had turned his attention back to Gabriel, who was still eyeing the nail gun. "This helps me to do my job," he said. "It pushes nails into wood."

"Like a hammer?"

"Sort of; except you don't have to hit it against the nail. You just…here, I'll show you."

Laine had stopped at the back door to watch Fran instruct Gabriel. As a teacher, she was often troubled by his easily-distracted mind. But she marveled at his ability to focus on things that captured his fancy. When he was interested in something, his retentive powers verged on the photographic. The trick was to get him interested.

Fran reached into his duffel bag which slumped next to him on the floor and groped around for a few seconds. He pulled out a short brace of two-by-fours that were already nailed together. He placed the wood on the floor and positioned the barrel of the nail gun over the top of the block. "Now watch…"

Jean watched Harry rub his hands over his face. "Please tell me I'm still asleep," he said. "Please tell me this is all just a dream." When he had come downstairs several minutes earlier she realized he was in a hurry. His unknotted tie looped over his shoulder as he rifled through the study and shoved a couple of documents into his briefcase. Even the sight and smell of his favorite breakfast dish—cheese and mushroom omelet—didn't slow him down very much. Jean had planned to unload Sunday's events on him very carefully as he ate. But he dug into his meal so quickly that she told her story much faster than expected, without all of the nuances and descriptions that she had rehearsed in her mind.

Now his elbows were propped on the table, his head was cradled in his hands over the half-eaten omelet, and he moaned quietly as if he had a bad case of indigestion. "You had to tell me this now. You've known about it for nearly twenty-four hours but you chose this moment—forty minutes before I have to meet with my boss—to let me in on the secret."

"Oh, Harry, you know what you're going to do," Jean said. "And we know you've gotta' do it. All we ask is that you treat this as an extremely unusual case. All we ask—"

"Who is *we*? Who else knows?"

"Well, let's see. There's Muriel, of course. Then there's Pam and Laine. Then Rick found out. Then we told Fran. And Sophie knows, too. Oh, and Gabriel."

"What? You haven't told the mailman?"

"Oh, hunneee," Jean exclaimed as she rose from the table and went to the counter. "It's not easy keeping this sort of thing a secret—"

"You did a damned fine job keeping it a secret from me!"

"That's different! You work for the D.A." She poured herself a second cup of coffee. "Wanna refill?"

"No," he moaned, "but I'll take a handful of antacids."

Jean sat next to him and stroked his arm. "Harry, please try to understand that this little boy has been through hell. He's seven years old—seven! Do you remember when Delaney was seven? Remember how frightened she was of thunder storms and TV monsters and being in a room alone? Well Jimmy is pretty much all alone in the world. His mother is dead. His own father kicked him to the curb. His only sibling is running around on some other continent. And, on top of everything else, this kid is battling against autism. The law-enforcement folks have gotta cut this little boy a big break. They can't just stick him in some foster home full of strangers, or hand him back to the unlovin' bastard who chased him away in the first place."

Harry sat back and folded his arms. "Okay, Jean," he sighed. "What do you want me to do?"

Fran squeezed the trigger and the nail-gun discharged with an unexpectedly forceful CA-THUNK! He then showed Gabriel the block. Though only the surface of the nail's head could be seen, Gabriel realized that the gun had rammed the steel missile into solid wood. "Wow!" my son's eyes lit up. "Can I try?"

Laine smiled. With her teacher's soul satisfied, she stepped through the back doorway. Tracey flashed a half-grin at me: "And they wonder where future N.R.A. members will come from." She followed Laine out to the bog.

SIXTY

S-53

TOM WANTED THE COFFEE TO INVEIGLE his nervous system and hijack his muscles; he wanted his body to do the caffeine rumba all the way back to Miami. Pensador's brew certainly packed a punch. He'd mixed so much powder into the mug that the scalding water took on the consistency of silt. But it wasn't potent enough to propel him out of the village. All Tom could do was pace the length of the tent as he tried to wrap his mind around everything Hitch had just told him. The whole story sounded like something out of Hindu scripture, replete with incarnations and apocalyptic prophecies. The problem was that Hitch told the story with an absolutely straight face, and no matter how much Tom didn't want to believe it, he suspected that it was the unvarnished truth.

When the engineer had worked for Lexel Corporation in the past, its officials always played it close to the vest, revealing very few details about their purposes and objectives. But now Hitch seemed determined to come clean about Lexel's mission. Tom felt a bit like a priest in a confessional booth listening to a man unburden his conscience. But as the engineer paced to and fro, he could also hear Lex addressing the Inucans in the middle of the village. The C.E.O. seemed to be givng a speech, but the words were in a language Tom didn't understand.

Hitch ignored his father's voice and continued with his explanation. "Our version of Surutas is different from anything that's ever existed.

Our final version—the one that matched our specifications—was Surutas number fifty-three. S-53 for short."

"You mean there was an S-1, S-2, S-3, and so on?"

"Yes, but each number represents an entire brood, not an individual creature. We started with about ten breeding females, each of which produced dozens of offspring in each brood. After years of breeding, neurological tinkering, and genetic transplants, the fifty-third brood produced the creature we wanted; hence: S-53. It has the right pigmentation, metabolic rate, cognitive capacity—"

"Cognitive capacity?" Tom felt a dull ache somewhere within. "You gave this thing the ability to think? To solve problems?"

"We wanted it to be smart enough to learn; we needed it to be trainable. So we tried to endow the various specimens in our labs with some of the mental capacities of higher mammals, like dogs, chimps, and dolphins. We failed trial after trial, year after year. But then there was one tiny breakthrough, followed by a slightly bigger success weeks later, followed by...well, you get the idea. After a dozen years we were almost too successful: S-53's mother was too smart for her own good."

"Mother? You mean one female produced fifty-three broods?"

"No, no," Hitch said, waving the bottle of tequila in front of him. "S-53's mother came out of the forty-first brood. She was an S-41. Her pigmentation was almost perfect. We actually considered using her as our final Surutas. But she was as mean as a Tasmanian devil. She didn't even kill its prey before devouring it; she ate her prey *while killing* the poor animal. Needless to say, she just didn't have a trainable temperament."

Outside, Tom could still hear Lex, who was speaking to the Inucans in his most diplomatic voice. But then he heard a raspy, defiant voice talking back to the C.E.O.

Hitch paid no attention to the exchange. "So instead of using S-41 as our final Surutas, we used her to breed more batches. We gave her a hyperactive metabolism to speed up her gestation periods, but it hiked her appetite and made her as predacious as a bull shark. Over time she became enormous. She also learned quickly from her experiences and became more unpredictable. Eventually she became so big and so cagey that we had to knock her out with sedatives before we could do any work on her."

"Big reptiles are scary enough," Tom said. "I can't imagine one with a big brain. Gives me the heebie-jeebies just thinking about it."

Hitch nodded. "It was a bit unsettling to look at her and find her looking back at you. For some reason that I don't fully understand, our genetic and neurological tinkering altered the eyes of our Surutases. Shape, size, color—their pupils and irises actually changed. Even the framework around the eyes seemed to change. This was very noticeable in S-41. Every time you looked at her you got the idea that she was wondering about things. It seemed as if she was on the verge of becoming some sort of self-conscious being." Hitch took another swig and then glanced at the bottle to gauge the amount of liquor that was left.

"Where is she now?"

"Rotting in a cranberry bog in Plymouth, Massachusetts. Though I don't imagine very much of her carcass remains at this point."

Tom considered this for a moment. "How did she die? She didn't fill the pockets of her overcoat with stones and jump into the bog, did she?"

Hitch laughed. "She was incredibly smart for a non-human, but not that smart—she wasn't capable of philosophical reflection. No, Tom, it wasn't suicide; it was reptocide, if you will. After she had served her purpose by producing the Surutas we wanted, Lex shot her with a lethal hypodermic. But I don't think it was the poison that killed her; she was too damned big. It would've taken two or three hypodermic bullets to put her down. We had her in a sealed room, but before Lex could reload the hypo-rifle she escaped."

"Didn't you just tell me she was dead?"

"She is. But I don't think it was the hypodermic that killed her. She was killed by the cold."

Tom shook his head and held up the fleshy white palms of his hands. "Wait a sec. Exactly how did the thing escape from a sealed room? And exactly how did she die?"

Hitch sighed. "To understand how it happened you've got to understand *where* it happened. We created a huge terrarium in the basement of Lex's house in Plymouth. That's where we kept almost all the Surutases. But we needed an enormous supply of water to recreate a rainforest environment. So we constructed a tunnel under the basement of the house and diverted a stream from a bog in the backyard. A steel hatchway was built into the floor right over the tunnel. We'd tap water from the stream and funnel it into a sprinkler system in the terrarium. Also, during the summer months, we'd leave the hatchway open so that the Surutases could go into the tunnel and swim to the bog."

"Didn't they just crawl away from the bog?"

"We had a specially designed fence constructed around the bog so they couldn't leave the area, and a much larger fence surrounded Lex's entire estate." Hitch paused and looked away. "I hope Lex pulled out the smaller fence before selling the house." He braced himself with another sip of tequila. "We made the decision to kill S-53's mother last December. The steel hatch to the underground tunnel was closed and locked with a simple hasp device. When Lex shot the first hypodermic into S-41, she crawled to the hatch, undid the hasp lock with her tongue, then curled her tongue around the handle and lifted the hatch open. Then she plunged into the tunnel and swam to the bog before Lex could reload and get another shot off."

Tom stared at Hitch; his speechless mouth hung half open.

"Yeah," Hitch nodded. "If I hadn't seen it with my own eyes I wouldn't believe it either. We never dreamed she'd become *that* clever."

"But if she got away—"

"There was no warm place for her to go. Remember: this happened on a December night in Plymouth, Massachusetts. The temperature outside was exactly 29 degrees. She crawled out to an environment that was literally freezing, and we slammed the steel hatch shut behind her. S-41 was a creature of the tropics—there is no way she could have survived for more than a few minutes in the December cold of the northern U.S.A."

"Did you find the dead body in the bog the next day?"

Hitch shook his head. "The bog was already icing over, so her body couldn't float to the surface. By the time winter ended, almost four months later, there was nothing left of her to float to the surface. Bacteria and parasites and scavengers probably nibbled her dead flesh down to nothing. She's long gone, Tom. Long gone."

SIXTY-ONE

THE BOG

TRACEY STOOD BEHIND LAINE AND WATCHED her slowly step into the bog. Waders covered her blue jeans up to her thighs, and she held an old hockey stick upside down in her hand. She used the stick to balance herself and to probe the floor of the bog. "Jeez Louise," she said, "this is a steeper drop-off than I expected. I don't think I can go much farther without drenching my jeans."

"I was afraid of that," Tracey said, scanning the bog. "Too bad you don't have a set of fisherman's overalls. Then you could go in right up to your chest."

"I don't know about that," Laine replied. "The bottom of the bog feels really mucky, and it gets muckier every step. The middle must be like quicksand."

"Oh," Tracey replied. She saw that most of the cranberries congregated in the center of the marsh, well beyond Laine's reach. But a few clusters pebbled the surface of the water around the fringe of the bog. "Maybe you can scoop up these berries over here, to your left."

"Good idea," Laine said. "Could you hand me the colander from the bag?"

As Tracey crouched down to get the colander she saw a hole in the ground next to the shopping bag. It was a perfectly circular opening, at least half an inch in diameter. She noticed another hole about a yard away, then another about a yard beyond that, then another... She stood up and realized that the holes had been drilled all around the bog. The sight of these strange apertures jogged something in her memory. Over the years she and Pat had visited many exotic sites throughout Central America, South America, and the Pacific islands. Her particular interest had been botanical displays, but Pat was drawn to zoological sites. Somewhere, during one of those trips, she had seen a similar configuration of holes, but she couldn't recall exactly where that was.

"Tracey," Laine said, distracting the veterinarian from her train of thought, "the colander."

Tracey tossed the quart-sized plastic strainer into the bog; it bounced off the hockey stick and plopped into the water, creating a ripple that gently expanded across the otherwise placid pond. But as Laine reached over to pick up the floating colander she slipped on the muck under her feet and thrashed around for a moment before regaining her balance. "Whew!" Laine exclaimed. After a few deep breaths she half-glanced over her shoulder at Tracey. "I hope your video camera didn't catch that act."

"I haven't pulled any of the cameras out of my pack yet. But I'd like to get a look at the rest of the vegetation around the place, if that's okay."

"Sure!" Laine said as she scooped up a cluster of cranberries. "Let me know if you find anything interesting."

Ripples stirred against the predator's face. It had been sleeping in the tunnel that led to the marsh, with its snout angled just above the surface of the water, when it sensed that something had either entered the bog or was moving around in the water. Now, as it became increasingly conscious, the diamond-shaped pupils of its eyes shrank in the morning light.

A deep pain ripped through the flesh somewhere in its body. For several days and nights, the pain had slowly gotten sharper and deeper. The predator had twisted, turned, stretched, and moved its body in every possible way to ease the ache, but the pain only got worse. Just above its head was the round, steel door that led to its old lair. The thing had spent part of the night trying to push this door open. But no matter how hard it pushed, and no matter how enraged it became, it couldn't break through. At some point during the night, exhausted from its efforts and its anger, the predator fell into an unsatisfying, pain-curdled sleep. Now, with its hunger inflamed by last night's exertion and rage, it awoke to the promise of easy prey, spluttering somewhere in the pond. Maybe food would ease its pain. The creature slowly moved through the tunnel, toward the source of the disturbance. Its senses were attuned to any sight, sound, or movement that might guide it to a living thing.

Gabriel walked up to Sky Palace. He wanted to tell Jimmy all about the nail gun. Sophie's dad had let him fire the gun into a chunk of wood, then he let him hold the gun while he worked on the front porch, though he removed the battery first. And before Mr. Sampson left to get more wood, he promised to teach Gabriel some things about hammers and nails later.

As Gabriel approached the treehouse, Twiggy the hamster crawled onto the threshold of the open door and sniffed nervously. Sophie called from inside: "Look out for her! Close the door!"

Gabriel got a glimpse of Jimmy as he obediently closed the door. But rather than keep Twiggy in the treehouse, the closing door pushed her out. The rodent slid down the slope of branch bark, rolled over twice, then bounced off the tree trunk before falling the last few feet to the ground. Gabriel rushed up and stared at the hamster's body; its little white paws were sticking almost straight up. Jimmy quickly climbed down and stood next to Gabriel. Sophie appeared in the doorway. "Oh, no!" she cried. "Bring her back up here!"

Neither boy moved. "You pick her up," Gabriel whispered to Jimmy.

"You do it," Jimmy whispered back.

"I didn't let her out," Gabriel said.

"I didn't, either," Jimmy replied.

"Yeah, but—"

"Oh, you sissies!" Sophie huffed. "I'll do it!" But just as the girl positioned her leg outside the doorway, Twiggy twitched. The boys jumped back just in time to see her twitch again. Then she rolled over onto her paws, sniffed the air, and scurried off. "Get her!" Sophie cried. "Don't let her get away."

Gabriel chased after Twiggy. The hamster ran to the end of the lawn, toward the fence that separated the Sampson's yard from the Delvecchio's yard. There it paused for a moment and sniffed the air. Just as Gabriel closed in, the rodent squeezed through one of the holes at the bottom of the chain-link fence. Jimmy, who was running slightly behind and to the right of Gabriel, saw Twiggy slip into the other yard. He veered to the teepee-shaped opening in the fence and quickly crawled through. Gabriel followed close behind. Together they chased Twiggy toward the bog, laughing as they went.

SIXTY-TWO

WHAT IF?

STANDING BY MARA'S SIDE on the outskirts of *la recognus*, Felipe listened as Richard Hitchens addressed the crowd from a makeshift stage. His tone was friendly; his words were carefully chosen but his purpose was vague. It had all the earmarks of a political speech. Hitchens wanted to convince the Inucans of something, but he didn't come right out and tell them what that *something* was. It seemed that he first wanted to lull the Amerindians into a state of charmed agreement, or sleepy submission, or some blend of the two. But Yoro, who stood directly in front of the stage, was having none of it. He had already interrupted the C.E.O. four times to ask questions. Each successive question was more challenging and each response from Hitchens was less cordial.

Felipe noticed that the three Brazilian workers had separated and positioned themselves about fifty feet away from the crowd. One man stood north of la recognus; another stood off to the east, behind the tribe; and the third occupied a spot to the south of the crowd, near Pensador's tent. The nurse also noticed that these men now carried holstered firearms. The mounting tension was as thick as the humidity. Felipe wondered where Pensador was. He turned and looked at his tent, and thought he saw movement through its slightly-parted front folds.

Tom had resumed pacing. Lex's voice sliced through the opening between double furls of tent fabric, and even though the speech was being delivered in the Inucan language, Tom knew that it was gradually becoming less of a speech and more of a debate. But Lex's son seemed strangely unconcerned by whatever was happening in the center of the village. He sat on his cot, balancing the bottle of tequila on his thigh, thinking about other revelations he might pass on to the engineer. The man whom the Inucans knew as Pensador had polished off almost a quarter of the bottle, yet his voice remained steady and his faculties seemed as sharp as ever.

"The important thing," Hitch continued, speaking over his father's voice, "was that S-41 had served her purpose: she gave birth to the creature we wanted—the creature that matched our specifications. S-53's temperament isn't perfect, but he has learned to respond to a simple set of instructions, which are given in the form of click sounds. As long as his behavior is reinforced with food within a reasonable time-span, he responds to the clicks just as he was trained to respond."

"What's 'a reasonable time-span'? Five seconds?"

Pensador smiled. "Even though we sped up the metabolisms of all our Surutases, he can go about twenty-four hours without a snack."

"What happens if he goes longer without a snack? Does he just drop dead?" The final word of Tom's question spiked upward in an unmistakable inflection of hope.

"Sorry to disappoint you," Hitch replied, "but S-53 only becomes surlier when he isn't fed. If he is being ordered to perform while raven-ous, he'll probably turn on the nearest person."

Tom shook his head and slouched back into the canvas chair. "You're talking about this stuff so...so casually. It's as if we're discussing cars or sports or some run-of-the-mill thing. But this is crazy business: intelligent reptiles; ancient legends; a plan to engineer a new breed of humans. You've gotta' be shittin' me!"

Hitch looked down at the orange floor of the tent. "I wish..." he said quietly.

Tom eyed his host and remembered last night's argument between Hitch and Lex. He began to understand Hitch's strangely detached attitude and his willingness to divulge the details of Lexel's project. When the engineer spoke again, his reflective tone invited more confessions. "Seems like you're not on board any more. Have you lost faith in Lexel's mission?"

A forlorn grin creased Hitch's lips. "That's an interesting choice of words, Tom. Maybe I've—"

The raspy voice outside the tent spoke out again, but this time it was louder and angrier. Lex responded in kind.

"What the hell is happening out there?" Tom got up and began to move toward the tent flap. Hitch quickly rose from his cot, still holding the bottle of tequila, and stepped in front of the engineer. But instead of pushing the tent flaps open and going outside, he turned and faced Tom.

"What are you doing?" Tom asked.

"I'd like to ask you a question."

The engineer, bewildered by Hitch's behavior, could only stare at him.

"What if you had met Vladimir Lenin in 1917, before he created the Soviet Union and all the mostrosities it would breed—"

"Monstrosities?"

"You know: party dictatorship, Stalinism, gulags, pogroms and purges... Would you have killed him? Would you have killed Lenin?"

"What?"

"And if you had killed him, would it be murder or would it be justifiable homicide?"

Tom looked intently at Hitch but couldn't detect any obvious sign of madness. Except for the bottle of tequila in his hand, he seemed like a perfectly self-possessed man, calmly thinking out loud.

"Or what if you had come across Adolf Hitler in a deserted field somewhere in Germany in 1932? And what if you knew a great deal about him, and you had some very strong intuition about what he was going to do…"

Outside the tent Tom could hear Lex's voice and the other, gravelly voice, fighting to be heard. Hitch ignored the argument and continued asking questions.

"And what if you had the means to get rid of young Adolf right then and there? Would it be murder? Would it be wrong? Or would it be right?"

"I don't know what the hell you're talking about," Tom said.

"I'm asking you a hypothetical question," Hitch replied. "Historians do it all the time. They ask each other 'What if this had happened instead of that? How would the world be different?'"

"I'm not a historian," Tom said. "I'm not a psychiatrist and I'm not a priest—I'm just a freakin' engineer." Outside the voices continued to clash.

"But you've got a mind," Hitch replied. "You've got the power to think about these kinds of things."

"I think I'd rather not think about them."

"But sometimes we have to do things we don't want to do," Hitch said. "For the greater good—for the sake of justice, or perhaps kindness—sometimes we have to do things we don't really want to do."

"All I want to do right now is get out of this village." Tom stepped forward and hoped that Hitch would move out of his way, but the tall man didn't budge.

"You don't want to go out there right now," he said.

"Why not?" Before his question could be answered, Tom heard Lex shout Hitch's first name.

"Because," Hitch said, ignoring his father's call, "something bad is about to happen."

"*Steven,*" Lex bellowed, "*come out here!*"

"I think your father is calling you," Tom said.

"Yes," the tall man said in a strangely reflective tone, "he has called me many things. Many of them weren't very nice."

Tom drew back and looked up at Hitch's steadfast blue eyes. "This is getting just a little too weird for me, Hitch. I'd think I'd really like to go now."

"You won't like it out there, Tom. It's going to get…ugly."

One of Lex's workmen pushed through the folds of the tent and said something in Portuguese to Hitch. Without turning to face the man, Hitch replied in the same tongue. The man looked surprised. He started to speak again but Hitch barked something at him. The worker turned and left.

Still looking at Tom, Hitch reverted to English. "You're free to go, if you want. But unless you keep your eyes closed when you step out of this tent, you're going to have nightmares for a long time." Hitch stepped aside to let Tom pass.

Outside, Tom heard Lex's voice rising to a fever pitch. The engineer didn't move.

"Wise choice," Hitch said. "You know, Tom," he continued in a matter-of-fact tone, "nature designed us so that we can close our eyes. But we can't close our ears." He held out the bottle of tequila, which was still a quarter full. "So you might want a shot of this stuff right about now."

SIXTY-THREE

REMAINS

TRACEY WALKED ON A DIRT PATH that led through the wooded area beyond the bog. With each step she was more impressed at the sheer size of the Delvecchio's yard. Now she understood why Jean had referred to it as an "estate." Then she came upon a far more delightful surprise: a cluster of red-petaled Lobelias. These strikingly beautiful plants, also known as Cardinal Flowers, had become a rare sight in the moist woodlands of the eastern United States, which was their natural habitat. But here she counted no less than six fully-developed stalks. They sprouted out of some bushes that fringed a small stream. The tallest stalk was nearly four feet, and, best of all, almost all of the crimson bulbs were in full bloom. She quickly unslung her backpack and crouched down to grab her digital camera.

Then something caught her eye. What seemed to be a large letter S had been etched lengthwise into the soil of the path. When she stood up to get a better look at the pattern she saw that it wasn't a discrete S but a continuous impression—about a foot wide—meandering down the trail all the way back to the bog. She had been so captivated by the plants and flowers on either side of the path that she hadn't noticed this strange, unbroken imprint beneath her feet. It was as if someone had taken a push broom and walked the length of the trail, weaving from one side of the path to the other, pushing

down hard on the broom all the while. She scanned the trail ahead
of her and saw that the brush marks veered off the path into some
hydrangea bushes about twenty feet away.

Her curiosity aroused, Tracey walked toward the hydrangeas,
still holding the *Nikon* in her hand. As she drew closer, she became
aware of an unpleasant odor. On the side of the trail where the
marks began, she saw a large pile of animal feces. A thick streak
of white uric acid laced the black, pulpy stool. From her veterinary
work she knew that this dropping had come from a reptile, but how
could it? She didn't know of any reptile that could produce so large
a stool. A section of vegetation behind the feces was flattened, as if
a heavy object had rolled over it.

Without going any farther, she reached over and parted the
upper twigs of the bushes that were still standing. A swarm of flies
buzzed noisily around her hand as the odor became heavier and
more repugnant. Holding her breath, she arched her head over the
parted shrubbery and looked down. There, on the opposite bank of
a small stream, was a large black sneaker. It was positioned upright
and its cord was securely tied. She noticed that the sneaker was
filled out, not saggy or shriveled the way abandoned sneakers are
supposed to look. Then she realized that a foot was in the sneaker,
but where the ankle should have been, there was a serrated mass of
bony, detached flesh.

A wave of nausea swept through her as the flies continued
to flit and drone. Before she could pull herself away, she saw the
bottom of a pant-leg dipping into the water farther downstream—
the same stream that fed the bog where Laine was scooping up
cranberries. Unable to restrain herself, she parted the bushes a bit
more to reveal a tall, armless body. There was no shirt; just a pair
of dungarees that looked as if they had been slathered in acid. A
slightly-twisted spinal column emerged from the waist; portions

of its tiered vertebrae were visible under clingy sinews of decaying flesh. Somehow, a head was still attached to the spine, but there were only gaping holes where the eyes should have been. A pocked, filmy underlayer of rotting tissue—clotted by blood stains and flecked by chunks of gristle—couldn't hide the distinctive shape of a human skull.

Tracey stumbled back to the path and fell to her knees. All of her training as a veterinarian hadn't prepared her for this moment. She fought the urge to throw-up, but was unable to keep her mind from seeing that rancid body. As the hideous image flashed again and again, the question *What is it?* infiltrated her racing thoughts. She sensed that she already held the answer to that question. Other images flashed: the neatly drilled holes around the bog; the sinuous, winding marks on the trail; the flattened vegetation; the pile of feces streaked by uric acid; the regurgitated body.

Regurgitated. The body had been regurgitated. Suddenly Tracey knew what *it* was.

Then another image appeared in her mind: Laine, standing thigh-deep in the bog, completely unaware. Summing up all of her willpower, Tracey struggled to her feet and began running toward the bog. Still holding her digital camera, she didn't stop to pick up the backpack on the path. It was all she could do to gather enough air in her lungs to scream.

SIXTY-FOUR

THE INCARNATION

YORO TURNED AWAY FROM THE STAGE and faced the tribe. His grizzled features were taut and Felipe could see that his patience had frayed to the snapping point. "This man is a deceiver," he cried, pointing back at Pensador's father. "See him clearly! See him through the cloud of pretty words! See him for what he is: an outsider who wants something from us, *but won't tell us what he wants!*"

"I will tell you," Richard Hitchens seethed through gritted teeth, "if you'll stop interrupting me."

"You've had enough time to tell us," Yoro shot back over his shoulder. "You've been talking long enough to tell us about the world and life and science...Why don't you just tell us *what you want?*"

"If you'll shut your—"

"And where is your son?" the Sartum continued. "Your men said that Pensador wanted to talk to us. Why isn't he here? He has earned the right to give us long speeches—you haven't."

Hitchens glowered down at Yoro, but the Sartum folded his arms across his chest and waited. The outsider suddenly called out: "Steven!... Steven, get out here!"

The Inucans thought the tall man on the stage was shouting at Yoro because his eyes were still fixed on him. But Felipe understood English well enough to know that the man was calling Pensador by his real name. Richard Hitchens gestured to the worker who had positioned

369

himself near Pensador's tent. The worker turned and disappeared into the tent, but reappeared a moment later and shook his head at the stage.

"Wake him up!" Hitchens shouted in Portuguese.

"He is awake," the man answered, "but he won't come out."

Felipe was standing off to one side of the crowd, about thirty feet from Hitchens, but even at that distance he could see his face turn pale and stiff. "I know you can hear me, Steven," the man shouted in English. "I want you to know that you are fired! Fired!" The Inucans glanced at each other and wondered what the outsider was yelling about. "As of this moment you no longer have a place in Lexel; and by the end of today, your name will no longer have a place in my will. I am finished with you! *Do you hear me? Finished!*"

Breathing heavily, Hitchens's looked down at the large box on the stage before turning his attention back to Yoro. He quickly mastered his rage, but continued speaking English: "Okay, Geronimo, you wanted me to hurry up and tell the truth? Well here comes more truth than you can handle." Hitchens pulled a silver device out of his breast pocket while his other hand undid the lock on the wooden box. Reverting to the Inucan tongue, he shouted a sentence that he had been reciting in his mind for over ten years: "My friends, the prophecies of your ancestors have come true this day!" With a powerful heave he flung open the box's lid. The large chunk of wood swung over, snapped off its hinges, and clattered off the back of the platform.

For a moment, nothing moved. Then Hitchens pressed the device in his hand, which produced a loud, metallic *click*. Immediately a white, triangular head—at least as large as Hitchens's head—arose from the container, followed by a white, serpentine body that was thicker than any human thigh. A chorus of moans, gasps, and screams came from the crowd.

Felipe tried to identify the creature: it had the massive body of an anaconda, but it had the head of a python—an abnormally large python.

Its eyes were unlike anything he had ever seen. Its pupils were distorted black rectangles framed against greenish-gray irises, surrounded by mustard yellow sclera. Staring at the eye on the right side of the creature's head, Felipe got the distinct feeling that the snake possessed some form of *awareness* far beyond its reptilian caste. Considering the size of the thing's head and the section of its body that he could see, Felipe estimated that it was about twenty feet long.

More and more of the snake's body unfurled from the box until its face hovered several feet above and beyond the stage. Felipe was too stunned to move or look away, but out of the corner of his eye he saw the entire tribe move back a step or two, beginning with the villagers who were closest to the platform. The only person who didn't step back was Yoro, who stood alone only several feet in front of the stage.

"Behold Surutas!" cried Pensador's father as he extended his arms toward the crowd.

"Science has brought the white incarnation to you. From this day on, everything will be different. Behold the incarnation!"

Some of the Inucans fell to their knees.

"Science has mastered your prophecies! Behold your god! Science is the master of your god!"

More villagers bowed down. Children followed their parents' example. Inucans who were too old to kneel sat on *chonta* stools and lowered their trembling heads.

"Behold the power!" Hitchens's triumphant voice reverberated through *la recognus*.

Soon almost all the Inucans had bowed, in one way or another, before the hideous gaze of the albino serpent. Some were lying face down, overcome with fear and wonder. Mara, who had been standing next to Felipe, sank to one knee but continued to stare at the white snake. Within ninety seconds of Surutas's appearance, the only villagers left standing were Yoro, Felipe, and Sarpay the elder, whose diminutive frame didn't become visible until all the people around her had bowed down to the incarnation. Like Yoro, she refused to kneel but, like her kins-people, she was awed by the creature. Felipe sensed she was fighting an inner battle to remain on her feet—a struggle that required all of her reason, willpower, and faith. As the nurse glanced around, he noticed that the three workers who had taken up strategic positions beyond the awning had their hands on their holstered firearms. Their eyes were wide with anxiety and astonishment, and Felipe realized that they too had no idea what had lurked in the box.

Hitchens stared down at Yoro. "Bow to the power, my friend."

Felipe couldn't see the Sartum's face, but his body didn't move.

As it inched ever nearer to Yoro, the serpent's long, angular head moved from side to side so that each of its shrinking pupils could gauge the distance to Yoro's face. A thin tongue, several inches long, darted in and out of a small hole in front of the snake's closed jaws. Each flick poked the air closer to the Sartum's face. Felipe thought that if the tongue had been a flame, Yoro's eyebrows would have been singed.

"Grandfather," Mara cried, "come away from there!"

"Bow to the power," the outsider said again, staring down at the Sartum. Felipe noticed that Hitchens's gray-tinged scalp moved left and right, almost imitating the movements of the serpent's head. As his face swiveled rhythmically from side to side, a strange gleam seemed to fill the outsider's eyes, no less freakish than the light that glimmered in the snake's eyes.

Yoro made no move to defend himself, but he stood his ground. Though his people were huddled or cowering, their faces popped up again and again as they became aware of the contest of wills that was unfolding between their Sartum and Pensador's father.

A double *click* filled the air and the snake writhed menacingly in front of Yoro's face. "Bow to the power," Hitchens thundered.

Yoro didn't turn, but he spoke loud enough to be heard by the entire tribe: "I bow only to goodness. I bow only to the Spirit." He seemed to be looking at the foot of the stage. Felipe moved forward and saw enough of Yoro's profile to realize that his eyes were closed. Suddenly Mara grabbed Felipe's arm and held it tight.

"Don't go," she pleaded.

"You must bow to truth," Hitchens advised the Sartum. "It would be foolish to deny the evidence that stares you in the face." As he spoke, the white snake hovered in front of Yoro, its head still angling right and left; its tongue flicking in and out. The beast seemed to be taking the measure of the old warrior.

Yoro kept his head down and his eyes closed; the only muscles he moved were those that enabled him to speak: "I do not deny the truth; but your truth is *un-whole*."

"My truth is science," Hitchens retorted, "and science is the *only real* truth. Here is the *proof*. Behold what my truth has created. See what my truth can do..." He clicked the device in his hand twice, and the snake again thrashed in frenzied spasms as if it had been prodded with an electrical charge.

"Grandfather!" Mara cried again. She was down on one knee, gripping Felipe's arm with both of her hands, but looking at Yoro. "Come away from there!"

"Yours is only a cold sliver of the truth," the Sartum's voice quavered as he defied the outsider. "It is only the sliver that can be proved to your hard mind—it is only the sliver that you can *fit into* your mind. But there is much more that cannot fit."

"You superstitious idiot!" Hitchens snapped. "There is nothing more! There is nothing else!"

Eyes still closed, Yoro's voice lost its tremor and took on a mildly rhythmic cadence as he recited the words of an Inucan poem: "The whole truth is infinite and eternal..."

"There is only what we have here and now!" Hitchens roared, overlapping Yoro's verses.

"...it cannot be squeezed into our heads..."

"Must Surutas make you suffer?"

"...it can only be touched by our hearts."

"Must you be sacrificed to Surutas?"

Yoro slowly looked up and faced Hitchens. "You can kill me, but the death of my body won't darken the eternal light—the light that we will all return to, sooner or later."

"Light?" Hitchens laughed and raised his arms searchingly. "Where is this light?"

"Those whose eyes see deeper truth," Yoro said, "see the light that shines through goodness and love. I would rather die on the side of good, than live as a slave of evil."

Out of the corner of his eye Felipe saw an Inucan rise to his feet near Sarpay. It was Destro, the warrior. Ashamed of his own cowardice, he spoke loud enough for Yoro to clearly hear him: "I bow only to goodness." Another Inucan quickly stood up at the back of la recognus. It was Hanoq, the elder, looking frightened, regretful, and defiant all at once. "I bow only to goodness," he intoned. Then Mara stood up by Felipe's side. Her fingers trembled as they gripped his arm. "I bow only to goodness," she said, as much to her grandfather as to the outsider on the stage.

Hitchens was speechless as he watched more Inucans stand up and repeat the Sartum's statement. Soon the entire tribe was on its feet, challenging the outsider with their still, silent, unbent bodies. When Felipe looked back at the stage he saw that Yoro hadn't moved, but the snake's head had sunk low to the ground in front of the platform. It seemed to be searching for something. The more it probed, the more its attitude seemed to change. Its pupils shrank; a fold of leathery flesh pinched down toward the iris, and its jaws opened just enough to reveal two rows of backward slanting fangs. Felipe wasn't sure if he could believe his own eyes, but the thing actually looked *angry*.

Hitchens, still staring at the tribe, didn't notice this change. His focus shifted to the three workers who nervously maintained their separate positions on the outskirts of la recognus. All three men still had their hands on the hilts of their guns. As the outsider's gaze settled back on Yoro, he seemed to be considering his next course of action. Slowly at first, but with an increasingly vigorous motion, he nodded. Hitchens was unaware that the snake's head was now only inches away from his knees and rising toward his chest.

Felipe began to call out but Hitchens's voice, thick with contempt, cut him off: "Very well! If a clearer demonstration is what you need..." He lifted his arm high in the air, but just as his hand pressed the metal device, the serpent's head darted upward. Felipe heard a *crunch* as the creature's jaws bit into Hitchen's exposed right arm-pit. He yelled and fell off the stage. More screams pierced the air as the Inucans pushed away from the platform and began to flee. The crowd disintegrated into chaos.

Felipe tried to move toward the platform, but Mara locked her hands around his body and refused to let go. Though Hitchen's had fallen to the ground on the other side of the platform, Felipe could hear him calling frantically for help. The snake coiled up and back, and for a moment its sinuous body formed a white question-mark above the stage. Its jaws separated to reveal slanted fangs, dripping with Hitchens's blood. A shred of the man's shirt hung from the front of the predator's mouth. Realizing that it was about to strike again, the outsider cried out in Portuguese, "Kill it! Kill it!" But the creature's head plunged downward and Hitchens's commands turned into screams.

As Felipe tried to free himself from Mara's tenacious grip without hurting her, he saw Yoro jump onto the stage and wrap his arms around the snake's body. The old warrior was trying to pull the serpent off the outsider. Hitchen's feet became visible at the corner of the stage—they kicked and flailed as if he was having a violent epileptic seizure. The man's body rapidly shimmied away from the platform so that his knees came into Felipe's view, followed by his thighs, hips, waist, stomach, chest, and neck. All the while the man's screams were strangley muffled. When Hitchens's head came into view, Felipe saw the reason why his screams were muted: the thing's fangs were clamped deep into the man's face, covering his mouth. Fighting for his life, Hitchens clawed at the serpent's jaws, but he couldn't pry them open. Red streams trickled out of the creature's mouth, forming rust-colored puddles as the blood mixed into the soil.

Gunshots suddenly ripped through la recognus. Felipe heard a bullet whiz by his ear. He turned on Mara, pushed her to the ground, and draped his body over hers.

SIXTY-FIVE

DEATH STRUGGLE

"OH NO!"

The cry reached up to my third floor study, but it took me a second to identify Sophie's voice. Though I'd only been working for a short while that morning, I was already looking for an excuse to take a break, so I pushed away from my drafting desk to see what sort of mischief the kids were into.

An ocean breeze carried the scent of moist sand and seaweed up to my veranda. Three floors below, Gabriel and Jimmy were chasing Twiggy toward the fence that divided our yard from the Sampson's yard. Crouching in the doorway of her treehouse, Sophie was urging the boys to catch her pet. For them it was a game, and their laughter filled our pastoral slice of Plymouth, garbed in its kindest colors. From my rooftop vantage point, the bushes and trees formed ridges and hillocks of luxuriant green, speckled by the pastel pinks, violets, and saffrons of flower blossoms. Deep summer seemed to shimmer from every living thing. If I possessed even a shred of artistic talent, I would've traded my draftsman's desk for an easel and set up shop right there on the portico. The reality of my situation hadn't ceased to amaze me: How could my name be on the deed of so beautiful a chunk of the world?

But I understood enough about human nature to know that we eventually devalue just about anything in our grip. From the first instant that we "have" something, its sheen slowly dulls in our minds, until we yawn at things that once took our breath away. Only the terrible ache of loss—or an inspired vision of the heart—restores our appreciation. But on that serene summer morning, as pastel petals and children's laughter floated on seabreezes, I was sure that it would be a long time before my human nature could diminish the beauty of this Eden.

A warning shriek speared my moment of peace.

The voice was so shrill that I couldn't make out the words. At first I thought it was Sophie, but the young girl was looking around from the doorway of her treehouse, just as startled and curious as I was. I quickly moved to the other side of the veranda. Gabriel and Jimmy had cornered Twiggy on the edge of the bog, but they had stopped to look at Tracey who was sprinting out of the woods.

"Get out of the water!" she screamed. "Get away from the water!" Her face was wild with fear.

Laine had already emerged from the cranberry bog. She was bending over, about to remove the waders from her legs, when she turned to see the veterinarian running toward her and pointing. I quickly realized that Tracey wasn't pointing at Laine; she was pointing at the marsh just beyond.

I looked down at the bog and saw a large, white S slowly float up through the murky water. As it came nearer to the surface, it looked less like a rope than a hose—a white, S-shaped rubber tube that became more enormous before my eyes. It must have been thirty feet long and at least two feet in diameter. I noticed that it was slowly moving toward the far side of the pond, as if it were propelling itself—as if it were actually alive.

But that was ridiculous. Dinosaurs had been extinct for eons, and there were no white reptiles—much less a white reptile as long as a bus and as thick as a grand oak.

Yet the thing in the bog undulated just like some absurdly gigantic snake.

I stared at the bizarre sight and something caught in my throat. I began to cough and choke. For a moment my heart seemed to stop beating. As I struggled to breathe, a sickening realization overwhelmed every reasonable assumption in my neatly ordered little world: The Thing in the bog was exactly what it seemed to be.

Pain stabbed again and again. Something kept biting and clawing at the middle of the predator's body, but when it turned to face its attacker, nothing was there except its own smooth flesh. How could its attacker be invisible? And how could the creature fight an enemy that it couldn't see or smell?

The only thing that could distract the predator from its unseen tormentor was the instinct to crush and eat. Warm, pulsing food would push the pain away. Driven by its hunger and drawn by the movement of meaty prey, the predator crossed to the other side of the bog. But whatever had been there had since left the bog. Fury shuddered through the predator's body. It wanted to turn its rage and agony into a howl. Yet it couldn't howl. It sensed, somehow, that it should be able to howl. But no matter how the predator flexed its mouth and strained its neck, there was no release of energy—no relief from the pressure and pain that mounted within. The predator lifted its head out of the water and wrenched its jaws wide, but a tortured hiss was the only noise it could make. Its fangs flashed for the whole world to see. As its tongue stretched toward the sky, it caught the musky scent of familiar prey. Following the direction of the smell, it saw the rodent at the edge of the pond. Though it was small—so small that the predator wouldn't have the satisfaction of crushing it to death—it would still provide a warm-blooded morsel.

With one thrust the creature glided to the shore-line, but the rodent was already running from the bog. The predator then saw two bigger animals on either side of the fleeing rodent. They were big-heads, and both were standing still. Though they were smaller than other big-heads, they weren't too small to crush; and either one would fill the predator's body with warm, oozing meat. The creature crawled out of the bog toward the nearest one.

My paralysis lasted for an eternal two or three seconds. During that endless moment, the giant Thing flashed a mouthful of gleaming white spikes skyward. Jimmy was standing almost directly below me, between the west end of the bog and the back door of the house. Gabriel was standing several feet farther out. Both of them seemed to be in a state of shock. Laine rushed toward the boys, but the bulky waders made her stumble and fall. She tried to kick the waders off as she yelled—as much at the Thing as at the boys—"Get away! Get away!" At the same time, Tracey was sprinting around the bog, screaming at Gabriel and Jimmy to run. She threw a small object at the Creature; an object which broke into silvery pieces against its head. The crash of metal and plastic jolted me out of my frozen state. I flew downstairs, sprawled onto the second floor landing, scrambled to my feet and kept running. As I plunged down the steps, my mind raced ahead of me, trying to think of anything that could be used as a weapon.

Tracey screamed another warning as she hurried around the bog toward the boys, but they seemed unable to move. The Thing was closing fast on them. She flung her camera, which shattered on the its massive skull, but this distracted it for only a second. In the blur of the moment, as she glanced around for a weapon, she thought she saw someone rush out the back door of the house. Tracey grabbed the only thing within reach: a metal rack from the outdoor grill. The Thing slithered to the blond boy's side and began to encircle him. Tracey was about to throw the grate when the person who had rushed through the back door took hold of the doomed boy's shoulders. It was a tall woman wearing black rags. With a ferocious grunt she lifted the boy just as the serpentine body constricted. Its sinewy flesh coiled around the boy's legs, but the woman pulled so hard that his feet came out of his sneakers, which remained trapped in the snake's leathery grip. She stumbled backward, still holding the blond boy in one arm, while scrambling away on her other three limbs like a crab.

It didn't chase her. Instead, it turned toward the other boy who stood just a few feet away. He was trembling and whimpering. Tracey knew that the boy's nervous system was so overwhelmed that it had virtually shorted out. He could not move. But the giant serpent was moving all too fast. It didn't try to encircle its prey this time; it simply lunged straight for the boy's head. Tracey jumped in front of him, holding the grate out with both hands as if it were a shield. The force of the reptile's thrust threw her back onto the boy and they both fell to the ground. The Thing snapped at her as she lay face up, but she again held out the rectangular grid with both hands. Enamel clanged on steel as the serpent's teeth clamped down on the outer edge of the rack. The predator's four longest fangs sliced between the bars. The Thing pulled back but Tracey refused to let go of the grate. Unable to extricate its fangs, the predator strained its jaws against the makeshift shield, and its steel bars slowly started to bend before Tracey's eyes. She was staring through the grid, directly into the predator's gaping mouth. The veterinarian saw fresh blood coating the inside of its throat, yet there was no blood on its fangs. Somehow, she realized, it was bleeding internally, but she didn't know why and she couldn't tell how fast it was losing blood. She gripped the grill grate with all her strength as the predator pushed it closer to her face. As its jaws slowly folded the metal rack, the predator's enormous, bony head loomed less than a foot away; its thorny, black pupils gazed menacingly into her eyes. Suddenly, a thin muscle shot out of the Thing's mouth. Before she could turn away, the slimy tongue struck her eyes. Tracey cried out as digestive acid stung her corneas. She let go of the rack and desperately tried to wipe the reptilian saliva from her eyes. With a sideways snap of its head, the Thing flung the grill off its fangs, then reared back to inflict a bone-crushing bite.

I was stumbling headlong through the kitchen when I saw the yellow-black nail gun on the shelf where Fran had left it—too high for Gabriel to reach, but not beyond my grasp. I grabbed the tool and plunged out the back door just as it coiled back to strike at Tracey. Gabriel was momentarily safe beneath her, but she was helpless as her fingers swiped at her own closed eyes. The serpent's triangular face burst toward her just as I threw my body against its jaws. The force of the collision snapped its head to one side, but it also sent the nail gun flying out of my hands.

As I got to my feet, Tracey—blinded and in pain—slid off Gabriel and clawed at her own face. My son, now exposed, was curled into a fetal position. His eyes were clenched tight and his hands were cupped around his ears. I rushed to pick him up, but the predator's attention was already locked on me. Its head moved faster than any boxer's fist, and its punch was far more powerful. The Thing's snout caught me just to the right of my stomach and sent me flying backward several feet. I hit the ground and rolled several more feet. With each turn of my body it felt as if jagged pieces of glass were stabbing out of the right side of my torso. I came to a stop at the edge of the bog, but when I tried to get up, excruciating pain wrenched me back down to the ground. The giant had shattered my rib cage.

"What's happening?" Tracey cried. "Someone tell me what's happening!"

Though I couldn't look up to see her, I knew she was blindly groping around. I couldn't answer her question; I couldn't even cry out to my son. Tracey was unable to see, and I was unable to speak or move. I could barely breathe. But out of the corner of my eye I could see the shadow of the Thing against the ground. Its head rose up and looped back; its jaws gaped wide. Only thin air separated the predator's fangs and Gabriel's body.

Suddenly, another figure, moving at breakneck speed, merged with the Thing's shadow. I heard a feverish snort and rolled back just enough to see that Laine had somehow fastened herself to the back of the snake—her legs and arms wrapped tight around it. In one hand she held the nail gun that had flown from my fingers moments earlier. But the creature was writhing so violently that Laine couldn't free her hand long enough to fire a nail. The moment she started to position the gun against the snake's head, she began to lose her grip and risked being thrown off the flailing monster. She hung on to the serpent like a bronco-buster as spasms of rage rifled through its monstrous body.

From my ground's-eye view I saw a tall woman with thatched blond hair creep toward Gabriel on all fours. About thirty feet behind her, Sophie was crying and hugging Jimmy, who had buried his face into her neck. When the woman reached Gabriel, she grabbed his arm and began dragging him toward the Sampson's yard. Tracey kept trying to open her eyes, but she flinched and groaned with each effort. The veterinarian cried out: "Get it from behind! From behind its head! That's its weak spot!"

Tracey had no way of knowing that Laine—perhaps by sheer instinct—had already flung herself on the predator's back and was desperately holding on. The serpent twisted its head left and right, snapping its jaws wildly, but it was unable to sink its fangs into any part of Laine's body. The maddened creature swung, gyrated, and coiled its massive hulk. Still, Laine held tight. A thin, foot-long muscle suddenly shot out of the mammoth mouth and slithered along the right side of its head, back toward Laine. But she turned her face to the left side of the serpent's head, and the tongue could only slather her arm with slime and blood. Then the predator's tongue slithered out of the left side of its mouth, but Laine quickly turned her face to the opposite side of its head. The tongue could do nothing more than leave streaks of reddish mucous on her arms, neck, and shoulders. Tormented by its elusive attacker, the reptile flopped down and rolled over. Laine grunted as the behemoth crushed her body into a puddle of mud. But when the Thing righted itself, Laine was still holding on.

The predator's face contorted with a sharp HISS and a crimson stream dribbled from its mouth. The Thing was bleeding from the inside out. It abruptly arched its head backward as if trying to bite its own tail. This movement left the creature vulnerable for a moment. Sensing this, Laine released her right arm and pressed the nozzle of the nail gun against the serpent's skull. She pulled the trigger, but there was no jolt. She quickly pressed it again and again, but nothing happened.

The tool had no power. Fran must have dutifully detached the battery pack so that Gabriel couldn't play with the gun.

"Damn!" Laine cried, dropping the tool to the ground. But before she could reclaim her double-handed grip on the Thing, it snapped its head and flung her off its back. She landed a couple of feet from me with a brutal thud. The blow left her momentarily senseless.

Finally free of its foe, the reptile coiled back to where Gabriel had lain seconds earlier. But our son was now safely on the other side of the fence. The tall, black-clad woman was hurrying him, Sophie, and Jimmy toward the Sampson home. I saw Pam rush down the steps of her back deck and embrace Sophie, whose body jolted from the force of her sobs. Gabriel and Jimmy, both crying hysterically, squeezed into the hug, and Pam embraced all three children.

Once I knew the kids were safe, a wave of relief washed over my pain. But my attention was quickly drawn back to the Thing, which slithered toward my wife and me. Something like malevolence—or a savage hunger for revenge—glowered from its eyes.

I tried to reach out for Laine, who was still dazed, but I could only move my hand enough to touch her arm. The serpent undulated to within a few feet, then it slowly reared up and loomed over us. I tried to say, "I love you," to Laine, but my voice was as powerless as the nail gun. The predator opened its jaws and a torrent of blood gurgled out of its mouth, foaming into red rivulets that ran down its neck. All at once the enormous head plunged down. I closed my eyes as the force of the serpent's blow sent shockwaves of agony through my body.

"What happened? Someone tell me what the hell is happening?" Tracey's frantic questions made me realize that I was still alive. My eyes slowly opened. A heavy weight was crushing my right hip and chest, and thick, warm liquid was flowing down my leg.

Though the slightest movement hurt, I tilted my head just enough to see the Thing's massive carcass almost covering Laine's body and its triangular head draping mine.

A yellow eye, the size of a baseball, was centered by a black thorn that seemed to be staring straight at me.

But the creature no longer moved.

I heard the sound of people running, coming nearer. Voices

shouted. I heard someone yell, "Call the police!" Then, though it was strained by dread and disbelief, I recognized Harry's voice: "Call an ambulance! Get more help right now!"

SIXTY-SIX

THE PROMISE

HUDDLED FACE-DOWN OVER MARA, Felipe couldn't see what was going on around him. The gunshots were getting louder and he knew that Hitchens's three workers were rushing toward the stage, firing at the snake. Mara's hands were cupped over her ears to block out the deafening shots, so the nurse couldn't ask her if she had been hit by any of the bullets. A quick scan of her body didn't reveal any wounds or blood. She was terrified but uninjured.

The gunfire abruptly stopped.

Felipe got to his knees and glanced around. Most of the Inucans had fled to the nearest huts where they crouched and waited. The trio of Brazilians held their weapons in shooting position and aimed at the upper part of the snake. But the creature was no longer moving. Its thick, tubular body was pocked with bullet holes and red streams flowed down its albino coat. Its lidless eyes, though dimmed by death, remained hideous. Destro and Sarpay rushed by the snake and the three men. As he ran, Destro held tight to the machete that hung from a cord which looped around his waist.

Felipe couldn't see Yoro. He was no longer standing on the stage. The nurse left Mara and reached the other side of the stage just as Destro and Sarpay knelt. Between them lay Yoro's motionless body. The Sartum was face down on the large wooden lid that had snapped off Surutas's box. Felipe immediately saw the hole on the upper part of

Yoro's back. As Destro and Sarpay turned him over, blood flowed from the wound and streamed around the old man's latissimus dorsi muscle, then drew a crimson streak across his ribcage.

Felipe dropped to his knees and examined the exit wound between Yoro's left shoulder and pectoral muscle. The old man's eyes stared straight up and his lips were turning blue. The nurse pulled a white handerchef from his pocket and gently placed it between the entrance wound and the wooden board. In a matter of seconds he judged the bullet's trajectory and feared that it had clipped an artery that branched from Yoro's heart. The nurse turned to call for Mara, but she was already kneeling beside him. Her face was etched with pain and fear as she took hold of her grandfather's hand. Felipe looked at her and spoke clearly but quickly: "Go to my cabin; get the big first-aid kit in the case by the front door, and the—"

"No," said a raspy voice from below. Yoro was looking up at the nurse. "Do nothing. I go."

Mara wept.

Yoro's eyes, glazed and calm, rolled to the other side until they focused on Sarpay's face. "You are Sartum now."

The anguish in her eyes was pierced by shock. She wanted to say *I am a woman*, but could only stare at Yoro.

Even as he strained to breathe, Yoro read Sarpay's thought. "You are the wisest elder; you have a brave and noble heart. Serve our people. Be Sartum." Yoro then looked at Destro. "Obey her as you obey me. Tell the others. It is my choice...my last wish for the people."

The young warrior swallowed hard and bowed his head. "Yes, my Sartum."

Mara's shoulders jerked and a sharp cry shredded the air. "Don't leave us," she blurted.

"Do not despair," Yoro said weakly. "All is mercy."

"Don't go," she pleaded.

"I return to Viro. The Son of Man is holding my hand."

Mara held tight to Yoro's forearm. Her head dropped down and tears fell into the open palm of his right hand.

Yoro looked up at Felipe, who struggled to keep his tears hidden. "Take care of my granddaughter...take care of my people."

Tears flooded Felipe's eyes. He tried to speak, but couldn't. He cleared his throat, and though his voice cracked, he finally voiced a promise loud enough for Yoro to hear: "I will, my friend. I will."

The Sartum stared up, his grey eyes reflecting the clouds that quietly clashed overhead. "Until you cross the river," he said softly, "farewell."

As he watched Yoro's eyes close, Felipe realized that those six words would be his last on Earth. The Sartum's labored breathing continued for several more seconds before fading into silence. Felipe reached out and gently placed two fingers against Yoro's neck. His carotid artery no longer pulsed. The old warrior's soul was gone.

Only the sound of Mara's sobs could be heard. Sarpay leaned over and kissed Yoro's forehead. Felipe and Destro wept quietly, their shoulders slumped.

The nurse then heard a distinct *snap*. He looked up to see that Destro had pulled his machete from the cord that had held it to his waist. In the split second that it took the young warrior to stand up, Felipe saw the dark glint in his eye and knew what it meant. Destro spun around and moved toward Hitchens's three workers.

Two of Hitchens's men were trying to remove the dead snake's fangs from their boss's face. But the third man turned toward Destro and quickly read his intentions. He leveled his pistol at the warrior. "Don't come any closer," he said in Portuguese.

"Stop!" Sarpay ordered, rising to her feet.

Destro halted within six feet of the gun barrel. His taut arm rippled as his hand turned slightly, gripping the machete.

"No more killing," Sarpay said.

Destro turned and looked hard into Sarpay's eyes. She did not flinch or look away. After several tense seconds, the warrior slowly tilted his head toward the woman.

Many of the villagers were returning to *la recognus*. Those who saw Mara weeping over Yoro's body quickly rushed to her side. Others began to gather near the stage. Felipe saw Pensador walking toward the platform. His height and blond hair made him clearly visible amid the crowd. "They were aiming at Surutas," he called out to Destro in the Inucan tongue, "not at Yoro. If you want to blame someone for this, blame me."

Felipe stood up. "Why should we blame you?"

Without answering, Pensador crouched down and helped the two workers unlock the snake's jaws from Hitchens's head. The nurse's sense of duty pushed him forward, but as he approached he realized that there was little he could do to help. The puddle of blood that formed around the prostrate figure was rapidly spreading. The man's only hope was an immediate transfusion, and Felipe had no way of quickly executing such a procedure. Blood was flowing from Hitchens's right armpit. Fang holes also lined his cheeks, jaws, and temporal lobes. Flaps of skin hung off his face, and reddish froth seethed from the intricate network of veins beneath. Felipe looked at Pensador, who was staring at his father. He seemed remarkably calm as he watched the man die. Then, in a voice tinged with polite consideration rather than sorrow, he said, "Sorry I let you down, Dad."

Lex heard his son's words but he was unable to move. He could feel life flowing out of his body, and he knew that no one could save him. He wanted his last words to be an eloquent and memorable summation of all his wisdom. But he hadn't given any thought to what those words would be, for he had expected to live well into his nineties. Nature had endowed him with a brilliant mind and an extraordinary physique, and he had always taken good care of both. So he assumed he had thirty good years ahead of him: three more decades in which to change the world and carve his name into the annals of history. This was to be his version of immortality. His fame would comfort him against the ravages

THE PROMISE

of time. The respect of his colleagues, the accolades of his admirers, and the profound gratitude of his beneficiaries all over the world... these were to be his reward for a supremely courageous and triumphant life. For years he had savored humanity's appreciation again and again—if only in his imagination—for he knew he wouldn't be able to savor anything when he was dead.

But now his life was slipping away all too quickly, and darkness was closing in from every corner. As a matter of intellectual reckoning, Lex had always believed in existential darkness. He agreed with the philosopher who said: *The cosmos is a flaw in the purity of non-being.* So, a long time ago, Lex made a separate peace with the darkness; he had bowed to the purity of non-being, for he concluded that absolute nothingness is the ultimate reality. But the darkness was coming too close now. It was seeping into his lungs, sliding around his muscles, oozing between his thoughts. His life was being absorbed by death, and it didn't feel very peaceful.

A final, frantic storm of thoughts and questions, spurred by death's stranglehold, burst in Lex's mind: *Nothing is literally "no thing"—the absolute absence of all existence or reality—so how can it be the ultimate reality? How can the antithesis of all substance and thought be the all-encompassing truth? "No-thing" is, by definition, devoid of existence, which means that it must derive from something real—like a shadow that is given shape and form by light. This must mean that being, rather than non-being, is the ultimate reality. Pure being might allow entire universes, renegade minds, and even nothingness to exist within its light, just as islands may exist in an otherwise shoreless and global ocean. All encompassing being. Infinite-eternal wholeness. God.*

At that moment, Richard Heinrich Hitchens breathed his last two words on earth: "Oh, shit."

The small group that had gathered around him watched his face go rigid, a look of dismay frozen in his gaping eyes.

"What did he say?" Destro asked Pensador after several seconds had passed. "What do those words mean?"

But Pensador didn't answer. Instead, he reached over and gently closed his father's eyelids. Felipe finally answered for him: "He asked us to say a prayer for his soul."

By nightfall, Inucan women had washed both bodies and wrapped each one in a traditional death shroud. Hitchens's body was placed in Felipe's cabin. It would be flown out by helicopter the following morning.

In the glow of the firepit at *la recognus*, Inucans gathered to take comfort in each other's presence. Pensador, after spending some time with his workers atop Kalsulnak, came into the village and asked Sarpay for permission to address those who had congregated around the fire. Felipe watched her grant his wish with a silent nod. The outsider made his way into the middle of the crowd. Every *chonta* stool was taken, so Pensador sat on the ground. He took a deep breath and looked around. Flickering shadows danced on the solemn faces. Though every voice was silent, every pair of eyes stared back at him: some flared in anger; some seemed adrift in memory; some were damp with grief.

"I am sorry," Pensador began. "I knew that my father would be attacked by Surutas. I allowed that to happen because it was the only way to stop him. If you had rejected his plan to build a laboratory on Kalsulnak, he would have taken control of the village by force."

Pensador paused and looked directly at Destro. "I knew that the Brazilians would shoot at Surutas once the creature attacked my father. But I didn't know that Yoro would risk his life to save my father. Your Sartum was a far better human being than my father or me, and I am truly sorry for the part that I had in his death. I ask…" Pensador stopped and looked down. Then he scanned the faces of the villagers again. "I don't blame you if you don't forgive me. But I beg for your forgiveness."

For a while only the crackling flames could be heard. Then Sarpay asked Pensador how he knew Surutas would attack his father. When Pensador answered her question, Destro followed with another question. Then Hanoq asked a question, and several more Inucans spoke up with their own queries. Pensador answered each one as clearly as possible. He explained about Lexel Corporation, genetic engineering, and his father's grand vision of a re-created human race. He told the Inucans that he had firmly believed in Lexel's mission. He was convinced that the destination would condone the journey.

"What changed your thinking?" Sarpay asked.

"A few things," Pensador said. "One of them was..." He glanced around until he saw Felipe's face in the crowd. A sparse smile formed on his lips. "...One of them was a long talk I had with the nurse in his cabin last Saturday morning."

Felipe was surprised to learn that the conversation had stayed with Pensador.

"There was no play of power during that talk," Pensador continued, "no selfish angles. Felipe didn't look up at me or down at me. He spoke and listened as a friend. I'm not used to being treated that way." Pensador gazed at the nurse a moment longer, then turned to Sarpay. "During our talk, Felipe said a few things that took root in my mind. He said that *the greatest truths cannot be devoured by our intellects: the finite cannot absorb the infinite. We may be able to grapple with ultimate truths, but we have to use all of our inborn resources, not just one of them. Even then, we cannot master those realities in the same way that we can comprehend a law of nature. At some point, truth exceeds our full human grasp. And at that point we take some things largely on faith. But this doesn't have to be blind, unreasoning faith—it can be sensitive, questioning, compassionate faith.*

"Those may seem like simple points to many of you; they may have been explained to you at a young age by your elders. But I never learned those lessons. I spent most of my childhood and young manhood living in the finest schools in the world. Such places taught me a great deal about scientific facts, pure logic, and social power, but they didn't teach me about the truths of the spirit.

"Lexel would have created a race of beings that would only know facts and logic and power: a race of beings engineered to dismiss every deeper, less measurable form of truth." Pensador paused and pursed his lips. "I am sorry that it took me so long to realize how misguided our goals were. Lexel's project seemed brand new to us. We thought we were walking on ground that had never been walked on before. But I'm beginning to understand that the mentality which breathed life into our plans is very old. It's what ancient peoples called *hubris,* and it's been around ever since humans first chose selfish power over compassion.

"Lexel would have put a new coat on that ancient evil. We envisioned human intelligence that would not have to share its conscience with any higher truth. We envisioned a world whose genius would be unrestrained by any form of goodness beyond its own egotism."

As these points settled into the minds of the Amerindians, Pensador heard several voices murmur the same word, *"Atola."*

"I cannot undo the damage that's been done," he continued, "but tomorrow morning all of Lexel's workers will leave this place, never to return. We will leave our tents, tools, and construction materials behind. You are free to do anything you want with them. As of this day, you are free of Lexel."

A youthful voice spoke up from the crowd. "Will you no longer have anything to do with us?" It was one of the teenage boys who Pensador had taught to use a fishing rod.

He smiled at the boy, then looked at Sarpay. "With your permission, I would like to remain until Yoro's funeral. Afterwards, I too will leave the village. But—" Pensador turned to face Felipe— "if the nurse wants to continue his work here, I will make sure he continues to get paid. And the weekly supply trips from Codajas will continue for as long as the Inucan people want them to continue. Also, I will leave one of my satellite cell phones—a special tool to call people far away—with Felipe. A fresh phone will be delivered from Codajas every week. If there is anything the people need or want, have Felipe call me. I will do everything in my power to help the Inucan people."

"Everything in your power?" Sarpay asked.

The right side of Pensador's lip curled up slightly. "Everything short of genetic engineering."

Mara was not present at the gathering. She was in Yoro's hut, where his children and grandchildren were anointing his body in preparation for the funeral pyre. Trackers had been sent to find Cotulko. Sarpay instructed them to tell the shaman what happened, and to ask him to return to his people. Runners had also been sent to the surrounding tribes. Their chiefs and elders would pay their last respects at a ceremony in the village at sunset the following day.

After the service, when darkness covered the Amazon, Yoro's body would be burned. Creatures for miles around would see the flames. The Inucan people would encircle the pyre and sing of death and hope. They would remember, and weep over their earthly loss, as Yoro's body was transformed into vapors. The wind would carry the wisps of smoke across all of the jungle's rivers to distant places—perhaps even across the sacred river that separated mortal life from eternal life.

Surutas had been chopped into pieces by Inucan warriors and buried in a cultivated field, where its meat and blood would nourish a fresh crop of maize. But the creature's jaws and fangs had been removed. Sarpay ordered the skeletal mandible to be placed at the back end of la recognus, where it would serve not as an object of worship, but as a reminder. The new Sartum wanted every Inucan to remember Yoro's final, heroic stand. She wanted unborn generations to know how close the tribe had come to being enslaved. This gleaming chunk of enamel was the symbol of their narrow victory over arrogance and deceit.

It would also serve as a warning to any person with a discerning soul: never bow to any *thing* that can be boxed up by human hands or to any *truth* that can be mastered by human minds.

EPILOGUE

THE MEDALLION

OUR ORDEAL NEVER MADE IT INTO THE NEWSPAPERS or onto TV screens. There were no digitally empowered bystanders to record the event, so it never even made its way onto *You Tube*. And the fact that the incident occurred on a dead-end street in a less-settled section of town helped keep it relatively quiet. Plymouth's finest did their best to squelch the story in its crib. The police were concerned that our near-tragedy would send shock-waves throughout the local community. If the details of our misadventure became public, people would probably wonder about other monstrosities that might have escaped from Lexel's breeding grounds, and such imaginings might set into motion a chain reaction that could have all kinds of grim consequences.

Of course, the EMTs, police officers, and those who saw the gargantuan carcass talked about it to their relatives and friends in spite of the gag order. As might be expected, rumors eventually swirled throughout Plymouth and beyond. In the days after the incident, Fran, Pam, Laine, and I each received calls from a couple of reporters who were investigating the scuttlebutt. But we didn't want our quiet road to turn into a macabre sideshow for townies and tourists, so we lied to the reporters. We told them that a large pet python had escaped from its cage, inflicted a few injuries, and had to be put down. The story, we explained, got blown way out of proportion. The reporters, though suspicious, eventually turned their attention to other happenings. Thus, the rumors about a huge, genetically-engineered predator remain just rumors. But, even as I write these words, the gossip about Bog Lane seems to be mutating into an urban legend.

On the night of our ordeal, a large truck pulled up to my house. Fran told me later that it looked like a large U.P.S. truck, except that it didn't have the U.P.S. logo. A group of men, working under cover of darkness and under the watchful eye of Plymouth's Police Chief, hauled the dead snake out of the backyard and placed it in the truck. Later we learned that the corpse weighed well over a thousand pounds—nearly the weight of an N.F.L. team's entire offensive line—so it required some time and serious effort for the group of men to load up the serpent. But when they were done, they departed as quietly as they had arrived.

The next day a team from the Envirommental Protection Agency came to Bog Lane. They were accompanied by a group of plainclothes men and women who arrived in an unmarked van. Working together, these teams carefully inspected the entire house, the six-acre yard, and the underground jungle. They also examined a laboratory which they found behind the beveled north wall of the huge basement. Fran watched the outdoor portion of their search from his own back yard, but if the searchers found anything of interest they didn't share it with him.

The following day a black woman with shoulder-length hair visited my room at Jordan Hospital. Decked out in a gray business suit, she flashed an impressive-looking badge, but all I really saw were three letters in bold print: F.B.I. She identified herself as Anne Killilea, and told us that she worked out of the Boston office. She then proceeded to tell Laine and me about the underground laboratory that had been discovered. All remaining equipment had been removed from the lab and the area had been scoured with a powerful anti-microbial solution. Agent Killilea told us that our property had been deemed "clean" of artificially-engineered organisms. But my wife and son were staying with the Powells, and they had no intention of moving back to #3 Bog Lane.

Laine then asked a question that had preyed on our thoughts: "What killed the snake? Why did it just drop dead?" Agent Killilea blinked at my wife and said, "I honestly don't know. Our lab is examining the creature now. If we can determine the cause of death, I'll pass it on." With that, she shook our hands and left. Laine and I got the impression we would never see her again. Agent Killilea didn't give us her card, or anything in writing, or even the phone number of a contact person.

But we still had Harry. As assistant D.A. for the county, he was able to use his connections to track the investigation and keep us informed...

Steven Hitchens, the second-highest ranking member of Lexel Corporation, was arrested by F.B.I. agents the instant he landed in Miami. In a matter of days he was sitting before a Senate subcommittee that was investigating genetic research. The panel was hastily convened behind closed doors and, before a single question was asked, Hitchens announced that he was ready and willing to cooperate with the investigation.

The first question concerned the whereabouts of Lexel's Chief Executive Officer. Hitchens reported that the C.E.O.—his own father—had been killed in an accident in Brazil on August 16. One of the senators began to discuss the likelihood of an autopsy, but Hitchens explained that his father's body had been cremated in Venezuela, and the ashes had been scattered over the Carribean Sea. His lawyer—the indefatigable Maxwell Burke—produced a copy of a contract for cremation and "final disposition of mortal remains" which had been signed by a funeral director in Caracas.

At that point one of the senators told Hitchens that a genetically re-engineered snake had terrorized several people at his father's former home in Massachusetts. Hitchens was reportedly stunned. He told the committee that he believed the transgenic reptile had been killed the previous winter. When asked how the serpent might have survived, Hitchens was silent for nearly a minute. Evidently, he was trying to explain the snake's survival to his own incredulous mind. Prompted for an answer, he speculated that as the creature was freezing to death, its transgenic brain must have prodded it to search for a winter den. Somehow, it must have discovered such a place in or around the bog on his father's estate. The shelter must have provided enough subterranean mud for warmth, and enough oxygen to keep the reptile's dormant body alive. Essentially, the serpent must have done what a garter snake does to survive a northern winter: it went into a form of hibernation.

The senators then asked Hitchens about Lexel's research, and the executive spoke for some time about his father's vision of a re-born human race—an entire species "purged of its maladaptive traits and tendencies." But Hitchens also testified that none of the corporation's researchers were told anything about Lexel's long-term goals. The company's chief scientist—a woman named Lynn Piao Lee—had already returned to Taiwan where she was pursuing a position as a university professor. Hitchens assured the committee that Ms. Lee, and all of Lexel's other employees, were uninformed participants in Lexel's larger mission. The senators seemed quite skeptical about this, but Hitchens insisted that all responsibility for any wrongdoing fell squarely on his father and himself. After some discussion between the committee's chairman and its chief attorney, the senators seemed content to close their eyes to the possible culpability of other Lexel employees.

At that point the redoubtable Mr. Burke spoke up. He didn't want his client to be punished more than once for the same offense. So he asked that the federal judgment against Hitchens include any indictments or penalties that might be levied by the governments of Arizona, Florida, and Massachusetts—the states where Lexel's labs were located. In making this request, Burke pointed out that his client had been "cooperative and forthcoming to the fullest degree." After a lengthy recess, the state attorneys agreed to this request. It would save their taxpayers the cost of expensive trials, and it would also keep Lexel's activities as quiet as possible.

On a Friday morning in September, Steven Hitchens appeared before a federal magistrate and essentially threw himself on the mercy of the court. Apparently satisfied with the defendant's contrite attitude, the judge imposed several conditions on Hitchens's probational release: Lexel would pay a considerable fine—somewhere in the vicinity of ninety million dollars—which would be portioned out among the federal and designated state governments. In addition Hitchens would be responsible for all expenses resulting from the attacks of Lexel's transgenic organism. Moreover, all of the company's research and related files were to be turned over to the E.P.A. Hitchens would also have to open all of Lexel's properties to government inspectors and then liquidate the corporation. Finally, he would have to sign a federal court order that contained several conditions: chief among them was the stipulation that he would never engage in, supervise, or be associated with any form of genetic research.

Hitchens signed every document that the authorities placed in front of him.

In fact, when the judge issued his sentence, the corporation was already in the process of being dismantled. Even before he left South America, Hitchens had ordered the company's chief accountant to issue an extremely generous severance package—which included one year's salary—to every Lexel employee.

So, after living on penitentiary food for four weeks, Steven Hitchens was a free man.

The smell of grilling steak, shrimp, and chicken teased my appetite as I sat on a lounge chair in a shaded patch of the Sampson's backyard. Summer was bidding its final adieus to the northern hemisphere, and it was parting on very gracious terms. Even as a few pre-autumn leaves fell lazily from the Sampson's oak tree, sunshine and warm breezes set the spirit of the day. The laughter of children—as resilient as hope itself—once again danced around Sky Palace.

About a month had passed since our bloody encounter with the man-altered predator, and though my ribs hadn't fully mended, I was able to walk, drive, and draft at my desk.

I just had to remember to move cautiously. "Until your bones heal completely," my doctor had advised, "try to think of yourself as a ninety-nine-year-old man." Unfortunately, my body had no problem remembering this advice.

Next to me sat Muriel. A pacemaker kept her heart beating on cue; she also needed to use a walker for indoor travel and a wheelchair for outdoor travel. Despite those limitations, my elderly neighbor was as genial as ever, and she was delighted to see Sophie, Gabriel, and Jimmy playing in the yard as if nothing had happened.

Next to Muriel sat Tracey. After an emergency operation at Massachusetts Eye and Ear Infirmary on August 16, she regained almost all of the vision in her right eye. But the serpent's noxious tongue had scored a direct hit on her left eye before slathering her face with its acid. The veterinarian had undergone a delicate procedure on her left cornea only five days before the Sampson's cookout, so she wore a post-operative patch over that eye. More surgical wizardry would be necessary before she had any hope of ever again seeing the world through her left eye. Pat Bishop, Tracey's partner, doted on her as if she was completely blind, and Tracey did nothing to discourage her attentiveness. But if Pat hadn't been around to assist her companion, I would've been happy to cut up Tracey's food every day and feed it to her by hand if necessary. This woman had saved my son's life. There was no way I could adequately thank such selfless heroism. But I would spend a long time trying to do exactly that.

Laine was up and about, helping Fran and Pam with the cook-out. She had suffered some dark bruises when the serpent hurled her off its neck, but none of her bones had been broken. She and Gabriel had been staying with the Powells since that monstrous Monday morning. However, when she arrived at the Sampson's backyard for the cook-out, she told me that she was ready to move back into our home.

I'd made a point of sleeping in the house since my release from Jordan Hospital. I wanted Laine and Gabriel to know that there were no more monsters, and that it was safe for them to come home. Did I have nightmares? Sure. Occasionally, in the middle of the night, I'd dream that a lissome tongue was sliding across my arm or foot. Suddenly I'd be wide awake: my heart pounding and my hand fumbling for the light switch. It's a rough way to wake up. But I suspect I'll be having such imaginings no matter where I lay my head.

This was to be the Sampson's last barbeque of the season, and they had positioned three picnic tables between their back deck and Sky Palace for the occasion. They had invited Harry and Jean, as well as Delaney and Jeff. Harry did his best to be civil toward his daughter's boyfriend, and Jeff did his best not to antagonize his girlfriend's father. At one point Fran opened the large "adult cooler" and asked Jeff what he wanted to drink. Among the cans of beer and bottles of wine, Jeff saw one small bottle of pinkish liquid sticking through the gleaming pile of chipped ice. "Thank you, sir," he said. "I'll have some lemonade, please." Delaney looked at Jeff, then at her father, then back at Jeff. She burst out laughing. Her laughter was so genuine and infectious that it melted her dad's stern façade into a smile.

The cookout's guest of honor came late, for she was shaking off her own legal and financial troubles. By the time Helga Kristiansund appeared at the back gate, the children had already started to eat. As the tall woman stood tentatively on the other side of the fence, I overheard Jeff say to Delaney, "That's the face I saw in the cellar that night. That's the face that scared the crap out of me."

Delaney stared at the visitor. "THAT face scared you?"

Jeff looked again at Helga and frowned. "Well, you had to be there," he said.

Delaney's doubts were understandable. Helga didn't have the kind of face that sent people scurrying in other directions; she had the kind of face that made male eyes look, and look, and look again.

Pam walked over and welcomed her guest with an embrace. She had met Helga six years ago during a visit to the States. A year later, Pam talked with Helga at Sonya's funeral. But Richard Hitchens, rather than aid their efforts to overcome the language barrier, did every legal thing in his power to keep the women apart.

Now, as the two women renewed their acquaintance, Gabriel cried out, "That's the yellow-haired lady, Dad! That's her!"

I nodded at my son and reassured him with a smile.

In the immediate aftermath of the snake attack, as Tracey, Laine, and I were packed into ambulances, the police led Helga away in handcuffs before any of us had a chance to talk with her. In the ensuing weeks, the Norwegian citizen had been in and out of jails, courtrooms, and psychiatric facilities. But as the details of Lexel's bizarre experiments came to light, the authorities finally realized that Helga Kristiansund wasn't nearly as crazy as they had thought. Indeed, almost all of her frantic claims—which had been dismissed for years as the ravings of an unbalanced mind—turned out to be true. The Norwegian Consulate won Helga's release from U.S. custody just two days before the Sampson's cookout. All charges against her were dropped. Psychiatrists pronounced her completely sane, and she was given a visa to remain in the United States for up to a year. It was the attorney general's way of saying, "Sorry."

Pam led Sonya's younger sister to the picnic tables and introduced her to each of us. The last time any of us had seen Helga she was wearing a pair of black pajamas that she had snagged at a Salvation Army outlet. Things apparently hadn't improved very much since then, for she now wore frayed sandals, baggy jeans, and an old plaid shirt that was too big for her thin frame. Her face was untouched by makeup, and her blond hair had been crudely cut so short that there wasn't enough to form a simple bun. But her destitute condition was like a field of dirt centered by a golden rose. The plainness of its surroundings only deepened one's appreciation of the flower's natural beauty.

When it was my turn to shake Helga's hand, I briefly considered asking her if she had somehow poisoned Lexel's serpent. I was still trying to figure out why the giant snake dropped dead. The notion that someone had infected it with a lethal chemical was the most likely explanation I could come up with, and Helga was the most likely suspect.

But her poor English, and my poorer Norwegian, didn't allow for such a complex exchange of thoughts.

Helga was surprised to see Jimmy sitting at a picnic table with

Sophie, Gabriel, Paige, and Corinne. Speaking slowly and using simple language, Pam explained to Helga that her nephew had been living with the Sampsons for about a month, and he had lost much of his shyness around them. The boy vaguely recognized Helga's face, and he seemed to realize that they were connected in some special way, but when she came close he instinctively drew back a bit. His aunt smiled at him and gently touched his shoulder. "No be afraid," she said in a soothing voice. "All okay. Everything okay."

Pam ushered Helga to the middle picnic table, but before she could sit a taxi cab drove down Bog Lane. The dead-end street seldom received unfamiliar vehicles of any kind, much less taxi cabs, so the car immediately drew Fran and Muriel's attention. Then Pam looked up, followed by Corinne and Paige. Soon all of us were looking at the yellow taxi that pulled to a stop in front of my house. The cabbie got out, opened the trunk, and placed two pieces of luggage on the sidewalk. A tall, blond man arose from the back seat and paid the driver. With his size, shape, and coloring, he could very well have been Helga's blood brother. The man said something to the cabbie, who nodded and got back into his car but didn't drive away. The visitor wore a blue sports jacket over tan slacks. We watched him remove a tie from around his collar and undo the top button of his shirt. All the while, he perused the Queen Anne Victorian as if mulling over the portrait of an old acquaintance.

Jimmy suddenly bolted from the table and flew through the open gate. "Stevie!" he cried again and again. The man turned as the boy raced toward him; he scooped Jimmy off his feet and the two hugged for a long, silent moment. This action, freely taken by a child who was supposed to be emotionally stunted, surprised all of the adults except Muriel and Pam, who had gained a first-hand appreciation of Jimmy's hidden resources.

Fran placed another steak on the grill, then handed the tongs to Harry and asked him to take over. Our host removed his apron and walked out to the lane, where Jimmy was talking excitedly to the visitor. Though I couldn't hear what the boy was saying, I knew enough about him to realize that a burst of chatter from his lips was a noteworthy event.

We watched Fran shake the man's hand. They spoke while Jimmy rested his head on the visitor's shoulder. Fran pointed back at us. The man nodded and paid the cabbie as Fran picked up the valises. As the trio approached the yard, Paige and Corinne looked at each other.

"That's the guy who was on the porch that day when we talked to Jimmy," Paige said.

"See!" Corinne whispered to her mom, "Doesn't he look like a movie star?"

Helga wasn't impressed. She stepped away from the table and stared through brooding eyes. Sensing the surge of tension, Pam looked at her and said, "Please, no trouble. No fight. He is also a guest in my home."

"I leave," Helga said. "I go now."

"Please, don't," Jean spoke up. "Stay with us. Let's hear what he has to say."

"He bad man!" Helga blurted. "He kill Sonya."

"No, I didn't kill Sonya."

The tall man had stepped to within several feet of Muriel's wheelchair, which was positioned at the end of the picnic table closest to the lane. With Jimmy's arms still wrapped around his neck, the man glanced around at us.

"I apologize for intruding," he said. "I'm Jim's brother, Steve Hitchens. I have a house in Duxbury, but I had to come here first. I've been away for almost a year, and I wanted to see my little brother more than anything on this earth." He paused for a moment, choosing his words carefully. "I know what happened here last month. My lawyer and an F.B.I. agent gave me most of the details. I'm sorry—truly sorry—to all of you. It was never supposed to... We thought we had killed the creature. We were convinced of that. I'm sorry that we were so horribly wrong."

Jimmy pointed to Sophie, Gabriel, Paige, and Corinne. "Those are my friends."

"I'm very happy to meet you all," Hitchens said as he lowered his brother to his feet.

Jimmy scampered back to sit among his pals. "That's my big brother!" he said proudly.

Hitchens smiled at the little group. "I'm grateful to each one of you. Friends are something that my brother has never had. He's been alone for most—"

"Because you father is monster," Helga cried. "Monster!"

Hitchens said something to her in Norwegian and gestured with the open palms of his hands as if to say, "Wait." Then he walked to where Muriel sat and knelt by her side. "This is something I couldn't do over the phone." With that, he gently lifted her hand and kissed it. "I cannot tell you how sorry I am for everything that I put you through, Muriel."

"You didn't put me through anything, Steven." she replied. "Your father...well, he was a different story, wasn't he? I'm just glad I could help in some way."

"If there is anything you need—a visiting nurse, physical therapy, a professional masseuse, anything at all—please let me know."

Muriel laughed. "Don't be giving an old woman any foolish ideas."

Hitchens rose to his feet and looked at Helga. The smile on his face slowly faded. "You're right," he said as he slowly walked toward her. "My father was a monster. And he created monsters. In the end, he was killed by one of his own creations."

"I thought he was killed in some sort of accident," Harry said. The lawyer was leaning over the deck, still holding the tongs in his hand. He was supposed to be tending the grill, but, like the rest of us, he was unabashedly eavesdropping on every word spoken by Hitchens and Helga.

"It was justifiable homicide," Hitchens said, still looking at Helga.

Harry blinked down at Hitchens. "As determined by a court of law?"

Hitchens looked up. "Are you a servant of the court?"

"As a matter of fact, I'm an assistant district attorney for this county."

"In that case," Hitchens said, "allow me to rephrase: My father was accidentally killed by one of his own transgenic organisms."

Harry studied Hitchens's face until a droplet of beef fat fell onto the gas burners and flared noisily behind him. He returned to his culinary duties without asking any more questions. I heard Jean breathe a sigh of relief.

Hitchens turned toward those of us who were sitting at the picnic tables. "Would anyone be offended if I spoke to Helga in her native tongue?"

No one said anything, so Hitchens walked to within a few feet of the woman and began speaking the language of Ibsen. At that point, everyone else—reluctantly or not—returned to their meals and allowed the couple to have some scant measure of privacy.

Everyone except me. I didn't much care if I was being rude. I wanted to know what was being said, and I also wanted to ask a few of my own questions. But even though I leaned in to hear every word that came out of Hitchens's mouth, I couldn't understand a single one. Still, I was able to discern a few things. Hitchens's tone was mild, his inflections had a feel that ranged from explanation to apology, and his pace was measured, as if he'd already given a great deal of thought to what he was going to say. As he spoke, the expression on his face was one of total, unflinching honesty. But Helga's face told me even more of the story: her blue eyes gradually went from a state of hostility, to surprise, to confusion, to understanding, and finally to pensive sadness. All of these emotional states transpired within a span of less than three minutes.

Helga moved back toward the table and slowly sat down. Hitchens walked around and sat opposite her. They looked at each other for a moment and then down at the utensils arrayed on the table. Fran poured wine into each of their glasses as Jean delivered a steak from the grill and placed it on Hitchens's plate. "I hope you like it well done, hunnee."

"No one even thought to ask the man if he's a vegetarian," Tracey said.

Hitchens smiled. "I confess to being a carnivore, and well done is fine. Thank you."

Laine offered Helga and Hitchens a serving dish full of various kinds of fish as Pam put a tray of vegetables within their reach. "Please help yourselves," she said. "We've got tons of goodies. If you don't see what you want on the table, just ask."

I looked at the agreeable faces all around me and scowled. The puffy white cloud of conciliation that had rolled in was more than I could take. "That's it?" I said, making no effort to hide my annoyance. "No more fireworks? No more answers?"

"Rick, it's between them," Laine said. "Let it go."

"No, no, no," I said, wagging my finger. "I'm entitled to a few answers too."

"I'm sorry," Hitchens said politely. "I don't think I got your name."

"My name is Americo Delvecchio. I'm the guy whose ribs were busted by your father's pet." I lifted up my shirt to show the large bluish bruise that still stained the right side of my midsection. "More importantly, that thing nearly killed my son, it nearly killed my wife, and it DID kill my dog. So don't tell me that it's none of my business."

"I didn't say it was none of your business," Hitchens replied calmly, touching a napkin to his lips. "In fact, I quite agree with you: You are entitled to answers. What would you like to know?"

This took me by surprise. I was ready for a verbal boxing match, but Hitchens's pliant attitude left me without a foe. My combative instincts abruptly wilted, leaving my mind a complete blank. The more I tried to remember all of my questions, the more they receded from my reach. I must have looked like an idiot, frothing at the mouth one second, stammering mutilated adverbs the next.

Fortunately, Laine cut short my moment of embarrassment. "Helga, did you write the word 'Lindorm' on our bathroom wall?"

Hitchens translated the question. Helga spoke Norwegian to Laine, but Hitchens gave us the English version. "She was trying to warn you to get out of the house."

"But what is Lindorm?" Delaney asked. "What does it mean?"

"I think I can answer that one myself," Hitchens said. "Lindorm refers to an old Scandinavian legend about a sea serpent that sometimes crawled up on land to kill and eat livestock or even an unwary person. Supposedly there were a few sightings right up to the late 1800s. The legend is fairly well known in and around Norway. I think Helga assumed it was well known in this country too."

"If she wanted to warn people to get out of the house," Pat Bishop asked, "why didn't she just come right out and warn them?"

Hitchens again explained the question to Helga and then translated her answer as she spoke. This became the pattern of conversation for every question directed at Helga for the rest of the afternoon. She would look at the person who asked the question and give her answer while Hitchens translated. "I was afraid of being arrested by the police before I could prove anything. One day, when the serpent was sunning itself in plain view in the back yard, I screamed for someone to come and see. But before anyone came the serpent disappeared into the woods. It was smart. It knew it had to hide from people." Helga looked directly at me. "Do you remember the night when you were standing by the bog? The night when your son screamed and you ran into the house?"

Laine and I nodded. We remembered that night all too well.

"I was standing on the rooftop veranda, looking down," Helga said. "I saw the serpent slowly approaching you."

"What?" Laine and I gasped with one voice.

"Yes," Helga nodded. "The monster was in the bog, and it swam to within several feet of you. From my vantage point I could see it clearly; from your vantage point you could only see the moonlight on the surface of the bog. If I had screamed for you to get away, you would have looked up at me, and you would have thought to yourself, 'Who is that crazy woman standing on my roof?' You would have called the police ON ME. Meanwhile, the serpent would have sunk back into the bog. I would've been babbling in Norwegian, the police would've learned that I was the woman who had been deported, and then I would've then been taken away and deported all over again. You see, I had to be very, very careful at all times."

"So instead of screaming, you woke up my son and made him scream?"

"Yes," she replied. "I was afraid I would be too late. But your son screamed just in time to send you running upstairs—away from the serpent—while I ran up the back stairway to the third floor."

It seemed as if a cannon ball had just whooshed by my head.

Realizing how close I'd come to dying a horrible death that night, I couldn't even force a grin at Helga's clever ploy. A lengthy pause followed. Everyone seemed to be imagining the same horrible 'What if...?' scenario that was skulking through my mind. Though I had no wish to relive that night, I began to experience every detail as if an imp in my head had hit a rewind button.

But, once again, Laine came to the rescue by asking a question that commanded my full attention. "How did you get into our house? We had the locks changed even before we moved into the place."

"I used to visit Sonya for one week every year," Helga said. "She showed me the whole house. I knew every hiding spot and passageway, including a secret entrance to the laboratory from the side yard. It was deliberately hidden, just as the inner entrance was deliberately hidden. I'll show you later, if you like."

"Yes, please do," I said, feeling strangely violated.

"How did you get out of the mental health facility in Oslo?" Harry asked. "You were supposed to be confined for several years, as I recall."

"The doctors let me go. I learned to stop talking about Richard Hitchens, the experiments, the serpent, Sonya's death, all of it. I learned to only talk about nice things to the doctors, every day things. After a couple of years the doctors were convinced that I was cured."

"Okay, but how did you get back into the States?" Harry asked. "I'm surprised the Norwegian authorities allowed you to return to a country where you had committed a serious felony. Attacking anyone with a knife—even someone as unlikable as Richard Hitchens—is a serious offense."

"No one allowed me to come back. But it wasn't terribly difficult to get into America. I traveled to Iceland. From there I went to Greenland. From Greenland it was a short trip to Canada. As a Norwegian citizen, I had no trouble getting into those countries. Once in Canada, it was easy getting into America. I passed over the border into Maine. There were no border people to stop me. But I almost got stomped by a moose while peeing in the woods," she laughed as she revealed this bit of information. It was the first time any of us had seen her smile, and it was a strikingly pleasant sight.

With each question, answer, or comment that was shared, the boxes that encased our private lives faded away, for a while at least. As the hours passed, all of us seemed to draw closer in some peculiar way. No one said it out loud, but we all seemed to sense it; we realized that we were united not only by a disquieting secret, but by a truly unique experience and a seminal lesson. Every person in the Sampson's back yard on that summer afternoon had, in one way or another, endured the same malevolent presence. I'm not referring to the serpent. I'm talking about the mind behind the serpent— the man who conceived of the transgenic snake as a means to an end. The fearful ordeal unleashed by that mind had changed us for the better. Although none of us would willingly go through such a nightmare again, the truth is that the nightmare deepened our humility and strengthened the bonds that unite us. Our singular experience made us more aware of our human power to—in the words of a poet—"make the mountains ring or the angels cry."

Toward the end of the afternoon another unfamiliar car drew my attention to Bog Lane. It was a silver Chrysler LeBaron and it pulled up next to the Sampson's fence. Hitchens seemed to recognize the woman who got out of the car. Then I remembered her as well: it was Anne Killilea of the Boston F.B.I. Office—the woman I never expected to see again. Fran met her at the gate and led her into the yard.

"How the hell did they know I was here?" I heard Hitchens murmur.

"Maybe they've got some sort of secret, sub-dermal tracking device on you," I suggested. "You would not believe what science can do these days."

Hitchens slowly turned and squinted at me. The corner of his lip curled up just a tiny bit.

As Anne Killilea approached, I noticed that she wasn't dressed in her official capacity as an agent of the law. Instead she wore a sleeveless blue blouse and a pair of cream-colored slacks that ended just below her knees, showing off her nicely-curved calves. She caught the worried look on Hitchens's face. "Don't worry," she said as she walked by him, "this has nothing to do with you." She continued moving toward me.

"Is that authorized weekend attire for F.B.I. agents?" I asked.

"I'm heading to Barnstable for the week," she said. "Even employees of the Bureau get vacation time every now and then."

"I'm afraid you're many miles short of your destination," I quipped.

"Gabriel is your son, isn't he?" she asked. "Is he here? I'd like to talk to him."

Her questions wiped the grin off my face. "Why? What's wrong?"

"Oh, nothing's wrong," she said. "It's just that we found out what killed the snake."

My eyes popped wide and several people quickly stepped toward us, all asking their own versions of the same question: "What killed it?"

"May I talk to your son?" she asked, ignoring the swarm of questions. "I have something for him."

I gave her a mystified look and then turned toward Sky Palace. "Gabriel," I called, "come down here."

His head appeared in the small window of the treehouse. "I didn't do anything, Dad," he protested.

"You're not in trouble. There's someone here who wants to talk with you."

Laine, who was with Pam and Jean on the deck, saw what was happening and came toward the small gathering. "What's going on?"

"I'm curious to find out myself," I said.

Gabriel made his way out of Sky Palace and climbed down the tree, followed by Sophie and Jimmy. He warily moved toward the cluster of people at the picnic table.

Agent Killilea smiled warmly as he approached. "Hi Gabriel," she said, extending her hand, "my name is Anne and I have something for you."

He limply clasped her hand and was about to ask what she wanted to give him, when he realized that she had already passed it from her hand to his. He opened his fingers and looked at a silvery rectangle in his palm. Tears slowly filled his eyes. Looking over his shoulder, Sophie gazed at the object in his hand and read aloud:

"Gabriel and Biscuit: Friends Forever."

Tears streamed down my son's face, but he didn't make a sound. Laine crouched down and held him close. When he wrapped his arms around her neck, I reached into his hand and slowly lifted out a silver medallion. It was about two square inches. On one side was the generic image of a dog, and on the other was the passage Sophie had read, inscribed across the middle of the ornament in two lines.

Then I remembered. Gabriel had seen the medallion in a jeweler's window during a visit to Boston last December. He begged me to buy it as a Christmas gift for Biscuit and I finally gave in. The jeweler said he could inscribe it with any message that wasn't too wordy. It took Gabriel less than five seconds to come with the sentiment that now adorned the medallion.

"I'm sorry," agent Killilea whispered to me.

"It's okay," I said softly. "He's been living under a storm cloud ever since Biscuit disappeared. I think a cleansing rain is probably the best thing that could've happened."

As Gabriel sobbed onto his mother's shoulder, I tightly clenched the medal in my hand. Suddenly I felt a sharp stab in my middle finger. I opened my hand to see a small cut on the fleshiest part of the finger. "Damn," I muttered.

"Now you know what killed the snake," said agent Killilea.

"What?"

"When the snake..." Killilea looked over at Gabriel, whose face was still buried in his mother's embrace. She chose her words carefully. "The pathologist told me that a snake's digestive system is pretty tough. It can usually pass along teeth and claws without too much trouble. But that medallion was different. Its substance, size, shape, and the sharpness of its upper left corner—the corner that just cut your finger—all made it very difficult for the snake to safely pass the medallion. That upper left corner gouged into the snake's internal tissue. The more the snake's body tried to eliminate it through normal processes, the deeper the medallion cut. Over a period of days it sliced through a whole section of the snake's intestines, which caused internal hemorrhaging. The more it exerted itself, the more it bled. That constant cutting and bleeding finally brought the snake down. Your dog's medallion was more than the snake could handle."

Gabriel, his eyes moist and red, faced agent Killilea. "You mean Biscuit killed the monster?"

She met Gabriel's stare with a sympathetic smile and nodded. "Biscuit didn't run away. Your dog faced the snake; he tried to scare it off to protect you and your parents. We found his teeth marks on the snake's hide. If Biscuit hadn't been so brave, his medallion never would've killed the snake. Your dog gave his life to protect the people he loved. So, yes, you could say that Biscuit killed the monster."

Gabriel sniffled and caught his breath. "I wish I could tell him how much I miss him."

"You can tell him," Muriel said from the circle of onlookers. "You can tell him when you say your prayers, and God will make sure Biscuit hears you."

"Does God care about dogs?" Sophie wondered out loud.

"Child," Muriel said, "God loves anything that truly loves."

"Why?" Gabriel asked.

Muriel didn't hesitate. "It's like the good book tells us: 'God is love.' And in the end, love always finds a way. Our bodies may hurt and our bodies may die, but, like the book says, 'Love never faileth.'"

Gabriel looked down and thought about Muriel's words before making a vow: "Then I'm gonna tell Biscuit how much I love him. I'm gonna tell him…" But his voice trailed off and he began to weep again.

Sophie hugged him. After a moment's hesitation, Jimmy stepped forward and put his arms around Gabriel and Sophie.

None of us spoke. At that moment every adult and near-adult in the Sampson's yard became a silent witness to the sweetest prerogative of childhood: the freedom to bare the tenderest of emotions, without shame or apology.

"Come on," Sophie said, "we'll send Biscuit a message from Sky Palace."

The three friends walked toward the treehouse with their arms hooked around each other's shoulders. The sun's amber rays slanted over the picnic tables and slid up the giant oak. Like a tide that swells by imperceptible dribbles, the shadow line crept ever higher against the Sampson's home. But the children were undaunted by the falling night. Willowy hope buoyed their hearts as they pulled themselves toward Sky Palace. They ascended carefully and encouraged each other as they went. With each step, they rose out of the gathering dusk and reached up toward the light.

AUTHOR'S ACKNOWLEDGMENTS

To objectively judge one's own work is the most challenging task of all.

Those words apply to any creative undertaking, and they lead inexorably to an even rougher maxim: *No matter how helpful it may be, criticism is seldom easy to take.*

Fortunately for me, I occasionally get to rub elbows with the following special people: Kayla Furbish, Helen Hoffmann, Mary Ann Killilea, Anne Nee O'Neil, Pamela Hultman, Henry W.D. Bain, Dustina Bennett, Francis Maloney, and Carolyn Bishop. These sweet souls not only took the time to read drafts of my manuscript, they also provided feedback with such gentle strokes that even *my* delicate feathers weren't ruffled.

And a very special thank you goes to my beloved wife, Laine Tulipano, who supported my efforts with a patient ear and a beautiful smile.

My gratitude is boundless.

ABOUT THE AUTHOR

AMERICO TULIPANO is a first generation American and a life-long lover of well told tales. He graduated with a master's degree from the University of Massachusetts, where he studied literature. He lives in Watertown, Massachusetts, along with his wife, nine year old son, a Labrador retriever, and two cats—both of whom know how to keep a secret.